THE GRIM COMPANY

LUKE SCULL was born in Bristol and lives in
Warminster with his wife. Luke also designs computer
roleplaying games and has worked on several acclaimed
titles for Ossian Studios and Bioware. His latest project,
iOS fantasy game *The Shadow Sun*, is scheduled for
release in 2013. Visit his website at: www.lukescull.com

'Scull spins a gripping tale with expertise and relish.'
GUARDIAN

'Packs an impressive amount of violence, hazy morality
and betrayal, crafting an energetically cynical read.
Showcasing thrilling action sequences alongside effective
plot twists, it'll please fans of the darker edges of epic
fantasy... An entertaining page-turner.' SFX

'If you like your gizzards glistening and your mages mean,
this rollicking debut will suit. Hugely enjoyable.'
DAILY MAIL

'One of the bright new voices in epic fantasy.'

THE GRIM COMPANY
LUKE SCULL

HEAD of ZEUS

First published in the UK in 2013 by Head of Zeus Ltd.
This paperback edition published in the UK in 2013
by Head of Zeus Ltd.

9 7 5 3 1 2 4 6 8

A CIP catalogue record for this book is available from
the British Library.

Paperback ISBN: 9781781852125
eBook ISBN: 9781781852132

Printed and bound in CPI Group (UK) Ltd.,
Croydon CR0 4YY.

Head of Zeus Ltd
Clerkenwell House
45-47 Clerkenwell Green
London EC1R 0HT
www.headofzeus.com

Contents

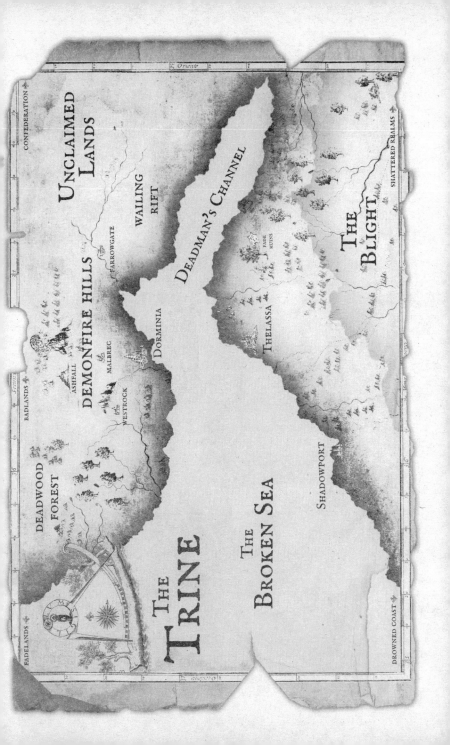

For Yesica

A Tyrant's Wager

THE WIND WHIPPED the flag of the warship swaying at anchor, the stylized 'M' wrought in silver thread on a black background proudly proclaiming her the head of Shadowport's triumphant fleet.

The conflict that had bloodied the waters of the Trine for the last six months was over. Two hundred miles to the north, across the Broken Sea, Dorminia was counting the cost of pitting its navy against the superior firepower of the ships from the City of Shades.

Tarn watched the crew of the *Liberty* swagger onto the docks to be engulfed in an adoring crowd. Joyous laughter and breathless chatter rolled across the wharf; tears flowed as family and friends welcomed their returning heroes.

Tarn stared for a moment longer, then turned and spat into the deep blue water of the harbour. He watched the phlegm bob for a moment before the choppy water disintegrated it. A passing woman gave him a hard look as she moved to mingle with the disembarking soldiers.

He would have been among the first on the ships when the hostilities with Dorminia had escalated, but his lame leg had made that impossible. On the Broken Sea, as everywhere else, he would be useless: an anchor weighing down those who depended on him.

Out of habit he glanced down at his hands. Crusted scabs and old bruises stared back, and he winced. Shame surged up like a geyser. He needed to see Sara. He needed to say sorry.

Head bowed, Tarn began the slow limp home.

To mark the city's victory in the war for the Celestial Isles in the Endless Ocean far to the west, Lord Marius had issued an edict for three days' suspension of labour. Revellers flitted in and out of the shadows cast by the dying sun, which this late in the day was a crimson half-orb slowly sinking beneath the waves of the Broken Sea.

Tarn felt his anger mounting as he made his way through the jumble of buildings beyond the harbour. Marius's decadence was extreme, his appetite for both food and flesh legendary. Like the Tyrant of Dorminia, and the mysterious White Lady who ruled Thelassa to the east, Marius was a Magelord: an immortal wizard of vast power who had brought about the Age of Ruin.

A damned *Godkiller*.

The crowd drifting towards the harbour had grown larger. Many of those heading down to the docks were whores, scantily clad and trailing cheap perfume, desperate to empty the purses of the disembarking soldiers.

Sensing early custom, one stepped in front of Tarn. She pushed her chest out and gave him a smile. Her teeth were crooked, but her eyes were a lively blue and her dirty brown hair framed a face that might be called attractive.

'Thirsty, darling? I got a cup that'll wet your tongue and no mistake,' she said, brushing her hands quickly down her thighs. Somehow she managed to raise the hem of her short dress as she did so. Her legs were pale and slightly bruised, like the white cheeses Shadowport exported up the coast of the Broken Sea to Thelassa and beyond. The sight triggered unpleasant memories.

Tarn cleared his throat. 'Ain't interested. Got a wife waiting for me at home.' He pointed to the plain band on his finger, trying to ignore the slight dent in the cheap silver.

The whore tutted softly in disappointment, an ingratiating gesture designed to flatter, but the deceit was plain as her eyes swept over his ruddy face, his thinning hair, his expanding paunch.

'Might be I can do you a special price, what with the celebrations and all. What your wife don't know won't harm her none, ain't that so?' The woman's voice held a note of disinterest now, as if she'd decided she'd already worked hard enough for whatever meagre rewards she might glean. The assumption angered Tarn, not least because it was correct.

'You know what it feels like to be loved? To have someone there for you no matter what, whatever stupid damn thing you do to drive 'em away? A woman like that deserves a man who stays faithful.'

'Whatever you say, mister. Plenty more like you will pass this way tonight. Most with better spirits and deeper pockets, I'd wager.' And the woman shoved past him.

Tarn snorted in annoyance. His left knee was beginning to ache as it always did, ever since the accident.

He resumed his slow journey home.

The light was beginning to fade. Dark clouds had sprung up in the half-bell it had taken Tarn to reach the industrial sector known locally as East Tar, adding yet another layer of grey to the smog-filled skyline. The forges lay cold and dormant in the midst of the city's celebrations, but little evidence of the festivities had permeated this part of Shadowport. East Tar was a dreary, moribund place; for Tarn, it was home.

He cursed his bad leg as it sent a fierce stab of pain down into his knee. The sudden jolt caused him to stumble forwards into a suspicious damp patch on the ground.

A boy's laughter reached his ears. 'See that, Tomaz? Fat bastard nearly flopped face down into your piss!'

'He's probably drunk again.'

Tarn's fists balled, the anger surging within him. There were six of them, local lads. An ugly bunch.

One of the youths swaggered right up to him and sniffed. 'He's not drunk.'

3

'For once. Guess his wife is safe tonight. You saw those bruises he gave her?'

'Yeah. Her face was all yellow and brown, like a dog turd.' The speaker, now safely back among his fellows, gave Tarn a sly look. 'Still, put a bag over her head and it'd make no difference, know what I mean?' The youth thrust his hips forwards and made grunting noises, much to the delight of the rest of the gang.

Tarn began to shake. He stepped towards them, his face bulging in rage. In an instant the youths' casual amusement switched to deadly seriousness, their feral eyes locked on him, hands straying to their belts. Tarn knew the odds weren't in his favour. He didn't care. He just wanted to hurt them.

At that moment the first patter of rain began to fall. With it came something intangible and unseen, a convergence of vast energies that all present sensed but could not articulate.

'Huh,' said one of the gang, and looked around at his fellows.

'Best get back,' Tomaz said. 'I have to let Tyro in. He don't like the rain.'

The others nodded, murderous thoughts replaced by concern for their friend's dog. They melted away into the gathering rain, shooting Tarn baleful glares but saying nothing.

Tarn bowed his head against the acidic rain as he made his unsteady way through the slippery streets. He needed to get home: Sara would be waiting for him. The wind had picked up, gusting cold water into his face. He blinked it away. Night had settled over the city like a blanket.

He hated what he'd become, but what could he do? The drink had broken him – broken him as completely as the falling cargo had shattered his leg. All the coin he had put aside for the last ten years, a full ten gold spires, gone on a physician who had saved the limb but left him crippled and broke. Sara deserved better.

He was almost home. What if she'd left before he had the chance to apologize? She was younger than him, a woman in her prime. She hadn't been able to provide him with any children, but there were apothecaries in the city that might have helped with that. Shadowport's recent advances in the sciences had been the talk of the Trine before the war.

There was no chance of hiring an apothecary now, not with his pockets near empty.

He approached the door to his modest home. There was no light from within. All was silent apart from the steady patter of rain rolling off the slate roof and down the red-brick walls to splash on the cobbles below. Tarn felt a moment of panic.

A light suddenly flickered on and the door opened. Sara stood there before him, the candle in her hand illuminating the fading bruises on her face. Without a word, she turned and moved into the kitchen. He followed her.

The small dining table was set with two bowls. He took his seat as Sara placed the candle down and walked over to the iron stove. She returned with the battered old stew pot and ladled a generous portion of the warm casserole into his dish and a smaller portion into her own, and placed two wooden spoons on the table. Then she sat down opposite him.

A half-bell passed. Sara barely glanced at him. She hardly touched her food. The dull ache in his skull was returning. He sat back and searched for the words he'd been waiting to say.

'Sara... I never meant to touch you. You know that. I'm a bloody fool. A useless, crippled fool. I'm so—'

The bowl flew past his head, missing it by scarcely an inch. Sara's face was a cold mask, yet her hands shook.

'You bastard,' she said. She pushed herself to her feet. 'How could you do this to me?'

'I couldn't help myself, Sara. I told you. You deserve better.'

'You're damn right I deserve better!' She looked around in sudden fury, grabbed the pan off the stove and moved towards him threateningly. Tarn slid out of his chair, cursing as he jarred his knee. She swung the pan and it struck him hard, right on the side of the head.

'Ow!' he bellowed, blinding light exploding in his vision. He felt blood running down his cheek, dribbling over his chin. It hurt like hell. Sara raised the pan again.

He caught her arm and squeezed tight. The pan fell from her weakening grip. The anger that had been bubbling within him all day suddenly surged upwards, unstoppable, a mindless fury. He squeezed tighter and she gasped. He raised the scabbed knuckles of his other hand, clenched them tight. Her eyes met his. His fist wavered.

And then they both heard it. A crashing like a thousand waves striking a cliff. The patter of rain on the roof became a fierce drumming. The ceiling shook. Leaks began to appear, streams of water showering down and soaking the table, the floor, the furniture. Screams echoed from the street, barely audible above the roaring and splashing.

Tarn released his wife's arm. Together they rushed outside.

The waters of Dusk Bay raged and boiled a hundred feet above the city, blanketing the skyline from horizon to horizon. A billion tons of water hung in the sky, suspended by some unimaginable power, streaming droplets that splattered onto the city below. Some men and women huddled on the street, frozen by fear; others locked themselves inside their houses. A few elders closed their eyes and prayed to gods they knew couldn't hear them. The gods had been dead for five centuries, murdered during the Godswar, their corpses cast down from the heavens by the Magelords who now ruled over the shattered continent.

Tarn stared at the impossible spectacle above him. He felt no fear. No sorrow. His mind was numb, unable to comprehend the scale of what was happening. A dog barked wildly nearby, running back and forth in terror. A young man cried a name – *Tyro?* – and threw his arms around the animal to soothe it.

Tarn felt a hand in his, soft skin against his grazed knuckles. Gently, he pulled Sara close to him.

'I'm sorry,' he whispered, and kissed her forehead.

Sara buried her head in his chest. He stood there stroking her wet hair, blinking up at the raging maelstrom. Without warning it ceased to move, hanging still for a heartbeat. He could make out a ship, the prow and half the deck protruding from the water almost directly above his head. The *Liberty*.

The sky fell.

Angel of Death

EARLIER THAT DAY...

THE WATER SEEMED to crush him with a giant's grip, forcing the air from his lungs. He thrashed wildly and shook his head, willing his body to resist just a moment longer. His chest burned.

He could do this. Three minutes. That was all. A few more seconds and—

It was no good. With a mighty exhalation, Davarus Cole's head burst from the water. He beat the sides of the iron washtub furiously with his fists, cursing the Magelord whose death was his life's goal. The tyrant who ruled this city with an iron fist.

Salazar. We'll have our reckoning one day.

He placed a hand on each side of the tub and pushed himself up. He stood there for a moment, blinking water from his eyes. His gaze went to the small mirror in the corner of the room. It was a rare item in Dorminia, where only the nobles could normally afford such extravagance. His mentor and foster father, Garrett, had procured it for him at some cost. As far as Cole was concerned it was a luxury he fully deserved.

After all, he thought, a hero has to look the part.

His lean, sinewy body looked back at him from the mirror, neck-length black hair and short goatee contrasted sharply with pale and glistening skin. The chill water in the tub had sapped what faint colour he possessed, and he looked almost ghostlike. *An angel of death.*

Cole narrowed his grey eyes and marvelled at his forbidding appearance. He imagined the look on Salazar's wrinkled old face when Magebane slid home, the soft sigh of recognition as the tyrant's blood spilled from his mouth and his body sagged. *Remember my father, you old bastard? What you did to him? I'm Davarus Cole, and I've come to take what's mine.*

He frowned. What was his? Vengeance, certainly, but there had to be more than that. It wouldn't do to tarnish his moment of triumph with doubt as to the true meaning of his grand utterance. Then again, perhaps it summed up Davarus Cole perfectly. *A man of mystery.* He liked the sound of that.

On an impulse Cole tensed and leaped backwards out of the tub, somersaulting in the air and landing in a crouch several feet away. He rose slowly and turned back to the mirror for one last admiring glance. His mind drifted again to the moment of his inevitable glory. *Not now. Not today. But someday soon.*

Lost in thought, his usually sharp ears failed to detect the approaching footsteps until they were almost at the door of his apartment. With a sudden feeling of dread, Cole realized he'd forgotten to turn the key. He froze. The door thudded open and Sasha bustled in.

They stared at each other. Sasha was a couple of years his senior, tall and slender, with dark brown hair that reached her shoulders and captivating eyes. He watched in rising panic as they made their way down his naked body.

A ghost of a smile danced on Sasha's lips as she said, 'Well, that's a less than impressive sight. I thought you possessed a weapon that could absorb magic and skewer Magelords like a hog. I have trouble believing an instrument like that could slay a farm girl.'

Cole looked down at his shrunken manhood. He quickly covered it with his left hand and gestured towards the washtub with the other. 'It's the water,' he mumbled. 'It's extremely cold.'

Sasha watched him for a moment, her oddly dilated eyes glittering with amusement. 'You might want to lock the door next time.' Her smile faded. 'Garrett wants us all at the Hook a bell from now. Make sure you're there on time – I think this is serious. No messing around, Cole.'

'Right,' he said meekly as she turned back to the door. She paused.

Without looking back, she said, 'Don't worry. As far as I'm concerned, you're still a prize cock.' And with a small laugh, Sasha swept out of his apartment.

To most in the Trine, Dorminia was known as the Grey City. The title was apt in more than one way: almost all Dorminia's buildings were constructed from granite quarried in the Demonfire Hills, which rose up just beyond the city's north wall. The hills had once been home to tribes of wild hill-folk, but the random magical abominations and other terrors that had blighted the land since the Godswar had driven those tribes north into the Badlands. A few ancient records mentioned a catastrophe in ages past that had given the Demonfire Hills their name, but the exact details were vague; much of the world's history had been lost in the cataclysmic aftermath of the deicide.

The wind grew fierce as Davarus Cole exited his small apartment and made his way up the Tyrant's Road. The wide thoroughfare sloped gently down towards the harbour in the south; to the north, it passed through the large circular plaza known as the Hook and up into the Noble Quarter, where a pampered and privileged few governed Dorminia in the name of the Magelord Salazar.

Cole could just about see the pinnacle of the Obelisk piercing the skyline. A monolith of magically reinforced granite in the centre of the Noble Quarter, the Obelisk had become the symbol of Salazar's tyranny.

The city's despotic Magelord had founded Dorminia almost five hundred years ago, shortly after the cataclysmic Godswar altered the region beyond recognition. The death of Malantis and his plunge from the heavens into the Azure Sea flooded the Kingdom of Andarr and eventually formed the inhospitable Drowned Coast, which now ran for hundreds of miles south and west of the Trine. Despite the fact they had murdered the gods, Salazar and his fellow Magelords were the only protection the survivors of the devastated kingdom had to cling to while chaotic magic ravaged the land. They fled north and east to Thelassa, which survived the flooding, and helped build the cities of Shadowport and Dorminia. Even life under a deicidal wizard was preferable to a certain death.

In the centuries since the Godswar, the Trine had grown into one of the largest pockets of civilization north of the Sun Lands. True, the Confederation dwarfed the Trine, but that alliance of nations, which had reclaimed their independence after the Gharzian Empire fragmented, was a month's ride to the east, beyond the abomination-plagued Unclaimed Lands.

Cole had never set foot past the hinterland settlements that supplied Dorminia's demand for food and other resources. He remembered escorting Garrett on a business trip to Malbrec three years ago, and feeling terribly bored. The provinces were the homes of farmers and miners and other common sorts, not men like him – men destined for *greatness*.

The gurgling waters of the Redbelly River accompanied Cole as he walked up the Tyrant's Road. The Redbelly ran almost parallel, a hundred or so yards to his left, winding down from the Demonfire Hills into the harbour. Few vessels plied the waters of the river this time of year; winter's bitter touch was still heavy in the spring air, and the cold would last a while longer. There was also the matter of the war with Shadowport. What had begun late last autumn as a dispute over the newly discovered Celestial Isles in the Endless Ocean hundreds of miles to the west had ended in Dorminia's humiliating defeat.

As far as Cole was concerned, any blow against Salazar was a victory for the people of Dorminia, even if they didn't yet realize it. The failure of the city's navy proved that the Tyrant of Dorminia was not infallible. It was this kind of setback – together with the efforts of men like Davarus Cole – that would ultimately loosen Salazar's grip enough for the good people of Dorminia to rise up and overthrow their eternal overlord. If Cole didn't kill him first.

The thought made him smile. One day the entire north would know him for the hero he was.

A screech rent the air and Cole looked up in alarm. A mindhawk wheeled in broad circles overhead. Its silver head vibrated slowly and its sapphire eyes scanned the city below. Those men and women unfortunate enough to find themselves in the area immediately began to hurry away.

Cole almost scurried off as well. Then he remembered the pill he had swallowed before leaving his apartment and breathed more easily. The drug was a soporific of sorts, numbing the parts of the brain that could inadvertently transmit treasonous thoughts to the magical mutations in the sky above. He would have a headache the next morning, but it was a small price to pay to avoid the Black Lottery. The Crimson Watch randomly selected those guilty of perfidious thinking and subjected them to brutality, imprisonment and, in some cases, outright murder.

A disturbance ahead brought his attention back to the street. Two Watchmen were approaching, herding a frail old man. One of the red-cloaked soldiers gave him a vicious shove from behind and he stumbled, falling on his face. When he regained his feet, Cole saw that he now bore an ugly graze from scalp to cheek. The old man turned to his tormenters and began to protest, but a fist from the other Watchman dropped him to the ground again.

Cole went perfectly still. Incidents like this were not uncommon. Ostensibly the Crimson Watch served Dorminia and its territories as both standing army and city guard. In reality, they were little more than a network of thugs and bullies who terrorized the populace on the orders of the city magistrates and their ruthless master in the Obelisk.

The sensible course of action would be to slink away and avoid drawing attention to himself. Hadn't Garrett urged caution? 'The collective outweighs the individual,' his foster father always said. 'We can't right every wrong. Acting rashly places us all in danger. Choose your battles wisely and remember that Shards cut deepest from the shadows.'

Cole frowned. Garrett probably hadn't been referring to *him*. After all, it was obvious that his abilities and quick wits outstripped those of his peers by no small distance – and besides, hadn't Garrett always said he would one day be a great hero, like his real father? A man such as he met injustice head on, enchanted blade in hand and epic destiny propelling him forwards with a righteous fury no petty villain could withstand.

His mind set, Cole strolled towards the Watchmen as assuredly as he could. He couldn't help but notice the smattering of a crowd had melted away entirely. Its disappearance left him entirely exposed. His throat suddenly felt very dry.

The soldier kneeling over the old man looked up as Cole approached. He gave his colleague a questioning glance, removed his sword from his victim's neck and straightened. 'What the *fuck* do you want?' he demanded coldly.

The other Watchman moved closer to Cole and dropped a hand to his scabbard. His voice was full of malice. 'You'd better have good reason for interrupting official Crimson Watch business, boy, or I'm gonna drag your arse to the cells.'

'That's enough!' commanded Cole, in a voice he fervently hoped rang with authority. He reached under his cloak and placed a hand around the hilt of Magebane. For some reason his hands had started trembling. That wasn't supposed to happen.

He pushed ahead with his ruse. 'Since you two sons of whores are too stupid to work it out, you're speaking to an Augmentor. This man is wanted at the Obelisk. Hand him over.' Sweat had begun to bead on his forehead. He tried to will it away, without success.

'That so?' The soldier to the left of Cole sounded unimpressed. He was a cruel-looking man of middling years, with small, squinty eyes and a pockmarked face. 'Then you'll take no offence if we ask you to prove your credentials.' He waited expectantly.

Cole swallowed hard and drew Magebane in one smooth motion, holding the long dagger in such a way that his shaking hand was mostly concealed. He nodded at the weapon. 'This is enchanted. See the glow? No one except an Augmentor may possess such a weapon. I trust that satisfies your curiosity.'

Please, just nod and leave in peace, he silently prayed. What he said was, 'Now get the fuck out of my sight before I shove this dagger so far up your dick eye it tickles the back of your throat with your balls!'

The Watchmen glanced at one another. An understanding seemed to pass between them. Pock-face shrugged and spat at the battered fellow on the ground.

'Right you are. He's yours. We'll bid you good day.' The two men moved slowly past Cole and continued south down the road.

He watched the fluttering red cloaks retreating. Elation flooded him and he couldn't help but grin at his impromptu wit. He might be better educated than the rest of the Shards – the rebels he called comrades – but he could still cuss like the roughest of them when the occasion called for it. He was an everyman, he supposed, able to empathize effortlessly with both the noblest and the most inconsequential of men.

He looked down at the groaning old fellow at his feet. His left eye socket was heavily bruised and blood caked his cheek and neck. 'Can you stand?' Cole asked.

'Uh...' the man replied. He tried to rise but failed. Cole felt a sudden flash of impatience.

'Did you even see what just happened? I saved your life. They would have killed you.' He softened his voice and placed a comforting hand on the man's shoulder as he struggled to his knees. 'It may not seem like it now, but fate had a purpose in your being here. You were supposed to witness this. One day you'll look back and laugh and wonder if this wasn't the birth of the legend— What? What is it?'

The man's uninjured eye had gone wide, as if he had seen something terrible approaching behind Cole. The young Shard turned.

Pock-face was standing there, an evil sneer on his face. The other Watchman had his sword raised. As if in slow motion, Cole's eyes swivelled to the right to stare up at the pommel that was descending on his head. He managed to jerk back quickly enough to take the brunt of the blow on his nose.

Crack. An explosion of pain. Ridiculous pain. He tried to scream, but his voice broke and it came out as a piggish squeal. White light blinded him. When his vision returned he found that he was lying on top of the old fool. *How did that happen?*

Slimy liquid in his mouth, tasting of salt. *Blood*. He shook his head and struggled desperately to orientate himself.

Pock-face was standing over him. Sunlight glinted off his raised longsword, reflecting onto his chainmail. Cole tried to focus. He saw the Obelisk against a red sunset on the Watchman's white tabard. Red bloodstains too. *My blood?*

The soldier brought his longsword whistling down. Cole managed to roll out of the way just in time. It cut the air where he had lain but a moment before and cleaved the head of the old man in two. Bone fragments and brain matter defaced the cobbles.

Gritting his teeth against the pain in his skull, Cole raised Magebane and stabbed at the leg of the Watchman. The glowing dagger scored a shallow wound and the soldier cursed, readying his gore-covered longsword for another strike. His companion advanced, his own blade raised.

Cole scrabbled madly backwards as Pock-face launched a savage overhead swing. The sword descended and suddenly Magebane was there, turning aside the larger weapon as if it weighed nothing. Pock-face aimed a kick at Cole's chest. It connected with a sickening thud and sent him sprawling. The Watchman snarled and sprang forwards, intending to end the fight. He slipped on a pool of gore and his wounded leg buckled. He struck the ground hard, uttering a string of vile curses.

Get up! Get up! Cole forced himself to his feet. His nose and chin dribbled blood, but at least his arms and legs still functioned. The other Watchman was closing fast, his sword raised.

Cole took a deep breath to steady his nerves. This is what it came down to. He couldn't overcome the soldier in hand-to-hand combat – not with his injuries and the Watchman's superior armour. His own leather would offer scant protection. He raised his left hand and lined up Magebane, as he had so often practised. He couldn't miss; fate wouldn't allow it. It was in moments like these that heroes performed deeds for historians to marvel upon.

He threw the dagger, watching as Magebane pivoted unerringly end over end through the air towards the soldier's head. It was a magnificent throw, as he knew it would be. Practice makes perfect, particularly for a natural marksman with an instinct for—

The blunt hilt of the dagger struck the Watchman's right eye. He bellowed in anger and reached for his face as Magebane clattered to the ground. His comrade had regained his feet and was now limping towards Cole, his mouth a twisted snarl of fury. 'Kill the fucker!' he screamed, spittle spraying over his chin.

Cole whimpered and ran for his life.

He'd been running for several minutes. His chest felt as if it was on fire. Every breath was agony.

He coughed and spat out blood. He could hear them pursuing through the winding alleyways that led south-east of the Hook. He shouldered past everyone he met – in these slums, the poor and the destitute – knocking one old woman into a pile of refuse and wincing as her cries drew the attention of the soldiers chasing him.

His breathing became more laboured. Something was wrong with his lungs. He slowed to a walk, and then to a complete halt. By a warehouse stinking of rotten fish, he sank to his knees and listened as death approached. A single tear rolled down his cheek.

A sorry end, he thought bitterly.

Back on the Run

H E PUSHED WITH all the strength he could muster. It was like trying to force a pebble through the eye of a needle. *Or an arm through one of the Shaman's wicker cages.*

The High Fangs were a world away, but there were some memories you couldn't leave behind. No matter how far you ran.

Brodar Kayne bit down and grunted with the effort. His large, scarred hands trembled around his manhood. The pain was excruciating. Spirits be damned, the pain was *unholy*. He'd taken arrows and blades in the gut that hurt less than this. At least, he thought they had. That was the problem with age. It played tricks on the mind.

Concentration. That was the key. Shut out the maddening noise of the street and focus on the job in hand. It was easier back up in the Fangs, where the wind was a constant whisper broken only by the howls of wolves or other beasts and a man respected another's privacy enough to let him take a piss in peace. Here in the big city it seemed everyone wanted to interfere in his business. Merchants thrust their wares into his face as if he was a pleasure maid at a chieftain's war gathering. It was madness.

He'd knocked one trader near-unconscious earlier in the day. The merchant had grabbed his hand, apparently intending to press some cloth into it. Brodar Kayne had apologized when he realized the fellow had meant no harm.

Gradually he felt the pressure in his bladder begin to relent.

Obstructions of the purifying mechanisms by which the body is cleansed, the physician had told him. He'd wanted to make a small incision, and had only just escaped without his metal tools wedged somewhere unpleasant. Kayne hadn't survived this long by allowing men with sharp implements to poke around his body.

Ten, nine, eight, seven... He mentally counted down in a silent ritual. If there was one thing he'd learned over his many years it was the importance of routine in defending the human body against the depredations of time. It had nothing to do with superstition. Or getting old.

Five... four... three... and he sighed in relief as the pain eased and his bladder prepared to empty itself. *Two... one...* 'Shit.' The sounds of a noisy pursuit interrupted him as he was on the cusp of release, a few drops of discoloured piss dribbling down his leg before his cock seized up like a dead man's chest.

Kayne thrust his treacherous member back inside his breeches and strode out of the side alley determined to find out what all the fuss was about.

Someone was going to pay.

A lad slumped against the side of an old warehouse a little further up the street. His head rested on his chest and his breathing was ragged, as if he had an internal injury that made every inhalation a struggle. Faces peered out from behind doors and then melted away as Brodar Kayne approached the miserable figure. He grabbed a handful of sweat-matted hair and pulled the boy's head back.

A mouthful of bloody spittle missed his eye by a finger's width. A hand groped up, desperately seeking a weapon but succeeding only in prodding him painfully in the groin.

As swift as a snake, he grabbed the youngster's arm and twisted it, eliciting a yelp. His other hand cuffed the insolent bastard in the head hard enough to bounce it right off the wall behind. He reached down and hauled the fool upright.

'You picked a bad day to start something with me,' he

snarled down into the blood-smeared face. He was a lad of around twenty winters, Kayne saw, fair-skinned like most of these city folk. His steel-coloured eyes were unfocused and slightly watery, as if he'd been crying. Kayne shook his head in disgust.

'You know you've lived too long when a smack upside a fellow's head is enough to set him to tears. At your age I'd killed more men than I could rightly remember. Took some wounds that could kill a man too, and came through 'em none the worse for it. You got yourself a broken rib, I reckon, and that nose won't ever be as straight as it was. Still, you'll live – assuming I let you.'

He heard the rustle of chainmail behind him and turned, releasing his grip on the Lowlander, who promptly flopped to the ground.

'Out of the way! This is Crimson Watch business.' The speaker was an ugly little man with a plague-ravaged face. He dragged his right leg as he approached. A trail of blood glistened behind him.

The other fellow was younger and somewhat broader but still half a head shorter than Kayne, who saw that he sported a fresh bruise beneath his right eye. The red-cloaked soldier scowled up at him.

'You're a Highlander. What are you doing so far south? A man of your years ought to be tending goats or sitting around a campfire spinning bullshit tales to convince some maiden to suck your cock – or whatever it is you mountain folk do. You're not welcome here. Lord Salazar has no love for the Magelord of the High Fangs.'

Kayne shrugged. 'Can't say I blame him,' he replied. 'The Shaman and me, we got our differences as well. Enough to make the frozen north an unsafe place for an old barbarian.' The youth at his feet had begun to moan. 'I was down this way. Thought I'd see the sights of the city. Tell me, what's the boy done?'

'What business is that of yours?' said the pock-faced fellow.

'He's guilty of interfering with the application of the law. The fucker stabbed me in the leg with this dagger. It won't stop bleeding.' He gestured at the weapon at his belt and then to his leg. There was a hint of panic in his voice.

Kayne's eyes swept over the weapon and noted the telltale glow. 'Magic, if I ain't mistaken,' he said. 'I'm no expert but I reckon that wound won't be closing by itself any time soon. Best find yourself a decent physician.' He folded his arms and fixed the two soldiers with his best implacable stare.

The younger soldier's hand went to his sword. 'Not without this shit-eater we're not. Come on, move aside.'

Kayne flexed his neck. It clicked slightly. He sighed in satisfaction. 'No,' he said.

'Then you'll die with him. Merrik, you take his left side.'

The Watchmen advanced on him slowly, their scarlet cloaks fluttering in the breeze.

Come at me, he thought, reaching behind him to the hilt of the greatsword slung on his back. He felt its familiar grip beneath his fingers. He stepped away from the prone lad, sparing the twitching figure an annoyed glance. This wouldn't make things any easier. His opponents circled around him.

The soldier to his right feinted low and then brought his sword around in a vicious backhand chop. Kayne thrust his hips backwards and drew his chest in. The sword whistled past, barely an inch away.

He caught movement out of the corner of his left eye and spun, dropping into a crouch. As he felt the steel pass harmlessly over his head, his right elbow rose and crunched into the cheek of his assailant, who flopped to the ground. He pulled his greatsword loose of its scabbard with his other hand as he completed the rotation, raised it just in time to parry the other soldier's follow-up attack.

His opponent stepped back and blinked. 'Fuck,' he said.

'Aye,' nodded Brodar Kayne. 'Let's get this over with. I need to piss.'

Greatsword and longsword came together. Kayne hardly moved as he casually responded to the wild thrusts of the Watchman. In desperation, his opponent launched an overhead slash intended to cleave his skull. Kayne neatly sidestepped it and brought his own blade sweeping around at waist height.

The Watchman stared at the entrails spilling from the bloody mess where his midriff had been. He dropped his sword and moved to gather the glistening, snaking things in his hands, but then dropped them in disgust.

Always bad when that happens, Kayne thought sympathetically. He raised his greatsword and cut the man's head from his shoulders.

Wiping the blade clean on the corpse's tabard, he sheathed it behind him and then walked over to the other Watchman, who was struggling groggily to his feet. He grabbed the soldier's head and smashed it four, five, six times into the side of the warehouse. Holding the body upright with one hand, he took the dagger from the dead man's belt with the other and let him fall.

He turned the dagger around in his hands. It was a fine enough weapon. The hilt and guard were plain, but the pommel was inset with a large ruby and the slightly curved blade radiated the soft blue glow that signified an enchantment of some kind. He sheathed it at his belt and was just starting back to the tavern when a cough got his attention.

'Almost forgot about you,' he muttered to the moaning lad. 'Suppose I should thank you for this. Might be tough finding a merchant who'll take it off my hands here in Dorminia, but it'll fetch a tidy sum elsewhere.' He hesitated for a moment, then raised a boot and placed it over the boy's neck. 'Sorry about this,' he said. 'More of those rotten bastards will show up soon. If they find you here, you'll be wishing you was dead a hundred times over before the day is out. I'm doing you a favour.'

The lad's face turned blue as Kayne's boot pressed down on

22

his windpipe. His hands flapped weakly. A pathetic gurgle escaped his lips. Grey eyes met his, wide with the terror of death.

They were begging him. Pleading with him.

Kayne looked away. He remembered eyes of a similar hue on a face much the same age. Recalled the mad agony as Mhaira's wild screams hammered at his skull and the sickening stench of burning flesh filled his nostrils while he scraped his arms bloody on a cage that refused to yield.

He looked down at his forearms. The marks were still visible, though it hardly mattered a damn. There were other, worse scars to carry. The kind that changed a man forever.

Sighing heavily, the old barbarian removed his boot from the lad's throat and hauled him upright, tossing him over his shoulder with an ease that belied his years. With a final grunt, he turned and loped away as fast as his creaking legs would carry him.

The Wolf was well into his cups by the time Brodar Kayne stumbled into the grimy tavern near the slums. The patrons of the smoky dive cast curious glances at him as he dropped his groaning burden to the ale-spattered floor. His back ached like a bastard.

He'd grown soft, that was the problem. They could be on their way east to one of the Free Cities by now. He doubted any of them could compare to this sprawling, stinking place – but they were well within the Unclaimed Lands, where no Magelord held sway and magic wasn't contraband as it was in the Trine. The dagger at his belt would fetch a chieftain's ransom from the right people.

But no. Instead he'd been unmanned by the bloody fool who was now writhing around at his feet.

Jerek had spotted him. He was sitting in the dingiest corner of the tavern, hunched over his beer, casting dark scowls at anyone foolish enough to meet his gaze. His bald head reflected the torchlight, giving him an angry red glow. His eyes narrowed further as Kayne stalked over.

'Time to go, Wolf. I had a run-in with the local authorities. They'll be all over this place like a rash within the hour.' He waited expectantly as his friend slowly drained his cup and refilled it from the pitcher in the centre of the table.

Jerek looked up at him briefly. Then he raised his cup and drained it again. 'Who the fuck's that?' he asked in his gruff, rasping voice, slamming the cup down and nodding at the youth across the tavern. His tone was almost conversational. An ominous sign.

Kayne sighed. *Might as well get this over with.* 'The lad? He was about to be murdered by a couple of those bastards with the red cloaks. They told me to step aside. I weren't that way inclined.' He waited patiently for the outburst he knew was coming.

Jerek stood up suddenly. He wasn't a tall man by Highlander standards, though he was plenty broad. Fire danced in his dark eyes as he stared at the boy. He stroked his short beard, which was black and shot through with grey. The stroking became a tug. His mouth began to twitch. *Here it comes*, Kayne thought.

'*Fucking unbelievable!*' the Wolf growled. He slammed his fists down on the table, upsetting the pitcher, which tumbled off the edge and spilled its contents on the floor. He reached behind him and drew his twin hand axes.

The Wolf gestured at the boy with a shake of his left axe. 'That cunt? Who's he? Nobody. Let him die. Makes no difference to us. You had to go and get involved, didn't you? Thought we'd done well. Made it here alive. Looked forward to a night of drinking. Well deserved. Can't say it ain't, all the shit we've been through. Planned to get myself some pussy tonight, did you know that? Don't look that way now, does it? Always the hero, that's you. I've had it with this shit. *I'm fucking tired.*'

Kayne waited patiently for Jerek to finish his rant. The Wolf might be the angriest person he'd ever met in a world full of angry men, and he might be quick to draw blood when a calm word was all that was needed to defuse a situation, and he might have a tendency to alienate just about anyone who spent more than five minutes in his company, but at the end of the day he was the closest friend he had ever had. You take the rough with the smooth, as his father always used to say.

Jerek had stopped to draw breath for a moment. The old Highlander seized his chance. 'Calm, Wolf. We'll steal a couple of horses and ride east to the Unclaimed Lands. We'll be there inside a couple of days. See this?' He drew the glowing dagger from his belt and held it up. 'Magic. Belonged to our friend over there. I reckon it will fetch us thirty gold spires. Maybe more.' A thought occurred to him. 'Didn't you say you were desperate for female company? You've been drinking for the past three hours. Plenty of whores over in the corner there.' He pointed to the opposite end of the tavern where a small group of scantily dressed women were attempting to solicit business.

Jerek scowled. 'Fancied a drink first. Can't a man wet his whistle? I'd empty this tavern's cellar and still do 'em all raw and you fucking know it, Kayne. Impugning my manhood. The front on you.' The Wolf's grip on his axes tightened and his knuckles turned white.

'Nothing meant,' said Brodar Kayne hurriedly. 'Just an observation. Let me have a quick word with the owner of this joint and then we'll be out of here.'

He moved over to the bar, where a man with a monstrous boil on the side of his nose watched him suspiciously. Kayne rummaged around inside the pouch at his belt and withdrew two silver sceptres. He placed the coins down on the bar. 'See that lad twitching around on the floor over there? I want a roof over his head for as long as he needs to get himself up and on his feet again. He's got a few cracked ribs and his head will hurt like hell for the next day or two, but he'll live. If the Watch happens to stop by here, you never set eyes on him. We understand each other?'

The bartender's eyes went to the coins and then to the struggling youth. He shook his head and pushed the silver away. 'My life's worth more than your sceptres can buy, Highlander. If the Watch discovers me sheltering an outlaw they'll burn this place down. I have a wife and a daughter—'

He was interrupted as the door of the tavern swung open and a rotund man wearing a blacksmith's apron burst into the common room, sweat trickling down his soot-plastered face. He spoke in a high-pitched voice completely at odds with his appearance.

'Important news, fellas! The city's under lockdown! No one is allowed in or out of Dorminia until further notice. The order's come straight from Lord Salazar himself.'

Brodar Kayne glanced across at Jerek. The Wolf was tugging at his beard again. 'Since when?' he asked the blacksmith. He had a sinking feeling.

'Since just now,' the man replied in his girlish voice. 'Something big's happened. Something to do with Shadowport and the war over those bloody islands.' He rubbed at the bristling whiskers on the sides of his face. 'There's a group of Watchmen just south of here. They're searching for someone. Apparently a pair of the bastards got murdered nearby.'

Shit, Kayne thought. *How did they react so fast?* He turned to Jerek.

'We'll make for the harbour and find somewhere we can lay low.' He felt a tugging at his trousers. The lad was struggling to pull himself up. Kayne reached down and hauled him to his feet.

The boy immediately bent over, his hands curled around his chest, drawing in ragged gasps of air. Then, remarkably, he straightened up. Pain was writ large across his blood-caked face, but there was a determined look in those steel-coloured eyes. *So. You've got some backbone after all.*

Jerek had stalked over and was now staring balefully at the youth. To his credit, the boy met the Wolf's gaze and didn't flinch.

'My name's Davarus Cole,' he said, in a voice that held a curious strength in spite of his obvious pain. It was almost as if he was reciting some kind of speech. 'I know a place north and west of here where we can seek shelter from the Crimson Watch. We'll be among friends.' He coughed and spat out a glob of blood. For a second he looked as if he would faint. Then he seemed to notice the two Highlanders watching him, and he shot the bloody spittle a hard glare.

Kayne scratched his head. This Lowlander was a strange one all right. 'I'm Brodar Kayne. This is Jerek. Can't say I have a better plan, so we'll take you at your word. What is it?' He noticed the boy staring at the belt on his waist. 'Ah. That. I'll be keeping hold of this dagger for a while, on account of me saving your life.'

Cole looked as though he was about to protest, but Jerek shot him a look that screamed brutal murder and he promptly closed his mouth.

Kayne reached over and gave young Davarus Cole a reassuring pat on the back. 'Right then. Lead on.'

Crossroads

THE CITY WAS abuzz with activity as Davarus Cole led his new companions through a winding maze of side streets. Fortunately, they encountered no Watchmen among the bustling crowds.

Fate smiles on me once again, Cole thought in satisfaction. His chest throbbed and blazing pain shot through his skull with every laboured step, but at least he was alive.

He cast a quick glance behind him. The older Highlander was of impressive height, almost a head taller than Cole himself. He looked to be around fifty. Despite his advancing years, the man's lean muscles were evidence that he'd lost little of his strength. His broad-nosed face was weathered and creased. An ugly scar began just beneath his left eye and ran diagonally to just below his cheek. The Highlander's grey hair had receded slightly and thinned a little at the crown, but the mane still fell impressively to the nape of his neck. Silver stubble covered his face, but his deep blue eyes were undimmed by age.

All in all, Brodar Kayne looked exactly as Cole imagined the stereotypical Highlander barbarian would look – albeit one who was a score of years past his prime. Cole suspected that women would still consider him handsome, in a fatherly kind of way.

The same couldn't be said of the silent figure stalking alongside him. Cole judged Jerek to be somewhat younger than

Brodar Kayne, perhaps in his early forties. Shorter than his compatriot yet still a few inches taller than Cole, he was a burly man with the kind of countenance that gave children nightmares. His dark eyes stared out from a scowling face horribly burned on the right side. His head was hairless save for a short beard.

Jerek's eyes met Cole's own and bore into them. 'Problem?' the Highlander growled at him. His hands shifted slightly towards the twin axes on his back.

Cole cleared his throat. They had arrived at the Hook. 'We're nearly there. You see the crumbling building on the other side of the plaza?'

Brodar Kayne squinted as if it were an effort to make out the old belfry a hundred yards ahead of them. 'I see it. Seems a risky place for a secret hideout.' His expression turned grim. 'Are those gibbets?' He nodded at the cages hanging from the large wooden frame on a raised platform in the centre of the plaza. The wind had picked up with the onset of dusk, causing the swaying cages to clank together in a grisly rhythm.

'Salazar keeps them well stocked,' Cole replied. He was taken aback at the look on Brodar Kayne's face. The man's expression had turned to stone. 'The tower is part of an old abandoned temple to the Mother. The Shards meet there once a month. The vestibule collapsed long ago, but there's a secret entrance at the back.'

'The Mother,' Jerek rasped. 'Ha. Ain't no goddess looking out for us now.' He spat on the ground.

Cole decided to move the conversation along. 'We'll go around the outside of the Hook. I might get recognized if we try and cut through.' He suddenly remembered the old man whose skull had been split by the Watchman's sword. He thought he could see a dark smear of blood on the Tyrant's Road. It appeared the body had already been hauled away and likely divested of any valuables it had possessed. Such was life in Dorminia.

Cole gestured to the Highlanders and they set off around the edge of the Hook. His keen ears picked up fragments of conversation from passers-by as they made their way along the perimeter of the large plaza. Talk seemed to focus on the lockdown and what it meant for the city. Cole could only vaguely recall the last lockdown, which had occurred when he was a young child. A massive abomination had besieged Dorminia's walls and a squad of Augmentors had been dispatched to nullify the threat. Not all of them had returned.

He overheard a pair of old women chattering about the weather. They were pointing at the horizon. They quieted as Cole and his companions strolled past, and he felt their curious eyes tracking them as they made their way to the opposite side of the Hook.

Highlanders were exceptionally rare in the Trine. Their homeland bordered the very edge of the world far to the north, beyond the tortured Badlands that were once the vast steppes of the nomadic Yahan horse-tribes.

Cole glanced at the grim figures following behind him. The mere fact they had survived the epic journey this far south was telling enough. These were hard men.

Perhaps almost as hard as he was.

They were nearing the ruined tower. The first droplets of rain began to fall. Cole could see a dark blanket of cloud rolling in from the south-west. He paused for a moment and tilted his head back, intending to wet his face and wipe away some of the blood from his chin. Jerek barged him in the back and he stumbled, hot pain shooting through his ribs.

'Keep out my fucking way,' the Highlander snarled. Cole's mouth dropped open. He had half expected an apology, or at least some acknowledgement that the collision had been accidental. He wanted to call the man to task for his rudeness, but the Highlander's tone unsettled him. Instead, he gave a sickly smile.

'Jerek doesn't like the rain,' Brodar Kayne said, almost

kindly. 'Causes his scars to itch something rotten. Don't take it personally.'

'No offence taken,' Cole replied casually, though in his mind his fists had already made a bloody mess of the bastard's face. 'Almost there.'

They skirted around the side of the ruined tower and the crumbling walls of the western court and vestibule. The skeleton of the building was snaked with ivy. Cole led them around to the rear of the temple where the walls had subsided and the cracked pediment leaned out at a dangerous angle. Warehouses had sprung up near to the rear of the temple. The close proximity of the buildings created a mostly enclosed space hidden from prying eyes.

With a quick look around to ensure no one was watching, Davarus Cole bent down and pulled aside a large patch of ivy. Behind the vegetation was a gap just small enough to squeeze through. He pushed himself through it and gestured at the Highlanders to follow him. Brodar Kayne made it inside with surprising ease, his long limbs negotiating the aperture with impressive flexibility. Jerek proved less supple. A torrent of foul curses accompanied his grunts of exertion as he finally forced himself through the opening.

'We're here,' Cole said. He stared down the stone passage to the steps leading up to the sanctuary. The Shards were doubtless even now fretting about his absence. He felt a shiver of anticipation. He had sustained wounds that would have surely incapacitated a lesser man, and yet here he was, the stoic hero breezing in, doughty new companions in tow. He could hardly wait to see the look on Sasha's face...

'Something the matter?' Brodar Kayne enquired, jolting him out of his reverie. Cole shook his head in response.

'The door ahead leads to the sanctuary. The Shards will be up there. Let me do the talking and everything will be fine.' Cole strolled to the end of the corridor and climbed the handful of steps, then rapped out a complex sequence on the door at the top. He waited for a few moments, hearing muffled whispers from just beyond. Finally a bolt was released and the door swung open.

'*Cole!*' exclaimed Sasha. Her eyes assessed his battered face without a hint of compassion. 'You'd better get up here.'

The Shards were gathered around the remains of the large altar that had, at one time, sat proudly at the heart of the Mother's sanctuary. When, centuries ago, the goddess's last few worshippers finally accepted her demise and abandoned the temple, they had stripped away the gold statues of the Mother in her various aspects, along with everything else of value. Now the place was bereft of adornment. Rainwater pooled near the base of the altar from a large crack in the temple ceiling above. It proceeded to trickle down into the nave, collecting dust, rat droppings and other assorted filth as it went.

To add final insult to the Mother's memory, Garrett had his considerable arse propped up against the altar as he watched Cole approach. Ten other pairs of eyes turned to regard the young Shard. It was hard for Cole to be certain in the dim light, but they didn't seem to contain the expressions of sheer relief he had been expecting.

'You're late,' said Garrett. He tapped the pocket watch in his hand. It was a lavish device, a new invention from the City of Shades. Garrett had purchased it from a Shadowport trader at extravagant cost just before the conflict with Dorminia had exploded.

'Better late than never, eh?' Cole replied, giving his best rueful smile. 'I was sidetracked by an incident with our friends in the Crimson Watch. No harm done.' He pointed to his face. 'Except to the nose. Don't worry, Sash, it will heal.'

Someone coughed. Sasha shook her head and looked at the floor.

'No such luck for the Watchmen, though,' Cole continued.

He paused dramatically, and then gave a nonchalant shrug. 'They're dead.'

Silence met his words. Eventually, Garrett spoke. His voice was soft. 'Who are those men lurking behind you, Davarus?'

Cole glanced back at the door behind him, where the Highlanders were waiting in the shadows. His palms were beginning to sweat. 'I was just getting to that. I met them on the way here. One of them, ah, lent me some assistance with the Watch. They needed a place to lie low, so I thought—'

'Fucking unbelievable. Place is a shithole. What, you want us to hide out here? How about you fuck off. I ain't staying here. This ain't fair.' Jerek emerged into the light and barked the words right in Cole's face. The young Shard reeled back from the Highlander's sour breath. Brodar Kayne melted from the shadows an instant later and placed a hand on his friend's shoulder.

As one, the Shards went to their weapons. Crossbows were raised and levelled at the two strangers. Jerek's hands immediately went to his axes.

Cole closed his eyes. This wasn't going quite as well as he'd hoped.

'Enough,' commanded Garrett. 'Lower your weapons. These men are not with the Watch.'

'Damn right we ain't,' said Brodar Kayne. 'It was me that saved your lad here. He's got some fruits on him sure enough, but it seems the blows he took scrambled his memory. He was down and out before I intervened.'

'Is this true?' Garrett asked. He was using that tone he had so often in the past when his protégé had done something to disappoint him. Cole winced. It still held a certain power.

'Well, yes, but I had a plan,' he replied. Looking back, he realized all he'd needed to do was distract one of the Watchmen long enough to steal his weapon and then run them both through. He was a hero, after all. Success was practically guaranteed.

The old Highlander's brow began to furrow. He had that same look Cole had seen back at the Hook. For all of his compatriot's aggression, something told Cole that getting this man angry would be every bit as dangerous as aggravating Jerek. 'Plan or no plan, I'm grateful for the help,' he added quickly.

'Right,' said Brodar Kayne. The Highlander's expression turned thoughtful and he scratched at his jaw. 'The fact is, we've got a city full of soldiers searching for us and nowhere to run. Not with the lockdown in effect. Young Cole said we might hide here for a time.'

Garrett suddenly leaped off the altar, his ample gut bulging out of his jerkin and his twin chins wobbling in a manner Cole would have considered comical, were it not for the seriousness of his words. 'Tell me you gave these Highlanders a soporific before you led them here, Davarus!'

Sudden dread struck Cole like the pommel of the Watchman's sword. 'I didn't think... There were no mindhawks in the sky...' His voice trailed off before the collective fury in the many pairs of eyes now boring into him.

'You may have given our location away to the Watch,' Garrett said quietly. 'They could be on their way here even now.'

'Not likely,' said Brodar Kayne. 'There ain't been a mindhawk in the High Fangs for years. Turns out we don't give up our secrets as easily as you Lowland folk. Stronger wills, I reckon.'

'You've learned to hide your thoughts?' Garrett asked. He sounded surprised.

'Can't say I know anything about that,' Kayne replied. 'Thought-mining just don't work on us. The Shaman roots out dissenters the old-fashioned way.' His voice trailed off as he spoke. The old warrior suddenly had a troubled look in his remarkable blue eyes.

Relief flooded through Cole. He glanced over at Jerek, who was standing with his arms folded, a dark scowl on his face.

'Well then,' said Garrett. The merchant's panicked expression had been replaced by one of careful consideration. 'That eases my fears somewhat. I am Garrett, and I lead the men and women you see before you. We are the Shards, a rebel group opposed to Salazar's tyrannical rule.'

Jerek snorted. His voice dripped with derision. 'A *rebel group*. Fucking priceless. I ain't gonna stand here and listen to this shit.' Without another word the angry warrior stormed off down the stairs leading to the nave and began examining the ancient stone benches arranged there. He chose one, threw his pack down on the floor next to it, and then lay down on his back, hands folded behind his head.

Several of the Shards had raised their crossbows again. The Urich brothers were red with anger, murder in their eyes. Garrett gestured frantically. They relaxed a fraction at his command but continued to shoot furious glares in Jerek's direction.

His compatriot looked mildly embarrassed. 'The Wolf's just a bit irritable,' said the old barbarian apologetically. 'He gets like that when he's tired. He don't mean no disrespect. I'm Brodar Kayne—'

A bitter voice echoed up from the nave, interrupting the tall Highlander. '*Well, ain't this the very lap of luxury. A just fucking reward for surviving the deadliest places known to man.*'

'Nice place you got here,' Kayne finished. He cleared his throat. 'Now that we're acquainted, you mind getting us something to eat? All this excitement is making me hungry.'

Cole stared into the flames and listened to the rain drumming on the ruined dome of the temple. They'd managed to get a small fire going away from the damp, in a spot where the roof was mostly intact. Loud rumbles of thunder competed with the crackling of fire and Jerek's snoring to overwhelm Garrett's droning voice as he informed Brodar Kayne of the finer details of the group. The tension had eased somewhat, though certain of his colleagues still appeared uncomfortable with the presence of the two grizzled warriors.

'—and this is Sasha, our best seditionist,' Garrett continued. 'She plots to stir up resentment against Salazar and his Grand Council. It is a fine line to walk. Hatred, as with every other strong emotion, is like a flare to the mindhawks. We have to be cautious.'

Too afraid to do what needs to be done, Cole thought. If it was up to him, the Shards would be taking the fight to Salazar in a far more direct manner.

'Vicard here, our alchemist, manufactures the narcotics that allow us to shield our thoughts from those magical mutations in the sky. Consuming too many of the drugs can be dangerous – and our supplies seem depleted as of late.'

'The more we push, the greater the demand,' Sasha said, somewhat hotly. 'We've spoken about this, Garrett.'

'I know,' Cole's mentor replied in a soothing tone of voice. 'It was simply an observation. The ingredients grow ever more expensive and difficult to get hold of. I keep us as well stocked as I can.

'You've seen our physician in action,' Garrett continued, gesturing towards the thin old man sat opposite him. Cole's eyes narrowed. He was sure Remy had taken a sick pleasure in clicking his nose back into place. It was all he could do to stop from screaming as tears poured down his face. At least his ribs were only bruised and not broken. Remy had warned against any kind of physical exertion for at least a fortnight, but Cole had quietly decided to ignore his advice. Heroes didn't sit around waiting for their wounds to heal.

Brodar Kayne gave him a broad grin. Despite himself, he couldn't help but smile back at the Highlander. Like Cole, the old barbarian was clearly a man of action.

'And these two strapping fellows?' Kayne asked, nodding across the fire. Cole frowned. He disliked the Urich brothers, who had given him a hard time as he grew up in Garrett's care.

'Aram and Garmst,' answered Garrett. 'Twins, if you hadn't guessed. They're the fiercest fighters in the group,' he added, to Cole's displeasure.

'If there's killin' needs doing, we's your boys,' growled Aram, shooting Brodar Kayne another glare.

Cole couldn't help himself. 'Just don't ask them to do anything more complicated than hit something,' he quipped. 'I've heard they check each other's trousers each morning to make sure they're not back to front.'

He grinned at the faces around the fire. Brodar Kayne chuckled softly. The Urich brothers gave him looks that promised grim retribution. Everyone else stared back at him coolly except for Sasha, who wore a faint smile. In Cole's estimation, that made it worthwhile.

'On to business,' Garrett said. 'I received news last night. News that could not wait. Salazar has summoned his Augmentors to the Obelisk. Every single one of them.'

What? Cole could hardly believe his ears. 'The Augmentors are Salazar's elite force,' he added, in response to Brodar Kayne's puzzled expression.

Garrett shifted on his haunches and exhaled slowly. He looked every inch the wealthy and successful merchant – and as far as his colleagues in the Grey City Cartel were concerned, that was exactly what he was.

None of Garrett's peers could have suspected that he spent much of his considerable wealth funding a rebel organization dedicated to overthrowing the Tyrant of Dorminia. Cole loved his foster father dearly, but he knew that when the time came for him to take the reins of leadership and guide the Shards, he would achieve more than the humiliation of a few magistrates. He would see the Magelord *dead*.

'The war over the Celestial Isles will not end with our navy's defeat,' Garrett was saying now. He placed a hand on his stomach and made a sour face. 'The political situation in the

Trine is on a knife edge. Marius of Shadowport and the White Lady of Thelassa know Dorminia is weakened. Salazar will seek to strike back, and quickly. He will not accept being relegated to the position of third power in the Trine.'

'But why gather all his Augmentors to him?' Vicard said, rubbing at his nose. He did that a lot, Cole noticed.

'He's working great magic. Magic on a scale that has not been attempted for many years. He's siphoning.'

'From his Augmentors?' Sasha exclaimed. 'Is that possible?'

Garrett nodded. 'Salazar is served by at least forty Augmentors. The raw magic he has spent decades accumulating is invested in swords and spears, shields and helms that elevate an Augmentor above any normal soldier. Yet that magic is still tied to him, to be drawn upon and added to his own formidable reserves. He could be working a spell to wreak devastation on a scale not seen since the Godswar, when he and his peers slaughtered the deities. Murdered the very goddess whose temple we now shelter in.'

Everyone was silent for a time. Eventually Cole spoke. 'Salazar's Augmentors defend Dorminia's territory from abominations and other threats. If he consumes their magic, they'll be useless. He can't afford to lose his enforcers. Can he?' He suddenly felt a surge of possessiveness towards Magebane. He looked across at Brodar Kayne and the magical dagger at his belt. As if reading his thoughts, the Highlander placed a hand over the weapon. With his other hand he took a huge bite out of the old apple he was eating and spat the core into the fire, where it sizzled slightly.

'Salazar is utterly ruthless, as we all know. He will do whatever it takes to further his aims,' said Garrett. He rubbed at his stomach again before continuing. 'The Celestial Isles are the greatest source of raw magic in the known world. Dorminia's existing supplies will have dried up within a decade. A Magelord who holds the Celestial Isles will ensure their domain goes unchallenged for centuries. Augmentors can be replaced, new items of power forged and bound to those Salazar considers worthy.'

Sasha leaned forwards. Cole couldn't help but notice that her eyes looked huge in the firelight. 'With his Augmentors at the Obelisk, Salazar's assets are suddenly vulnerable,' she said. 'This could be our chance. Our chance to do something big.'

Garrett's heavy moustache twitched and he smiled at the group. 'The Wailing Rift,' he said. 'Dorminia's only active magic-mining operation, and hence of great value to the Magelord. It is usually guarded by at least a dozen Augmentors. We are going to sabotage it.'

'But the city's under lockdown,' protested Garmst. His brother nodded sagely, as if this detail had escaped everyone else around the fire.

'Let me worry about that,' Garrett replied. He turned to Sasha. 'You will lead a small group down to the harbour where my contact awaits. I'll give you the exact location when I brief you. Vicard is going with you. Remy, your presence would also be useful.'

'Not me,' the drab physician replied. 'I've no taste for adventure. Besides, I must spend the evening with a patient, one of the city magistrates. He won't be happy if I fail to turn up.'

Garrett sighed and then turned to Brodar Kayne, who had finished the apple and was now attempting to dislodge a particularly stubborn pip from the back of his teeth. The merchant's expression became grim. 'I would have you speak your intentions, Highlander. You and your friend now know enough to get us all killed.'

The old barbarian raised an eyebrow. 'I saved young Cole's life. I reckon we've earned your trust.'

Garrett had that calculating look Cole had seen on those occasions he had accompanied the merchant to negotiate business. 'I have made my fortune out of my ability to read people,' his foster father said slowly. 'There is little that escapes me. I note, for example, that your compatriot's breathing seems to have slowed a fraction – and that his hands are mysteriously closer to the axes at his side than they were a moment ago.'

Cole glanced across in surprise, just in time to see Jerek's eyes shoot open and witness his silently mouthed *shit*. He felt a sudden rush of admiration for his wily old mentor.

Brodar Kayne, too, appeared vaguely impressed. 'You got my word,' he said. 'I ain't never broken it except once, and in the circumstances I would have called any man who acted differently a damn fool.'

Garrett nodded. 'As I said, I have made a living out of judging men. I suspect that, even outnumbered five to one, the two of you would turn this temple into a bloodbath if it came to it.' He shook his head ruefully. 'But enough of such talk. I have a proposal for you.'

'Go on.'

'The Rift is at the very edge of the Trine. Bandits often cross over from the Badlands to the north. And the area is plagued by abominations.'

Brodar Kayne raised an eyebrow. 'Bandits and abominations? I reckon I got more experience with them than most.'

Garrett nodded. 'Sasha and Vicard will require some muscle to accompany them. I would send the Urich boys but they're needed elsewhere. How does ten gold spires sound?'

The old Highlander stopped picking at his teeth for a moment. 'The way I see it, this magical dagger is fair reward for rescuing your lad Cole. I reckon I would get more than twenty spires for it in the Unclaimed Lands.'

Garrett shook his head. 'You will find that Magebane is useless to you and most anyone else who attempts to wield it.'

Brodar Kayne looked puzzled. 'Why's that?'

Despite his growing annoyance, Cole couldn't help but grin. He knew the answer to that question.

'Magebane's magic will only work for those possessing the blood of a true hero,' Garrett replied. He shifted a little as he said it, as if the words made him slightly uncomfortable.

Brodar Kayne scratched his nose and then grinned. 'Counts

me out then. I never claimed to be no hero. But what's to stop you refusing to pay up after I've fulfilled my part of the deal? It ain't like I could find you again in a city this size.'

The leader of the Shards pursed his lips and said nothing. In the silence that followed, Cole could hear the *tick tock tick tock* of the timepiece in Garrett's pocket.

'I'll hang onto this dagger,' Kayne said eventually. 'When our business at the Rift is concluded I'll hand it back to your lad here. Just as soon as I've got the thirty gold spires you're about to offer. Fifteen each for both me and the Wolf there, I reckon.'

Garrett narrowed his eyes. 'You barter like a merchant,' he complained. 'Fine. We have a deal. Just be sure to keep that dagger safe. Its value cannot be underestimated. It is the one thing that can negate a Magelord's magic.'

'I won't let it out of my sight,' said Brodar Kayne.

Cole had heard enough. He rose angrily. 'It looks like I'll need to find another weapon. What time are we leaving?'

'You're not going anywhere, Davarus.'

Cole paused. What was Garrett talking about? 'Look, my ribs are fine,' he said in exasperation. 'Even with these injuries, I'm still quicker than anyone here.' He swept his gaze over the assembled Shards, daring any of them to gainsay him.

'It's not about your injuries.' Garrett's voice was heavy with weariness. 'You nearly got yourself killed today. You disobeyed my explicit instructions and almost drew disaster down on us all.' His voice softened slightly and grew sad. 'I've raised you since you were eight years old. I love you like my own son, Davarus. But you refuse to do as I ask. You think only of yourself and glory. You must learn to act as part of a group before I can trust you again.'

Cole could hardly believe what he was hearing. He felt like he'd been stabbed in the gut. 'This is ridiculous,' he protested. 'I'm the best man for this mission! You know I am! This is what I was born to do!'

'I'm sorry, Davarus,' Garrett said.

Cole looked around, desperately seeking support. No one

met his gaze except the old Highlander, who remained silent.

'I'm Davarus Cole!' he shouted furiously. 'My father was a man without equal! You can all cower around and pretend you're making a difference. I won't stand by as an innocent is murdered in the street.' He reached down under his leather vest and withdrew the green quartz crystal Garrett had given him on his eighteenth naming day, when he had been officially sworn in as a member of the Shards. It hung on a simple cord of leather. He gave it a hard tug and the cord snapped around his neck.

He stared at the crystal for a moment as it rested in his palm. He remembered how proud he'd been when Garrett had presented it to him. Twelve years the man had been as a father to him. Over half his life. And *this* was how he treated his prodigal foster son?

Cole shook his head in disgust and, to the collective gasps of those seated around the fire, tossed the crystal into the flame. Then he stormed out of the temple of the Mother and into the stinging night rain where two hundred miles to the south the city of Shadowport had at that moment ceased to exist.

The Implacable Weapon

'YOU MAY RISE.'
    Barandas did as he was commanded, shocked at the exhaustion in that ancient voice. The undisputed master of Dorminia and arguably the most powerful man in the north had never sounded so decrepit. It was an unsettling revelation, even for the city's Supreme Augmentor.

He risked a quick glance at the men sitting before him as he straightened. Lord Salazar slumped forwards in his obsidian throne, his age-spotted hands clutching at the sides for support. Those voluminous robes of deep scarlet he always wore fell around his thin body like a shroud. The harsh lines of the Magelord's dusky face were accentuated by fatigue, and his eyes were sunk even deeper than usual, shadowed by circles almost as black as the throne he sat upon. Even the beard and moustache he kept so meticulously well oiled, an ancient Gharzian custom he had never discarded, seemed to droop with weariness.

In contrast, Grand Magistrate Timerus, sitting to the left of Lord Salazar, positively glowed with satisfaction. Like the city's ruler, Timerus was not of Andarran ancestry; though he had been born in Dorminia, the Grand Magistrate shared the unmistakable features of the men and women of Ishar to the east. The chief steward of the city's affairs placed a long index finger to the side of his hawk-like nose and gave Barandas an appraising look.

On the other side of the Magelord, Marshal Halendorf of the Crimson Watch sat with his hands folded on his lap and a ghost of a smile on his corpulent face.

Go ahead and gloat, gentlemen, Barandas thought irritably. *You won't find it so amusing when the White Lady discovers the city's Augmentor force has been shattered.*

'I trust you are sufficiently recovered,' Salazar said eventually. As it happened, Barandas still felt weak, but he would never admit to such. Not in front of the Magelord and the city's two most powerful magistrates.

'I am fine, my lord. However, I regret to inform you that twenty-one Augmentors lost their bondmagic. Fortunately, none of them died in the process.'

Salazar pursed his narrow lips. 'Over half my Augmentors,' he stated, a hint of annoyance in his voice. Barandas felt a flutter of apprehension. The Tyrant of Dorminia might be exhausted to the point of tottering from his throne, but he could snuff out the lives of everyone in this chamber in the blink of an eye – and would, given reason to do so. Shadowport's fate was a testament to that.

'Yes, my lord. Mostly the new and inexperienced. We lost one or two veterans, but the core of your Augmentors remains strong.'

Timerus leaned forwards. 'I expect your erstwhile colleagues will need something to lessen the discomfort. I understand that being parted from one's bondmagic can be a traumatic experience.' The Grand Magistrate's beady eyes were mocking. He felt nothing but hatred and contempt for the Supreme Augmentor. The feeling was mutual.

'They'll suffer for a week or two. Most of them will survive it,' Barandas replied. 'After the worst has passed, I would like to see them given positions elsewhere. I'm sure their skills would be useful in the Watch.' He gave Halendorf a pointed look.

'I'll consider it,' the Marshal said. 'I should say that the Crimson Watch has little use for addicts.'

'Which is precisely why they won't be swapping magic for narcotics,' Barandas replied, narrowing his eyes at Timerus. The Grand Magistrate said nothing, simply smiled his lizard's smile.

Salazar raised a hand for silence. 'You will do as the Supreme Augmentor asks, Marshal. I will tolerate no further discussion on this issue.' He snapped his fingers and a maid scurried over with a golden goblet full of the red wine the Magelord favoured. He swirled the blood-coloured liquid around in the chalice almost absently, staring into its depths as if seeing events and places long past.

'Shadowport is gone,' he said. 'Though I won't presume Marius is dead until I see his corpse. He was ever a superb strategist, plotting schemes within schemes. His cunning served us well, back when the Congregation began cleansing the lands of those with the gift.' He sipped the wine and closed his eyes. For a moment Barandas thought Salazar had drifted off to sleep. Then his eyes shot open and his voice once again rang with the iron authority they were all accustomed to. 'With Shadowport out of the picture the White Lady is certain to move against me. There will never be a better time for Thelassa to consolidate power in the Trine.'

Marshal Halendorf cleared his throat nervously. 'My lord, is war with the City of Towers truly unavoidable? After what happened to Shadowport, the White Lady has every reason to be cautious.'

A hint of annoyance crept into Salazar's voice. 'The destruction of the City of Shades was no small feat, Marshal. The ritual lasted over a month – a month in which I have not slept. It cost me half my Augmentors, as well as the raw magic we have stockpiled over the last three years. My personal reserves are spent. Without raw magic to siphon, it will be months before my power recovers to what it once was.'

The commander of the city's military looked very uncomfortable. Still, he ploughed ahead. 'But, my lord, the

Celestial Isles… can they not be divided between the two city-states? The White Lady would risk much going to war with us. Are the Isles so important?'

Barandas was mildly impressed. Halendorf was a brave man when he was speaking with a subordinate and backed up by his captains and lieutenants, but he was far less sure of himself when it came to proffering an opinion to the city's forbidding Magelord.

This time Salazar's eyes flickered dangerously. 'The Celestial Isles are a fragment of the heavens themselves. There is more magic in those islands than anywhere east of the Fadelands. You suggest I hand the White Lady enough power to conquer the Trine and beyond.'

Halendorf sat back in his chair, his face pale.

Salazar took another sip of wine. Barandas and the other two magistrates held their breath. 'We require more Augmentors,' said the Magelord eventually.

It was the turn of Timerus to shift uncomfortably. 'Lord Salazar,' he began, 'our mining operation at the Wailing Rift is proceeding as efficiently as possible. We cannot go any faster—'

'Silence,' Salazar commanded, interrupting the Grand Magistrate, whose narrow brow immediately moistened with sweat. 'We will search further afield. Three days' sailing west of here, on the edge of the Broken Sea, is a deposit of magic that will serve to replenish my power – both for the creation of new Augmentors, and to defend the city when the White Lady eventually shows her hand.'

Marshal Halendorf swallowed hard. 'My lord, you refer to the *Swell*?' His voice faltered on the last word.

'Yes,' the Magelord replied coldly. 'Inform Admiral Kramer that he has a singular opportunity to redeem himself. He will captain a crew and sail to the Swell. There he will oversee a new mining operation.'

Timerus licked his lips. 'My lord, the Swell is the very reason the Azure Sea is now named the Broken Sea. Even in death, the

Lord of the Deep punishes those who would violate his resting place. Sane men will not venture near the Swell for all the gold in Dorminia.'

Salazar frowned. 'Then we will send the insane, the desperate, those already condemned to death. I trust you will not fail me in this, Grand Magistrate.'

Timerus bowed his head obediently. *Wise man*, thought Barandas.

'Fear not, Supreme Augmentor,' continued the Magelord. 'We will see your force restored. For now, however, there is a matter that requires your attention. The Grand Magistrate will explain the details.'

The Magelord rose unsteadily from his throne. 'I must rest now. Ensure I am not disturbed.' After draining the last of his wine, Salazar shuffled slowly from the chamber.

Barandas emerged from the Obelisk in the early hours of the morning. A fierce storm still raged, plastering his blond hair to his face and sending his crimson cloak dancing wildly behind him. Droplets of rain rolled down his golden armour and somehow worked their way into his boots. He gathered his cloak around him as tightly as he could and bent his head to the storm. If he hurried, he could catch a few hours' sleep before sunrise. Tomorrow would be eventful, and besides, Lena would be waiting for him. He imagined the scent of her hair and smiled despite the foul weather and the squelching in his boots.

Barandas wasn't blind to the suffering of those less fortunate than he was, and he knew the city could be a hard place for many – but at least it *worked*. Long ago, Salazar had taught him that a strong man does what is necessary and not always what is right. Barandas had reflected on this over the years. He had concluded that, as always, the Magelord had been correct. Who could understand the necessity for difficult actions as well as a man who had overthrown the very gods?

Mindhawks, the Black Lottery, the creative methods used to

extract information from potential insurrectionists and traitors... these things were regrettable, but how else was a city to survive and prosper in the face of threats both from within and without?

A faithless population, Salazar had once declared, was like a leaf carried in the breeze, quick to twist and turn in whichever way the wind pulled it. Strange notions could be born and then spread like wildfire. In the absence of the gods a soul searches elsewhere for nourishment, and in such circumstances insurgency was but one determined demagogue away. Better to ensure compliance through fear than to see Dorminia torn apart.

When Lord Salazar's justice needed to be imposed upon those wishing the city harm, the Supreme Augmentor was its implacable weapon.

Barandas approached his large estate in the south-east corner of the Noble Quarter and nodded at the doorman sheltering under the veranda. The man saluted quickly and unlocked the ornate entrance doors. Barandas strode through into the hallway and up the winding staircase, ignoring the muddy footprints his boots left on the new carpet.

A soft light flickered from beneath the bedroom door at the end of the corridor. He approached and knocked softly, not wishing to startle Lena if she was sleeping.

He needn't have worried. The door opened almost immediately, and then she was standing before him, her beautiful face filled with worry. She pulled him into the room and threw her arms around him.

'I was terrified, Ran,' she whispered into his chest. 'Kyla told me what happened. How could you agree to it? It's different for you. You could have died!'

Barandas ran his fingers through her hair. It smelled of jasmine, as always. 'I had no choice. What kind of commander would I be if I stood aside while my own men placed themselves in danger?' He wriggled his arms free of Lena's embrace and reached behind him, unfastening the buckles that held his breastplate in place. Lena pulled it away and lowered it gently on the floor, then helped him remove the padded jacket he wore beneath. She stared at his naked chest for a time, tracing a finger down the jagged scar that began just below his clavicle and divided his well-muscled torso down to the base of his sternum. Then she drew her hand away, as if afraid she might inadvertently harm him.

Barandas smiled at her. 'Really, I'm fine,' he said gently. He bent his head forwards and kissed her deeply. Her mouth tasted of plum wine. He glanced across to the dresser beside the bed where a candle illuminated a pitcher next to a half-empty glass. 'You've been waiting up for me all this time?' he asked.

'You know I have,' she replied. 'I tried to finish the poem I've been working on for the last week, but it was no good. I was sick with worry.' She seemed about to say something else, only to change her mind at the last moment. Her face became grave. 'Tell me, Ran, is it true? About Shadowport?'

Barandas nodded grimly. 'They were our enemies,' he said, in response to her shocked expression. 'Better to end this now than for yet more of Dorminia's soldiers to die.'

Lena looked unconvinced, but she nodded and helped him with the rest of his armour.

'I have a busy day tomorrow,' he said. 'But we'll make some time for each other, I promise. I love you, Lena,' he added, watching her undress. 'I do what I do for you.'

'I know,' she replied. 'I love you too.' She blew out the dying candle and joined him under the blankets. He felt her warm body press up against his.

A man does what is necessary. For his lord. For his city. For love.

The Joys of Laughter

***

BRODAR KAYNE'S KNEES ached.

They'd departed the ruined temple just after midnight to find the storm hadn't let up. An hour spent trudging through the sodden streets had caused all his old scars to chafe against his damp leathers, and to add to the discomfort his bones had started to protest.

It don't get any easier, he thought ruefully. At least Jerek had calmed down now, retreating into a sulk after his little outburst. He splashed along sullenly at the rear of the group, cussing under his breath occasionally and shooting dark looks at the world in general.

The streets sloped gently downwards as they made their way south towards the harbour. They passed sagging groups of buildings that loomed in the darkness like gigantic beasts. Occasionally a flash of lightning would illuminate the night sky and render the individual buildings in ghostly shades of monochrome. He saw warehouses hard by tanneries, coopers' establishments nudging chandleries, and apothecaries' shops abutting brothels, the last no doubt by design. He'd never seen so many different trades packed so tightly together.

Vicard the alchemist had pointed out his shop as they passed nearer to the docks, but Kayne hadn't been able to make out a damned thing. Fact was, his eyes weren't getting any better.

The alchemist was just ahead of him now, having dropped slightly behind the girl at the head of the sorry band. The man's nose was like a busted cistern and his long sleeves were covered in as much snot as water. Vicard was the sort of fellow Jerek would take an instant disliking to, so Kayne took care to keep himself positioned between the alchemist and his belligerent friend.

The outline of ships suddenly appeared and the sounds of the sea became audible above the persistent hammering of the rain. The girl – what was her name? Sasha? – slowed, and Kayne saw a cloaked figure emerge from the shadows. The small group drew to a halt. He shifted a fraction for easier access to his greatsword, should he need it. It always paid to be careful.

The stranger threw back his hood to reveal a face of devastating blandness. He looked to be in his mid-twenties and was of average height and build, but aside from those few details Kayne struggled to identify a single distinguishing feature about the man.

Sasha stepped forwards. 'The night is black,' she said carefully. 'Yet hope burns in the darkness. Do you know where we may find succour?' She made a complex gesture that involved lots of finger wiggling and ended with her hands locked together in front of her chest.

The man looked confused. 'Are you here for the master?' he asked. 'He told me to meet some guests here. Well, he didn't use the word "guests" exactly, but he's in a dark mood what with his haemorrhoids playing up again and you shouldn't hold that against him.'

Sasha's mouth worked silently for a moment. 'The merchant Garrett. Your master knows him?' she finally managed.

The unremarkable fellow thought for a moment, then nodded. 'The fat man? He's been around a few times. Eremul always says he could give him gout just by looking at him. Or he could if... well, you know.'

Kayne had heard enough. 'I ain't one to grumble,' he said, 'but it's pissing down something fierce and this conversation don't seem to be going anywhere fast. I don't suppose you could lead us to this Eremul fellow?'

The man blinked, and then gave a bland smile. 'Of course,' he said. 'The depository's a bit of mess but that's my fault. I've had no time to put everything back in its proper place yet. Let's go.' He pulled his hood back up over his head and set off west along the docks.

Kayne glanced around at everyone else, shrugged, and followed after him.

'Really, Isaac. I don't know why I put up with your incompetence. I swear, you're a boil on the arse of humanity. If it wasn't vaguely amusing to see you blundering around like a blind man in a brothel, I'd have turned your flesh to stone and had you tossed in the harbour years ago.'

Kayne stared in amazement as the venomous insults continued to drip from the tongue of the man sitting before them. Dark-haired and olive-skinned, he didn't seem that much older than his manservant, except that his eyes were as cynical as the other man's were cheerful. Oblivious to the torrent of abuse raining down on him, Isaac smiled and continued pouring steaming tea for each of them from a large pot.

'Maybe he misunderstood my hand signals,' Sasha said, sipping from her cup and watching their contact warily. 'It was dark and raining heavily. I wouldn't blame—'

'Nonsense,' the man seated behind the desk cut in. 'Isaac is a cretin of the highest order. If I didn't know better, I might think he was placed on this mortal plane simply to annoy me.' He grimaced as he finished speaking and shifted uncomfortably on his seat.

Kayne watched as Sasha raised an eyebrow.

I can see why young Cole has a thing for you, he thought. *You're an attractive lass, though too sharp for my tastes. And far too young*, he quickly appended, feeling somewhat guilty.

'Garrett said you could help us reach the Wailing Rift,'

Sasha said. 'Dorminia is under lockdown. How do you propose to get us out?'

'To most in the city I am simply Eremul, a rather tedious fellow with a love for cataloguing books,' the man responded, repositioning a particularly large volume on his desk. The whole interior of the building was filled with stacks of books and reams of paper; tomes of all shapes and sizes filled endless shelves and covered almost every available inch of floor space. 'To a select few,' he continued, 'I am known as Eremul the *Mage*.'

'You mean the Halfmage,' Isaac corrected gently. 'They call you the Halfmage.'

Eremul froze. 'I distinctly recall asking you not to call me that, you buffoon.'

'You're a *wizard*?' Sasha gasped. 'Impossible. Salazar would never tolerate another mage in the city. Not after the Culling. Everyone with the gift of magic was put to death.'

Eremul sneered, his thin lips curling up unpleasantly. His voice was soft, but the bitterness was almost tangible. 'I was a scribe at the Obelisk when the order was given. I was young and talented. I dare say I was a favourite of his lordship. He must have seen a use for me, since he allowed me to keep my life.' He put his hands on the edge of the desk and pushed against it.

All those sitting around the table gasped, save for Jerek who gave an amused snort. Large wheels had been affixed to the bottom of Eremul's chair, allowing it to slide effortlessly backwards to reveal the mage in his full glory – or more appropriately, his half-glory.

Eremul's legs had been removed just above the knee. His dark green robe had been shortened to fall just below the stumps.

The Halfmage sneered at the faces gawking at him. 'Never let it be said our benevolent lord is without mercy. Salazar only butchered half of me, which is a half less than every other wizard in Dorminia. I was given enough coin to set up the depository here. As long as I bequeath certain information to the city's magistrates when required, they leave me in peace. I suppose I was the lucky one,' he added sardonically.

Vicard twitched and rubbed at his nose. 'You... You would dare to help Salazar's enemies, despite what he did to you?' he stammered.

'He thought me broken,' Eremul replied. He tapped his head with a finger. 'Yet I still have my wits and some small amount of magic... pathetic though it is in comparison to a Magelord. Most of all,' he continued, 'I have my *hatred*. I won't rest until Salazar's corpse is strapped to the bottom of this chair and I'm free to shit on his face for the rest of eternity.' He laughed suddenly, a horrible choking sound. 'You think I'm scared of what they'll do to me? They can't do anything to me. Look at me. I'm the *Halfmage*!'

Another sound chimed in with the mage's broken gasps, and Brodar Kayne realized that Jerek, too, was laughing: a harsh bark that formed a duet of tragic amusement. Sasha and Vicard looked deeply uncomfortable. Even Isaac appeared perturbed.

'Right then,' Kayne said slowly, attempting to restore some sanity to the room. 'Back to business. I can't say I'm fond of magic of any sort, but if you can get us out of Dorminia without being seen, I reckon I can live with it.'

Eremul abruptly stopped laughing, or at least making the noise that passed for laughter. 'You'll leave shortly,' he said. 'You will sail east into Deadman's Channel for sixty miles, following the coast. You will put in to shore when you see the Tombstone in the distance. From there, the Rift is a couple of hours' trek to the north.'

Vicard didn't sound happy at the prospect. 'In this weather?' he protested. 'We'll be washed away! And how will we get out of the harbour? There are ships patrolling everywhere.'

Eremul gave the alchemist a scornful look. 'I've enchanted your craft so that it is quite impossible to submerge,' he said. 'As for the patrolling ships, your boat is also cloaked in a spell that will conceal your passing. The charms will hold until you return, so long as you do not tarry. My personal reserves of power are small, and I have no raw magic to siphon.'

Brodar Kayne sat back and sighed. Out in the rain once more, except this time they'd be on a small boat in choppy waters with only a lunatic's magic keeping them afloat. It didn't get any easier.

'Get your stuff together, Isaac,' Eremul said to his manservant. His mouth twisted into a mockery of a smile. 'You're going too.'

Despite Kayne's reservations about the man's sanity, Eremul proved true to his word. The sailing boat they boarded at the docks drifted right past the huge galleons guarding the harbour. A half-hour later and they were out into Deadman's Channel, where they hugged the coast in a trajectory that proved strangely unwavering. Brodar Kayne wondered if the Halfmage hadn't placed some additional spell on the small cutter to ensure it maintained its course.

The rain continued to assault them. Sasha and Vicard huddled at the stern of the boat and rested their heads on their packs, which had been coated in wax to protect them from the elements. Isaac stood at the tiller nearby, watching the passing coastline. He was a strange one, Kayne reckoned. He hadn't complained at being sent on such a dangerous mission. In fact, he'd seemed vaguely excited at the prospect of adventure. His enthusiasm reminded the old Highlander of the lad he'd rescued from the Watch.

He'd felt some sympathy for the youngster back at the temple, but it wasn't his place to interfere with the decision of his gaffer. Certainly Davarus Cole had displayed unusual courage for a Lowlander – even if the boy was clearly obsessed with self-glory and winning a reputation.

Kayne couldn't blame him for that. He'd been young once.

While his motivations had been similar, his deeds hadn't been anywhere near so noble.

The Wolf ambled over and sat down next to him. 'Fucking weather's doing my head in,' he complained. 'Wetter than a whore with gold in her sights, and just as evil.' He spat over the side of the boat.

A short silence passed. 'This is almost pleasant, compared to what we faced fleeing the Fangs,' said Kayne. 'The world seems a great deal smaller down here. Apart from all the people, I mean. I reckon you could fit the Grey City and this entire hinterland into the East Reaching and still have room to spare. You got any thoughts about how we approach our mission at the Rift?'

Jerek snorted. 'We get in there, kill who we can, fuck up that mine and whoever gets in our way.' He rubbed at his beard and his voice became a low growl. 'I don't like the alchemist,' he said.

Kayne sighed softly, though the words came as no surprise. He'd known Jerek a long time.

'Something about him rubs me up the wrong way,' the Wolf continued. 'Always playing with his nose. I reckon he might be some kind of faggot. Better not look at me funny or I'll tear his nose right off his face. Prick.'

'Best you ignore him,' the old barbarian replied. 'We'll need his alchemy later. Don't go causing no trouble.'

Jerek shrugged. Kayne thought about saying more but decided it wasn't worth it. The Wolf could be relied upon when it mattered.

The girl had risen and was walking towards them. Jerek got to his feet as he saw her approach and turned his back, strolling over to lean against the mast. Kayne shook his head. The Wolf had a peculiar way with women.

'Not long now,' said Sasha. The rain had created a sopping mop of her pretty brown hair, but she seemed in better spirits than she had at the start of their journey. Her dark eyes looked big in the light of the torch she carried. 'Do you know the history of the Wailing Rift?' she asked.

'Can't say I do,' he replied. 'Never been one for books, though I got some skill with letters. There ain't many Highlanders that can say that.'

'The Rift was formed during the Godswar,' Sasha explained. 'A minor goddess called Alundra was cast from the heavens and sent crashing down to earth, where the impact created a gigantic fissure. Her corpse still leaks wild magic. Some of it crystallizes into the surrounding rock, which the miners extract and transport to Dorminia. The stuff that doesn't crystallize... Well, there's a reason there's such a large Augmentor presence at the mine. Abominations are physical manifestations of chaotic magical energy. They appear randomly and without warning.'

Kayne nodded. 'Saw my share of abominations up in the High Fangs. Demons, too – more and more as the years passed. They come from the Devil's Spine and kill without mercy until someone put 'em down.'

'Demons?' Sasha asked. 'I thought they only existed in legend.'

'Maybe in these parts they do. Up north, they're as real as the sword on my back.' He was quiet for a time, remembering. 'This mine we're headed to. How did it get its name?'

'It turns out gods take a very long time to die. Alundra sometimes cries out in agony. Apparently she can be heard from miles away.'

The old Highlander stared far into the distance. 'The world's full of wonder,' he said. 'Or at least horror that looks wondrous from afar.'

Sasha looked at him curiously. 'What were the two of you doing in Dorminia anyway? What happened in the High Fangs?'

He sighed. *Bad things, lass. The kind of things that, once I told you about 'em, you'll wish you hadn't asked.* He was about to reply when Isaac suddenly turned to them and pointed to the south-west. His forgettable face was rendered momentarily more interesting by his intense look of concern.

'What's that?' he asked.

Kayne turned to where the man pointed and squinted, tried to force his eyes to make sense of the blurred nightmare before him. The horizon looked as if it had risen somehow – and it was getting bigger. 'Shit,' he swore.

Jerek had noticed the disturbance too. He took one look at the disaster heading towards them and raised his hands in a gesture that expressed his complete disgust at this unlikely turn of events. 'This is bullshit,' he said. 'One thing after another. Fucking unbeliev—'

He was interrupted as the wall of water hurtled into the cutter and lifted it into the air, tossing it with alarming speed towards the onrushing coastline.

Smoke Ceilings

THE SUDDEN CACOPHONY of animal noises from outside told her the Brethren had arrived.

Yllandris rose hastily, brushing ash from the silk shawl straining against her breasts. Sweat moistened her bronze skin, running in beads down her perfectly flat stomach. Her hair was so dark as to appear almost purple, complementing the violet paint she wore on her lips and under her eyes. She gave it a shake and it fell almost to her waist, an impressive mane of hair that resembled that of the great Highland cat: a regal, graceful creature, yet utterly vicious when provoked.

Yllandris smiled, revealing perfect white teeth. Regal, graceful and deadly was exactly how she would describe herself.

She kicked dirt over the embers of the dying fire. The modest wooden hut that was her home disgusted her, but she wouldn't have to suffer it for much longer. Yllandris was the favoured paramour of Magnar, King of the High Fangs, and, if the spirits were good, before the year was over she would sit beside him in the Great Lodge as his queen and consort.

She pushed aside the bearskin that covered the entrance to her hut and stepped out into the early-morning air. The freezing wind buffeted her immediately, depositing snowflakes on her skin and causing it to prickle where moments ago it had perspired. Snow blanketed Heartstone as far as the eye could see. The capital and largest city of the High Fangs was a sea of white, dotted by mounds and hills that were all that remained of the huts and longhouses buried beneath the night's snowfall. The tall wooden wall surrounding the town rose menacingly from a thick fog that obscured the frozen surface of Lake Dragur beyond.

Yllandris could feel damp cold on the bottom of her bare legs. The snow had swallowed her boots and now reached almost to her knees. She paid it no mind – she was a sorceress and a daughter of the Highland people. The soft fops in the Lowlands might quail at such hardships, but she was made of sterner stuff. Besides, she would not appear weak in front of the Brethren.

There were eight of them. Gaern had led this hunt; he sat on his huge haunches at the front of the pack, panting heavily. Frozen blood clung to his snout, though whether it belonged to him or another Yllandris could not be certain.

She narrowed her eyes. A massive silver boar lay with his head resting on the snow. The animal's breathing was shallow and a jagged wound ran down the length of his left flank. It looked deep. It was a small miracle he had made it back to Heartstone.

It took her a moment to remember the beast's name. *Thorne*. He had been with the Brethren for twenty years. Already greying when he had transcended, he was old even by the standards of the most grizzled warriors in the High Fangs. For a boar, the animal the Highlander had merged with during the Shaman's ritual, he was positively ancient.

'What did this to you?' she snarled. Thorne measured eight feet from the tip of his snout to the end of his tail and weighed close to half a ton. Even a pack of Highland cats would shy away from attacking such a formidable beast – especially when they saw the human intelligence shining within those gimlet eyes.

Yllandris placed a hand on Thorne's boulder-like head. Thought-mining was next to useless when attempted on a Highlander, but the Brethren were no longer human. The natural resistance her people possessed towards mental intrusion evaporated when they transcended.

Images formed in her mind. She saw giants, ugly hulking creatures half again the height of a man, wielding crude clubs and axes of wood and stone. The Brethren had fallen upon them on a ridge overlooking a pine-crowded valley. Despite their size and strength, the giants had been outnumbered and overwhelmed by the speed and cunning of their foes. She witnessed Gaern take a club to the face and then rise up with a mighty roar to wrap his arms around the giant that had struck him. The transcended bear closed massive jaws around the giant's neck and tore out its throat in a shower of blood.

Some of the Brethren had taken minor wounds, but the encounter with the giants had proved to be little more than a distraction. It was not giants they hunted.

Yllandris mined deeper and concentrated. Scattered recollections came to her: visions of snow-encrusted vales and frozen streams; a herd of elk scattering in alarm as the Brethren passed by. Then she saw it and she could not stifle a gasp. It was impossibly tall, towering over even Gaern: a lithe, black-skinned reptilian monstrosity with bat-like wings and claws resembling scythes. It had ambushed them as they crossed the surface of a frozen lake, plummeting down out of the sky to rend Thorne with its enormous talons. The others had immediately surrounded the demon, but it had dodged their attacks with terrifying speed. One of the pack, a white cougar unknown to her, leaped onto its back and sank its claws into the fiend's scaly skin. The creature took to the wing again, pulled the transcended great cat from its back and disembowelled it while those below looked on.

The Brethren had retreated then. This was a fight they could not hope to win. Thorne had somehow kept pace with the others, leaving a sticky red trail across the snow for miles. Now, though, his strength was all but gone. His fading mind had become hazy, the images indecipherable.

Yllandris quickly withdrew her hand and listened to the final exhalations rattling from that great chest. They had lost two of the Brethren. The King would need to be told.

She spun around to face the small crowd that had gathered to watch. Fur-clad men and women stared back, all much paler than she. The men wore their hair loose and long, and their beards were flecked with snow. The women had their hair braided. Many wore small trinkets of bone and copper around their necks and wrists. Not a few of them regarded her with barely disguised hostility.

Go ahead and hate me, she thought, sneering back at them. *I'm young and beautiful, a sorceress high in the favour of the King. I could have any one of your husbands in my bed in an instant, and you all know it. I will be a queen. None of you will amount to anything, you sour-faced pack of bitches.*

'Find a healer,' she ordered the greybeard closest to her. 'The rest of you, fetch a pallet. Thorne must be brought to the Great Lodge. Move your feet before I light a flame under them.'

She strolled away from the crowd in the direction of the Great Lodge, confident that her orders would be followed. Many of the assembled Highlanders might desire or despise her, depending on what they had between their legs, but they feared her even more. Besides, the Brethren were their sacred protectors. None would dare anger the Shaman by dishonouring one of the beasts.

The snow continued to fall. Yllandris made sure no one was looking and then pulled her thin shawl tighter around her shoulders.

In marked contrast to the vast majority of the structures in Heartstone, the Great Lodge was a huge and sprawling edifice. It occupied the centre of town where it rose higher than any other building, gazing down on its domain like one of the great alpha wargs that roamed the highest peaks. The Shaman would be up there, she knew, unless he was off hunting. Their Magelord had become less and less a part of the world of men, preferring to dwell alone under the stars when he was among them at all. Whatever ancient tragedy had driven him to isolate himself so far from his peers had slowly stripped away his humanity.

Yllandris paused for a moment to stare up at the Great Lodge before entering. She always felt a shiver of excitement when she approached the massive building. It represented the pinnacle of power among her people here in the secluded north of the world.

She had always admired strength. Ever since she had stumbled across her mother's broken body on the floor of their hut as a child, had met her father's eyes and saw what he had done, that terrible, irrevocable moment when he had pushed things too far, she had sworn to achieve power at all costs. It was the only thing that mattered.

Her father had been exiled for his crime. She had become a foundling, hunting for scraps and shelter where she could find it. The High Fangs were a hard and unforgiving country, and her life might have taken a much darker path had she not come into her magic shortly after her first blooding. The circle of sorceresses in Heartstone had seen her potential and taken her under their wing. They were a bitter and spiteful brood of old hens, but their teachings had proved invaluable. What they didn't realize was that one day their prodigal daughter would become queen, and their precious hierarchy would be turned on its head.

The massive warrior stationed outside the entrance to the Great Lodge nodded as she approached and beckoned her to go on inside. She stepped past him through the huge gate, inhaling the pungent odours of ancient darkwood, smoke, fur and leather that hung in the air. *This is what home will smell like, so very soon.*

She followed the vast entrance hall down towards the throne room, practising a regal smile on the men standing guard on either side. The Six were among the finest warriors in Heartstone, sworn to guard the King with their lives. The weapons and shields of legendary Highlanders hung from the darkwood walls, glistening in the smoky light of the torches arrayed on sconces down the length of the hall. Some day she would have sons, and no doubt their own arms would have pride of place among these of heroes from ages past.

She paused for a moment before entering the throne room and adjusted her shawl one final time. With a nod to the guards on either side of her, she swept through the great double doors.

Magnar, King of the High Fangs, watched her enter from his mighty oak throne at the head of the long trestle table dominating the room. Eight of the ten smaller thrones positioned lengthwise down the table were empty. The Butcher of Beregund, Krazka One-Eye, watched her hungrily from the throne immediately to the King's right. On Magnar's left, Orgrim Foehammer scowled and crossed his meaty arms over his expansive paunch.

Yllandris slowed. She hadn't expected Magnar to have company. Not these two men, at any rate. Krazka and Orgrim were the most powerful of the chieftains who ruled the ten Reachings under the King, who in turn answered to the Shaman – when the Magelord bothered to involve himself in matters of state.

'Yllandris,' drawled Magnar in his cultured voice. 'What brings you here?'

'A *woman*?' interrupted Orgrim, distaste plain in his voice. He slammed a fist down on the table. 'We're here to discuss war!'

Krazka licked his lips. Yllandris wasn't sure which made her more uncomfortable: the leering eye on the right of that cruel face or the dead, colourless orb staring blindly on the left. 'This the one you spoke about, Magnar? Your pet sorceress, aye? No wonder you like to keep her close.'

The King beckoned her to approach. He was young compared with the chieftains beside him, only a few years past his twentieth winter. Muscular and exceptionally tall, he regarded her with eyes the colour of steel. It was said Magnar's prowess with a sword matched that of any of the Six, his elite bodyguard. He had proved a shrewd ruler during his short reign.

A formidable man. One who deserves a woman to match. She gave him a small curtsy. 'My king, a pack of the Brethren returned just moments past. They were attacked by a demon of a kind I have never before seen. Two of the pack were killed: Thorne, and a white cougar whose name I do not know.'

'This is troubling news,' said the King. He was an educated man; perhaps *too* educated for the tastes of certain of his chieftains. His personal prowess and the ruthlessness he had displayed during his rule had ensured their muttering went unvoiced in public, but Yllandris knew some of them bore Magnar a grudge, and not only because of his learned manner.

'Describe this demon to me,' the King commanded.

'It was hugely tall and as black as the night. It flew with wings near as wide as this chamber. Its talons were the size of longswords, capable of rending a man apart with a single swipe. I saw all this from Thorne, before he passed away.'

'The Devil's Spine continues to fuck us up the ass,' Orgrim growled. 'That accursed place spews up more demons by the day. How many of the Brethren have we lost this year alone? At this rate the High Fangs will be overrun.'

Krazka finally tore his gaze away from her breasts. He rubbed at his weeping dead eye with the back of his hand, where it left a trail of sticky slime. 'It ain't just the demons crawling out of the Devil's Spine that's the problem. They're chasing out the giants and the wargs and fuck knows what else. This latest attack is just the tip of the iceberg.'

The King frowned and leaned forwards. 'This has come at a bad time. We plan to move on Frosthold in the next few days. I had intended to send the Brethren with our main force. With the Shaman's approval, of course.'

Yllandris was confused. *Frosthold?* That was the principal

town of the North Reaching under the rule of Mehmon, one of the oldest and most respected chieftains of the High Fangs. Why would they move against Frosthold?

The King noted her puzzled expression. 'Mehmon has declared independence,' he said. 'He no longer wishes to honour the Treaty, claiming his own people are starving. If his mutiny is allowed to go unpunished, other Reachings will follow his lead. Mehmon must be brought to justice and Frosthold put to the sword as an example to the rest. Orgrim and Krazka will return to their Reachings shortly and ready their men.'

Yllandris noticed the eager look on Krazka's face. The Butcher of Beregund had earned his reputation three years ago, when he had led the ruthless massacre of the town of the same name. The Green Reaching had rebelled and the town of Beregund had been slaughtered to a man. No doubt he was looking forward to a repeat of the bloody work that had made him infamous across the High Fangs.

'This demon will wreak chaos if it is left unchecked,' she said. 'It is capable of destroying entire villages.'

Magnar nodded. 'Then I will split the Brethren. Half will accompany the war party to Frosthold, while the other half will hunt down this fiend—'

'No,' said a deep voice from a dark corner of the chamber.

The Shaman stepped out into the torchlight. His tanned body rippled in the orange glow, naked save for a pair of tattered brown breeches. He wasn't tall by the standards of the men in the room, but he was incredibly wide, three hundred pounds of muscle packed onto a frame a shade under six feet. Deep veins threaded his bulging biceps and heaving chest and shoulders. His straggly black hair ran down to his waist, which seemed chiselled as if from stone. He looked like a god, or some heroic figure of legend.

He is neither. He participated in the killing of the gods and the bringing about of the Age of Ruin. She wondered how long he had been in the chamber. The Magelord could have slipped

66

unnoticed into the throne room at any time, wearing the form of any number of creatures – even that of an insect. There was said to be no greater Shifter in the known world than the Shaman.

'I will hunt and slay this monster,' the Shaman growled in his low, rumbling voice. 'Send the Brethren to Frosthold. You will need them.'

'As you command,' said Magnar. Yllandris felt a tickle of disappointment at his easy deference. The Shaman rarely interfered with the governing of the High Fangs, except to place a new king on the throne when the previous one had passed away. Magnar's obedience reminded her that no matter how high she rose, there would always be a ceiling to her ambitions. The King's will would forever come second to that of the Godkiller standing before her. No mortal outranked a Magelord where he or she claimed dominion.

The Shaman crossed his massive arms. Even Orgrim Foehammer looked small when sat so close to the hulking figure. 'Frosthold's circle is powerful. Send as many sorceresses as you can.'

'There are seven in Heartstone, including Yllandris,' the King replied. 'That gives us fifteen in total, including the circles from the East and the Lake Reachings.' He glanced at the chieftains to either side of him. They nodded in confirmation.

'Adequate,' said the Shaman. He looked up at the ceiling and raised his mighty arms in the air. 'Search the High Fangs. Find any man who possesses the spark of magic and bring him here. I will create more of the Brethren.' And with that he began to shimmer, his body seeming to stretch and elongate. All of a sudden his shifting form imploded, condensing so that only a tiny ball of light remained floating above the ground.

The glow faded away, to reveal a large black raven hovering in the air. The transformed Shaman croaked once and flew upwards, disappearing through a smoke vent in the wooden ceiling above.

Magnar, King of the High Fangs, looked at Yllandris and pursed his lips. 'You had best prepare yourself for travel. Tell the rest of your circle to do the same. The North Reaching is ten days away at the very least, and the journey is a hard one. I will see you when you return.'

Yllandris cursed silently, shooting venomous glances at the amused faces of Krazka and Orgrim. 'Yes, my king,' she said, slightly too sweetly. His eyes narrowed. She ignored his displeasure, dipped a perfunctory curtsy and turned on her heels to stride out of the throne room.

She had expected to find herself in his bed by now, as had been their routine for the past few months. Instead she must prepare herself for an unpleasant sojourn to the frozen North Reaching and a confrontation with a hostile circle.

One thing she did know. When Yllandris and King Magnar of the High Fangs finally underwent their joining and emerged as husband and wife, she would not sit quietly on her throne and be dictated to by a half-mad immortal.

A Magelord could die like any other man, of that she was certain.

The Hero's Journey

COLE WOKE SOME time after tenth bell. His head pounded and his mouth tasted foul. A glance at the vomit-stained clothes strewn over the floor of his cramped sleeping quarters confirmed his worst fears.

What hour had it been when he'd left the Gorgon to stumble home in the rain? He couldn't remember the short walk back to his modest apartment. He could recall only fragments of the preceding four hours or so he'd spent drinking himself into oblivion. All in all, he was extremely lucky to have made it back in one piece. The Hive was one of the roughest parts of the city, and a man wandering drunk and alone in the middle of the night was a ripe target for thieves and cut-throats.

He hadn't intended to end up in such a state. After his dramatic exit from the temple of the Mother, Cole had entertained some vague notion of attempting a daring robbery on one of Dorminia's powerful magistrates and returning triumphantly to his shamefaced comrades. 'Witness!' he would have declared. 'A king's ransom in gold and jewellery, enough to fund a strike at the very heart of Salazar's power!'

As it happened, his ribs had begun to ache fiercely a few hundred yards from the temple and he'd decided that such valour would have to wait for another night. He had chosen to head home, only to become unaccountably sidetracked along the way.

Cole frowned. Somewhere in the hazy recesses of his mind, fragments of memories began to unveil themselves: a pair of women laughing at him; a kindly old man with his arm around him, calling him 'boy' and telling him everything would be all right. He looked at his clothes again. He hoped he hadn't embarrassed himself.

Cole thrust his blanket away and slid gingerly from the straw mattress. He rose unsteadily to his feet, remaining perfectly still as the room swam around him and a wave of nausea threatened to heap further agony on his ribs. He breathed steadily for a few moments and the sensation passed.

He walked from the small bunk room into the main quarters, and then caught sight of his reflection in the mirror propped in the corner.

Cole stared in horror. His nose was hideously swollen and coloured an ugly shade of red from the bridge almost to the tip. He had a large purple bruise under his right eye and his cheeks were scraped and scabbed from thrashing around on the floor during yesterday's exploits.

He felt a flash of rage. What had he done to deserve this? He reached for Magebane, half intending to hurl it at the foul visage staring back at him from the mirror. Too late he remembered that he no longer had the weapon. That only made him angrier.

Storming across to the armoire on the wall opposite the mirror, he quickly selected some fresh clothes and pulled them on. Then he strode over to the opposite corner of the room and knelt down, feeling around for the loose floorboard. He levered the board up slightly to hook a hand under and remove it.

He examined his hidden stash. He selected a plain dagger and a handful of copper crowns and silver sceptres, which he stowed away in his trousers. A tiny container at the very back of the shallow recess contained a dozen pale green pills. He placed one in his mouth and swallowed it down. He was just about to move the floorboard back into place when he noticed the small leather bag in which he had often stored his pendant.

He felt a sudden pang of regret at having tossed it into the fire last night. Despite the disgraceful way they had treated him, he was still a Shard.

In a sudden burst of charitable feeling, Cole decided that after he had purchased what he needed at the market he would seek out Garrett and give him the chance to apologize. Other men might hold a grudge, but not him. His heart was just too big.

With one last mournful look in the mirror at his battered face, Davarus Cole exited his home in the western half of the city and headed south towards the market.

The sun was high in the sky by the time he arrived at the Bazaar, a sprawling collection of tents and stalls that operated all year round and brought folk from all over the Trine together to gossip, trade and otherwise interact in a relatively peaceful confluence. Goods from Shadowport were currently forbidden, as were merchants from that city. Two had been apprehended and dragged to the Hook in the last fortnight. They now hung in gibbets, their ample girth serving only to prolong their suffering inside the tiny cages.

The lengthy walk had given Cole time to clear his head. He had calmed down and examined the situation from every angle and had concluded that, in truth, there was only one person to blame for last night's unpleasantness.

Brodar Kayne. The Highlander had stolen Magebane, his precious heirloom. Not content with undermining the respect he enjoyed among his fellow Shards, he had then sat idly by as Garrett announced that Cole had no place on the mission. He had expected the old warrior to speak up for him, to proclaim that, despite his youth, he possessed exactly the kind of courage that could aid their quest. Instead he had simply stared into the fire and continued picking his teeth.

And what right did an over-the-hill barbarian have to even borrow a weapon such as Magebane? He was no hero, unlike

Davarus Cole, whose own legendary father had passed it to him on his deathbed.

The young Shard smiled sadly, as he often did when remembering his father's tragic death. Illarius Cole had been a great rebel leader, and it had taken three of the Magelord's best Augmentors to best him during a vicious and lengthy battle. Illarius had killed two of them before escaping, mortally wounded, to find young Davarus and deliver his final words.

'*Take this weapon, son,*' his father had said, choking back blood. '*One day you will lead the city to freedom. I have seen the spark in you. Listen to Garrett and try to be a better man—*'

Illarius had died before finishing his sentence, but he hadn't needed to hear the rest. He knew Garrett's limitations. While he loved and respected his mentor, he could not deny that his father's wish for him to be a better man than Garrett was wise. For all his resourcefulness and organizational skills, the merchant lacked the ambition to ever achieve a truly significant victory for the Shards.

Cole tried not to blame his foster father. Greatness was a gift bestowed upon few, after all, and Garrett had done the best he could. It was up to Davarus Cole to lead the Shards to new heights when the time was right.

He heard his stomach growl and sudden hunger overwhelmed his ruminations on future glory. A food vendor was hawking his wares just ahead. Cole handed over four copper crowns for a chunk of pale goat's cheese, a crust of hard bread and an overripe pear. He bit into the fruit and almost gagged when he saw the trio of tiny white worms twitching around inside.

He hurled the spoiled pear to the ground in front of the vendor's stall and crushed it with his boot; then, on an impulse, he grabbed hold of the large basket in which all of the seller's fruit was presented and upended it on the street. *Let that be a lesson to you*, he thought. Satisfied he had made his point, he strolled away from the stall, the outraged merchant's curses following him down the narrow aisle.

He was feeling in better spirits now. The clouds that had blanketed Dorminia for the past week had finally dispersed and the sun was shining. In fact, it was unusually warm for a late spring morning. The pear aside, the hasty breakfast he'd just eaten had settled his stomach. Most important of all, he had a purpose.

That was the thing about being a hero. When you took a knock, you got right back up and came back stronger.

A bellman's cry abruptly split the air, coming from somewhere on the other side of the Bazaar.

'*Attention, good people of Dorminia. Your glorious master has cast down the treacherous Marius and cleansed his city of sin with the very waters of the Broken Sea. The war is over. All praise Lord Salazar!*'

It took a moment for the crier's words to sink in. When they did, Cole hurried as fast as he could towards the man. A crowd was already forming around the crier, who repeated the announcement and ignored the flurry of questions darting at him from every angle.

'This can't be true,' a gap-toothed farmer said numbly as Cole drew closer. 'I got a daughter in the City of Shades. What does he mean by "cleansed"? I wish this bloody lockdown would end.'

Cole didn't bother to reply. He shouldered the man aside and pushed deeper into the unwashed mass of citizenry chattering in alarm over the news. One woman in particular seemed anxious to air her views to as many folk as possible. He watched her for a time. Eventually her eyes met his and she wandered towards him. He was about to turn his back and pretend to have pressing business elsewhere when he noticed her swaying hips. Although she wore the drab clothes of a goodwife, her bosom, too, was impressive.

As she approached, Cole saw that she wasn't as old as he'd initially thought. Her strawberry-blond hair caught the sun and glimmered prettily. All in all she was quite pleasant to look at. Worth a minute of his time, he supposed, though he couldn't help feeling a bit self-conscious about his bruises.

'I take it you've heard,' she said, standing in such a way that her cleavage seemed to drag his eyes downwards with irresistible force. 'Shadowport's no more. The City of Shades has been destroyed by Salazar himself.' The tone of her voice changed slightly, a hint of sarcasm creeping in. 'Strange that he waited to act until *after* our navy was crushed.'

Cole said nothing, settling instead on a non-committal shrug. He wasn't about to voice treason against the Tyrant of Dorminia in the middle of a crowded market. He wasn't stupid.

The woman leaned in close to him and her voice became a whisper. 'I lost my husband to the Black Lottery four years ago, you know. He was a brave man.' Tears welled up in her eyes. 'There aren't many like him around these days. Men prepared to take a stand.'

Cole puffed out his chest and placed a comforting hand on her shoulder. *If only you knew*, he thought. *If only you knew.*

'I'm sorry for your loss,' he lied. 'I'm sure your husband and I would have had much in common.' He gave her a winsome grin, and was rewarded with a shy smile in response.

'How did you come by those bruises?' she asked, placing a gentle hand to his face. He felt his body respond and shifted uncomfortably.

'Let's just say the Watch and I don't always see eye to eye,' he replied. He couldn't resist giving her a conspiratorial wink. She looked thoughtful and bowed her head.

He noticed abrupt movement in the corner of his vision. One of the tradesmen the woman had been speaking with was suddenly grabbed from the back. His surprised face was visible for a split second before he disappeared behind the mass of humanity. There was a yelp, cut off as suddenly as it had begun, and then a young woman was also forcibly removed from the throng, her arms flailing before she faded from view.

A worried murmuring spread. Faces glanced left and right and behind them. Two more people were suddenly pulled from the crowd: an old woman and a man of middling years.

A dark foreboding seized Cole. He stared at the woman opposite him. She frowned as if trying to figure out some puzzle. Her eyes had changed. The wetness was gone. There was no tender recollection there, no earnest longing. They were as hard as stone.

'I can't work this one out,' she said, and it took Cole a second to realize her words had been directed at someone behind him. He spun around to find a large man dressed in commoner's garb looming over him, preparing to grab his arms. He was about to go for the dagger concealed in his sleeve when he felt a prick on the back of his neck and suddenly his body refused to listen to his brain. He was completely paralysed. Even his chest protested at drawing breath.

Cole listened to the sound of air whistling through his nose as the woman moved to stand in front of him. She held a hairpin in one hand, its pointed tip glistening red. With her other hand she removed a stud from her right ear, which had been hidden underneath her hair. Both adornments glowed softly.

'Magic!' he tried to exclaim, but nothing issued from his frozen mouth save for an unintelligible moan.

'What shall we do with him, Goodlady Cyreena?' the burly male asked.

The woman stared at Cole as she might an insect that had performed an interesting trick. 'My earring could not read his thoughts,' she said. 'This has never happened before. Carry him to the safehouse on Kraken Street. I would experiment.'

Davarus Cole struggled with all his strength, but the best he could manage was to close his eyes. The day had suddenly taken a turn for the worse.

'Look at me. Look at me or I'll tear your prick off and feed it to you.'

75

Cole opened one eyelid a fraction. His whole body ached from being thrown across the shoulder of the disguised goon and carried like a sack of potatoes. He appeared to be lying on a stone table in an abandoned warehouse. A small torch provided the only illumination.

The woman who had instigated his kidnapping, Goodlady Cyreena, hovered next to a table covered in evil-looking metal instruments. Her face was as passionless as death. She regarded him with those pitiless eyes. There was something vaguely familiar about them, he thought, but he couldn't quite work out what it was.

'Can you feel the sensation creeping back into your muscles?' the goodlady asked. 'It will be hours before you can so much as *walk* unaided. Don't think about escaping.'

Cole tried to work his mouth and found that his tongue had loosened enough to form mangled words. 'Why are you doing this?' he asked. 'I'm innocent!'

Goodlady Cyreena pushed her hair back from her face, revealing the silver stud gleaming softly in her ear. 'Words weren't necessary,' she said. 'I could tell by the way you reacted to my mummer's show that you harbour treacherous appetites. Usually, my bondmagic' – she tapped the glowing metal at her ear – 'confirms the intentions of those I suspect of treason.' She walked over to him and placed one smooth hand on his brow. 'You, however, refused to yield anything. No thoughts at all. That should not be possible. You are going to explain to me why I cannot read your mind.' She looked down at him expectantly.

'I don't know,' slurred Cole. 'I was drinking last night. Maybe—'

The woman looming over him grabbed a handful of his hair and slammed his head down onto the table.

'You will tell me how you are immune to thought-mining,' the Augmentor said calmly, 'or I will cut open your skull.' She crossed back over to the table and picked up a wicked-looking scalpel. 'I can send part of your brain for analysis,' she said.

'You would not survive the process. Alternatively, you can save us both some unpleasantness and tell me the truth.'

Cole felt dazed and nauseous and his mouth was suddenly as dry as a desert. He hacked up phlegm from the back of his throat to moisten his mouth. 'I took a soporific,' he managed. 'A friend gave it to me.'

Goodlady Cyreena said nothing for a time. Finally, she nodded. 'I will require a urine sample.'

'Yes,' Cole hastily replied. 'I'll need help with...' His voice trailed off as the woman reached down to the table and picked up a huge needle connected to a tube, which in turn was affixed to the bladder of an animal. She walked over to him and began to untie his breeches, tugging them down over his boots and ankles. For the second time in two days, Davarus Cole's flaccid manhood was subjected to a humiliating inspection.

The Augmentor's lips pursed. 'Do you find me attractive?' she asked. Her face betrayed no emotion. She simply waited for his response.

Only the spot right between your eyes, Cole thought. He wished he had Magebane to hand. Not that it would have done much good, since he couldn't even *move* his hand. 'Yes, very much so,' he said. He licked his lips nervously.

Her face melted into a smile. His own lips twitched upwards in response. She might be an Augmentor and quite possibly a sadist, but when it came right down to it a woman was a woman and he was Davarus—

'*Argh!*' he bellowed as her balled fist smashed him right between the legs. An explosion of pain surged upwards through his entire body. He could hardly breathe for the agony. She hit him again, even harder, and bright lights danced in front of his eyes. He wanted to curl up and die, but his body simply wouldn't respond. He was helpless.

The goodlady raised the unfeasibly long needle she held and positioned it just above his groin. Sudden horror filled him. 'Wait!' he gasped. 'You don't need to do that! I can—'

White piercing agony reduced his words to a whine as the Augmentor pushed the needle through his skin and deep into his bladder. Tears streamed down his cheeks and he prayed desperately for Garrett and the Shards to storm in and rescue him. Whenever he had been in trouble in the past, the fat old merchant had always been there to bail him out.

'Does it hurt?' Goodlady Cyreena asked in a mocking tone. She had a faint smile on her face as she steadily leached the piss from his body and listened to his shrill screams. 'Consider yourself fortunate. You won't die on this table. Lord Salazar has a need for healthy young men.'

To his relieved gasps, the Augmentor finally removed the needle. 'That's it,' she said. 'Rest now. You have a taxing voyage ahead of you.'

Her final words seem to drift towards him, as if floating from some great distance. 'Tonight you set sail for the Swell...'

Hearts of Iron

BARANDAS ADJUSTED HIS sword one last time and surveyed the street before him. The Hook had emptied almost immediately once he and the other Augmentors arrived on the northern edge of the plaza. A horse and cart trundled away towards the east gate, heading towards one of the farms or villages dotting the fertile stretch of land beyond Dorminia. With the city under lockdown, however, the cart's owner would not be going anywhere fast. Further down the Tyrant's Road, small crowds stared up at them, fear and curiosity warring on the faces of young and old alike.

All in all it was a pleasant morning. The storm had broken during the night, leaving the streets smelling of damp. There was something else in the air too – something aside from the sour, slightly rotten stench that was always present when one passed the gates of the Noble Quarter. It was the smell of death.

He looked up. The gibbets in the centre of the square hung sullenly, their occupants in varying stages of desperation, madness or decay. One of the cages was empty: Admiral Kramer had been released by the Watch earlier that morning, a development with which Barandas was quietly pleased. He'd always respected the erstwhile admiral of Dorminia's navy, who was loyal and forthright if somewhat uptight. Kramer would need all of his experience to handle a crew comprised mainly of convicted criminals, especially out on the Swell. The corpse of the god Malantis corrupted the waters of that dreaded stretch of the Broken Sea. Mining the region for magic was so fraught with peril that it had never been seriously attempted in the past. Still, desperate times called for desperate measures. Barandas supposed anything was better than dying in a gibbet.

He turned to the three men he had chosen to accompany him on this bloody assignment. In truth, there wasn't a great deal of choice in the matter. Most of his Augmentors were still recovering from the siphoning. Goodlady Cyreena was a notable exception, but her skills did not lend themselves to the nature of the black work the four of them were about to undertake. He cleared his throat.

'You know why we're here. One of the most powerful merchants in the city has been secretly funding a terrorist group for the last decade or more. It is time they faced justice.'

He stared at the dilapidated old temple across the way. Whoever this rebel leader was, he had succeeded in evading discovery for longer than most. He had to admire the cunning of the man, to have chosen a base so conspicuous and yet so widely shunned that few ever gave it a second thought.

'Our informant told us to expect a dozen rebels.' Barandas paused for a moment. It was unpleasant, but it couldn't be helped. 'We are to execute them all. Including the girl.'

'There's a girl? Huh. First we get to kill. Then I get to fuck.'

Although they were standing in the morning sun, the looming presence of Garmond the Black seemed to sap the very colour from the world. Fully seven feet tall and as wide as two normal men, the huge Augmentor wore a suit of enchanted plate armour that devoured nearby light. As a result, he resembled a gigantic shadow. The horned helmet that enclosed his entire head only added to his nightmarish appearance.

Garmond carried no weapon – his reinforced iron gauntlets and terrifying strength were enough to shatter a man's spine or collapse a skull with a single punch. Behind his enchanted armour the huge Augmentor was near invincible.

Legwynd, on the other hand, wore very little protection save for a leather vest. His belt bristled with daggers of all shapes and sizes, and his boots glowed with the faint blue that signified magic. 'I'm ready,' he said. As if to prove it, his legs suddenly began vibrating in a blur too fast for the eyes to follow.

'Enough,' ordered Barandas. 'You're going to draw attention to us.'

'So?' demanded Thurbal. He was a burly middle-aged man with close-cropped grey hair and chainmail. His sword hand fell to the pommel of the terrible weapon at his belt. 'We're Augmentors. It does these peasants good to fear us.'

'I said enough.' Barandas dropped a hand to his own weapon.

Thurbal might be a bastard and a killer and a murderer rivalled only by Garmond the Black, but he knew better than to challenge the Supreme Augmentor. 'As you say, Commandant,' he conceded.

Barandas relaxed and drew a deep breath. 'There's our target,' he said, nodding at the ruined temple of the Mother. 'Ready yourselves. They won't be expecting us, but if any manage to get away... Legwynd, you know what to do.'

The wiry Augmentor flashed an almost beatific smile and licked his lips. Barandas shook his head and sighed.

Time to get this over with.

There was no response to their careful knocking at the door, so Garmond put his shoulder to it and literally tore it from its hinges. The massive warrior stumbled up into the sanctum of the old temple, holding the door out before him as a shield. Crossbow quarrels thudded into the wood and bounced off his armour, but not one of them managed to find flesh. With a roar, Garmond hurled the door across the room into a small group of the rebels, sending them scattering in all directions.

One of the men, calmer than the rest, took aim, his weapon locked on Barandas's head. There was a blur, and suddenly the man was staring down in confusion at the dagger buried in his neck. His crossbow bounced off the floor and he sank to his knees, blood welling up around his fingers as he clutched at his throat. Legwynd grinned and drew another dagger.

Two men ran towards Barandas, both clutching swords. The Supreme Augmentor parried one and then reversed his grip, thrusting behind him to skewer the third man who had tried to sneak up on him.

Thurbal sidled into view, his jagged scimitar raised in a defensive posture. The rebel who had swung at Barandas launched a diagonal downward swipe at the grey Augmentor, who casually raised his glowing weapon to parry. There was a screeching sound, and suddenly the rebel was missing the top half of his sword.

Thurbal took advantage of his opponent's confusion to launch a swing at his neck. The blow was almost desultory, lacking any real power, yet the scimitar sheared through flesh and vertebrae as easily as it had steel. The head lolled horribly for a second before tumbling to the ground. The body toppled down next to it and proceeded to pump blood all over the ruined floor of the temple.

Legwynd had closed the distance with the crossbowman lurking in the nave, and now they fought hand to hand, dagger against dagger. Almost too late, Barandas noticed another man targeting him from behind a pillar. The crossbow clicked. Time stood still.

The bolt bounced off his longsword and ricocheted harmlessly off a wall.

The Supreme Augmentor had devoted countless hours to studying every text on the art of combat that could be found in the city. He had regularly spent entire nights practising his swordsmanship, performing routines of such tedium and precision they would drive most men mad. It had cost him much, but Barandas had not achieved his current position by luck. He stalked towards his attacker. The crossbow clicked, and again his sword was there, deflecting the quarrel. He leaped forwards and came up in a roll just before the pillar. The rebel discarded his crossbow and went for the mace at his belt, but he fumbled it. Barandas waited for him to pick the weapon up off the floor. It would make no difference to the outcome.

A quick exchange of blows and the rebel was sagging back against the pillar, his punctured heart leaking blood down his chest to pool around his lifeless legs. The sight gave Barandas pause.

Battle cries split the air, and two large men burst into view. One wielded a hatchet, the other a wooden club spiked with iron rivets. Garmond, gore dripping from his bloodied gauntlets, immediately focused his attention on them. 'Mine!' he growled. The two rebels circled him warily.

The brother with the club – they were twins, Barandas realized – swung at Garmond, a powerful blow that would have flattened a lesser man. Garmond the Black raised an arm and deflected it with his vambrace. At the same time, the other brother yanked a loaded crossbow from where it had been hidden underneath his cloak and fired it. The bolt flew true, hitting the steel gorget around the Augmentor's neck. It should have snapped it, damaged Garmond's windpipe at the very least, but the enchanted metal held and the quarrel bounced away.

With incredible speed for a man of his size, Garmond launched himself forwards and unleashed a right-handed hook at his would-be killer, who had dropped the crossbow. The man twisted to avoid the full impact, but the gauntleted fist caught him a glancing blow and sent him flying to the ground.

Suddenly Garmond stumbled and went down to one knee. The other brother was attempting to tackle him from behind. The rebel was himself large by any normal measure, but Garmond the Black could not be compared to other men.

The Augmentor reached behind him with one arm, dragging his opponent away from his legs and along the ground towards him. With his other hand, he shoved his fingers into the rebel's eyes, pushing down with terrible strength. Screams erupted from his unfortunate victim and rivulets of blood welled up beside Garmond's fingers as they probed ever deeper.

A hatchet suddenly crashed into the back of the Augmentor's helmet with enough force to jolt his head viciously forwards. Barandas thought Garmond might be in serious trouble, but the giant stumbled to his feet in time to catch the follow-up blow in his open gauntlets. Blood dripped from his hands where the hatchet had made its mark.

Garmond didn't seem to care. Snarling from behind his horned helm, he tore the hatchet from the rebel's grip and sent it hurtling across the temple. The twin reached desperately at his belt for another weapon, but he was out of time. Garmond was upon him, his mighty fists shattering the man's cheekbones, then his jaw, and finally opening his skull with a sickening *crack*.

'Enough,' Barandas commanded. Garmond let the corpse drop to the floor. The other brother twitched once nearby, and then lay still.

Taking stock of the situation, Barandas saw that Legwynd had got the better of the rebel he'd been fighting. Bodies were strewn everywhere. He counted eight corpses. 'Do we have their leader?' he asked.

'Over here, Commandant,' Thurbal shouted. Barandas walked over to the shadowy alcove where his fellow Augmentor was waiting. He stared down at the grisly sight on the floor. 'What is the meaning of this?' he demanded.

Thurbal gave an insolent shrug. 'I thought he might try to make a run for it,' he said, 'so I cut off his legs. Then he tried to pull a crossbow on me, so I cut off his arms.'

The twitching mess of flesh at his feet moaned weakly. With the amount of blood he'd already lost, it was a miracle the rebel leader still lived. He was trying to say something, red froth spilling from his mouth down over his double chin. 'I can't understand you,' Barandas said. He put his ear close to the man's mouth.

'*Who...*' he croaked weakly. '*Who betrayed us?*'

Barandas shook his head. 'It's not important now. I regret what this man did to you, but you knew the price of treason. Go to your peace now.' With those words, he placed the edge of his sword against the rebel's fleshy neck and slit his throat.

He glared at Thurbal. 'You and I will have words. Your conduct is unacceptable.' He frowned suddenly. He could hear a faint ticking noise. He raised a questioning eyebrow, but his surly grey-haired colleague pointedly ignored him.

Before Barandas could press him further, a glint near the dead man's severed leg suddenly caught his eye. It was a small crystal, likely quartz, of a pretty green hue. *Like Lena's eyes*, he thought. It was slightly smudged with ash, as if it had been in a fire. He rubbed the grime away and put the stone inside one of the pouches hanging at his belt.

There was a slight sensation of wind brushing against his face and suddenly Legwynd was standing next to him. 'No sign of anyone else alive,' said the cherub-faced killer with a smile. 'But I found this.' He thrust a map at Barandas, who took it from his hands. It illustrated Dorminia and the surrounding region in impressive detail. A hastily drawn circle immediately got his attention. It outlined a specific location east of the city.

'The Wailing Rift,' Barandas muttered under his breath. *Nine corpses, none of them female. Our informant said there were twelve.* Sudden comprehension dawned. 'Legwynd,' he said. 'You will go to the Wailing Rift immediately. I believe these rebels were plotting to take advantage of our sojourn at the Obelisk.'

Legwynd grinned and threw a salute. 'I'll be there before midday. If I find any rebels at the Rift, they'll be in for a surprise.' He patted the daggers at his belt and then sped away almost as fast as the eye could follow.

Barandas looked around at the temple. He had been born into a godless world, yet the sight of so much bloodshed in this once holy sanctuary made him uneasy.

'Thurbal,' he commanded. 'Finish searching this place, and then burn these corpses.'

It was an unpleasant business, but a man did what was necessary.

An Unexpected Message

THE DEPOSITORY WAS a shambles.

Eremul wheeled his chair slowly forwards, circumnavigating the ruined piles of books and soggy reams of paper that had congealed together, becoming little more than clumps of worthless pulp. A soft squelching noise accompanied his slow circuit of the ruined archives. Most of the water had retreated back into the harbour, but the carpeted floor of the depository remained flooded.

He slumped in his chair. The project he had worked on for the last thirteen years was in danger of becoming a literal washout. *Thirteen years.* That was how long he had persisted in this farce, trying to build some wretched facsimile of a life for himself after his mutilation and exile from the Obelisk. The depository had been a welcome diversion, something to take his mind off the truth of his wretched existence.

Eremul fought back the urge to wheel himself out into the streets and rain fiery death down on anyone stupid enough to wander within his immediate vicinity. Why not go out in a blaze of fury? Why not give the slack-jawed fools a taste of the shit they had so gleefully flung at him over the years?

Come, one and all! Come and gawk at the legless cripple. Go ahead. It's not as if I'm a real person, after all.

The answer to his own question was, of course, staring him in the face. To abuse the gift of magic would make him no better than that monstrous shitstain Salazar – the bastard who had torn his life apart and taken his legs in the process. And what the Magelord had done to *him* was but a speck of dust compared with the avalanche of horror that was his latest crime.

The Tyrant of Dorminia had dropped a billion tons of water on a living city and instantly created the biggest mass graveyard since the Godswar five centuries past. Forty thousand men, women and children had died in an instant. One second they were alive; the next they were gone. All those lives, extinguished with the same callous lack of regard a farmer might show for an ant's nest as he drowned it in boiling water.

The ineffable *wrongness* of that act had shocked Eremul in a way he had not thought possible. That any man should have the audacity, much less the capacity, to enact such judgement on so many unknowing souls... why, it would be an affront to the gods, if the gods weren't already dead.

What use for boundaries, when a man has already cast down his makers? Salazar and the other Magelords know nothing of what it means to be human. They forfeited that right long ago.

The destruction of the City of Shades had caused ripples that would be felt for a long time to come. The most immediate was the tsunami that had surged north across the Broken Sea, hitting Dorminia earlier that morning. It had lost most of its energy by the time it reached the harbour, but even so it had destroyed several of the city's battered fleet and flooded the docks as far north as the Tyrant's Road. The homes, shops and taverns that clustered along the harbour had been damaged, some irreparably, and an entire community of Dorminia's poorest families had simply been washed away, along with the ramshackle huts that had sheltered them.

And what of brave Isaac and his companions, trapped out on the water?

Eremul couldn't help but feel a certain amusement at the irony of the situation. The enchantment he had placed on the cutter guarded it against capsizing, but he had no idea how the boat would fare in the grip of a tsunami. Would it be dashed against the coast? Would its passengers tumble out and drown in the hungry waters of Deadman's Channel before it hit the rocks?

Much as he hated to admit it, Eremul hoped neither was the case. He *needed* his assistant. Why, his arms were already starting to ache from the effort of wheeling around the cumbersome contraption Isaac had designed for him. If only he could float up off his chair and drift serenely through the air, like a noble genie riding an invisible steed from the stables of the heavens themselves.

Alas, that was the stuff of fairy tales and Magelords. His own powers didn't extend to being able to wipe his own arse effectively, and Creator knows he'd tried. No, if you wanted a party trick, some minor deceit or frippery to amuse the children, the Halfmage was the man for the job. Anything more substantial required a *real* wizard.

During his lowest moments – which tended to occur roughly four times on any given night – Eremul had pondered why it was that, in spite of the terrible suffering he had endured, his magic remained so pitifully weak. Surely losing his legs meant he should be compensated in other ways? If reality worked the same way as those awful stories he kept buried in the depository, he ought to wield power to rival the mightiest Magelords.

The truth was a very different matter. It seemed the Creator had decreed that if Eremul was to be a man, he would be the most pitiful of men; and if he was to be a mage, he would be the most pitiful of mages. The injustice of it all made him snigger for a second, until the strain set his haemorrhoids to throbbing once again. He shifted around on his chair, searching in vain for a position that would ease the discomfort. Isaac possessed an ointment that helped considerably when applied, but it seemed the bastard had taken it with him – most likely out of spite.

A fine way to reward years of gainful employment. In his

experience, if a man extended a hand to you, it was probably intended as a distraction while he cudgelled you around the back of the head with the other. The most sensible solution was, therefore, to ignore the hand altogether.

Or else simply to steal the cudgel and scramble the bastard's brains before he did the same to you.

He stared around at the wreckage of the depository one more time. He needed some air. Pushing open the sodden door of his ruined archive, the Halfmage inhaled deep the smells of his beloved city.

Saltwater. Rot. Shit? The city's ageing sewer system had been hit by the deluge and had leaked its contents onto the streets above. The late-afternoon sun had barely begun to dry out the abused lanes of the harbourside sprawl, and the incessant sound of trickling water formed an almost pleasant background to the sight of turds floating down the flooded avenues.

Ah. Dorminia in all its glory.

Squelching footsteps suddenly caught his attention. He wheeled his chair around, startling the boy who had been approaching behind him. With his threadbare clothes and grime-covered face, Eremul judged him to be one of the homeless urchins who operated in the city's markets and ran errands for those too savvy or dangerous to pickpocket. Most of them failed to make it to their adult years, desperation driving them to reckless deeds that earned a public execution. Some, the comely ones, were sold in clandestine auctions to powerful men in government. Their fates were the most tragic of all.

This particular orphan gawked at him in amazement, the sealed scroll in his grubby hands forgotten as he stared at the man with no legs.

'What is it?' Eremul asked irritably. He wasn't in the mood for this.

'Got a message for you, sir,' the boy responded, his eyes still glued to the spot where most men sprouted additional limbs. Eremul snapped his fingers and the urchin suddenly seemed to remember where he was. He proffered the scroll. 'A lady asked me to find you and hand you this. Gave me six copper crowns. Said you'd give me the same when I delivered it,' he added hopefully.

Eremul narrowed his eyes. 'What did this lady look like?' he asked.

The boy's brow creased in confusion. 'I can't rightly remember,' he admitted. 'She was mighty strange. Made me nervous. Olly wanted nothing to do with her, but he's a pussy.'

'Indeed. Six crowns is more than generous for a brief jaunt across the city. As you can see' – he pointed to the interior of his ruined depository, then at his ruined body – 'I'm hardly Gilanthus the fucking Golden himself. Hand me that and run along.'

'Who's Gilanthus the Golden?'

Eremul sighed. 'The Merchant Lord. God of wealth and commerce. Not one of the Primes, and besides, he's been dead these last five hundred years.' He reached across and took the scroll from the lad's unresisting fingers. 'Well, what are you waiting for?' he added. 'Piss off.'

The urchin blinked and suddenly began to cough. He raised his hands to his mouth and hacked into them. Eremul rolled his eyes.

'Ah, that old chestnut,' he said. 'Let me just reach into my robes and withdraw a nice big bag of fuck-all to hand to this poor afflicted youth, whose sad lifeless corpse I will surely encounter at some point in the near future...' He trailed off as the boy continued coughing. He was bent over now, his body convulsing in wild spasms. When the urchin finally recovered enough to stand up straight, Eremul saw that blood flecked his chin and stained his small hands.

The boy would, in fact, be dead within the year.

The Halfmage slipped a hand inside one of his pockets and withdrew a silver coin. 'Buy yourself something to eat,' he mumbled. 'And drink plenty of honeyed tea. It will help with the cough.' He tossed the coin at the lad, who didn't react quickly enough. It struck him on the side of the head and rolled into a puddle. The urchin picked it up off the muddy ground, his eyes wide with disbelief.

'Thank – thank you,' the boy stammered, but Eremul had already turned his chair around and wheeled himself back inside the depository, slamming the door shut behind him.

The scroll was blank. He had known it would be. Only a fool would entrust an unencrypted message to a street urchin. The Crimson Watch was known to employ street rats for the sole purpose of diverting literature meant for the eyes of malcontents and using it to track them down.

He ran his fingers down the parchment. The enchantment was faint, absolutely undetectable to anyone not skilled in the arts of magic. In this post-Culling era, when mages were about as welcome in Dorminia as the plague, that meant there were precisely two people in the city capable of discerning its message: himself, and a certain genocidal Magelord.

Muttering an incantation, Eremul summoned forth the latent energy that hummed within him. Every wizard was born with a certain capacity for the harnessing of magic. Salazar and the other Magelords possessed a veritable ocean of power to draw from. For Eremul, it was more like a puddle. Raw magic – the essence of the gods – could be siphoned to replenish or augment a wizard's strength, but it was consumed by the process. Without such external help, a wizard was restricted to the limits of the power they were born with. While that tended to increase with age, the speed with which it recovered once spent slowed at a similar rate.

Of course, Salazar and the other Magelords controlled the distribution of raw magic with an iron grip. Already possessed of power that dwarfed mortal wizards, they widened the gap further still by maintaining exclusive access to the corpses of the gods.

Magic was fading from the world, and as soon as the last divine corpse was sucked dry, there would be nothing left, unless further discoveries like that of the Celestial Isles were made. The murder of the gods had broken something fundamental in the world: the land was slowly dying, refusing to rejuvenate itself as it had prior to the Godswar.

Eremul finished his evocation and then waited. Slowly but surely, spidery words of glowing white energy seeped up from the blank page to float a fraction of an inch above the parchment. The message was starkly simple: *Attend us at the abandoned lighthouse north of the harbour two nights from now. Be there at midnight precisely. Do not be late.*

And that was it. Eremul hissed in frustration. The lighthouse in question was a good mile to the north, situated on top of a large bluff overlooking the harbour. It was an uphill slog most of the way. He hoped Isaac had returned by then.

The cryptic note bore all the hallmarks of the enigmatic individual whose attention he had been seeking for many months now.

The White Lady.

And if there was one individual in the Trine capable of deposing the Tyrant of Dorminia, it was the enigmatic Magelord of Thelassa.

No Brother of Mine

He could hear footsteps. Torchlight flared, and it seemed to burn as brightly as the sun. He squeezed his eyes shut immediately, blinking away tears and the crust accumulated from countless days spent in impenetrable darkness. A harsh voice reached his ears.

'The Sword of the North. Huh. That's a fancy fucking title for a man as wretched as this old greybeard.'

The footsteps slowed. Sounded like three of them, though he couldn't be sure. Another voice.

'He ain't seen the outside of that cage for nigh on a year. It's a wonder he ain't as mad as a wolverine.'

Silence. One of the men coughed. He opened one eye a fraction. How long had it been since his last meal?

The first voice again. 'Fucker's awake. Listen up, Kayne. The Shaman wants you brought to the Great Lodge. Guess who the Brethren found holed up in a cave up in the Devil's Spine?'

Sudden terror. Had they discovered her? He wanted to scream. Bracing himself on the fouled floor of his prison, he pushed himself up, willing his atrophied muscles into life. The weeping sores covering his body chafed agonizingly with his every movement. He didn't care. He squeezed the bars of the cage, trying desperately to force them. They didn't move an inch. He remembered exhausting himself attempting to escape when he'd first been imprisoned. He had no chance now, not after a year of wasting away, yet he grunted and redoubled his efforts.

The harsh voice again, this time amused. 'That got your attention. Your wife. What's her name, Mhaira? She did well, evading the Brethren for all this time. And she ain't a young thing either, though that didn't stop the Butcher having his sport.'

His teeth ground together. His eyes felt as if they were going to explode and he tasted blood. Still the bars wouldn't budge.

A third voice, this one known to him. 'That's enough. Let's just get the cage on the platform.'

He stopped struggling. Stared at the speaker, met his eyes. Saw shame there. Shame and regret.

'My son?' he managed. His voice cracked; it sounded like a foreign thing to his ears after all this time. 'Where is my son?'

The man who was known to him looked down at the ground. 'You'll learn soon enough,' he said, and his tone was apologetic. 'Don't struggle, Kayne. You can't change what's coming.'

He sank back to the floor of his prison. Covered his face with his hands. He'd suffer a thousand agonies, embrace an eternity of torment for the chance to avert the atrocity he knew would be committed at the Great Lodge.

But it was no good. He couldn't change what was coming.

'Kayne.'

The rasping voice dragged him awake and into a world full of misery. His body hurt all over. He opened his eyes to be confronted by the unpleasant sight of Jerek's scowling visage staring down at him. The Wolf had a few bumps and bruises but otherwise appeared unscathed.

'Shit,' Brodar Kayne muttered. 'Help me up.'

Jerek reached down, grabbed hold of his wrists and then hauled him roughly upwards. He tottered for a moment, a hundred little niggles assailing him like a pack of wolves trying to bring down a bear. The old Highlander breathed deeply. His knees ached like buggery and his chest felt as if it had been bludgeoned by a giant's club, but he could tough it out. You had to, when you were stupid enough to keep doing this kind of shit at his age.

'The others?' he asked. Jerek nodded over his shoulder in reply, and Kayne turned gingerly to survey their surroundings.

They stood on a mushy grass slope overlooking the coastline hundreds of yards distant. A little further down, Vicard lay motionless on the edge of a wide shingle beach covered in pools of saltwater. Sasha was kneeling over him. He couldn't tell if the alchemist was alive or dead.

The wreckage of their boat littered the hill around them. The upturned hull rested a mere dozen yards away, its keel broken and sagging in the middle.

'Isaac?' he asked, fearing the worst. Jerek said nothing, simply shook his head and spat. Kayne sighed and began to make his unsteady way down the slope towards the other survivors. 'Evil luck to lose one of the group so early on this expedition,' he said. 'Don't bode well. The Halfmage ain't going to be best pleased—'

'Bastard's over there,' Jerek interrupted. He pointed down the coastline to a rocky outcrop that marked the beginning of a promontory in the distance. Kayne could just make out a figure sat perched over the edge.

'Is he... fishing?' he wondered aloud. The blurred shape seemed to notice him staring and waved an arm in greeting. 'I'll be damned. He's tougher than he looks.' *Or maybe I'm just old and brittle.*

The two Highlanders climbed down the sodden hill until they reached the girl and the figure at her feet. The alchemist was still breathing. He was also making pitiful whimpering sounds, much to the disgust of the Wolf.

'How's he doing?' Kayne asked. Sasha had a nasty cut on her forehead, but aside from that she didn't seem too much the worse for wear.

'Bruised ribs,' she replied. 'Twisted ankle. One of his

shoulders popped out of its socket but Isaac managed to tease it back into place. I didn't know he was a physician.'

'And an angler,' the old barbarian replied. He was beginning to understand why the Halfmage kept the man around.

Sasha held a strip of wet cloth and was wiping at Vicard's brow. He made a soft moaning sound and reached weakly for her hands, taking them into his own and holding onto them as if for dear life. Jerek shot him a baleful glare. Even Sasha pursed her lips in distaste.

'Wolf, go fetch our talented friend,' Kayne said, thinking it best to give Jerek something to do before he ended up throttling the alchemist where he lay. His friend grunted his assent and stalked off towards the distant crag.

Kayne glanced up at the sky. How long had it been since they'd washed up on the pebbly coast? He reckoned two, maybe three hours. The sun still rode low in the scattering clouds, bleeding golden light into the newborn day and reflecting serenely in the now-calm water of Deadman's Channel. All in all, the morning was shaping up to be a glorious one. It reminded him of another morning, many months past. That had turned out to be the darkest of days.

'Do you still have Magebane?' The girl's question brought him back to the present. He felt around at his belt.

'Aye, it's right here. That wave knocked us a few miles off track. I figure we head north and east until we see the Tombstone.'

Vicard whimpered again. Sasha looked down at him doubtfully. 'He's going to struggle on one leg. We can't leave him here.'

The alchemist pushed himself up so that he rested on his right elbow, moaning all the while with the effort. 'My bag,' he panted. 'Where is it?'

Sasha walked over to where Vicard's pack rested next to the handful of possessions that had survived the wreck. 'You're lucky,' she said. 'I've already checked inside. Most of it is intact.'

She brought the pack over to the alchemist and dropped it down beside him. He rifled through it with his good arm, becoming increasingly frantic as he failed to locate what he was looking for. Pouches and strange containers were cast aside as his hand probed deeper. A sheen of sweat appeared on his face. Sasha watched him anxiously.

Eventually Vicard found what he'd been searching for. With a delighted yelp, he tugged a small brown leather pouch from the bottom of the pack. The alchemist fumbled with the cord for a moment, then lifted the pouch to his face and buried his nose inside, snorting deeply. When he finally removed it from the pouch it was covered in a white powdery substance. He sighed in satisfaction and grinned stupidly.

Brodar Kayne observed the scene with a deep frown on his lined face. He'd seen Highlanders become hopelessly addicted to *jhaeld*, the fireplant found in the most desolate reaches of the mountains. The powdered resin of that rare plant could cause a man's blood to feel as though it were on fire, inciting his passions and lending him the courage to smite his enemies as if he were the Reaver, the Lord of Death himself. Such men inevitably died young, attempting feats beyond their true prowess. Over-confidence could get a man killed.

The powder Vicard was snorting was white rather than the rust-red of the *jhaeld*, but the ecstasy on his face was the same, and unmistakable. Kayne cleared his throat. 'I reckon that's enough of that for the moment. Can you stand?'

Vicard carefully replaced the pouch in his pack and retied the straps. With another unctuous smile, he stuck his uninjured arm out towards Sasha. 'Pull me up,' he ordered. She gave him a dirty look but complied, heaving him to his feet. He hopped around for a bit before risking some weight on his dodgy ankle. It seemed to hold.

'Don't look like too much damage has been done,' said Kayne. 'But you might want to wipe that smirk off your face. The Wolf's returning and you don't want to get his dander up unnecessarily.'

From the looks of it, though, Jerek's dander was already at neck height and rising. Isaac followed behind him, a faint smile on his insipid face. A rod was hung over his back and in his arms he carried a net teeming with fish. A few still twitched every so often.

'I caught us some fish,' he said, stating the obvious. 'Most of our provisions were lost in the wreck. I thought you might be hungry. No, don't look at me like that. *Of course* I don't expect you to eat it raw! I found some kindling untouched by the wave, and there's plenty of flint on this beach. We'll set forth on full bellies. Correct nutrition is essential to any endeavour, as so adroitly articulated in Gnoster's *Food for the Soul*.'

Kayne looked at his companions. 'I don't know about you, but I won't pass up the opportunity to get some grub down me. We have a dozen miles to cover before midday. Get your hand out of that pack,' he added, noticing that Vicard was once again rummaging around for his mystery pouch.

'The pain!' the alchemist protested. 'It's unbearable! Just one more sniff and I'll be able to walk on my own. I wouldn't want to slow you down…' Kayne fixed him with his best icy glare and the man hesitated and finally withdrew his empty hand. 'Fine!' he said petulantly. 'I'll need someone to lean on.'

'I ain't touching the faggot,' Jerek growled.

Kayne rubbed at his temples with callused thumbs. 'Throw an arm around me,' he said. 'I've travelled with worse baggage.' Vicard looked at Sasha with a hopeful expression, but she was having none of it.

'Fine,' he said sullenly.

They'd been walking for a little over an hour. The sun had cast off its wispy shackles and was well on its way to fulfilling its earlier promise. Brodar Kayne wiped sweat from his brow and tried to ignore the incessant sniffling from the man limping alongside him. He could just about see Jerek in the distance, stalking along by himself. The group had become strung out, with Isaac ambling happily along some way behind Jerek and the girl following a similar distance behind the manservant. Kayne and Vicard brought up the rear.

Hardly the merriest of companions. He glanced at the alchemist beside him. Vicard had been eager to engage him in conversation at first, babbling about all manner of topics until it became clear Kayne wasn't interested in talk. Now he dragged himself along in miserable silence, his good arm thrown around the Highlander's neck and the other held uselessly at his side. Snot dribbled from his nose and hung in slimy threads from his chin. The barbarian was beginning to regret offering the man a shoulder to lean on.

The monstrous wave of water had flooded the coastline for miles inland. With every step his boots sank into the saturated turf. They'd held a consistent line just above the flooded shingle, but the land rose at a steady pace and it made navigation awkward, especially with Vicard clinging to him like a limpet.

It don't get any easier. He couldn't recall a time when he had felt so old. His body protested with every step. In all likelihood, he needed a physician to tend his injuries. Still, there was no point grumbling. You had to grit your teeth and get on with it.

Where did that damn wave come from? He had never seen anything like it. Truth be told, he'd almost pissed himself when he first set eyes on the wall of water barrelling towards them. He couldn't remember the actual impact, but the terror he'd felt was clear enough in his mind. It was a miracle they'd all survived.

Jerek had stopped far ahead. Kayne saw him glance back at the rest of the group, point to the north, and without further ceremony begin climbing the shallow promontory that overlooked the coast. The ascent was difficult, but the headland rose up sharply a little further on and if they delayed any longer it would become impassable. Vicard groaned when he saw the path they had to take.

'Chin up,' the old barbarian said. 'Once we've made it to the top, it'll be easy going until we reach the Rift. I hope whatever it is you've got in store for the mine ain't been spoiled by damp.'

Vicard managed a weak smile. 'The powder's still dry,' he said. 'They won't know what hit them.'

Brodar Kayne nodded in satisfaction. Bringing down the mining operation would be a mighty kick to Salazar's balls. He didn't have anything personal against the Tyrant of Dorminia, but a job was a job.

Sudden movement caught his eye. *Thirty yards ahead, behind those boulders.* He halted, pulling Vicard back behind him. The alchemist looked at him questioningly and he raised a finger to his lips. Isaac and Sasha were well ahead of them and Jerek was out of sight. *Damn.*

'Wait here,' he ordered. He inched slowly forwards, hands poised to reach behind him and draw his greatsword at any moment.

'I'm Brodar Kayne,' he said loudly. 'Once named the Sword of the North. That's in the past and I ain't one to live on old glories, but the title might mean something to you. I don't like killing but I'll be damned if there was anything I was ever half as good at. If you want to walk away from here, and I'm guessing you might, best show yourselves now.'

He waited. A hawk burst from a clump of bushes near the largest boulder and screamed loudly before soaring off towards the sea. *Maybe I was mistaken. Bloody eyes.* He shook his head in disgust. *Spooked by a bird.*

And then they emerged from behind the rocky outcrop. A tangle of furs and shields, bristling with weapons of murder. Faces as hard as the stone of the High Fangs, five of them. His breath caught for a moment. He recognized one of the men.

Borun.

He drew his greatsword slowly, rested it point down on the moist earth and leaned upon it. 'It's been a while,' he said evenly.

The largest of the five men raised his hand and the others halted, hands on their weapons. They eyed him warily. He could hear Vicard's breath quicken and smell the alchemist's fear.

'It has,' Borun replied. 'Two years, I reckon. You look much better than the last time I saw you, though age gets to us all.' He had more grey in his beard and a few more lines on his face, but Borun looked as hale as ever. He was younger than Kayne by a good handful of years, the same height but plenty broader.

'Ain't that the truth.' He drew deep, even breaths. Borun was one of the finest warriors in the High Fangs. He should know, he'd fought alongside him often enough. His palms tightened on the pommel of his greatsword. 'How long you been watching us?'

Borun shrugged. 'Half an hour. I see you got the Wolf with you. He marched right on by us. The two of you make strange companions.'

It was Kayne's turn to shrug. 'Funny thing, that. You never really know a man until he's called upon to keep his word.'

Borun had the decency to look ashamed. 'It was nothing personal, Kayne. You know that. I got a wife and three daughters. Krazka—'

'Raped Mhaira so bad she couldn't walk, then grinned as the Shaman burned her alive. *My wife*, Borun. The woman you gave away during our joining.' He paused. He could remember their wedding ceremony as if it were yesterday, every detail. Proudest moment of his life, with maybe one exception.

'I called you brother,' he said. He tried to keep his voice level. As well try holding back a river with his bare hands.

'Aye, you did. Don't think it ain't a weight I carry about my neck every moment of every day.' The two men stood in silence for a time. Borun's men shifted uneasily. *Probably expected to be knee-deep in blood by now. Not listening to a couple of old men reminiscing about the past.*

Borun blinked and then hefted his great two-handed

battleaxe. Its oak shaft was covered in notches. 'You gonna try and add one more to that?' Kayne asked, nodding at the brutal weapon.

'Aye,' Borun replied. 'The deepest cut of all, I reckon.' He shook his head ruefully. 'Only one of us can walk away from here.'

One of the warriors next to Borun, a young heavy-browed fellow Kayne didn't recognize, jabbed his spear in the air and spat. 'We're gonna fuck you up good, old man. Don't expect any help. Not unless that streak of piss knows how to handle a blade.' He leered at Vicard, who had slowly begun backing away. In the distance Kayne saw three more Highlanders emerge from behind rocks and shrubbery to cut off Sasha and Isaac.

Borun gestured and his men moved forwards, weapons raised and eyes eager for blood. 'You still got it after all these years, Kayne?' he taunted, his massive axe glittering cruelly in the sun.

Brodar Kayne didn't respond. He simply waited, hands on the pommel of his greatsword, his body perfectly still. 'You'll want to run, I expect,' he hissed to the cowering figure of Vicard behind him. No sooner had the words left his lips than he heard the alchemist break into a scrabbling half-hop, half-sprint punctuated by pained gasps.

The ugly fellow with the spear suddenly thrust the weapon at Kayne's head. He shifted his neck, felt it brush past his ear. The jagged edge of a half-rusted longsword slashed at him from the right and he swivelled, watched the blade whistle through the empty air. *All right. Now it gets serious.*

He forced a smile onto his face. 'That the best you got?' he said. 'I might be old, but I ain't dead. Put some effort in. *Come at me.*'

The spear-wielder duly obliged, lunging forwards and aiming for his chest. With lightning speed, Kayne thrust his body to the right to avoid the jab, grabbing hold of the shaft with his left hand and pulling it towards him. He glimpsed the surprised look on his attacker's face a split second before his head shattered the man's nose.

Still with one hand on his greatsword, he grabbed the stunned Highlander by the neck and pulled him to one side, positioning the warrior between his own body and the descending blade of his other opponent. Blood spurted as the rusted blade tore into the spot right between the neck and shoulder of his human shield and then stuck there.

Silently thanking his luck, Kayne raised his greatsword and buried it in his shocked opponent's sternum as he struggled to free his snagged weapon from the other man's body. It burst through his back in a splatter of gore. He slid the blade free and watched as the dying Highlanders sank to the earth in a tangle of limbs and iron.

Borun stared at the carnage with a look of consternation. His two remaining men suddenly seemed a great deal more wary, the eager looks on their faces draining away with the lives of their comrades. 'You told me age had caught up with you!' Borun said accusingly.

Kayne shrugged. 'I ain't what I used to be. Can't piss in a straight line, if at all. I got aches in places I didn't know *could* ache. But if there's one thing I still know how to do,' he added, moving towards the three men, 'it's killing. You never really lose the instinct for it.' He nodded at Borun's axe. 'There was a time when I thought to record my kills,' he said quietly. 'When I ran out of room on one weapon, I'd choose another, a different kind. It'd be rough going for a while.'

He was opposite the three Highlanders now. They spread out and moved to surround him. He met the eyes of each in turn, and then focused his attention on Borun. 'You remember me back in the day. All fire and thunder and fury. Fact is, a year spent caged like an animal changes a man. Seeing your wife get burned alive changes a man. You learn to accept what can't be undone and bend so you don't end up breaking. You *adapt*.

'For example,' he said, as Jerek finally reached them and his axe split the head of the Highlander to his left, 'you don't pass up an advantage when it presents itself. What's honour to the kind of men who'll rape a woman and then burn her alive? The Code ain't worth two shits as far as I can see.'

Borun and the remaining Highlander had spun the instant they became aware of Jerek among them, but it was too late. The Wolf was already stalking towards the warrior on Kayne's right flank, twin axes raised.

Borun snarled in anger. 'Coward's tactics that, distracting us for your dog to sneak up behind.'

'Like I said, the Code don't mean anything. I reached that conclusion long before the Shaman stuck me in a cage. Couldn't stomach the hypocrisy no more. Course, I was stupid enough to tell him that to his face. Just goes to show that it don't matter how well a man *thinks* he understands something. He never really does, not until he's taught the lesson at first hand.'

'I'll teach you a fucking lesson,' Borun bellowed, and he pounced. His axe came flashing down. Kayne raised his greatsword and caught it, turned it aside. The two men came together in a flurry of feints, parries and clashing steel. Borun was every bit as good as he remembered. Unlike him, Borun hadn't spent a year in a cage, his muscles withering away to nothing. He hadn't spent the best part of two years running from the Brethren, giants, and even worse things. He hadn't just survived a damned shipwreck.

The haft of Borun's axe caught him a glancing blow on the face and he stumbled backwards. He felt blood dampen his right cheek, trickling down to his chin. His body hurt all over and his heart hammered. Borun feinted, punched forwards with the head of his huge axe and then brought it swinging around in a devastating overhead slash. Kayne ducked and rolled out of the way, his body screaming in protest. No sooner had he finished his roll than Borun was upon him, his axe swinging downwards in a fierce overhead chop. He caught it with his greatsword, but the effort sent pain jarring through his neck and shoulders. He was on his knees, the weight of the muscular warrior pushing down on him.

Ten years ago, maybe even five, he would have summoned up the strength to push back. Borun might be the larger man, but he was *Brodar Kayne*, and his strength had been legendary.

That was then. This was now. Try as he might, he could not overpower the huge, stinking warrior looming over him. Fact was, he wasn't the man he used to be.

You have to adapt.

He dived to the left, heard the heavy steel head of the axe thud into the turf an instant later, missing his head by a hair's breadth. There was an angry grunt and then Borun was on him again. Still on his knees, Kayne parried the first blow. He dropped a hand to the magical dagger at his belt and parried Borun's second slash one-handed, his arm almost buckling with the effort.

With his free hand, he drew the blade and slammed it hard into Borun's stomach.

The big Highlander gasped and stumbled backwards, staring down at the hilt quivering in his midriff. Blood seeped around it, dribbling between his legs.

Brodar Kayne clambered back to his feet and stalked forwards. 'I reckon that'll about do for you,' he said, swatting aside a diagonal chop aimed at his neck. Borun was already weakening. The dribble of blood had become a steady patter. 'I should leave you here to die a slow death. Ain't like you don't deserve it.'

Borun drew a shuddering breath. 'Couldn't rightly blame you for that,' he said. He wavered and suddenly his axe tumbled from his grasp into the mud with a squelch. He placed both hands around the hilt of the dagger, where they hesitated.

'Lost count of the times I dreamed of killing you,' Kayne said. 'Sometimes it was all that kept me going. I guess I should be feeling mighty satisfied right about now. Truth is, though, I don't. You can't change what's been done.'

'Aye,' said Borun. He rocked on his feet again. His hands

had begun to tremble. 'And sometimes you can't change what's coming.'

Kayne closed his eyes for a moment. Memories came back to him. Swimming down the Icemelt on his twenty-first naming day, his skin so cold it had turned blue. Borun laughing his arse off, little more than a boy. He had swum to the shore and hauled the younger man in, to much laughter from them both.

Hunting in the Long Pikes together, Borun bringing down his first boar after they'd spent the best part of a day fleeing an enraged mountain lion.

The look of pride on Borun's face when Kayne asked him to be Spirit Father for his bride-to-be.

The same face staring at the ground while he scraped his arms raw on the Shaman's cage.

Mhaira's screams.

He raised his greatsword high above his head. The sun bathed it in a red glow, the colour of blood. 'Sometimes you can't change what's coming,' he said, staring down into Borun's eyes. 'But a man who looks away and accepts it without as much as a whimper, he's no man. And for damn sure he ain't no brother.' The sword flashed down. Borun's head thumped onto the ground and rolled for a good few yards before coming to a stop against an outcrop of granite.

Jerek walked over, his twin axes dripping red. 'You told that cunt,' he said simply. Specks of blood dotted his face and short beard.

Kayne glanced at the bodies of the two Highlanders the Wolf had killed. It wasn't a pretty sight. 'You could have stepped in,' he said. 'Borun almost had me.'

Jerek snorted. 'That's some fucking gratitude. You'd never have forgiven me, Kayne, and you know it.'

The old barbarian thought about it for a moment, and then nodded. 'Aye, you're right. The others?'

'Isaac and the girl are fine. He ain't bad with a sword. Held them off until I got there. As for the faggot, fuck knows.'

Brodar Kayne shook his head. The Halfmage's manservant was full of surprises. 'Vicard fled. I expect he's hiding under a rock somewhere.'

'Up here,' called a strained voice. They looked up. The alchemist knelt on a narrow ridge some distance above them. He had a stupid smile on his face. 'I found a path,' he exclaimed. 'I was preparing a little something for those brutes, but it turns out it wasn't necessary.' He tossed the small ceramic ball in his hand into the air to demonstrate. The barbarian winced as he almost fumbled it.

Vicard wiped his nose with the back of his hand and grinned again. Kayne could see the brown leather pouch on the ground near his satchel. 'Pack your things and get down here,' he bellowed. 'If I see you snorting that shit again, the whole pouch goes up your arse and that's a promise.' The adrenalin was wearing off and his whole body was aching worse than before. He glanced down, saw Borun's sightless eyes staring back at him. He grimaced.

It don't get any easier.

Hard Decisions

COLE RETCHED ONE more time, heaving until there was nothing left inside him and he thought his innards were going to spill out of his mouth. Between the constant rocking sensation and the foul stench, scarcely an hour passed when he didn't feel the need to empty his gut. Puddles of piss and dark mounds of excrement lay mingled with vomit, blood and other assorted filth on the floor beneath him. The one saving grace was that it was too dim to see the putrid mess in all its glory. Cracks in the planking above allowed a few narrow shafts of light to illuminate the faces of his fellow prisoners, but they didn't reach far enough to penetrate the darkest recesses of the cargo hold.

Someone kill me, he thought miserably. The *Redemption* had set sail the night before, and while the small carrack was making good time they still had the better part of a day and night before they reached their destination.

Of the forty men on board, almost half were consigned to the cargo hold. Their ankles were shackled to ensure they didn't try to escape. The rest of the ship's passengers were above decks: Kramer, the disgraced former admiral of Dorminia's fleet, now captain of the *Redemption*, and his first mate, a bald-headed brute of a man named Vargus; their crew, ten of the bravest – or stupidest – men they could convince to sail the ship; a dozen Crimson Watchmen to maintain order and help operate the small arsenal of heavy artillery in case of attack; and finally

Falcus, the lisping Augmentor overseeing the expedition. He'd already murdered one captive for refusing to return to the hold after they'd been allowed on deck for their morning meal. The Augmentor had clucked in annoyance, whipped out his crossbow and put a quarrel through the man's head at point-blank range. The body had been hurled overboard to sink to the bottom of the Broken Sea.

Cole's ankles were chafed raw from his shackles, his ribs still ached and he'd been pissing blood ever since Goodlady Cyreena had clobbered him in the balls and shoved a needle in him.

She had been waiting down at the docks to watch them depart. Cole had longed to spit in her face or break away from his captors and drown her in the harbour. When she'd met his gaze with those strangely familiar eyes of hers, however, he'd felt his legs turn to jelly and promptly vomited all over the Crimson Watchman beside him. That had earned him a rough backhand across the face.

I want to die. He'd never known suffering like this. He was trapped on a cramped and filthy ship, his body a mass of agonies, any single one of which would likely incapacitate a lesser man. Even a hero had his limits.

Not for the first time Davarus Cole cursed his ill luck. He was on his way to the Swell, a place sailors spoke of only in the most fearful of whispers. The odds of him returning to Dorminia and the glorious future he had been promised were growing worse by the hour.

'Stop your snivelling, boy,' spat Three-Finger. He was an evil-looking fellow, with dirty grey stubble covering his scabrous face and piggish eyes staring from beneath a brow that seemed permanently furrowed. His left hand was missing its index and middle fingers. As a boy he had been caught stealing in the Bazaar.

From the other captives Cole had learned Three-Finger was also missing half a cock, having more recently been charged with numerous counts of rape and sentenced accordingly. He

110

scowled at anyone he caught looking at him whenever he decided to take a piss, which was often.

'My nose is broken,' Cole replied sullenly. 'I wasn't snivelling. You don't know what I've been through.'

Three-Finger laughed. 'Aren't you a special snowflake. Take a look around, kid. Every man in this shithole has a sorry tale to share. You think I want to be here? It was this or swing in the Hook until the crows pecked off the rest of my prick. I figured the Swell would be quicker and a good deal less painful.'

One of the other captives coughed, a horrible hacking that told of some illness in his lungs. 'I didn't even have a choice,' the man said, once he'd wiped the blood away from his mouth. 'The Watch burst into my home. They told me I'd been found guilty of treason.' He coughed again before continuing. 'Taxes were raised so high to fund the war with Shadowport that my business collapsed and my wife had to take to the streets to support our family. I called Salazar every name under the sun, didn't see the mindhawk until it was too late. Then the Black Lottery chose me.'

'What kind of trade you in?' Three-Finger asked. He had a rash on the side of his face and kept scratching at it with his maimed hand.

'I'm an engineer,' the sick man replied. 'I ran a business. Soeman's Solutions on Artifice Street.'

'I know it,' Three-Finger said. 'You're Soeman, then?'

The engineer nodded and lapsed into another fit of coughing. 'Those in charge of this operation must have thought I'd be useful to them,' he said once he recovered. 'Otherwise I'd be dead. Armin is directing the mining operation. Maybe he requested an additional engineer aboard the ship.'

'The *Swell*,' exclaimed a red-nosed man of advanced years chained nearby. 'I've sailed the Broken Sea for thirty years – travelled to the Drowned Coast and the ruins of old Andarr, and west further still, out onto the great Endless Ocean. Yet never once did I venture near that accursed place. They say the

Swell marks the spot where Malantis plummeted from the heavens. His corpse rots there still.'

The old seadog's voice suddenly dropped to a whisper. Cole struggled to hear him over the creaking of stressed wood and the murmuring of waves washing against the hull.

'A ship can be sailing happily along one minute – and the next, it's twenty feet under water. That ain't the worse though. I've heard tales of craft that have crested a wave only for the sea's surface to plummet a hundred foot or more in an instant. He might be dead, but the Lord of the Deep don't rest easy in his watery grave. His rage is unquenchable, they say, and he'll scupper any ship that dares disturb his resting place.'

The old sailor's words sent a shudder of fear rippling through Cole and the other captives within hearing distance. Danger was one thing, a calculated risk to overcome. What the veteran sailor described amounted to playing roulette with the very sea itself.

'This is suicide!' he gasped.

Three-Finger grinned, revealing crooked yellow teeth. 'I hope those wankers know what they've let themselves in for.'

The hatch above them suddenly banged open and sunlight flooded the hold. Cole blinked tears from his stinging eyes. Once his vision had cleared, he saw the weather-beaten face of First Mate Vargus staring at them. Sweat ran in rivulets down his bald head and scarred cheeks.

'Captain Kramer wants you all up on deck,' he barked at them. 'We're coming down to open your shackles. Any of you so much as *looks* like causing trouble, that man gets to feed the fishes.'

He disappeared. A rope ladder was lowered, and four men of the Watch climbed down into the hold. Each wore chainmail and carried a steel longsword in his hand.

Cole briefly considered trying to overpower the soldier unlocking his shackles, but a glance at the open hatch revealed Falcus and a half-dozen Watchmen positioned around the edge of the hold, crossbows at the ready. The young Shard's appraising gaze became a sickly grin when the Augmentor caught him staring at them. Cole gulped and quickly looked away.

Ten minutes later and the captives were huddled together on the main deck. The Crimson Watch surrounded them, swords in hand. Captain Kramer stood on the forecastle. Falcus was to his right, fondling his crossbow as if looking for any excuse to shoot someone. Vargus brooded to the captain's left.

Kramer placed his hands on the forecastle's rail and surveyed the men arrayed below him. The stress of recent events had affected him: he looked thin, almost frail. His grey hair was cropped close to his head and his weathered face looked tired. Even so, his voice was strong and clear.

'By now, you all know where we are going,' he said loudly. 'The Swell, a place said to be haunted by the restless spirit of the Lord of the Deep. Be that as it may, we are all here for a reason. Many of you are convicted criminals who have chosen to be part of this voyage rather than face the noose or the headsman's axe. Some of you are free men who possess the courage to risk your lives in pursuit of greater fortunes. I salute your bravery.

'I am here because I failed Dorminia and our lord. In his wisdom and mercy, Salazar saw fit to grant me a second chance. I will *not* fail him again.'

Cole looked around as Kramer's words rolled across the deck. The wind was a constant whistling presence, shaking the mainmast looming over them and buffeting the sails high above their heads. The *Redemption*'s flag displayed a white background, but in an ironic modification of the arms borne by the Crimson Watch, the Obelisk had been replaced by a gibbet. The significance couldn't have been lost on Kramer or anyone else aboard the carrack.

In the distance, *Red Bounty* struggled vainly to keep pace alongside the swifter carrack. The huge cog was loaded with mining equipment and a skeleton crew of sailors and miners desperate enough to risk their lives in an expedition to the Swell. The dark waters of the Broken Sea lapped hungrily at her sides.

Closing his eyes for a moment, Cole imagined drowning in that sea, thrust into an abyss of crushing saltwater that squeezed the very life from his lungs. The thought made him nauseous again.

'Pay attention to the captain, dog!' ordered a Watchman to the side of him. The soldier placed a hand on the hilt of his sword. Cole's eyes obediently shifted back to Kramer.

'Tomorrow morning we will arrive at the Swell's boundary,' the captain was saying. 'If all goes as planned, our mining operation will be under way within a day or two. We could be stationed at the Swell for as little as a fortnight. I am a hard man, but I am also a fair one. Do as I command and you might well live long enough to return to Dorminia.'

All across the deck men perked up at the captain's words. Cole wanted to shake them, yell at them that Kramer was just another of Salazar's puppets, feeding them a line so that they would work themselves to death. They would be disposed of once their usefulness was at an end. He was a Shard – he knew how the Magelord operated.

'Bullshit,' he muttered, louder than he had intended.

'What?' It was the same Watchman who had warned him before. The soldier's eyes narrowed dangerously. 'Did you just call the captain a liar?'

Everyone turned to look at him. He swallowed. 'Not at all,' he replied. 'Everyone knows that Admir— uh, Captain Kramer is an honest man. As honest as stone, I've heard folk say.'

'And just as dumb,' Three-Finger added loudly, to Cole's disbelief. There were gasps followed by chuckles. The face of the Watchman turned an ugly shade of red and he drew his sword. The other soldiers followed suit.

'Halt,' ordered Kramer from the forecastle. 'What is the meaning of this?' Next to the captain, Falcus had his crossbow

114

raised and was sweeping it over the prisoners assembled below them.

'These two clowns called you a liar and a dullard, Captain,' the Watchman answered. 'Say the word and I'll put them overboard.'

Captain Kramer looked almost pained. 'I am loath to waste more lives so early in our mission. Yet insubordination cannot be tolerated, especially from a rapist and a child-fiddler.'

A child-fiddler? Cole's jaw dropped. A rational part of his mind told him to keep quiet, but the injustice of it all was too much to bear. 'Forgive me, Captain, but you're mistaken,' he began. 'I—'

'Silence!' Kramer screamed. He was shaking with anger. 'You disgust me. Full details of your crimes were provided for each and every one of you. Some are more unfortunate than others to be here, true, but you, and you' – he pointed at Three-Finger, and then at Cole – 'deserve everything that might befall you on this ship. You're the lowest form of scum.'

Cole bit down on his tongue so hard he tasted blood. This was a travesty!

'Enough of this,' Kramer said irritably. 'You prisoners will be returned to the hold, where you will remain until your evening meal. If I so much as hear a complaint about the food from either of you,' he added, glaring at Three-Finger and Cole, 'you'll both go over the side.' That said, he turned his back on the crowd and disappeared off towards the bow. Falcus pointed his weapon at Cole, smiled, and then followed after the captain.

'You crazy idiots,' Soeman said, once they were back in the hold. 'You almost got yourselves killed.' He coughed and spat blood onto the soiled planking beneath them.

Three-Finger shrugged. 'Death by drowning don't seem so bad. I can think of nastier ways to go.' He had an evil look in his eyes that made Cole uncomfortable.

'Ain't nothing worse than the Swell,' the old sailor, Jack, spat. He made a warding sign in the air with his left hand. 'I want to stare death in the face. Not be swallowed up by the sea when I least expect it.'

Three-Finger raised his mutilated hand and scratched at his scabrous cheek. 'Most of us haven't got any sailing experience. Know what that tells me? They mean to use us for all the dangerous shit – stuff no sane man would do. We won't make it out of here, none of us.'

Cole cleared his throat noisily to get their attention. He'd had an idea. It was crazy and dangerous and some might even say foolish, but desperate times called for desperate measures.

When hard decisions need to be made, hard men step up to take them. He had read that in a book once, and it had struck a chord.

'Once we've reached the spot where we're to begin mining, what happens?' he asked softly.

Soeman answered. '*Red Bounty* will drop anchor. We'll board her and begin unloading the equipment. It will be heavy work.'

Cole dropped his voice to a whisper so that only Soeman, Three-Finger and Jack could hear. 'What if we create a diversion on the *Bounty*? Soeman could sabotage a piece of equipment and draw the attention of the Watch. If we can empty the *Redemption* of soldiers, we could sneak back aboard this ship and steal it before they realize what's happening.'

Three-Finger grinned, flashing yellow teeth. 'And what about her crew? You think the four of us can handle a dozen men? You're deluded.'

'Not just the four of us,' Cole replied. 'I can convince some of the others to join us. The sailors on board this ship are poorly armed. They're no warriors. On the other hand,' he said, waving an arm at the shadowy figures scattered about the hold, 'most of us here know how to fight. Am I right, Three-Finger?'

'Aye, I'm a surgeon with a shank,' the convict replied. 'And there's plenty more killers among us. But we're unarmed. We'll be cut to shreds.'

Cole just about stopped short of tapping his head knowingly. He had them right where he wanted them. 'The mining equipment is sure to include objects that can be used as weapons. Picks and hammers, that sort of thing. While the Watch are distracted, we'll arm the other captives, board this ship and force the *Redemption* to sail before those aboard *Red Bounty* know we're gone.'

It was old Jack's turn to speak. 'I can captain this ship, that I can. *Red Bounty* won't stand a chance of catching us. But where would we go?'

Cole shrugged. 'Anywhere, so long as it's away from Dorminia.'

Soeman shook his head slowly. 'This is madness. We're better off working the Swell and hoping for a pardon from the magistrates. I have a family to think about.'

Coward, Cole wanted to hiss at him, but he forced a look of compassion onto his face. 'I understand your fears, Soeman,' he said gently. 'But do you think your family would want you to die out here alone in a freak accident? Or swallowed up by the Swell? No. They would want you to die *fighting*.'

He had a sudden flash of inspiration. 'Besides, you're sick. You've contracted something bad, Soeman. You can't risk exposing your family to whatever disease it is you have. Better for them to discover that their beloved husband and father spent his final days a free man, sailing the sea alongside boon companions like the storied heroes of old.'

The engineer sagged. 'You're right,' he said. 'I'll make my family proud of me. Maybe... maybe we can send some gold home to my wife. Just so she doesn't have to work the streets any more.' His voice had turned hopeful.

Cole smiled. 'Of course we will,' he said. *If we have anything left to spare. Organizing a rebel army isn't going to be cheap.* 'I need to share my plan with the others,' he said. 'I'll wait until this evening when it's dark and I can move freely above decks.'

'I'm with you, lad,' said Jack. 'I've wanted my own ship for years. Hah, I got caught trying to steal a pretty little schooner from the harbour. Turns out it belonged to a powerful magistrate. I was up for hanging until the *Redemption* called.'

'Count me in too,' said Three-Finger. 'I'll die with a weapon in hand if I'm going to die at all.' The convict rubbed at his ravaged face again. 'You still haven't introduced yourself, kid. Or explained how it is you think you can convince a bunch of criminals to work together and pull off the escape of the century.'

Cole squared his shoulders and gave each of the three men a weighty stare, aches and pains forgotten in the sudden rush of pride. At last he was getting the respect he deserved! He could already see the amazement on Garrett's face when he unveiled the full depth of his brilliance in years to come.

'My name's Davarus Cole,' he said. 'As for the exact details of how I'm planning to pull this off, you don't need to worry yourselves. I have a lifetime's experience with this kind of thing. You see...' He paused momentarily for effect. '... *this is what I do.*'

The Ultimate Lesson

YLLANDRIS HAD THOUGHT she understood what it was to endure the deepest cold. The last couple of days had taught her otherwise.

She squinted, trying to make out the town a scant few hundred yards ahead of the war party. The blizzard that had buffeted them for the last few hours persisted stubbornly, slowing their advance and piling on the misery that had blighted the march since it began.

'Fucking spirits be damned,' Krazka spat, wiping frost from his beard with the back of his hand. His dead eye had frozen over and gleamed malevolently from his cruel face.

Standing beside the bloodthirsty chieftain of the Lake Reaching was Orgrim Foehammer. The grizzled old campaigner hefted his infamous great maul and scowled at the small army of Highlanders bustling behind them.

The war party numbered around five hundred men. The two Reachings provided the bulk of the force, with a further century of Heartstone's finest warriors supplied courtesy of King Magnar. Somewhere in the swirling snow up ahead the menagerie of beasts that was the Brethren lay in wait. They would swarm out of the mist the moment hostilities with Frosthold began, a deadly whirlwind of claw and fang rending all before them.

The war party had lost seven men on the trek northwards. A mountain bear had burst out from an unseen hollow and killed the first, shaking him like a leaf until his arm tore away at the shoulder. The huge predator had begun disembowelling the screaming warrior before the first of half a dozen spears had buried themselves in its hide.

Two more Highlanders had plummeted to their deaths after a gust of wind stole them from the side of a ridge. Another three died of hypothermia.

The last man simply disappeared overnight. None of his fellows could recall his departure. That incident was the most troubling of all, as Wulgreth had originally hailed from the North Reaching before swearing loyalty to King Magnar. If he had deserted to warn Frosthold of their coming, the invasion of the town would prove all the more difficult.

And difficult it was likely to be. The capital of the North Reaching was home to almost three thousand Highlanders, a full quarter of them men of fighting age. However, that wasn't what bothered Yllandris most. Frosthold's circle was both large and powerful. Even with her sisters and the circles of the two Reachings beside her, the young sorceress felt a hint of trepidation.

Fifteen sorceresses against eight. The High Fangs will not have witnessed such a contest in many years.

'Pay attention, sister,' snapped Shranree. The woman's plump red cheeks were accentuated by the freezing cold so that she resembled an oversized apple buried within a bundle of furs. Yllandris only just suppressed a snort of amusement. Old Agatha shot her a withering glance, a bead of frozen snot hanging from the end of her ridiculous nose.

Yllandris couldn't stand either of the two sorceresses, but they were the most senior members of her circle and she was bound to obey them. *Not for long*, she thought. *A queen acquiesces to no one*. Then she remembered the Shaman and the way Magnar had kowtowed before him, and her momentary satisfaction wilted and died.

'We will accompany the warriors at the head of the force,'

Shranree announced, her voice muffled by her hood. 'Our allies from the Lake and East Reachings will focus their power on nullifying the threat from the enemy circle. We,' she added, looking at each of the six women in turn, 'will rain fire down upon the town. Our task is to force the men, women and children from their huts so our warriors may cut them down.'

Yllandris felt a moment of unease. 'I don't see how the murder of children accomplishes anything. What part do they have in the rebellion?'

Old Agatha tutted softly. 'Do you know nothing of our history, girl? Bad seed must be culled lest it corrupt the entire herd.'

Shranree nodded, her flabby jowls wobbling. 'The children of traitors inevitably grow to adulthood with the same poison festering in their hearts. They must die.'

'You were too young and inexperienced to play a part in the razing of Beregund,' added Old Agatha. 'Now you have the opportunity to prove yourself. Failure could cost the entire circle.'

Yllandris glared at the old crone. 'I won't let you down.'

Shranree gave her a patronizing smile. 'I trust you won't. Now, the men are preparing to advance. We should join them.'

Yllandris wiped snowflakes from her face, pulled her wolfskin cloak tighter around her body, and followed her sisters as they made their way over to the warriors.

The light was dying. The snow continued to fall.

Like Heartstone, Frosthold perched on the edge of a great lake. However, unlike the capital and the surrounding Reachings that made up the region known as the Heartlands, this far north spring had yet to gain any kind of foothold. The North Reaching was frozen and would remain that way for all but a couple of months of summer.

Yllandris watched her breath mist in the frigid night air as she and the other sorceresses approached the high wooden gates. She saw no sentries on duty, but a couple of shapeless bundles gathered snow near the gatepost to the left of her. It seemed the Brethren had already begun their silent work.

Krazka glared at the gates with his good eye. He turned to Shranree, who was waddling along beside him and Orgrim Foehammer at the head of the war party. 'Blow the fucking gates off,' he barked. 'Let them know we're here.'

'I reckon they already know,' Orgrim replied. There was a flicker of light behind the gate, and then the sounds of boots crunching on snow.

Everyone readied their weapons. Yllandris reached down deep inside, evoking the power that throbbed within her veins and teasing it to the tips of her fingers. She saw her sisters doing the same.

There was the sound of a bar being raised. Very slowly, the gates creaked open...

To reveal four ragged figures: a man, a woman and two girls. Yllandris narrowed her eyes. She seemed to recall seeing the man before.

Mehmon.

It was indeed the chieftain of the North Reaching – but he was no longer the imposing figure she remembered from his audiences with the King in months gone by. He had been a proud warrior then, his long beard streaked with grey but his back broad and unbowed.

Now he was a broken old man. He hobbled towards them, his beard turned to white and his frail body robbed of the girth that had made him such a feared warrior even in his twilight years.

After a moment of confusion had passed, Krazka held up a gloved hand. 'Mehmon? Is that you? You look like something my hounds shat out.'

The chieftain of the North Reaching halted. He stared across at his counterpart, his expression empty of hope. 'Krazka... I didn't expect you here.'

The Butcher of Beregund grinned, a predator's smile completely devoid of humour. 'This is quite the little reunion. I'd like to say you're looking well, but that would be a barefaced lie, wouldn't it? These your wife and girls?' He nodded at the women shivering behind Mehmon. Each held a torch, revealing them to be emaciated.

Krazka gave a dramatic tut. 'The poor lambs shouldn't be out here. A girl could catch her death on a night like this.'

Orgrim frowned. 'I ain't got no quarrel with you, Mehmon. Fought alongside you in many a battle. Got a lot of respect for the warrior you once was, back in the day. But you know why we're here.'

Mehmon turned to the leader of the East Reaching and raised his hands in a pleading gesture. 'Foehammer, I ain't doing this by choice. You got to believe me. We ain't got a scrap of food between us. Our larders have been empty the past six months. My people are starving.'

The big chieftain looked uncomfortable. 'These ain't easy times for any of us, Mehmon. We got demons and all sorts pouring down from the Spine. More with every passing season. My own Reaching has taken the brunt of it. That doesn't excuse our obligations to Heartstone. It never has.'

Mehmon shook his head. 'Listen to me, Foehammer! I taxed my villages until they had nothing left to give me but their blood. Even that's turned to dust. Frosthold's about the only settlement left for a hundred miles. And we're on the brink. We're *fucked*.'

Orgrim stared at the ground and then squinted up at the sky. He seemed about to speak, but the sound of scraping steel drew everyone's attention.

'You bleat like a sheep, old man. You call yourself a chieftain? You've grown weak with age, and that's the fact of it. Just like the Sword of the North, who was too damn proud to step down when the fire went out.'

Krazka had his sword in his hand, a wide, single-edged

123

blade that was said to have cut more throats than an executioner's axe. His dead, frozen eye glinted evilly in the quivering torchlight. 'You know something, Mehmon? I fucked his wife and now I'm gonna fuck you. Except this time I'll do it with steel.'

Mehmon's wife and daughters were trembling, sending shadows dancing all over the snow. Yllandris felt her breath quicken and then her own body began to shake. She bit down on her lip, silently cursing her weakness. This hadn't happened in years, not since she was a child, when her father used to come home and she had smelled the mead on his breath and knew her mother would be searching around for lost teeth on the morrow.

You're not that girl any more. You are Yllandris, a sorceress of the Heartstone circle. Soon you will be Queen of the High Fangs.

Those thoughts calmed her. She felt her breathing slow and her body relax.

Mehmon looked at Orgrim in desperation. The Foehammer's jaw was clenched and his teeth ground together, but he said nothing.

Krazka spat on the snow. 'Draw your sword, Mehmon. Show some backbone before your wife and girls, at least. You wouldn't want them to die knowing their old man was a coward.'

In reply, the haggard chieftain of the North Reaching snarled and pulled his broadsword free from the scabbard at his side.

Yllandris watched, transfixed. Mehmon had been a warrior of great renown back in his day, but that day had long passed. Krazka, on the other hand, was possibly the most infamous killer in the High Fangs, a warrior with nerves of ice who had climbed a mountain of skulls to claim his position as chieftain of the nation's most powerful Reaching. Unlike Orgrim Foehammer, whose muscle had turned to fat over the years, the Butcher of Beregund carried not a pound of excess weight on his athletic frame. This was only going to end one way.

Mehmon lunged forwards, but he slipped and his charge became a stumble. Krazka sidestepped him effortlessly, then spun around and planted a boot on his arse to send him crashing face-first into the snow.

'On your feet, Mehmon,' Krazka said. 'I ain't done with you yet.'

The rebel chieftain of the North Reaching tried to push himself up, but his arms gave way and he collapsed again.

Yllandris glanced across at Orgrim Foehammer, who was staring off into the distance. Contempt filled her. *Coward*, she thought.

Krazka placed one hand on his chin and assumed a position of mock consideration as Mehmon struggled to rise. 'I reckon you need a bit of encouragement,' he said. He stalked over to Mehmon's wife, yanked her head back and ran his sword along her neck before she had time to gasp. A bloody smile blossomed on her throat and she sank to the ground with a soft gurgle. The two girls began screaming.

Mehmon made a noise like a strangled animal. This time, full of maddened fury, he managed to scrabble to his feet. Krazka dodged his first wild swing, caught the second on his own blade and then turned it aside. With frightening speed, his cleaver-like sword came whistling down and severed his opponent's hand.

Krazka stepped back, a satisfied smile on his face. 'Well now, looks like you're just about done—' he began, but then he stopped and rocked forwards suddenly. There was a slight tearing sound.

One of Mehmon's daughters clutched a small wood knife in her trembling hand. Yllandris could see the hole in Krazka's magnificent white cloak where the knife had ripped the pelt. Apart from the damage to his prized mantle, the Butcher of Beregund appeared unhurt. He was, however, incredibly angry.

'You bitch,' he growled. 'I've had this cloak for years. Killed a Highland cat for it with nothing but a hunting knife. It was that beast what took my eye. And now you've put a *hole* in it.'

'Run,' Mehmon croaked. He was on his knees, staring dully at the bloody stump at the end of his arm. His daughters heard him and made a break for it. Krazka watched them flee. Then he turned back to the fallen chieftain.

'I might have been persuaded to grant you a swift death,' he said. 'That ain't happening now. You're coming back to Heartstone. It's the flames for you.'

Sudden screams filled the air from the direction in which the girls had fled. The grunts and roars of savage animals punctuated the obscene sounds of tearing flesh. Yllandris felt sick.

'Looks like the Brethren caught up with your girls, Mehmon. That's that.'

Krazka turned and faced the war party. Most of the warriors had watched the confrontation unfold in silence. He raised his bloody sword high in the air and then pointed it at the gates.

'The show's over. We attack now and kill every last man, woman and child within these stinking walls. No mercy.'

No mercy. Yllandris took a deep breath, glanced at her sisters, and prepared to bring the King's justice to Frosthold.

The sounds of clashing steel rang out ahead of her. Snow continued to fall, obscuring her view of the fighting, but it was clear that Frosthold's defenders were offering scant resistance. Mehmon had not been lying. Famine had brought the town to its knees.

A shape loomed out of the darkness up ahead. It was a cart, overflowing with snow from which frozen limbs jutted out at odd angles.

A corpse wagon, Yllandris realized. They had piled the dead on the back of the cart but lacked the strength or will to carry them away.

They passed a cooking pit. She glanced down and saw the bones of various animals, most of them oddly sized. It took a moment before Yllandris realized they were the remains of the town's dogs. She half expected to see a human thighbone or skull among the grisly remains, but it appeared things hadn't quite become that grim. Not yet.

To her left, Shranree was breathing heavily. The woman was winded already by the short walk from the town gates. Flanking their circle to either side were the sorceresses from the two Reachings. They were a motley collection of the young, the old and the ancient: soothsayers and healers and wise women from numerous backwater villages and towns hastily assembled for the war party. In Heartstone, sorceresses lived alongside one another and formed a permanent circle; out in the Reachings, they were permitted to gather only for specific occasions.

Sorcery was tolerated and occasionally even honoured, but it was not liked, and it certainly was not trusted.

A grunt ahead drew her attention. One of the town's defenders was running towards them. The filthy furs he wore engulfed his wasted body, but there was fury in his eyes and he had an ugly club raised and ready to strike.

Old Agatha raised her walking staff, mumbled a quick incantation under her breath, and then pointed at the man with a bony finger. Fire leaped out from her extended digit and wreathed him in red flame. He screamed once and then toppled to the snow with a loud hiss. The flames sizzled out almost immediately, leaving a charred mess of bone and roasted flesh.

One of the sorceresses from the East Reaching retched. Yllandris narrowed her eyes. He had been coming straight at her. Had Old Agatha not acted...

I would have done what was necessary. The future Queen of the High Fangs will not perish here in this forsaken place.

'Stop!' Shranree hissed suddenly. The group halted abruptly. 'Magic is being worked ahead of us,' she explained. 'I can sense it. Sorceresses from the Reachings, now is the time.'

Yllandris felt the hairs on the back of her neck rise. The tang

127

of magic was in the air. There was a flickering in the distance, and phosphorescent green globes of energy suddenly appeared in the black sky, moving closer at terrifying speed. She held her breath.

A translucent blue barrier sprang into existence above the heads of the sorceresses. Yllandris watched the women from the Reachings straining with effort as they maintained the magical shield above them.

It was not a moment too soon. The globes splattered down and struck the barricade, where they exploded into bubbling ooze that hissed and popped. One of the women from the Lake Reaching slid on a patch of ice, causing the section of barrier above her to wink out of existence. Green slime rained down, covering her head and shoulders, which began to steam. She uttered a high-pitched shriek and clawed madly at the corrosive material, but it had already eaten through her flesh and was now dissolving bone and sinew.

Yllandris tore her gaze away from the terrible sight. There was a glimmering in the sky up ahead, and then more globes were rising in the air to arc towards them.

'Sisters, lend me your power!' shrieked Shranree. In response, Yllandris drew upon all her magic, felt it shoot down her veins and make her skin prickle with energy. It begged to be unleashed. Instead she held it there, until she felt Shranree's gentle probing. With a shudder, she surrendered the magic.

Shranree's head tilted back in exultation. She raised her arms high into the air, fire dancing around her hands. Euphoric with the accumulated power of her sisters, she thrust her arms in the direction of the enemy circle ahead.

Motes of orange streamed skywards and then disappeared. All was silent. Nothing seemed to happen. Yllandris glanced at the round little woman and felt her lip curl.

You exhausted us for that? A pretty display of dancing lights? You aren't fit to lead this circle, you useless lump of—

Glowing spheres of golden fire suddenly appeared in the sky.

There were thirteen of them, forming a pattern hundreds of feet above the town. The central sphere floated directly above the spot where the green globes had appeared. It vibrated violently, seemed to shrink down on itself—

A towering pillar of flame roared down from the sky. They were bathed in a warm glow as superheated flame incinerated everything it touched.

The other spheres began to vibrate and then they, too, transformed into columns of raging death. The entire northern half of Frosthold had become a furnace. Yllandris's breath caught at the sight of the devastation before her.

Shranree clapped her hands together happily. She wore a self-satisfied smile on her glistening face. 'Wonderful,' she said. 'It's a shame we had to lose a member of the Lake Reaching circle. Such are the perils of carelessness.'

Yllandris stared again at the unfortunate sorceress who had slipped on the ice. The body had stopped twitching and now the corpse lay huddled up on the snow like a child. She had barely been more than a girl – a couple of years younger than Yllandris herself. Fortunately, the look of hatred she shot Shranree at that moment went unseen by the senior sister.

'We should begin cleansing the rest of the town—' Shranree began, but she was interrupted by shouting. Fleeing the carnage to the north, a mob of Frosthold's defenders appeared, rushing furiously towards them.

Bestial shapes suddenly emerged from the shadows and several of the shouts turns to shrieks, but even the intervention of the Brethren couldn't stop some of the mob from reaching the sorceresses.

Starving men and women fell, torn apart by magic. A warrior managed to bury his axe in the head of one of the East Reaching sorceresses. Two more grabbed Old Agatha and dragged her away from her sisters. They beat her into the snow with their spiked clubs even as magical flame stripped the flesh from their bones.

Madness, Yllandris thought. *They have gone mad.* A woman lunged at her, a long gutting knife in her hands. She evoked enough power to thrust her attacker away from her, but her reserves were nearly empty and the effort almost made her scream. Her attacker hit the ground. There was a blur, and suddenly a snow leopard had its jaws locked around the woman's skull.

'Retreat,' Shranree cried, and they fell back. The bulk of their own warriors had caught up with them by now. They met the desperate men and women of Frosthold head on, cutting them down without mercy.

The sorceresses retreated until they were almost at the gates. They were safe now, shielded by lines of their own warriors. With the town's circle burned to cinders and their chieftain already captured by the invading force, Frosthold's defenders were lambs to the slaughter, caught between the fires raging in the north of the town and the warriors under the command of Krazka and Orgrim to the south. Desperate and weakened from lack of food, they fell like wheat before the scythe.

Yllandris tried to catch her breath. The sheer carnage had shocked her. Breathing deeply, she examined the smattering of structures nearby. The taverns, longhouses and other important buildings were all in the centre of town where the remnants of the fighting were taking place. There was nothing here but modest homes and hovels. She saw a small face peek out from behind the door of one and then dart back inside.

Shranree hadn't missed it. 'The worst is over,' she said. 'We are victorious. Now we flush these rats out of their holes and snuff the life from them. Spare no one.'

The senior sister turned and launched a ball of flame at a nearby cabin, where it exploded in a storm of fire. Screams echoed from within and then slowly died. Shranree clapped her hands together again and waddled off in search of more targets. The other sorceresses followed her for a time before breaking away to hunt their own prey.

Yllandris looked around. There, over near the wall: a small hut with a faint wisp of smoke curling from its roof. Someone had been foolish enough to forget to extinguish their hearth. *Foolish... or so desperate for warmth they kept the fire going even with a murderous army on their doorstep.*

The young sorceress felt increasingly uneasy. Highlanders followed the Code, a set of rules meant to uphold the martial tradition that had made the warriors of the High Fangs feared throughout the known world. That way of life had existed for centuries. And then the Shaman had come, and though he had created the Brethren to defend them and ensured their freedom from the tyranny of other Magelords, he had altered the Code.

The Shaman had decreed that strength was the only true virtue. By its nature, weakness invited the imposition of will from the strong. The weak deserved neither sympathy nor mercy, as their very existence was akin to that of a deer providing sustenance for the hunter. The weak became strong or they perished. That was the natural order of things.

Yllandris *was* strong. She had refused to be weak, had broken the insidious shackles of a troubled childhood to achieve true greatness. Was she not a living demonstration of the Shaman's ideology? She smiled to herself. *One day I will be the Shaman's ultimate lesson. The last he ever learns. I wonder if he will appreciate the irony.*

Her power burgeoned, the magic sufficiently recovered from her earlier exertions. Blue flame flickered around her hands as she approached the hut. Let Shranree and the others deal death from afar. Yllandris would deliver this particular lesson personally.

She struck the door with such power that it tore away from its hinges. Then she stepped inside the hovel and raised her glowing fists.

She lowered them again when she saw the terrified eyes staring up at her. There were three of them: two girls and a boy, none older than eight winters.

Their mother lay next to the hearth. The woman knew she was there, but she was too weak even to raise her head. The entire family looked near starved. The children shrank away from Yllandris to huddle closer to their dying mother as if she could protect them. The boy was too afraid even to look at her.

The ultimate lesson...

Yllandris felt her body begin to tremble. She turned away and stumbled out of the hut. A warrior emerged from the home opposite, his sword bloody and a wide grin on his gap-toothed face.

'More in there?' he asked jovially. 'I'll deal with them.' He nodded respectfully and made to walk past her into the building.

Her force-shove sent him flying forty feet through the air to crash into the side of the town wall. Bones cracked. His lifeless body slid to the ground.

Yllandris pulled her cloak tighter about her and before she knew it she was running, tears streaming down her face and turning to ice on her cheeks. She reached the gates, ducked outside them and then sank down onto the snow, silent sobs racking her body while inside the city blood continued to flow and fire consumed everything it touched.

Sudden motion caught her attention far above, and she looked up with wet eyes to catch the dark shadow of something huge and inhuman. It circled once, moving at terrifying speed, and then whirled away eastwards.

Its passing left her shivering uncontrollably, and not from the numbing cold.

More Haste, Less Speed

THE SUN WAS at its zenith by the time the small band finally approached the Tombstone. The massive column of basalt jutted out from the small outcrop of hills surrounding them, and was visible from a good few leagues away once a gap in the ridge line finally opened up.

To the west, a day's ride on horseback would carry them back to Dorminia. The city was too far away to be seen from this distance, but the dark line of the Demonfire Hills was visible even to Brodar Kayne's ageing eyes. Small villages and towns dotted the ancient road that ran all the way from the city to terminate just below the mine ahead of them. He and Jerek had followed the same road only a month past. The last stretch of their epic journey had turned out to be fairly pleasant, all things considered. For one thing, no one had tried to kill them.

He couldn't say the same for the Badlands a couple of days' ride to the north. A vast, treacherous stretch of country filled with hidden gullies, the Badlands were haunted by gangs of bandits that preyed on the Free Cities of the Unclaimed Lands to the east – and, when they could get away with it, those settlements in the small hinterland that swore allegiance to the Grey City. The bandit tribes that pursued a life of lawlessness in the Badlands had to choose their targets carefully if they wished to avoid deadly retribution.

'Carefully' had not included a pair of ragged Highlanders passing through, at least not at first. Kayne and Jerek had left a trail of bodies in their wake as they fought their way south through the Badlands to the Trine. That particular part of their trek had taken many weeks.

North beyond the Badlands, many days' travel further still, and through places he would as soon forget, the land began to rise. The temperature dropped, becoming cold and then bitter, and slowly the High Fangs emerged, marking the place where the very world ended. It was an enormous country of sheer ridges and plunging valleys, fast-flowing streams cold enough to freeze a man to his bones and forests of snow-capped pines so tall they towered over anything built by the hands of men. It seemed like another lifetime away.

Or at least it had, until Borun appeared like a ghost from his past.

What were they doing this far south?

He supposed he ought to have asked before the encounter had taken its inevitable turn for the worse. The fact was, a meeting between him and Borun was only ever going to end one way.

Jerek strode beside him in silence. The Wolf looked almost content, which wasn't something you could say about him often. Nearby, Sasha struggled along with Vicard, who had been whining ever since Kayne had taken his pouch away from him. Isaac ambled along at the rear of the band, whistling a jaunty tune. *He's an odd one and no mistake*, the old barbarian thought. There was something troubling about the man, but nothing he could quite put his finger on.

Sasha stopped suddenly, flicking sweat-matted hair away from her face. 'The Rift is just ahead,' she said.

From his current vantage point, Kayne could just about see the top of a wooden tower protruding from the yawning pit that opened before the Tombstone. Dark smoke and noxious fumes rose above the pit, staining the sky above a murky grey. A huge pile of earthen waste dominated the eastern side of the chasm.

'According to the brief Garrett provided, almost a hundred

men work the Rift,' said Sasha. 'The Augmentors could return at any time, so we'll need to make this quick.'

'What about the Watch?' asked Vicard. 'There's sure to be a few soldiers around.'

Sasha's eyes narrowed as she searched for any sign of movement around the edge of the chasm. 'I don't doubt it.'

Brodar Kayne flexed his neck. 'I reckon the Wolf and me can handle a few of those red cloaks, if it comes to it,' he said. 'You'll want to stay out of the way if there's any trouble, lass,' he added. 'Keep an eye on that one.' He nodded at Vicard, who shot him a dirty look. Sasha didn't look too pleased either.

Isaac raised a hand to get their attention. 'I'll fight. You might need the help.'

'Where'd you learn to handle a blade?' Kayne asked. 'I thought you might struggle to tell one end of a sword from the other, but you held your own back there and no mistake.'

The manservant shrugged. 'I like to read. Swordplay isn't so different to any other craft. You just need to pay attention to the instructions.'

Something about Isaac's words struck him as being off, but once again Kayne struggled to pinpoint exactly what it was. 'You're a fast learner, I'll give you that,' he managed. 'How did you end up at the depository anyway? The Halfmage don't seem like the most grateful employer, if you don't mind me saying.'

A bland smile appeared on the manservant's face. 'He's not as grouchy as he appears. Sometimes his worries just get on top of him, you see. Especially his— Oh. Oh, no...'

'What's wrong?' Kayne asked in sudden alarm. Isaac wore a look of such concern the old Highlander was certain he had just spied an army of Augmentors marching down the road towards them.

'I forgot to leave his ointment behind,' Isaac groaned. 'He's going to be furious! I knew I'd overlooked something.'

'Ointment?' Kayne asked, puzzled.

Sasha coughed unconvincingly. Everyone turned to look at

her. 'I don't mean to be rude,' she said, 'but we have important business ahead of us. Let's get that over with and then we can all return to Dorminia and whatever urgent matters await us there. The Halfmage can look after his own arse until then.' Without another word she set off towards the Rift, dragging Vicard along behind her.

Jerek rubbed at his beard thoughtfully. 'Bitch has a point,' he said, and followed after her.

Kayne glanced at Isaac, who still looked crestfallen at having committed such a heinous error. With a sigh, the ageing barbarian set off after the rest of the group.

The Rift was much larger up close than it looked from a distance. The chasm spanned a good eighty feet across and ten times that in length, a vicious scar in the earth belching foul gases that made the eyes sting. Worse than the gases, though, was the stench. The odour was unmistakably that of death, as if something huge rotted at the bottom of that stygian pit. Brodar Kayne squinted down into the depths of the breach but saw nothing but darkness at the bottom. *Just as well*, he thought.

They were gathered around the edge of the gigantic fissure. A narrow path had been carved into the face of the rock, folding back on itself as it descended into the chasm. Rope bridges spanned the drop from one side to the other at various points along the length of the gap. The sound of metal clanging on rock echoed from far below. Through the miasma of smoke drifting around the mouth of the chasm, Kayne could just about see small figures hard at work.

Jerek grabbed his arm and pointed to the top of the wooden tower just below them. The path ran above it along the face of the gorge for a few hundred feet before switchbacking to cut back directly beneath. If they tried to follow the path, they would likely be seen by the men on the platform before they could stop them raising the alarm.

Kayne nodded at Jerek, who grunted, and then at the top of the tower. He turned to the others. 'Stay here,' he said. 'We need to take out those guards before they see us.'

The two Highlanders lowered themselves onto the wooden structure as quietly as they could manage, crawling on their bellies until they were able to peer down over the edge. Two miners were standing on the platform directly beneath, talking heatedly and gesturing at the work going on below them. A Watchman lounged on a stool in the corner, taking swigs from a flask.

Jerek pointed down, put a finger to his lips and removed an axe from the harness on his back. With his other hand he lowered himself carefully over the edge and disappeared from sight. Kayne heard the *thump* of boots hitting wood and then a couple of strangled moans followed by the sounds of a short scuffle. All was silent for a time. He tensed, expecting the worst.

Right on cue, the Watchman soared from the platform. The unfortunate soldier twisted in the air like an unwieldy and vastly oversized robin, his limbs flailing around and becoming hopelessly entangled in his scarlet cloak. He unleashed a mighty shriek as he fell, which seemed to last for an eternity. Jerek emerged on the path below a second later, his face twisted in rage. He spat something inaudible after the plummeting figure.

Brodar Kayne uttered a silent curse. For a minute there he'd almost hoped they might do this the easy way. He watched Jerek sprint back up the path, and then he hurried back to the others.

'Get ready,' he said. 'They know we're here.' He reached behind him and drew his greatsword, taking comfort in its familiar weight and the way the steel whispered against the scabbard. Isaac drew his own sword.

Jerek arrived just as the shouts from below reached their ears. 'They're coming,' he panted. He was breathing hard.

Kayne gave him a withering stare. 'Aye, I figured a screaming Watchman tumbling to his death might get their attention. You'll be the death of me, Wolf.'

His old friend grinned in response. 'Might be I saved your life earlier,' Jerek said. 'Take the rough with the smooth, I reckon.'

Vicard was rummaging around in his backpack. 'Hold them off,' he said. 'I have enough explosive powder in here to bring the whole thing crashing down.'

'Hang on—' Kayne began, but a quarrel whistled past his ear and he threw himself to the ground. Another one sailed over his head. Two Watchmen were rushing towards them up the switchback trail, furiously reloading their crossbows. Three more of the bastards were scrambling to reach the bridges on the other side of the Rift, their swords already in hand.

'We need to close them down,' he yelled at Jerek, but the Wolf was already halfway to the two crossbowmen. Kayne pushed himself to his feet and sprinted after him, sharp pain stabbing in his creaking knees with every step. The fumes caused him to choke and squeezed the air from his lungs, but he barrelled on regardless, tears streaming down his face.

Suddenly Jerek stumbled, barely staying on his feet. Brodar Kayne heard his growled *fuck*, saw him stagger again as another quarrel hit him in his right arm. The Wolf slowed and then sank to one knee. *Shit*.

Willing his ageing body forwards, every muscle screaming, Kayne reached the two men just as they were preparing another salvo. His greatsword caught one of them under the arm, almost cleaved his torso in half in a spray of red gore. He kicked the other soldier dead in the chest. The Watchman flew backwards off the path and tumbled down out of sight, screaming all the way.

The soldiers crossing the bridges were almost upon him. One of them fell to his knees and clawed at his throat. Kayne glanced back to see Sasha reloading her own crossbow. There was a flash, a warning shout from Vicard, and then the bridge with the two remaining Watchmen exploded in a torrent of hemp, timber and sizzling blood. The searing heat from the blast drove Kayne back and knocked him to his knees. The sound of the explosion hit next, a deafening roar that sent agony screaming through his ears to pound at his brain with the force of a hammer blow.

He coughed, spat blood. He'd bitten through his tongue. More men were coming up the path from the depths of the Rift, though their progress was decidedly hesitant having just witnessed the carnage above them. Regaining his feet, Kayne turned and saw Jerek struggling to rise. Blood soaked his arm and pooled on the ground at his feet. A bolt quivered in his thigh.

'Come on, Wolf,' he snarled, dragging his friend upright and throwing an arm around his shoulders to stop him from sinking back down again. The two Highlanders half ran, half stumbled back to the others. Jerek snorted in agony every time his wounded leg struck the turf. Most men would never have made it up from the ground after taking two quarrels from near point-blank range, but Jerek was the hardest bastard Kayne knew in a world full of hard bastards.

Sasha was gritting her teeth and aiming hopelessly down at the swarm of men climbing the chasm. The miners weren't trained fighters, but they didn't need to be. Not when they outnumbered the tiny group twenty to one. You didn't survive those odds.

Vicard suddenly bustled forwards, or at least limped at an impressive pace. He held a bundle of what looked like thick red tubes in his hands.

Kayne felt a tiny shiver of fear run up his spine. 'What are you doing?' he asked carefully.

'Saving the day,' the alchemist replied. 'Isaac, pass me some flint.' The manservant immediately obliged and Vicard withdrew a small knife from his belt. He looked up at the rest of the group. Sweat beaded on his brow. 'When I say get down,' he said, 'you get down. Understand?' He placed the knife blade against the tangle of cords poking out of the tubes and struck the flint several times. It took a few attempts, but eventually the sparks caught and one of the wicks began to burn down.

'Five... four... three... two... *get the fuck down!*' The alchemist hurled the bundle at the path and dived for cover just as the first miners arrived on the scene. Brodar Kayne pushed Jerek gently to the ground and then threw himself down next to him, covering his ears with his hands.

The world turned red.

An indeterminate amount of time passed before he risked opening an eye a fraction. The rumbling had finally subsided, though the cloud of dust floating above the wreckage of the Rift continued to mushroom above them. He glanced at Jerek. His friend had gone pale and his breathing was shallow, but he was still conscious. Vicard climbed to his feet and began dusting himself down. Sasha and Isaac stared at the scene with horror on their faces.

Brodar Kayne got up and peered over the edge of the chasm. The southern side had partially collapsed in on itself, raining thousands of tons of rock down on the unfortunate miners below. None could have survived that avalanche. *Shit*, he thought, and not for the first time that day. The plan had been to put a halt to the mining operation and destroy whatever equipment they could find, not cause a full-blown massacre.

'Vicard. What the hell was that?' growled Sasha, her large eyes full of anger. 'Those were innocent men. Men just doing their jobs.'

Vicard flicked at a patch of dirt on his shoulder and shook his head. 'I didn't have any choice in the matter. We would have been killed. And *you* would have suffered even worse things.'

'There's nothing worse than being dead,' Sasha replied. She walked over to where Jerek lay. 'How's he doing?' she asked.

Kayne closed his eyes for a moment. Things hadn't exactly gone as planned. The chances were that they'd get a whole lot worse. 'He's bad. Lost a lot of blood.'

Isaac knelt down and examined the Highlander. 'None of the major vessels are punctured. He might still have a chance. Vicard, can I have your knife?'

The alchemist tossed his small blade over to the manservant and hobbled over to Kayne. 'I want my powder back,' he whined. 'Fair's fair. I saved your life.'

'Take your bloody pouch,' he growled back, throwing it at the alchemist's feet. Vicard retrieved it and then went to stand alone. He pulled the flap back and raised it almost reverently to his nose.

'Those explosives were worth twenty gold spires,' he said. He inhaled deeply from the bag. His face became slack and then broke into that stupid smile. 'You have no idea how much of this stuff twenty spires could afford. I tell you, I could be sitting on a whole mountain of *hashka*. The best money can buy. I—'

There was a blur behind him and suddenly the alchemist gasped. A barely audible whine escaped from his lips and for a moment he stood there swaying, blood leaking from his mouth. Then he toppled forwards onto his face. The hilt of a dagger was buried in his back.

'Right through the spine,' said the baby-faced killer who had appeared from behind Vicard. He smiled in satisfaction, revealing a perfect set of pearly-white teeth. The assassin flicked a blond curl away from his blue eyes and drew another dagger from his belt.

Brodar Kayne saw the glow around the man's feet and tensed. *Those boots. Magic. Bastard's an Augmentor.* He took a deep breath and stepped forwards. 'Takes some courage to stab a man in the back. Why don't you take off those boots you're wearing and face me like a real warrior?'

The Augmentor smiled again, as if he found the thought terribly amusing. He picked casually at his nails with his dagger. His hands were perfectly manicured, like those of a noblewoman. 'You'd like that, wouldn't you?' he said eventually. 'Look at you. So old I doubt you can get your prick up, and yet you bluster like a man thirty years your junior. There's nothing quite as sad as an ageing savage.'

Bastard. Clever bastard. His hands tightened on his greatsword. Isaac rose from where he had been kneeling beside Jerek. Sasha was surreptitiously reaching under her cloak for her crossbow. He gave them an urgent shake of the head. A moment passed, and then their hands inched back away from their weapons.

'Tell you what, old man,' said the Augmentor in a conversational tone. 'Give me some sport and I promise I'll make the deaths of those two quick. I'm not like Garmond or Thurbal. They'd make the girl scream something fierce.' He gave a rueful chuckle. 'That's hardly fitting behaviour for a gentleman like me. One has certain standards to maintain.'

Kayne narrowed his eyes. 'Best we get to it then,' he said. He raised his greatsword and waited.

There was the faint sensation of a breeze prickling his skin and suddenly the Augmentor was directly before him, dagger stabbing at his neck. At the last possible instant the old barbarian threw back his head, and the blade scored a shallow flesh wound. He brought his greatsword swinging around to cleave the bastard in two, only to slash at empty air. The Augmentor was back where he had been before, a full thirty feet away. Kayne felt blood trickle down his neck and dribble onto his chest.

'Not bad, grandfather,' said the smiling killer. He raised one hand in a mock salute. 'Let's see you evade this one.'

There was another blur, and before Kayne had time to react the Augmentor's dagger was plunging into his stomach. He felt his hide shirt give way, the burning hot sensation of cold steel tearing into his guts. '*Urgh,*' he grunted. The cherubic face in front of him flashed another white smile and then it was gone. The Augmentor reappeared twenty feet to his right.

He sucked in air as he felt the warm blood flooding his breeches. Fire burned in his stomach. He risked a glance down at the steel buried there. Nausea threatened to unman him. *Look at your opponent. Look at him.*

The Augmentor casually drew yet another dagger. This one was cruelly hooked, a weapon intended to catch and tear at flesh. The killer smiled at him once more, but just before he did so his eyes flicked to a spot on the barbarian's chest.

Suddenly Brodar Kayne understood.

'What are you waiting for?' he gasped. 'Come at me.' He took a deep breath, saw the muscles twitch in the Augmentor's arms...

In that same instant he dropped to one knee, brought his greatsword arcing around. He felt the slight rush of air, the *thud* of his sword connecting with flesh. A dagger clattered out of the air above his head and hit him on the shoulder before tumbling to the ground. Ten feet away, his would-be killer appeared. He had a confused expression on his cherubic face.

'What—' he began, and then his right leg fell away just above the knee in a gush of blood. He toppled over.

Brodar Kayne walked over to the squirming Augmentor. 'You ought to have listened to me and taken them boots off,' he said. 'Your legs might move like the wind, but the rest of you ain't no quicker than anyone else.'

He raised his greatsword. 'That's the problem with magic. It warps a man's measure of himself, makes him lazy. The only place where speed really counts is in here.' He tapped the side of his head with a finger.

Then he brought his greatsword down, plunging it through the Augmentor's chest and driving it deep into his heart.

He released the hilt. The blade stood there, quivering. He stumbled a few steps, looked down at the steel protruding from his own body. He felt weak suddenly. There was movement behind him, but he was too tired to care. He just wanted to lie down and rest. He was allowed that much, wasn't he? *I'm too old for this sh—*

This time the world turned black.

Friends in High Places

EREMUL WIPED SWEAT from his brow and attempted to dry his hands on his filthy robes. He succeeded only in smearing mud, sweat and other assorted scum further over his palms and fouled garments. With a muttered curse, he squinted down the hill that overlooked the harbour, attempting to catch sight of the utter bastard who had upended his chair and scampered off with a handful of coins he had spectacularly failed to earn.

The White Lady's agents will be positively awed to make my acquaintance. Filthy, bruised and stinking of mud and shit. Perfect.

Of course, the lout Eremul had hired couldn't have guessed the pitiful cripple he was pushing uphill was a mage. If he had, there wasn't a chance in hell he would have tipped him unceremoniously onto his arse and run off back down the hill.

He had come within a whisker of evoking a powerful wind to sweep the treacherous son of a bitch from the bluff and send him hurtling towards a messy death on the rocks far below. Perhaps the only reason he hadn't was the sudden shock at finding his useless body flopping around on the muddy ground. It had taken all of his strength to right his chair and somehow pull himself back on again.

Damn it, Isaac. Where are you?

The small band of rebels had not returned to Dorminia and Eremul was beginning to worry. Isaac was loyal and usually competent when it really mattered, despite his frequent

145

buffoonery. The fellow he had hired to manoeuvre him to the top of Raven's Bluff, on the other hand, was typical of the lowlifes he had no choice but to tolerate on a daily basis. Only a select handful of Dorminians knew he was a mage and therefore treated him with a modicum of respect. The rest saw a scrawny, bookish cripple who was known to be irascible and hence the perfect target for all manner of cruel japes.

About the only use they have for books is to fuel their hearths during winter's coldest months – or else wipe their arses with in the case of an emergency.

He had considered moving to a more affluent part of the city, but that would entail swapping honest ignorance for conceited superiority and insufferable pomposity. Frankly, that wasn't a trade he was willing to make. Besides, the unassuming nature of the locals suited his purposes. The more distance between himself and his masters in the Noble Quarter, the better.

The ruined lighthouse loomed ahead, illuminated by the crescent moon in the clear midnight sky above. The tower here at Raven's Bluff had once overlooked the point where the harbour opened up into Deadman's Channel. As Dorminia had grown the harbour had expanded. New lighthouses had been constructed further along the coast, leaving this old building obsolete.

The Halfmage squinted at the tower, searching for any sign of his mysterious contacts within. He could see nothing except darkness. The structure soared before him like some giant skeletal finger stuck in the ground, as dead and silent as a corpse.

The thought made him uneasy. Thelassa's enigmatic Magelord was said to practise strange magic, and maintained a strict isolationist policy. Merchants required a special permit to trade and visitors were strictly monitored.

Those who had spent time in the City of Towers reported it to be a wondrous place, as beautiful as Dorminia was ugly, where fairness and equality were there to be had by all. More disturbing accounts made reference to queer things such as apparitions that materialized and then disappeared just as suddenly, pale women who seemed normal apart from their eyes, which were as dead as those of a corpse, and last but not least mass orgies in the streets, so licentious that the white marble of the city itself seemed to pulse with pleasure.

The White Lady was potentially a very useful ally – but Eremul didn't approach anything without a healthy dose of scepticism. *Expect the worst and you can't be disappointed. Optimism is the luxury of the young, the foolish and the dullard.*

His arms shaking from exertion, the Halfmage wheeled his chair up to the rotting old door at the foot of the tower. It was overhung with a thick mass of cobwebs that had not been disturbed in many a moon. He sagged.

They aren't here. Have they been discovered? Dorminia and Thelassa are technically at peace, but any fool can see war is imminent. The White Lady's agents could be protesting their innocence in the dungeons of the Obelisk at this very moment.

Without warning, the door suddenly creaked open. Husks of long-dead spiders and ancient, clinging cobwebs showered him, torn away from the wall above the door by a sudden breeze. He cursed and shook his head violently, brushing his hands carefully over his robes. He hated spiders.

Yet another layer of finery to add to my glorious attire. Sweat, dirt, shit, and now dead arachnids and half-eaten insects. At least I haven't pissed myself. Yet.

'Enter,' commanded a feminine voice from within. Eremul plucked away a spindly leg dangling from one eyebrow and pushed his chair into the building. The interior was a damp and filthy ruin. A trio of thick candles on a table in the centre of the circular chamber provided the only light. There was a stairwell on the other side of the chamber, and the draught from that black maw caused the flames to dance as they illuminated the women around the table.

There were three of them. Each of the women was slender and pale and wore a plain white robe down to her ankles. They watched him expectantly. Something about their eyes seemed strange, he thought. And there was something else—

Eremul stared in shock. None of the women cast a shadow.

The tallest bowed slightly. 'We appreciate you coming here,' she said in a voice that was soft, controlled and completely devoid of emotion. 'You may refer to me as First Voice. I speak with the authority of the White Lady. These are Second Voice and Third Voice.' She gestured to the women to either side of her.

Eremul raised an eyebrow. *So it's going to be like this.* 'You can call me Halfmage,' he replied. 'I would bow in return and kiss each of your hands, but you would surely grow tired of lifting me off the floor. In any case, I find formality overrated.'

First Voice nodded, unperturbed by his poor attempt at humour. 'You are known to us, Eremul Kaldrian. You are far more than you appear.'

He shrugged. 'Not a particularly impressive feat, it must be said.'

'We uncovered one of your agents in Thelassa,' replied Second Voice. 'He was most forthcoming.'

Eremul nodded. He had expected as much. 'Is he unharmed?' he asked, almost fearing the answer.

'He is. When it became apparent that our interests were similarly aligned, we had no reason to use more... creative means of coercion.'

'What did he tell you?'

This time First Voice replied. 'He told us much about you. You were once a favoured apprentice of the Tyrant of Dorminia. When Salazar ordered the Culling and those with the gift were put to death, he chose to spare you. Why was this?'

The Halfmage frowned. He had asked himself the same question often enough over the years. 'I would like to think my wit and charm made me indispensable,' he began, 'but I fear the truth is somewhat simpler.' He leaned forwards in his chair.

'My magic was too weak to pose a threat. Even a ruthless murdering bastard like Salazar recognized that having another wizard around might one day prove useful to him. I was maimed and cast out of the Obelisk, with one final set of instructions.'

'Which were?' asked Third Voice softly.

'I was to act as a spy and informant for his lordship. Who better to masquerade as an insurrectionist than one who had suffered so visibly at his hands? I have thwarted many a nefarious and wholly incompetent plot against Salazar.'

Second Voice took a step towards him, and he saw immediately what was wrong with the eyes of the women. They were entirely colourless save for the black pupils at their centres. 'You serve the Tyrant of Dorminia? Tell us why we should not kill you now.'

Eremul sighed. 'Trust must be earned before it can be betrayed, no? Believe me when I say I hate Salazar more than anyone in this city. But the only way I can truly work against him, the only way I can *survive*, is by pretending I am a loyal servant of his regime. To maintain that illusion, I must sometimes feed the magistrates useful information.'

'Information that means the deaths of the unfortunates involved,' said Second Voice, again without emotion.

Eremul gripped the sides of his chair so hard his knuckles turned white. 'Those are the sacrifices that must be made.' He let out a deep sigh and sagged in his chair. 'Look, I *could* wheel myself up to the Obelisk while proclaiming Salazar to be a cunt of the highest order. Apart from a fleeting sense of satisfaction, that would achieve precisely fuck all, except to earn a rather messy death. So I play a longer game.'

First Voice held out a hand and beckoned to Second Voice, who returned to her side. 'If your intentions were truly in any doubt,' she said slowly, 'you would not walk away from here.'

Eremul raised an eyebrow.

'You would not *leave* here,' First Voice amended.

'Are you threatening me?' Eremul asked, almost pleasantly. He drummed his fingers on the sides of his chair.

'You have no idea what you face,' answered First Voice. 'Your magic would be of little use against us.'

'What are you?'

'You may call us... the Unborn. We walk in places others cannot. In time you will not remember our faces. I trust you are not planning to test your magic against us?'

The Halfmage shook his head. 'I prefer to avoid unnecessary violence. Waving one's prick around and spoiling for a fight always strikes me as the privilege of the barbarian or some other testosterone-fuelled brute. I'm a *survivor*.'

First Voice nodded. 'Then we are of accord. You will not betray us.'

'I don't plan to,' Eremul agreed. 'Now that we've established I am on your side, why did you summon me here? What do you want of me?'

'Nothing,' replied First Voice. 'The White Lady simply wished to establish your intentions. She will move against Salazar soon.'

'Salazar... or Dorminia?' asked Eremul carefully. 'I would rather this city didn't become another Shadowport.'

First Voice folded her hands beneath her breasts. Her strange, empty eyes gave nothing away. 'The White Lady wants to liberate Dorminia, not destroy it. She grieves for Shadowport and what was done to the people of that city. She has concluded that Salazar must die.'

For the first time in the course of this clandestine meeting, Eremul found himself smiling. 'Tell me how I can help.'

'You cannot,' First Voice said. 'Preparations have already been made. The risks are great, and it is possible we may fail. If we do not succeed, the White Lady will contact you again.'

'Any hints as to what you're planning? Give a poor crippled mage something to cling to. It helps keep me warm at night.'

First Voice shook her head. 'The less that you know of our plan the better.'

'Fine,' Eremul said, rather irritably. 'If we have nothing more to discuss, I'll bid you goodnight.' *Besides, my arse is throbbing and I desperately need to piss.*

'Remember,' said First Voice, as her sisters placed a hand on each of her narrow shoulders. 'Speak of this to nobody. Betray us and you will suffer consequences beyond your—'

'Bah, shove your threats,' Eremul interrupted. 'I've heard it all before. I've *suffered* it all before. I may be a traitor and a turncoat, but at least do me the honour of taking me at my word when I tell you—'

He stopped short. He was speaking to thin air. The candles on the table had burned down to tiny stumps that flickered feebly, surrounded by pools of wax. The pale women had simply disappeared.

Eremul shivered. There had been no magic at work, or at least none that he could sense.

He spun his chair around and wheeled himself back outside, breathing in the crisp night air and listening to the sounds of water lapping against the cliff below. He tried to recall the faces of all the men and women whom he had betrayed to the magistrates. People like him, united in their hatred for the city's despotic ruler and determined to bring about a future free from his tyrannical rule.

Sentenced to death. By me, the unassuming, maimed scribe hiding in plain sight among the fakeries of book and tome and scroll. A… spider, damn it, yes, the irony… a spider at the centre of a web of deceit. Bitterness welled up inside him. He swallowed it down. One day Salazar and his cronies would learn that this spider had venom.

Shoulders slumped and bladder bursting, Eremul forced his aching arms into motion and pushed his chair back down Raven's Bluff towards the harbour – and, for want of a better word, home.

The Great Escape

COLE TOOK A deep breath and tried to steady his nerves. He squinted up at the purple sky where the glowing orb of the sun was just about visible behind a thick band of clouds. Dawn was upon them.

The *Redemption* had crossed into the Swell in the early hours of the morning. The captives had been allowed on deck shortly after first light. They had enjoyed a breakfast of thick gruel, dried nuts and salted beef, washed down by a generous cup of fresh water from the barrels stored in the small hold near the mizzenmast at the stern of the ship. With strict rationing, the provisions on board would last for months.

He had spoken with eight of the prisoners while on deck the night before. Seven had agreed to his plan. The last had said nothing, only looked at him with a hard expression before glancing off in the direction of the captain. Cole's heart had felt as if it was lodged in his throat as he waited for the lank-haired fellow to run over to Kramer and tell him everything. Instead, the man had simply looked down and spat on the deck.

Still. Eleven men. With the exception of the engineer, Soeman, every one looked like he could handle himself in a fight. If everything went smoothly they would be sailing away to freedom before the morrow.

He looked around one last time, meeting the eyes of each participant in this daring plot. He saw the hint of worry on one face, excitement on another. Three-Finger positively smirked at him. Cole gave his co-conspirator a confident nod, a gesture he hoped conveyed an iron certainty that, for some reason, he wasn't really feeling.

Red Bounty's small crew waited by her railing for the men on the smaller carrack to board. A small rowing boat had detached from the cog and now bobbed alongside the *Redemption* on her starboard side. Rope was thrown down and the first group of prisoners was lowered onto the vessel under the careful gaze of four Watchmen. It took only a couple of minutes for the boat to cross the small expanse of water. The passengers were hoisted up the side of the cog, and then the rowing boat swung around to collect more men.

Cole was ferried across in the third and final group. Soeman sat next to him, his thin face ashen and his hands twitching with nerves.

Not that the soldiers staring across at them had any cause for suspicion. Just about everyone aboard the two ships was feeling the strain of sailing on the Swell. Prisoners, sailors and Watchmen alike had reacted poorly to the news they had crossed into the dreaded stretch of water. The hold had been an unpleasant place to be at that moment, with prisoners retching all around him, others moaning in fear, and Three-Finger accidentally pissing on his leg as he shifted to avoid another man's vomit.

He reached across and squeezed Soeman's arm. A Watchman saw the gesture and sneered. Cole frowned in response and then turned and spat over the side of the boat, just as he imagined Brodar Kayne would have done.

He immediately regretted the gesture. It was because of that old bastard he was in this mess in the first place. To make matters worse, the Highlander still had his birthright, his precious dagger. He wanted Magebane back. If he had to take it from the old barbarian by force, so be it. That was *exactly* what he would do.

The boat bumped against the hull of the cog and Cole

shipped his oars. The old seadog, Jack, clambered up the hanging rope like some wiry monkey. Soeman tried to haul himself up next but slipped and crashed back down into the boat, sending it lurching to one side and soaking everyone with cold seawater. A Watchman hauled him to his feet and shook him so hard Cole thought his teeth were going to fall out.

He wouldn't have minded giving the man a shake himself, but he needed Soeman for his plan to work effectively. It came as a relief once the engineer was finally over the side of *Red Bounty*.

'You next,' ordered a Watchman. Cole glanced around and stretched theatrically to make sure everyone was focusing on him. Then he sped up the rope like an acrobat. He reached the top and vaulted onto the deck of the ship, landing in a smooth roll.

He immediately regretted his bravado. Agony exploded in his swollen groin. His bruised ribs hurt even worse. He wanted to fall to the deck and wait for the pain to subside, but everyone was watching him. Teeth clenched, he shrugged and strolled over to the rest of the captives.

'What was that about?' asked Three-Finger, a puzzled expression on his ugly face.

'Morale,' Cole replied. 'The men can't fail to have been impressed by what they just saw. A leader has to inspire confidence in his ability.'

'Whatever you say.' Three-Finger looked around the ship and counted under his breath. 'There are six Watchmen aboard this vessel. That means there are six more back on the *Redemption*. And that cocksucking Augmentor.'

Cole nodded. The rowing boat was now back alongside the other ship, where the sailors were attending to the rigging. Captain Kramer stood near the rail, conversing with his first mate. Falcus lurked nearby.

A booming voice brought Cole's attention back to *Red Bounty*. The speaker was a huge bear of a man with a bristling beard. His assistants cowered behind him on the aftcastle as he stared down at the indentured workforce with undisguised contempt.

'I'm Foreman Armin,' he bellowed. 'I'm supervising this mining operation. If any one of you so much as puts a foot out of place, I'll have the flesh stripped from your hide.'

Cole glanced at the soldiers behind him. They wore eager looks on their faces, no doubt keen to get stuck into the business of mistreating their prisoners. Whatever one might say about Kramer, the captain ran a tight ship. Armin, on the other hand, gave the distinct impression he would be the taskmaster from hell.

'We have the whole day ahead of us,' the foreman continued. 'When I say the word, you cretins will begin unloading equipment from the cargo hold. I want everything tested to ensure it's operational before work begins on the morrow. Any man not pulling his weight gets to feel the leather of my boot up his arse. Where's Soeman?'

The engineer hesitated for a second, and then raised one thin arm.

'You'll oversee the construction of the platform,' Armin said. 'I want it assembled by the time we finish work this evening.' He paused a moment, savouring his next words before he spoke them. 'Tomorrow a handful of you bastards will test the water. My men will operate the drill. You lot' – he smiled grimly, gesturing at the captives – 'will search the sea floor.'

The uproar was instantaneous. Men cursed and shook their heads. Others looked for weapons as if they would mutiny right then and there. Crimson Watchmen waded in, laying about them with the pommels of their swords and lashing out with cruel whips. The man next to Cole was knocked down and stomped on. He turned his head and spewed bloody spittle and loose teeth all over the deck.

Within the space of a minute the protest was over. Captives groaned, wiping blood from their faces and nursing bruised bodies. Cole shook his head in annoyance. This wasn't going to make their escape any easier.

'Now that we understand each other,' said Armin, 'let me explain how we're going to do things. You will search for blue veins in the rock. When you find one, follow the vein and extract as much of the rock containing blue material as you can. That stuff is solidified magic. These waters are rich with it, so you shouldn't have much difficulty locating good hauls.'

'How are we supposed to dive to the bottom?' asked a long-faced fellow behind Cole.

'The sea is shallow here. Less than thirty fathoms. You will be provided with special helmets to help you breathe.'

'What kind of helmets?'

Armin frowned. 'The kind you wear on your head. They're a Shadowport invention, based on old Fade designs.'

'I thought the Fade were just a myth.'

The foreman was starting to grow annoyed. 'The Fade are no myth, you gormless fool. Almost everything we know of engineering and the sciences is taken from their ancient teachings. Why do you think Shadowport's navy defeated our own? They had access to knowledge we did not.'

'But no one has crossed the Endless Ocean for centuries—'

'*Enough!*' Armin roared. His beard bristled with anger. 'You're here to do a job, not talk my bloody ears off. You criminal scum will keep your mouths shut and do as you're told. I want the cargo hold emptied before midday. And if any piece of equipment so much as gets scratched,' he added, 'the idiot responsible loses a finger. Get to work.'

Cole glanced at the prisoner whose face had been ground beneath the boot of the Watchman. It was the fellow who had rejected his scheme the previous night. He had a hand in his mouth and was taking a painful account of his remaining teeth. He caught Cole staring at him and nodded once, a grim gesture whose meaning could not be lost. *One more.*

He hoped it would be enough.

*

Dusk arrived.

Cole's body ached all over from hauling equipment around. *Red Bounty*'s cargo hold was enormous and it was a wonder she hadn't sunk under the sheer weight she carried. One poor fool had accidentally dropped a section of the huge drill Soeman was assembling, opening a considerable hole in the deck. Just as Armin had promised, the worker had lost a finger.

Three-Finger might have sympathized with the man's loss, but he didn't seem the sort to offer much in the way of compassion. The convict sauntered up and flashed an evil grin. 'Soeman thinks the Core can be sabotaged to start a fire,' he said.

Cole had seen the Core earlier that day. The blue orb of permanent energy had been created by Salazar many years ago at an exorbitant cost of raw magical material. When connected to the platform that floated a hundred yards to port, the Core would cause the gigantic drill underneath the platform to rotate at unimaginable speeds, tearing up the sea bed faster than a hundred men with picks and axes. Of course, the machine still required that divers identify spots for drilling, as well as gather up the loosened material and place it in nets to be hauled to the surface.

'How long before we move?' asked Cole. Nightfall was almost upon them.

'A half-bell,' replied Three-Finger. 'They're going to take Soeman over to the platform now and have him test the drill.'

'Perfect,' replied Cole. If Soeman could cause the Core to malfunction and start a blaze on the platform, the soldiers over on both ships would need to cross over to investigate. In the ensuing confusion, the twelve conspirators would make for *Red Bounty*'s rowing boats and then the undefended carrack nearby. They would overpower the crew, and then cut and run. *Red Bounty* would never catch them.

A thought occurred to the young Shard. 'What about Soeman?' he asked. 'He'll be stuck on the platform.'

Three-Finger shrugged. 'If the man has any sense, he'll leap off and swim for the *Redemption*.'

'Good enough for me,' said Cole, though he still felt a certain amount of trepidation. What if the engineer's obvious lack of backbone caused him to falter at the last moment? Not everyone possessed the iron resolve he had been blessed with. 'And the weapons?' he asked. This was an important part of the plan.

Three-Finger grinned again. The scabrous convict only ever seemed to smile when the topic involved inflicting misery on someone.

'You see that barrel over there? The third one in? There's more than water inside it. Six pickaxes, four hand axes, a hatchet and a crowbar, to be precise. All gear capable of smashing a man's head in.'

Cole rubbed his hands together in satisfaction. Everything was going exactly as he predicted. If only Garrett had possessed the foresight to acknowledge the brilliance of his young charge, the Shards would probably have liberated Dorminia already.

Three-Finger scratched at his festering cheek. 'Are you sure about this, kid? I'm seeing some margin for error if things don't go to plan. We'll need to be ready for a fight if it comes to it.'

Cole rolled his shoulders and clenched his fists as if a fight was exactly what he was hoping for. In actual fact, he had slipped off into pleasant thoughts of Sasha and her reaction when he told her about his heroics. He could hardly wait to see the adulation in those dark eyes—

'Kid?' said Three-Finger again. 'I asked if you were ready for a fight.'

He tore himself away from his daydream. 'I was born ready,' he replied, as grimly as he could manage. 'And my name's Davarus Cole. Don't you forget it.'

Three-Finger narrowed his eyes. 'If you say so. We'd best get into position. The show's about to start.'

Ten minutes later the conspirators were crowded near the railing, watching the platform floating out at sea. Soeman was there, along with Armin and two of his assistants. The engineer was bending over a metal frame situated next to the base of the drill. The rest of the huge contraption was submerged in the water below. Soeman fiddled with the frame for a moment, and then took the glass box housing the Core from Armin and motioned at the other engineers to step back. He bent down and placed the glowing blue orb inside the frame.

There was an instant humming noise and the sensation of energy gathering in the air. Cole felt his hair standing on end. The smell of sulphur reached his nostrils.

With a monstrous whine the base of the drill began to turn. It spun faster and faster, until the whole platform vibrated beneath it. The magical core was first a vibrant blue, and then an odd shade of purple, and finally all colour bled from it until it became a white sphere bright enough to make Cole's eyes water.

There was a blinding flash of light like a small sun exploding. Suddenly the night sky was lit by fire. Tongues of flame lapped greedily across the platform. Armin was on his knees, his two assistants smouldering gently nearby. Soeman had disappeared, apparently vaporized by the energy unleashed from the malfunctioning Core.

Concerned shouts went out all over *Red Bounty*. A boat was lowered. Cole glanced across at the *Redemption* and saw the explosion had also caught the attention of the soldiers on the carrack. They began to board their own boat. Everything was going as planned.

'Now!' he shouted to the men around him. As one, they ran over to the barrel where they had spent the best part of a day secretly stashing implements for the bloody work to come. Cole reached in and pulled out the crowbar. *Damn it.*

The boat from *Red Bounty* reached the wreck of the platform at the same time as the vessel from the *Redemption* drew level with the big cog. The voice of Falcus hissed at them from the boat. 'What happened? Someone put those fires out!'

159

Cole took stock of the situation. *Red Bounty*'s small crew were standing around gaping at the burning platform, completely oblivious to the mutiny happening on their ship. This was the moment.

'Make for the boat!' he yelled. He bounded across the deck, leaping over coils of rope and piles of crates. The cog's second rowing boat was secured near the mizzenmast. Three-Finger and Jack fell upon it with hatchet and axe, cutting away the lines that held it in place. The twelve men lifted the boat above their heads and lowered it over the side of the ship with a splash. Jack fetched up a coil of rope and tied one end to the railing. Then he hurled the rest over the side, where it unravelled all the way down to the water.

'Down the rope,' Cole yelled. Each of the prisoners took hold of the rope and slid down into the waiting boat. It was only designed to carry eight passengers but they piled in regardless, each man grabbing an oar and paddling for dear life towards the *Redemption* in the distance.

We're going to do this, thought Cole in elation. After what seemed like an eternity they reached the carrack. There was a grappling hook in the boat, and Jack threw it with masterful aim so that it snagged the prow of the ship above them. One by one they scaled the rope and climbed up onto the deck of the *Redemption*.

A young sailor stared at the newcomers with confusion. 'Hey, what are you doing—' he began, but Three-Finger's hatchet took him in the middle of the head and split his face in half.

Captain Kramer ran over, flanked by two soldiers who hadn't boarded the boat sent to investigate the burning platform. 'What is the meaning of this?' he demanded.

Cole stepped forwards. 'We're taking this ship, Captain. Turn her around and sail due west immediately.'

Kramer's jaw clenched and he ground his teeth together as if he was trying to chew rocks. 'Not a chance! Men, kill these bastards!'

The two Watchmen raised their swords and were met by Three-Finger, Jack and four other captives. It was brief and bloody. The soldiers were better armed, but the escapees were desperate and outnumbered the red-cloaked soldiers three to one.

The man whose teeth had been shattered took a sword through the chest, but the Watchmen were soon stabbed, bludgeoned and stomped to death by the remaining runaways.

The *Redemption*'s small crew had fetched their weapons in the mêlée. They now stood facing the escapees uncertainly. Three-Finger had an arm around Kramer's throat, the edge of his hatchet tickling the captain's chin. 'Tell your men to back off and turn this ship around,' he snarled.

'Fuck yourself,' Kramer replied.

Three-Finger's voice dropped to a deadly whisper. 'I don't know what you've heard about me,' he said, 'but whatever it was, it doesn't come halfway near the truth. I can do things to you that'd make a trained soldier piss his pants. Turn this ship around or I'll decorate it with your body parts. Beginning with your cock.' The convict withdrew the hatchet from Kramer's neck and positioned it just above his groin.

The disgraced admiral swallowed and eventually his shoulders sagged. 'All hands to deck,' he commanded his crew, his voice full of resignation. 'We sail west.'

The *Redemption*'s crew responded immediately to the order. Cole watched *Red Bounty* anxiously, expecting to see boats full of Crimson Watchmen closing on them at any moment, but the soldiers were still busy trying to put out the flames on the floating platform. Soon they were under way. With the wind strong in her sails the *Redemption* would soon outpace even the most determined team of rowers.

'Movement portside,' yelled Jack. 'A hundred yards distant.'

Cole squinted at the dark shape bobbing slowly in their direction. The last of the light had almost fled and every second put more space between them, but the struggling figure was unmistakable.

Soeman.

He seemed to be slowing down. Every so often the engineer would dip below the waves only to emerge again a moment later.

Three-Finger wandered over to the bow and stood next to Cole. 'Now that's rotten timing,' the convict said. He flashed that evil smile of his. 'He won't ever make it. We're not even at half speed yet and he's falling behind.'

Cole shifted uncomfortably. 'We can't just leave him there. He risked his life for us.'

The convict narrowed his eyes. 'Don't be foolish, kid. If we heave to, the *Bounty* will catch us. Soeman's missed his opportunity.'

Cole stared around him at his crew. They were looking at him. Looking *to* him, no doubt. There was only one thing to do.

'No man gets left behind,' he said loudly. 'I'm going after him.'

Three-Finger scowled. 'What's wrong with you? Soeman's a dead man walking. You saw his cough. Why be a hero?'

Cole drew himself up to his full height and shot Three-Finger his best steely gaze. 'It's the only thing I know how to be.'

The young Shard ignored the flash of irritation on Three-Finger's face and his muttered '*For fuck's sake.*'

'Tell the helmsman to slow the ship and bring her around to the north,' he ordered. 'Give me five minutes. If we're not back by then, sail as though your lives depend on it.'

Sucking in one final deep breath, he pushed himself up over the railing and dived into the rolling water far below.

Troubling Times

'AND WHAT IS your opinion on this matter, Supreme Augmentor?'

The question snapped Barandas out of his pleasant reverie. He glanced across at Grand Magistrate Timerus, who sat with his elbows propped up on the table and his palms pressed together in front of his face, one eyebrow raised expectantly. What had the man been blathering on about?

Ah yes, our prospects in a war with Thelassa.

Barandas cleared his throat. 'Our navy has been destroyed. However, Thelassa has never possessed much of a fleet – and, if the rumours we have been hearing are true, the White Lady has secured the services of no less than three companies of mercenaries from Sumnia. The men from the Sun Lands have little taste for maritime warfare.'

'What are you saying, Supreme Augmentor?' persisted Timerus. 'That we have nothing to fear from our neighbour in the Trine?'

Barandas sighed. 'I am saying that trying to rebuild our navy is likely a waste of time. The White Lady will seek to invade over land, not sea.'

'And when might we expect this invasion?'

'Sumnian mercenary companies are famously expensive. The Magelord of Thelassa will not want them sitting idle for long.'

Chancellor Ardling raised a hand. He was a grey man, with

white hair, thick silvery eyebrows and a sickly complexion. Even his magistrate's robes were the colour of charcoal, boasting none of the devices displayed on those of the twelve other magistrates seated around the massive darkwood table in the Grand Council Chamber. He might be capable of making a corpse seem vivacious, but Ardling was a shrewd master of coin and managed Dorminia's coffers with the deftness of a virtuoso. Money was said to be his only passion. His wife had reportedly committed suicide by leaping from the top of their five-storey mansion, and the only noticeable effect it had on her husband was his slight air of frustration at needing to hire additional house staff.

'Our treasury is near depleted,' the Chancellor was saying now in his monotone voice. 'We simply cannot afford to invest more coin in the construction of ships. Last year's harvest was poor, and a considerable sum of gold has been earmarked to pay for produce imported from the Free Cities. We still owe Emmering in excess of one thousand spires.'

'Pah,' spat Marshal Halendorf of the Crimson Watch. 'Who cares how much we owe? What's Emmering going to do, demand we hand it over?' He winced and rubbed at his stomach as he spoke.

Barandas narrowed his eyes at the commander of Dorminia's army. In his estimation, Halendorf was neither a socially inept genius like Ardling nor a cruel but competent schemer like Timerus. He was a buffoon. How the man had reached his current position was anyone's guess.

'We are not the only ones to trade with the Unclaimed Lands,' Timerus said. 'If we fail to pay our debts, the Free Cities will simply cease to do business with us. Any attempt on our part to bully them will be met with hostility from the Confederation. We do not need more enemies.'

'No,' whispered the Tyrant of Dorminia. 'We do not.'

The chamber fell silent. All eyes turned to the wizard in the high-backed obsidian throne at the head of the table.

Three days had passed since the destruction of Shadowport, and the Magelord still appeared almost as exhausted as he had then. The colossal energies he had harnessed to flatten the city under the waters of its own bay had left a permanent scar on Salazar. And the damage wasn't just physical. There was a distracted look in those ancient eyes.

'The Confederation has made its position clear,' he said. 'Their rulers will tolerate no interference in the business of the Free Cities. It seems the brotherhood we once shared is no longer of any value to them.'

Barandas was well aware of the frustration his master felt for the cabal of Magelords who ruled the lands far to the east. The Confederation was hundreds of miles away, but the influence it extended seemed to reach into every pocket of the continent.

Salazar leaned forwards slightly. Barandas found himself inching backwards. He saw other magistrates doing the same.

'If the White Lady desires war, war is what she will receive,' snarled the Tyrant of Dorminia. His hands curled into fists. They were so thin and wrinkled that together with his long nails they resembled withered claws.

'That accursed woman always was unpredictable. She sided with the Congregation when they declared war on magic.' He paused for a moment. 'When she finally decided to change sides, it was with a fury that would shame Tyrannus himself.'

Tyrannus. Barandas recognized that name. The god known as the Black Lord was one of the last of the thirteen Primes to perish in the Godswar. A score of mages were said to have died in order to bring him down, strangled with their own entrails or turned into piles of oozing flesh after their skeletons had been torn whole from their bodies. The image made even him queasy, and he had seen some awful things over the years.

Thurbal's gruesome handiwork back at the abandoned temple wormed his way into his mind. Barandas closed his eyes and tried to think instead of Lena and the morning they had spent together. He still had the scent of jasmine on his fingers.

'This is the Age of Ruin,' Salazar intoned. 'We cannot afford to compromise. Marius made a mistake in opposing me, but he understood the necessity of claiming the Celestial Isles. Year after year crops fail. The waters of the Broken Sea retch up as many dead fish as they do living. Our existing supplies of raw magic are almost exhausted. We cannot leach from the corpses of gods forever. *We need those isles.*'

Tolvarus cleared his throat suddenly. He was in charge of Dorminia's judicial system, such as it was – a particularly sick joke given he possessed a well-known penchant for young boys. 'My lord, I cannot help but consider the potential in a more considered exploration of the... ah, land across the Endless Ocean. I know the voyage presents many challenges, not least of which is the sheer distance one must cross. However, Admiral Kramer was adamant that with the right preparations—'

'*No.*'

The Magelord uttered the word with the finality of a coffin lid slamming shut. Tolvarus blanched and looked at the floor. 'You will not speak of the Fadelands. None of you. The next man who dares defy me on this will be sentenced to death.'

Barandas swallowed hard. Admiral Kramer had received a similar reaction when he had broached the subject a year ago. Tolvarus was either very brave or extremely forgetful.

The silence was broken by Salazar. 'Magistrate Ipkith. I would hear your report on Thelassa, including all information pertinent to a possible military confrontation. First, however, I believe you have news to share.'

The red-bearded Master of Information ran a hand over his shaved pate. 'I received a report earlier this morning. Farrowgate came under attack yesterday afternoon. Another magical abomination. It killed scores of villagers. Men, women and children. I am led to believe that it... ravaged them internally, my lord.'

Salazar nodded. 'Go on.'

'The Augmentor Rorshan had been stationed at Farrowgate. I understand he was one of those... recently dispossessed of his magic.' Ipkith's voice trailed off into silence.

Barandas winced. *Rorshan. A good man. One of the few I have. Had*, he corrected himself.

The Magelord pursed his lips. 'We are in the process of recovering raw magic to create new Augmentors. These things take time. What news do you have of the Rift, Barandas?'

Here it comes. He had been dreading this. 'Legwynd has not yet returned, my lord,' he said. 'However, I believe two of the men who accompanied the insurrectionists were Highlanders. Formidable men, I am led to understand. They apparently killed two of the Watch in broad daylight.'

Marshal Halendorf slammed a meaty fist down onto the table. 'I'll have their heads!' he growled.

Salazar raised an eyebrow. 'Is it possible two Highlanders may have overcome one of your best Augmentors?'

Barandas shifted uncomfortably. He didn't like Legwynd on a personal level, but the man was an effective killer and had always been reliable. 'I have commissioned a ship to sail up Deadman's Channel and investigate the Rift,' he admitted. 'It should be back any time now.'

The Magelord sat back and closed his eyes briefly. 'More wine,' he ordered. 'We have much still to discuss, beginning with Magistrate Ipkith's report.'

A serving girl darted over and refilled Salazar's goblet from a large crystal decanter. Another maid appeared with a bottle of wine in each hand and passed down the table, filling the cups of each of the thirteen magistrates who governed Dorminia's fifty thousand inhabitants in the name of the Magelord.

Barandas raised his own cup to his lips. The wine tasted

sweet and fruity. He caught the serving maid staring at him and smiled back politely. There was something odd about her, he thought, but before he could think to say anything she had moved on.

'None for me,' said Halendorf, waving the girl away. 'My damned gut can't take it.' The Chancellor also passed on the wine. Barandas suspected Ardling could drink his own piss and find it too sweet for his palate, though he had to admit a grudging admiration for the man's determination to keep a clear head for figures.

Tolvarus coughed suddenly and violently, interrupting the Supreme Augmentor's musings. The Lord Justice wiped his mouth with the back of one hairy hand and cleared his throat. 'Excuse me,' he said. 'The wine must have gone down the wrong hole. Quite unpleasant—'

His words were interrupted by another spasm of coughing. This one lasted for much longer. He bent over the table, heaving spittle over the polished darkwood.

Timerus sneered at the struggling man. 'Someone give him a slap on the back,' he said with distaste.

Barandas got to his feet to assist Tolvarus. He knew something was wrong as soon as he tried to place one foot in front of the other. The chamber seemed to rock around him. Paintings of long-dead magistrates leered down at him from the walls, wavering in and out of view like mischievous phantoms.

He tried to focus, saw a sight that made his heart pound. He stumbled forwards. He could hear magistrates coughing the length of the table, but he paid them no mind, intent on reaching his destination.

The Lord of Dorminia was clawing at his throat. His face had gone purple. The golden goblet he had been drinking from lay beneath his throne, its contents spilling out across the floor. Approaching him were the three serving maids, and in their hands they held silver daggers.

Salazar tore a hand away from his neck long enough to gesture, and one of the girls exploded in a shower of blood and bone.

The torches went out, plunging everything into darkness. Confused shouts and the sounds of violent retching reached Barandas's ears over the heightened gasps of his own breathing.

The torches flickered back to life.

He was by his master's side, his longsword flashing to sever the arm of the girl whose blade had been closing on Salazar's chest. The limb tumbled away in a gush of blood, but the maid displayed no signs of slowing. With incredible speed, she reached around Barandas with her other arm. He gasped at the incredible strength in that grip. Her touch was like ice, and it crushed the life from him. His heart hammered as if it were about to explode...

And then the strange woman was hurled away from him, slamming against the wall of the chamber with enough force to break her spine. She slid down to the marble floor.

The remaining maid stared at him with strange colourless eyes. It was the girl who had served him his wine. She was unusually pale, the colour of milk. How had he not noticed that before?

'You,' she said, in a voice empty of emotion. 'I saw you drink. You should be dead by now.'

'What are you?' Barandas demanded in response. He glanced to the side, where Salazar was now doubled over on the throne, still clutching at his throat.

'Servants of the White Lady.' The girl stared at him with no expression on her face, but her ghostly eyes seemed to see right inside him. 'This man is a tyrant. He has murdered countless thousands.' She paused. 'You are not like him, nor these other men. Why do you defend them?'

Barandas stared back, shocked at her perception. How did she know? There had been times when he had wanted to hang up his sword in despair at some of the acts he had committed in the name of the city and its Magelord – this city where children starved down in the Warrens while the elite, the rich and powerful, enjoyed lives of luxury. But what was the alternative? The world was a brutal place. Dorminia needed a strong ruler to protect it from the horrors unleashed by the wild magic that ravaged the land – as well as the predations of other Magelords.

Salazar was that man. A man who had, as it happened, saved his life.

'Duty,' said Barandas. 'This is my *duty*.'

The pale woman nodded. 'I understand duty.' She raised the silver dagger she held in her sallow hand. 'Let us both do our duty, then.' She plunged forwards, the dagger slashing down towards his neck. She was incredibly fast, faster than any man Barandas had ever faced, almost inhumanly fast.

But he was the Supreme Augmentor, and he was faster still.

His longsword burst through the woman's chest, lifting her off the floor. She gasped, dribbling dark blood all over her chin. The blood smelled rotten, as if it had putrefied inside her. He almost gagged as he tugged the sword free. The lifeless corpse of the strange woman slid to the ground.

He immediately turned his attention to Salazar. The Magelord's breaths came in tortured gasps, as if he were sucking in air through a reed. The Supreme Augmentor cast his gaze across the chamber, desperately seeking help.

Most of the magistrates were dead. The body of Lord Justice Tolvarus flopped on his chair, a trail of drool running from his mouth to drip onto the terrified lap of Marshal Halendorf, who sat staring at the scene in horror.

Chancellor Ardling had gone a lighter shade of grey but was otherwise breathing normally. Grand Magistrate Timerus was also alive, though he was shivering uncontrollably and appeared to have vomited most of his wine back over his robes.

Barandas stared down at the Tyrant of Dorminia. A lump welled in his throat. He held the Magelord close, tears threatening to fall from his eyes.

With great effort, Salazar looked up at him and tried to speak. Barandas leaned in close to hear his words. They came out as a faint whisper, but he nevertheless caught their meaning.

'Fetch… the Halfmage…'

No Easy Choices

THE HALFMAGE STARED down at the book he was reading. *The Last of the Crusades* was a controversial work dealing with the conflict that came to define the Age of Strife, an extremely bloody period culminating in the cataclysmic Godswar. Armies had stormed across the northern continent. Kings and queens had fallen.

Eremul felt his lips twist into a wry smile. The followers of the disparate faiths of the north had spent millennia at each other's throats, yet somehow those ancient rivalries and vastly contrasting dogmas were thrust aside when the crusade against magic itself was declared.

Hatred. Hatred and fear. The twin mortars that bind the bitterest of enemies more closely than shared notions of virtue or tradition unite the best of friends.

The Congregation had been formed: a council of the ruling high priests and priestesses of the thirteen Prime divines. Their combined political and military strength had been immense and they had almost succeeded in cleansing magic from the land entirely. Of those who possessed the gift, none were spared. Parents had smothered their own children rather than see them burned alive on the Congregation's fires. For all that he hated the Magelord, Eremul acknowledged that Salazar – together with Marius, a mage named Mithradates, and several other leading wizards of the age – had proved instrumental in organizing a resistance. They had saved many of those blessed with the gift of magic from the flames.

He turned over the page. There, in all her ethereal glory, was an illustration of the White Lady. The high priestess of the Mother, the most widespread faith in the land, had also been a powerful wizard.

Eremul snorted in amusement. What had the Congregation done? Why, they had *embraced* her. Principles were all well and good, unless holding to them ran counter to self-interest.

Quite why the White Lady eventually underwent such a rapid change of heart was a mystery, but her betrayal of the Congregation gave the alliance of wizards the respite they needed to plot their assault on the heavens. The resulting Godswar had lasted an entire year. Only a handful of mages survived their odyssey to the celestial plane. Those that returned were no longer truly human. They had absorbed some of the essence of the gods and achieved immortality.

The tyranny of the old, replaced by the tyranny of the new. Such is the way of the world. He was about to close the book when he saw the place in the middle where several pages had been torn out. A few specks of dried blood marked the ancient parchment.

The author's chronicle of certain details of Salazar's role in the Godswar had displeased the Magelord. The Tyrant of Dorminia had ordered the unfortunate scribe put to death and the offending chapter removed. Even before the unpleasant events surrounding the Culling, years past, and the subsequent crackdown on freedom of expression that had seen the introduction of mindhawks into the skies, there were certain topics those in the Grey City did not talk about. Not if they valued their lives.

There was a sudden knocking at his door. Eremul sighed. It seemed half of Dorminia was intent on paying him a visit these days.

He wheeled his chair over, pulled the latch, and pushed open the door.

'Oh, *fuck*,' he muttered, as he stared into the hard eyes of four of the Watch's finest.

'Eremul Kaldrian?' asked the officer in charge. The Halfmage's heart hammered in his chest and a hundred thoughts whirled inside his head. *They know. Shit, they know. I'm a dead man. I'm dead—*

'You're coming with us.' The Watchman's eyes bore into his own. 'There's been an incident at the Obelisk.'

Dorminia was in a state of chaos.

Eremul gazed out at the commotion on the streets far below. The crowd was too far away for him to be able to make out individual faces, but he imagined the multifarious horde wore looks of fear, hope, and – in some cases – quiet satisfaction. By now most in the city were aware that the Tyrant of Dorminia had been the victim of an assassination attempt and that his very life hung in the balance.

He enjoyed a fleeting moment of satisfaction himself. The magistrates who had survived the murder plot were no doubt wondering how news of the incident had slipped beyond the Obelisk's walls. The truth was that the Halfmage had sent word to certain of his contacts as soon as he was able. If tidings of the Magelord's perilous condition inspired the braver of Dorminia's dissidents to push ahead with an insurrection, it would be yet another nail in Salazar's metaphorical coffin.

The more perceptive of the Magelord's lackeys had their suspicions about the source of the leak, he knew. The Supreme Augmentor, the blond-haired warrior with the golden armour who looked like some prince from a children's tale, he was a sharp one. The man's blue eyes had cut into him like the edge of a steel blade.

Which is exactly what will happen if Salazar dies.

Eremul's good humour suddenly evaporated. He was under no illusions about his fate if he failed to save the Tyrant of Dorminia from whatever unnatural poison coursed through his veins. There would be no consolatory pat on the back. No *oh well, you did your best* and *never mind, it was a valiant effort*. The Supreme Augmentor had been rather insistent on that point. If he failed, he would share the Magelord's fate.

And wouldn't that be a tragedy.

He remembered the sudden dread he had felt upon seeing the soldiers. He was certain they had learned of his meeting with the White Lady's agents at the abandoned lighthouse. Such a perfidious act could not be explained away as the scheming of an informant. Anyone truly loyal to Salazar's regime would have reported their presence to the Watch, not wheeled themselves back to the book depository for a good long piss followed by a lie-down.

He could barely disguise his relief when the Watch had revealed the truth – but his hidden delight at Salazar's condition was immediately tempered upon learning he was to be entrusted with the Magelord's life.

He glanced once more at his surroundings. He was inside a small guest room on the seventh and highest level of the Obelisk. The room was luxuriously adorned, with a four-poster bed covered in silk sheets and carved darkwood armoires that were worth more than most in the city earned in a year. And yet for all the luxury on display, the room was just as much a prison as the dungeons beneath the tower.

The door was locked and magically warded. Two Augmentors waited outside. The windows were barred and enchanted so that the metal was immutable and heat-proof and safe from all the tricks a journeyman wizard might employ to escape.

I suppose I should be flattered, he thought. The sad truth was that he barely even qualified as a journeyman. Even if he could somehow bypass the thick bars blocking the window, the only direction he would be going was two hundred feet directly down.

At least there would only be half a corpse. Whoever was tasked with cleaning up my remains could probably knock off early. Every cloud has a silver lining.

The lock on the door suddenly clicked and it swung inwards to reveal the Supreme Augmentor in all his golden glory. A pretty woman with hard eyes and a colossus of a man in black armour followed just behind him. Eremul squinted up at the shadowy figure.

He must be seven feet tall. The largest man I have ever seen, if indeed he is a man. The helm covering the giant's head made him look like some kind of demon from the old legends.

The Supreme Augmentor gave him a cool look. Eremul frowned back. He was troubled by the fact he could see no magic on the blond-haired commandant. The giant's armour was clearly enchanted, and the woman's hairpin omitted a faint blue glow, but the leader of Salazar's elite force of magically enhanced enforcers apparently walked around lacking the one thing that *defined* an Augmentor. It made no sense.

'His lordship grows worse,' said the blue-eyed commander. Concern was plain on his face. Concern... and sorrow? *Is it possible this fool actually loves Salazar?*

Eremul drummed his fingers against the sides of his chair. 'I will need more time to prepare.'

The Supreme Augmentor grimaced. 'Time is the one thing we do not have.' He paused for a moment. 'Lord Salazar carries the essence of the divine. What kind of poison can harm an immortal?'

'That's what I intend to find out,' lied Eremul.

The Supreme Augmentor fixed him with a hard stare. 'I know what was done to you during the Culling. I trust you would not be stupid enough to bungle your administrations out of some sense of vengeance.'

Eremul felt a prickle of fear. This one was perceptive.

'Whatever your feelings towards Lord Salazar, his survival is vital. To Dorminia. To the north. Fail and you will suffer. I will take no pleasure in it – but I will do what is necessary.'

Eremul couldn't stop the sneer that crept onto his face. 'Why, I desire nothing more than to see our esteemed ruler returned to full health. It wouldn't do to have this glorious utopia he has created fall apart were he to perish.'

The Supreme Augmentor's gaze narrowed, and for a moment he wondered if he had pushed the man too far. The hard-eyed woman to his left shot him a venomous scowl and reached up to unclasp the glowing metal accessory in her hair. Across from her, the armour-plated monstrosity towering over them all flexed his huge metal gauntlets.

Eremul sighed. He had already considered trying to fight his way out of this predicament. He decided he could kill one of the three before they reached him. Of course, that would give the other two ample time to kill him. Even if he somehow got lucky he would have six flights of stairs to contend with, followed by a dash through a courtyard packed with Crimson Watchmen. And truth be told, he was never much of a sprinter even when he *had* legs.

The situation was hopeless. Either he saved the life of a tyrant whom he despised or else he would be begging for his own death before the week was out.

The Supreme Augmentor held up a hand and shook his head, and his colleagues both relaxed. Eremul felt an odd sense of disappointment. Perhaps being killed by one of those two monsters would be easier than the choice he would soon need to make.

'Enough talk,' said the Supreme Augmentor. 'This may be our last chance, Halfmage. Do whatever is within your power to save Lord Salazar. Garmond, see to his chair.'

Eremul opened his mouth to protest as the massive Augmentor grabbed the handles fastened to the back of his seat, but after a moment he decided to suffer the indignity in silence. He might as well travel in comfort and enjoy the sights of the Obelisk on the way down to the Magelord.

After all, it might be one of the last things he would ever see.

*

The dungeons were just as he remembered them.

Thirteen years had passed since Salazar ordered the Culling. He had been in the Great Library on the third floor of the tower at the time, studying an old tome. The young Eremul had resolved to find out what he could about wild magic and the increasing number of abominations that were manifesting in the Trine. He recalled that he had been desperate to gain some unique insight and bring his research to Lord Salazar.

So eager for a pat on the head. The recognition that I deserved a place among the Magelord's apprentices in spite of my less-than-impressive powers. Ah, the naivety of youth.

Instead he had looked up to find three Augmentors standing over him. They had ignored his questions and forced his arms behind his back. One of them, a grey-eyed, slender man, had placed a dagger at his throat. Eremul had felt the blade leaching away his magic, sucking him dry until he was an empty husk. He remembered the fear that had gripped him then.

The three Augmentors had marched him down to the dungeons. What followed was still a blur, but he remembered the agony. Pain so terrible it made him vomit. The horrible feeling of weightlessness beneath his torso. He had looked down at what had been done to him and he had promptly fainted. He remembered praying for a release from the torment – for death.

He had not died. For some inexplicable reason, they had kept him alive.

Eremul glanced now at the slab he had been fastened to all those years ago. He fancied he could still see the scorch marks on the stone where the fire had been used to cauterize the stumps after his legs were cut from his body. They had been thrown on a huge fire, along with the corpse of every wizard that had perished during the Culling. No less than thirty bodies had turned the air black with smoke.

Of all the wizards in Dorminia, Salazar had permitted Eremul alone to live. Had he divined that his one-time apprentice would serve some purpose in the years to come? The mages who had survived the Godswar had returned changed, possessed of immortality and other traits that made them something more than human. Perhaps a certain amount of prescience was one of those traits.

Eremul's chair jerked to a halt, tearing him away from his reminiscences. They had reached the fallen Magelord. The Tyrant of Dorminia was lying on a makeshift bed, his head propped up on cushions the colour of blood. A wiry old physician wrung his hands together nearby, fear plain on his face.

The Supreme Augmentor walked over to the prone form of Salazar. He bent down and placed an ear to the Magelord's mouth. 'He is hardly breathing.'

Eremul stared, feeling hatred surge within him. How he would love to yank a cushion from under that ancient head and choke the life from the withered old monster! Or better yet, summon up whatever feeble magic he possessed and smite the murderous bastard. Set fire to his eyes and watch them run down his sagging cheeks. Burn his manhood to a cinder.

It would cost me my life, but I'd enjoy every second of it.

He almost did it. A look from the hard-eyed Augmentor looming over him changed his mind at the last moment. Her gaze seemed to promise him a fate worse than death. He thought suddenly of the Hook and the poor bastards left to die in the hanging cages. His nerve faltered.

'Move aside,' he muttered. He wheeled his chair to the side of the bed and looked down. Salazar's eyes were closed and his face was the colour of an old bruise.

'I've tried every remedy I know,' the physician whined. 'The poison refuses to respond to any of them. Perhaps his lordship should be taken somewhere more comfortable?'

The Supreme Augmentor shook his head. 'I don't want him moved. We can't allow anyone to see him in this state. There may still be assassins within the tower. This is the safest place for him.'

Eremul doubted there were any more of the White Lady's pale servants around. The would-be killers were most certainly the three he had encountered several nights past. They had come close, so very close, to succeeding. They still might.

'Begin,' the Supreme Augmentor ordered, placing a gloved hand on the hilt of the longsword at his belt. Eremul swallowed. *No easy choices.*

He touched the Magelord's neck, feeling for a pulse. It was there, but it was incredibly faint. He took a deep breath, closed his eyes, and plunged into Salazar's mind.

The stench of death filled his nostrils, so strong that he thought he might retch up his breakfast. He could *feel* the sludge crawling through the Magelord's arteries, could hear the rattling of the tyrant's heart as it fought to pump fouled blood through his body.

Then he sensed it. A third presence besides himself and the subconscious mind of Salazar. It was unnatural and cold and full of malign intent. He reached for it and it recoiled. It felt *dead*. He clenched his teeth together and probed deeper, grabbed hold of the presence and began to thought-mine…

He stood upon grey wastes of ash and bone and watched the robed figures scurrying to meet him. They dared challenge him here, in his domain? Humanity's hubris knew no bounds!

With a thought he raised a thousand thousand corpses from the dead wastes, sent them lurching towards the invaders in a wall of clawing limbs and snapping teeth a mile deep. A handful of wizards were torn apart, but then magic flared from the intruders, arcing up and back down to erupt in a wave of explosions that obliterated his army. Fragments of bone exploded into the air, a cloud of white dust so thick it momentarily blotted out the monochrome sky.

He snarled, skull visage twisting in anger. Then he exhaled mightily, and from his mouth issued a billowing darkness that swept towards the invaders. Three of them were caught up in it before they had time to raise their magical barriers, dancing in agony as the flesh was stripped from their bones. Their naked skeletons eventually toppled to the ground, breaking apart in the places where even their sinews had been consumed.

The rest of the insects had evaded the cloud, surrounding themselves in globes of energy or miniature whirlwinds that dissipated the pestilence before it could reach them. One of the wizards stepped forwards, an old man wrapped in scarlet cloth. The interloper raised both hands and a gigantic web of glowing energy shot from his outstretched palms.

He roared as the web landed on him and burned through his rotting flesh. He tried desperately to pull it off, but something massive hit him from the side and sent him crashing to his knees. It was a mammoth, as tall at the shoulder as he was at the thigh. It shifted shape and became a man, naked from the waist up and rippling with muscle. The wizard shifted again, and suddenly a huge eagle was before him, clawing at his eyes.

Missiles of the brightest energy struck him from all sides. The barrage of magic poured endlessly from his assailants as he struggled to free himself. He swatted at the eagle, and then saw movement below him. He raised one foot and crushed a man beneath it, felt bones crunch and bodily fluids splatter around his ankle. Even so, the pain was overwhelming...

Eremul gasped. He was witnessing the final moments of a god. But how? He felt the Magelord's consciousness beginning to stir. He reached out to it and was immediately assailed by a hundred thoughts and memories. One thread was brighter than the others, so he latched onto it...

The Reaver was on his knees. They had lost Raurin, and Zayab, and countless others, but they were winning. The god was unable to shake off the snare he had thrown. Mithradates clawed at the Reaver's eyes, tearing a gaping hole in the left orb with his talons. Foul pus welled out and the god screamed in pain. He saw Balamar crushed by one of those massive hoofed feet, leaving a broken pile of gore beneath.

He glanced to his right. Marius watched the carnage with

his hands clasped around his corpulent waist, his eyes fixed on the face of the ailing god.

'Marius,' he snarled. 'We almost have him! What are you doing?'

The other wizard started as if surprised. He wiped at the sweat on his brow, smoothed his robe down over his paunch. 'Catching my breath,' he replied. 'Let's finish this.'

Snaking tendrils of blue light erupted from the big man's palms and enveloped the Reaver, twining around the golden web that had entrapped him. The reinforced weave began to constrict, tugging tighter around its victim. Skin split and bones cracked as the god was compressed. With a final scream, the Reaver exploded in a torrential shower of black blood and whirling energy.

As the carnage settled, he noticed that Marius had a small smile on his face.

Eremul's head swam. He had just beheld the death of a god. And not just any god, but one of the thirteen Primes: the Reaver, Lord of Death himself. At that moment, he suddenly understood the nature of the poison afflicting Salazar.

He opened one eye and peered at the Augmentors waiting anxiously behind him. 'He needs to be bled,' he said. 'Open his wrists. I will do the rest.'

The Supreme Augmentor looked as though he was about to protest but then his mouth set in a grim line. He nodded and walked over to the bed. Then he drew his longsword in one smooth motion and placed the edge of the blade over the Magelord's left arm.

'If you are lying,' he said, 'you will hang in the Hook. You will be fed and watered to ensure you do not die quickly. I trust you understand this.'

Eremul rolled his eyes. 'Just cut his fucking wrists,' he said. The Supreme Augmentor bent to his work.

He summoned all the magic he could muster. He felt it blossom within him. *Now I must decide*, he thought. *I can save a tyrant and damn a city... or I can save a city and condemn myself.*

He was a double agent who had deceived a great many potential allies to maintain the fallacy that he was a loyal servant of the Magelord. He had ratted on the foolish, the desperate, those who never had a hope of bringing about any real change. They were the scapegoats that needed to be sacrificed to give him an opportunity like this.

To pass up that opportunity now would be the greatest betrayal of all – a slap in the face to all those he had sentenced to death.

He frowned. No one in the city cared a damn for him. He wasn't loved. He wasn't even respected. He wanted Salazar dead – but after a lifetime of suffering, the prospect of a drawn-out, agonizing death was not appealing. No, the Tyrant of Dorminia would die, but on Eremul's terms. He would not sacrifice himself. Not here. Not now. He wasn't a *hero*.

Coward, his brain screamed at him, but he ignored it and focused on the corrupted presence within Salazar. He poured his magic against it. Magic was life, the potentiality of creation, and it was anathema to the supernatural poison flooding the ancient Gharzian wizard's veins.

Black blood began to seep from Salazar's wrists. It dribbled out, running down his arms to gather in thick oily pools as the essence of the Reaver, the Lord of Death, was slowly purged from its withered old host.

The Magelord's pulse quickened. His breathing became audible. His eyelids began to flutter until finally they opened.

'Barandas,' he croaked. The Supreme Augmentor leaned over him, his eyes suspiciously moist and a joyous expression on his face.

'My lord! You are back with us. Lie still. Do not strain yourself. You have suffered a great deal.'

Salazar glanced at his wrists. The black ooze had ceased, and now his arms leaked simple, clean blood rather than living poison. He whispered something inaudible and the wounds began to smoke.

Eremul gasped. The Magelord's skin was knitting itself back together. *Such power*, he thought, aghast. *Such terrifying power.*

The Tyrant of Dorminia sat up. His gaze swept over the Augmentors assembled around him and settled on Eremul, who felt a shiver pass through him.

'Ah. The Halfmage. You have repaid my mercy most handsomely.' His voice became harder, growing stronger even as he spoke. 'You will say nothing of what you saw while our minds were linked. I will have your word or I will have your tongue. Which shall it be?'

Eremul swallowed hard. 'My word,' he said.

'Good. Help me up, Supreme Augmentor. There is no time to waste.'

'My lord?' the blond-haired warrior asked uncertainly.

Salazar looked at his wrinkled palms and brought them slowly together in front of his face. 'War,' he said. 'This attempt on my life was the White Lady's doing. Only she has the means to use the Reaver's own blood to poison me. We must prepare for war.'

The Measure of a Man

H<small>E CUT THROUGH</small> the water like an arrow, blinking stinging tears from his eyes. He was closing on Soeman fast. The engineer was only a hundred yards away. The flailing man went under again, and for a moment Cole thought he wasn't going to surface.

Don't you dare die on me, he thought angrily, spurring himself on. *This is my moment. I'll never forgive you if you drown.*

Of all his many qualities, Cole had always prided himself most on his athleticism. He could run faster and further than any man he knew, and he was as comfortable in water as he was on land. He could feel the eyes of Three-Finger and the rest of the *Redemption*'s passengers on him now, could well imagine the looks of awe and respect on their faces as they witnessed the deeds of a hero at first hand. It was time the world learned the measure of Davarus Cole.

Soeman's balding pate poked up above the waves once more, but this time he didn't resume his laboured swim towards the *Redemption*. Instead his arms flailed around desperately, and he sank back beneath the water.

Cole grunted with exertion and redoubled his efforts. He reached the spot where the engineer had vanished, took a mighty gulp of air and then swam downwards. He could see the man just below him. He was twitching pathetically. With a mighty snort, Cole grabbed hold of one of Soeman's arms and reversed direction, kicking frantically for the surface.

His head broke the water and he gasped for breath. He dragged the engineer up and held his mouth open with one hand, beating on his chest with the other as he desperately treaded water. With a strangled retching sound, Soeman puked out water and began coughing uncontrollably. Cole sighed with relief. *He'll live.*

'Hold on tight,' he said, and with one arm looped around Soeman's chest to keep him afloat he swam for the carrack ahead of them. Their progress was agonizingly slow compared with the quicksilver pace Cole had set in the opposite direction, but nonetheless the *Redemption* drew nearer.

'You saved me,' Soeman managed to croak once he was sufficiently recovered from his near-drowning.

'It's what I do,' Cole replied. 'Try to remain still. If you wriggle around you'll only hinder us.'

He had saved a man's life. He thought back to the Hook and his failed attempt to rescue the poor old sod who had been chosen by the Black Lottery. His anger at having let the man die still rankled with him, not least because things would have gone so differently back at the Shard hideout. Garrett and the others would learn to respect him soon enough, once he returned with Magebane and a crew of loyal men under his command.

'Uh,' Soeman mumbled. His right arm waved vaguely at something in front of him.

'What is it? I thought I told you to keep still...' Cole's words trailed off when he saw what the engineer was pointing at. There was a rowing boat full of Watchmen in the distance. It was closing the gap between them at frightening speed.

'Kick your damned legs!' Cole shrieked, pushing down on the water with all the strength he could muster.

The *Redemption* was within hailing distance. 'Lower a rope,' he shouted. Someone must have heard him, as a figure hurried across the deck and threw a line over the side of the ship. *Fifty more yards*, he thought.

His legs burning with exhaustion, so heavy they felt like they would drag him to the sea floor, Cole grasped the hanging rope and wrapped it around his body. He held Soeman close to him. 'Pull us up!' he yelled.

Whoever was above them complied, and they were hauled up the side of the ship and pulled aboard. Cole flopped out onto the deck, listening to the sounds of his heart thumping inside his chest. Eventually he looked up into the scabby face of Three-Finger. *My loyal sidekick.*

'You did well there, kid,' the convict said, giving him a nod. Soeman moaned nearby.

'The boat,' Cole panted. 'There are Watchmen closing on us.'

'Vessel spotted, five hundred yards to starboard,' someone cried.

'We can take them,' Three-Finger said. He offered a hand. Cole grasped it and grunted as the other man pulled him to his feet. His legs still felt unsteady and his left arm ached as bad as his ribs.

'The boat's packed with them,' the lookout cried again. 'Ten Watchmen, a handful of sailors, and... that bastard Augmentor.'

'Who here has a crossbow?' Three-Finger bellowed. One man raised his hand – the others looked around helplessly.

Cole clicked his fingers as another moment of inspiration struck. 'The artillery,' he shouted. 'We can sink them before they reach us.' He ran over to one of the small cannons mounted on the forecastle. 'Get me some powder, a small wad of cloth, and a flint and tinder,' he ordered one of the sailors close to him. The man hurried over to the hold at the stern. He returned with three small canvas bags, nondescript save for the red flames inked near their centres.

The young Shard reached down at his belt, grasping for the hilt of Magebane. With a curse he remembered that he no longer possessed his precious dagger. 'Pass me your knife,' he said. He took the blade from the sailor and cut open one of the bags, emptying its contents into the end of the cannon.

Artillery operated by alchemy was a relatively new invention. The components needed to create the explosive powder were rare and costly to obtain. Shadowport had enjoyed access to far greater reserves of the necessary materials, and the effectiveness of the City of Shades' cannons, combined with its considerably more advanced shipbuilding techniques, had effectively won the naval war with Dorminia.

Cole had studied a few of the books in Garrett's collection and he thought he knew enough to operate one of these weapons. They were cumbersome and potentially dangerous – but in the right hands, they could be deadly.

He grabbed a round iron shot from a crate near the cannon and fed it down the barrel with a wooden pole. 'Bring the ship around so I can get a clear shot,' he yelled at Jack, who spun the ship's wheel with relish. The carrack began to turn. The rowing boat was almost within his sights.

He took the cloth from his assistant, shoved it in the aperture just behind the powder chamber, and lit a spark which took to the small scrap of cloth immediately. He figured he had maybe fifteen seconds. *Just enough time.*

He thrust his head over the bulwark and pointed a finger in the direction of the furious men rowing towards him. 'I'm Davarus Cole,' he shouted down at them. 'You made a mistake when you signed up for this life of villainy. At least you can go to your deaths knowing you were slain by the best—'

'You forgot to swab the barrel!' the sailor beside him hissed. He looked down.

The fuse was halfway burned when the cannon went off. The force caused Cole's head to strike the bulwark and he came close to pitching over the side. The iron shot splashed harmlessly into the sea a dozen feet to the right of the rowing boat.

He looked around wildly, hoping nobody had witnessed his blunder. Everyone had. His head throbbed.

'Pass me more cloth,' he spat into the grinning face of the sailor.

This time everything went as planned. He cleaned the barrel, loaded the shot, lit the fuse and lined up his target. The soldiers were within fifty yards of the carrack when the cannon fired, sending its projectile whistling into the side of the boat. There was an explosion of timber and water and flailing bodies. Screams filled the air.

A loud cheer went up on the *Redemption*. Cole straightened and then stared out at the carnage. He froze. A moment ago he had faced a dozen men. Men with families, hopes and dreams. Now there was nothing but driftwood and a few corpses bobbing just below the surface of the sea.

His face split into a wide grin. 'Let that be a lesson to them!' he yelled, spinning around and pumping a fist in the air at the men celebrating on deck. He swaggered down to join them, savouring each slap on the back and happy smile as his new comrades gave him a hero's reception. Life had never felt so good.

'You did well, kid. You did well,' Three-Finger said.

He puffed out his chest. 'The name's Davarus Cole. I told you that already.' He sauntered over to where Soeman was shivering on the deck and hauled him up. 'Look at that,' he said to the engineer, gesturing at the setting sun and the dark water that stretched out across the horizon. 'This is ours. All of it. We're free men now.'

Soeman sniffed and then coughed. Despite the blood at the edges of his mouth, he smiled. 'I can't believe your plan worked. I admit, I thought it sounded crazy. You're a hero.'

'Yes,' Cole said quietly. 'I am.'

They stood together in silence for a time, watching the sun bid its final farewell. The last of the light faded. Soeman suddenly twitched and let out a faint gasp.

Cole shook his head. 'Your chest is getting worse. I thought the saltwater might have done you some good.'

There was no response. He looked at the engineer. Something was sticking out of the back of his head. He reached across and touched it.

A quarrel.

Soeman fell flat on his face. He didn't move.

There was a rustling sound above him and a dark shadow soared into view. Cole squinted up at the figure. It looked like a man...

Falcus! The Augmentor had survived the capsizing of the boat. His cloak billowed around him, glowing faintly in the night sky. He held a crossbow in one hand – and it was pointing at Cole.

Cole threw himself to the deck, shouting wildly to get the attention of the rest of the crew. One of the men ran over and levelled his crossbow at the soaring figure above them. He pulled the trigger, but the bolt missed. The Augmentor circled them, dipped low and then flew by barely a dozen feet away, taking aim with his weapon. There was a *thunk,* and the fellow beside Cole dropped to the deck, a quarrel protruding from his chest.

The young Shard turned and ran. He made it to the safety of the crowd that had gathered near the mainmast. Most still had no idea what was happening. 'Get down!' he yelled. One of the former prisoners was slow to react and ended up with a bolt quivering in his throat.

He felt at his belt for Magebane. This time he found the knife the sailor had lent to him. Falcus was preparing for another deadly pass. He tensed.

The Augmentor plummeted down out of the sky, arcing directly towards him. He waited until the last instant and threw the knife, aiming for the man's chest. It missed but snagged his cloak, cutting a large gash in the fabric.

Falcus cursed. Suddenly he was out of control, spinning wildly in the air. He crashed into the mainmast with a sickening thud and slid down it.

Three-Finger was on the fallen man in an instant, his hatchet taking chunks out of the dazed Augmentor. Within seconds it was all over. Three-Finger continued to hack away, dismembering the corpse and then tossing the parts overboard.

Cole got to his feet. They had lost three men, including Soeman. Jack was badly hurt too. He felt a sudden fury at his absolute triumph being sullied by the deaths of several of his crew – especially Soeman whom he had worked so hard to save from drowning. It just didn't seem fair.

Suddenly the air seemed to throb around him. He halted, staring around in shock, and then almost retched. A foul stench assaulted his nostrils. It smelled like a corpse left out in the sun, and it was overpowering, as if whatever was creating the smell was huge. All over the ship, men were leaning over and heaving onto the deck.

A roaring filled his ears and Cole staggered. The sea began to shimmer, so brightly it made his eyes water and forced him to look away. He opened his mouth to ask what was happening – but sudden, intense pressure stole his words away and cold water forced its way down his throat. He flailed wildly, hopelessly disorientated and surrounded on all sides by crushing water. The deck beneath his feet had disappeared; he was being dragged downwards. Ever downwards.

Darkness swallowed him.

'He will live.'

The words seemed to float into his ears from a long way away. He tasted bile and salt. His body shivered uncontrollably.

'Open your eyes.'

He did as he was ordered and stared up into the face of a beautiful woman. Her skin seemed almost supernaturally pale, but perhaps that was a trick of the moon behind her. There was something queer about her eyes. His own eyes felt full of grit, and he rubbed at them with salt-wrinkled hands.

'Where am I?' he asked.

191

'On *The Lady's Luck*,' the woman replied. 'The Swell almost claimed you. Your ship was lost, as were most of her men.'

'*The Lady's Luck?*' Cole noticed there were others near them, a crew of both men and women who glanced at him curiously.

'The flagship of Thelassa's fleet. We had orders to sink your carrack and the old cog trailing behind her.' His rescuer looked down at him without expression. 'The Swell saved us the bother.'

The Swell. Cole shivered again. He had come within a whisker of being yet another victim of the Lord of the Deep's undying wrath. 'What now?' he asked.

The woman's strange eyes narrowed on him. 'War is imminent between our two cities. We sail to Thelassa.'

'We?' Cole managed.

'Yes. You are our prisoner. The White Lady will have a great many questions for you.'

The Gathering Storm

His eyelids flickered open and the world shifted into focus. He was lying flat on his back, staring up at a huge grey cloud looming directly overhead. A gust of wind pushed at his hair, ruffled the growth of beard he felt bristling upon his neck. He tried to move his body, grunted at the sudden sharp pain in his midriff.

He felt weak. Weak and half-starved. Memories rushed back to him. The collapse of the mine. The fight with the baby-faced Augmentor and his belt of knives. Cold steel slipping inside his stomach. Waking in sweat-drenched fever, swallowing desperately from a waterskin shoved halfway down his throat before the blackness took him again.

'You're awake. About fucking time.' Jerek was there, crouched beside him. His right shoulder and thigh were wrapped in padded dressing. Blood had seeped through the bandages, but it had long since dried and turned brown.

Brodar Kayne forced himself up onto his elbows and glanced around. They were in a narrow depression, tree-covered hills rising on either side. The smell of rain was in the air. It was hard to be sure with the sun behind the clouds, but he reckoned it was late afternoon. *How long?*

'You been out the better part of a week,' the Wolf said, answering his unspoken question. 'You were gutted good and proper, Kayne. Isaac stitched you up but the girl thought you was done for. I told her you was a stubborn cunt.'

Kayne licked his lips. His mouth was dry and tasted foul. 'Where are they?' he asked.

The Wolf reached down and passed him his water bottle. 'Hunting,' he replied. 'Would have gone myself, but Isaac reckons my wounds still need time to heal. Turns out he's an expert trapper.'

He looked up at his friend. Jerek's face was unreadable. He scowled slightly when he saw Kayne studying him. *You've taken worse wounds and they ain't slowed you an inch, Wolf. You stayed with me in case I regained my senses.* Not that the grim Highlander would ever admit to the fact.

'Where are we?' he asked.

Jerek spat. 'West of the Rift, maybe a dozen miles. A shipful of the red-cloaked pricks turned up the day after we collapsed the mine. Followed our trail for a while, but I reckon we lost them. We been lying low ever since.'

Kayne sighed. How many had died at the Rift? The sabotage mission had turned into a massacre. 'They discover it was us that destroyed the place?'

Jerek shrugged. 'Don't think so. They never got close enough to see our faces. Still, ain't much chance of us swanning back into the Grey City now, is there? Not with the trail of bodies we've left behind. I say we escort the girl back to the city and get her to retrieve our gold, then put some miles between us and Dorminia. I'm tired of this shit.'

Kayne was of a like mind himself. He felt old. He felt *ancient*. Too many dead; too much sorrow. He was tired of running away, sick of killing. A man has to know when to quit.

A disturbance up near a line of alders caught his attention. Isaac and Sasha emerged from the trees, the manservant clutching a trio of coneys in one hand. He smiled happily when he saw his charge had regained consciousness.

In contrast, Sasha was looking mighty peeved. Her jaw clenched and unclenched in a manner not dissimilar to the Wolf when he got into one of his moods. She had a jagged tear down the side of her breeches and her left leg was caked up to the knee in mud.

'So you made it after all,' she said, somewhat coldly, hunkering down near to where he lay. She pulled her muddy boot off and turned it upside down, giving it a violent shake. Filthy water trickled out. 'It would be nice if Isaac paid as much attention to our footing as he did your recovery.' She glared at the manservant. 'I can't believe you led me into a bog.'

Isaac looked slightly embarrassed. 'I really am sorry about that. I was distracted.'

'Distracted? You were ambling along drawing pictures of birds.'

'I like to sketch. I have quite a collection back at the depository. Perhaps when we return to the city I could show them to you.' His vapid face looked hopeful.

Sasha snorted. 'Now *there's* an offer I can't refuse. Don't waste your time, Isaac. I'm not interested.'

Isaac's face fell. Kayne couldn't help but feel sorry for him. 'I guess I should thank you for patching me up,' he said to the dejected manservant. He lowered his voice conspiratorially. 'I shouldn't fret about the girl. I reckon she has her sights set on someone else.' He gave her a knowing look, thought about winking but couldn't quite muster the enthusiasm.

Sasha shot him a poisonous glance. 'As if you're in any position to know what I want. You Highlanders and your women. How does it go? You hit them on the head with a rock and rape them while they're unconscious? Or is it the other way around?'

The girl's words cut right through him. She might have been jesting, but if there was anything besides anger and contempt in those dark eyes he couldn't see it.

Her tone didn't sit well with Jerek. 'What's your fucking problem?' he demanded in an angry rasp. 'You've been bitching like a she-bear with a twig up her arse for the last week. Did the alchemist mean that much to you?'

'Vicard was a better man than you'll ever be,' Sasha spat back. 'I suppose I should consider myself lucky Isaac is around, or who knows what you'd have done to me by now. I'm not scared of you.'

Jerek's face twisted in anger. He stepped towards her. She stared back, unflinching. The Wolf's right hand went to his beard, tugging furiously. His left hand clenched into a fist. 'Fuck yourself. I'm going for a walk.' With that, he spun and stormed off into the trees.

Kayne watched him go. He released the breath he'd been holding with a tired sigh and closed his eyes for a moment. The first light patters of rain fell, cooling his face and releasing some of the tension in the air.

Isaac scratched the side of his head and risked a nervous smile. 'Well,' he said. 'I think we'd better find shelter from this downpour.' He gave the rabbits he was holding a small shake. 'Who's hungry?'

He watched the small fire dancing in the light breeze. The canopy of leaves and branches overhead shook with the strength of the downpour. Occasional droplets of rain splattered down through gaps in the foliage, but it was better than being out there in the open where the spring deluge was beating at the surrounding hills like an anvil. Isaac stirred the stew he was preparing with a stick, humming to himself. It smelled delicious. Even Sasha appeared to have relaxed somewhat.

The old Highlander was so hungry he felt sick but there was no point complaining about it. The food would be ready when it was ready. At least his stomach wound seemed to be healing. He'd managed to struggle to his feet and hobble up the hill without the help of the others. His knees hurt like hell and the piss he'd just taken had been two of the worst minutes of his life, but he reckoned he was on the mend.

He cleared his throat and glanced across at Sasha. 'Sorry for the loss of your friend, lass,' he said. He tried to think of something else to add but couldn't, so he stared at his scarred hands instead.

For a moment she didn't respond. Then she looked across the fire at him. 'I have a name, you know. *Sasha*. Not "girl", or "lass". Or even "bitch", as your brutish companion so endearingly refers to me.'

'I don't mean to offend,' he said. 'I've never been good with names, and my memory ain't getting any better with age. Besides, most everyone seems a girl or boy when you're as old as me.'

She seemed to ponder this for a time. 'Just how old are you?' she asked eventually.

'Can't say for sure. I killed my first man over forty years ago. I was, what, nine at the time. I guess that means I'm past fifty.'

She stared at him in disbelief. 'You killed your first man when you were nine years old? That's ridiculous.'

'Aye, well, the High Fangs were wilder back in them days.' He stared at the pot bubbling over the fire. 'My village had come under attack from a nearby settlement. Our warriors drove them off, but they left some of their wounded behind. One of 'em was right there before me on the snow, stabbed through his chest and sobbing like a babe. Father handed me his spear, told me it was time I became a man.' He shrugged. 'I did what I had to do.'

'You were a child,' she said. He saw disgust in her eyes.

Aye, I was. And yet in that moment I saw the truth of the world, and a smarter man would have heeded that lesson better than I ever could. Still. What's done is done. I wager your own past ain't all sweetness and light. Got some ghosts of your own, if I'm any judge.

'It was the way things were done,' Kayne said. 'Still is, though the Reachings don't war like they used to. The threat from the Devil's Spine has made everyone a bit more cautious about killing each other. Most of the time,' he added.

Isaac decided the stew was ready. The manservant passed over the cook pot. 'Have as much as you want,' he said. 'You need to eat. To tell the truth, I'm surprised you pulled through. You mountain folk are a hardy lot and no mistake.'

Brodar Kayne didn't respond. He was already stuffing his mouth. Hot stew spilled down his chin and burned his fingers, but he paid it no mind. He'd spent two years being pursued all over the High Fangs, never knowing where his next meal might come from. In that situation a man eats what he can, when he can, and in any way he can. There were times when he'd been forced to drink his own piss, and you know things are looking bleak when that prospect's almost appealing.

The other two watched him in silence. When he'd eaten as much as he could, he felt the weakness return. He was about to nod off when Sasha's voice drifted over and tugged him back to wakefulness.

'You never did tell me what you and Jerek were doing in Dorminia.'

He shifted, blinked a few times to shake away the sleepiness. 'We were on the run,' he said, after an uncomfortable silence. 'The Shaman has a bounty on our heads. Mine especially. Ain't nothing he'd rather see than my ugly face on a spear above the Great Lodge.'

'The Shaman? You mean the Magelord of the High Fangs? What did you do to upset *him*?'

'Ain't what I done, lass. It's what I didn't do.' He closed his eyes and thought back to the morning the Shaman uttered the words that had frozen the blood in his veins.

Beregund must be razed to the ground.

'I wasn't always the sorry old bastard you see now. The Sword of the North, they named me. I was the Defender of the High Fangs, the first bulwark against the fiends that came down from the Spine. In times of war I was the instrument of the Shaman's will.'

Sasha looked puzzled. 'You served the Shaman?'

He nodded. 'The fact is, I didn't much care for right and wrong when I was a younger man. I did many things I ain't proud of. Wasn't until I got older that the fame and respect began to lose their lustre. Once that happens, killing is the only thing that's left, and being the best at killing ain't enough. Not when the weight of a man's deeds begins to drag on him.'

He sat for a time, remembering. The wind had picked up, whistling through the boughs above them like the shrieks of a thousand lost souls. Sasha and Isaac looked at him expectantly. He cleared his throat.

'I met Mhaira when I was maybe half the age I am now. We had our joining within a year. She was a daughter of the Green Reaching, born to a couple of herders from Beregund. A modest family, but it didn't matter a damn to me. Not when I saw the laughter in her eyes. Thinking back, I probably thought wedding a shepherd's daughter added to my own legend in the making.'

'That sounds like someone I know,' Sasha said quietly.

He thought about that for a time. 'Aye, I reckon I can see shades of myself in the lad. I was arrogant. Proud. Conceited. Wedding Mhaira was the one thing I got right. Ain't a day goes by that I don't count my blessings for that one moment of good sense.'

'What happened?' asked Sasha, poking at the remnants of their campfire with a stick. Isaac looked on with his usual bland expression.

He closed his eyes for a moment. 'The Shaman ordered Beregund put to the sword. Mhaira's family. The friends I had there. All of them.'

'Why?'

He shrugged. 'It's how the Shaman does things. Aye, reasons were given: the town wasn't honouring the Treaty; they were withholding tributes due to Heartstone – that kind of thing. But what it came down to was the Shaman exercising his dominance. He was always pitting folk against each other. Culling the weak, as he called it.'

'You refused to do as he asked.'

The old Highlander nodded. 'The Shaman gave me a day to make my decision. I figure he thought to test me. Knowing he wouldn't like my answer, I fled east with Mhaira. The Brethren caught me a few days later but I bought her some time to escape. Or so I thought.'

Tears threatened his eyes. He blinked them away. 'I spent the best part of a year inside a wicker cage. The Brethren found Mhaira huddling in a cave in the Devil's Spine and had both of us brought before the Shaman. He burned her alive. Would have been me next but for Jerek. Whatever else a man might say about him, the Wolf ain't one to forget a debt.'

Sasha pursed her lips and stared down at the ground. 'That's a horrible story. Do you have any children?'

He flinched at the question. 'I had a son. Pride of his mother and me, he was. Had his mother's wits and his father's skill with a sword. He... died, the day Mhaira burned.'

Silence followed his words. Isaac's plain face was sympathetic, and even Sasha's eyes had softened. The fire had burned down to embers. Kayne stared at the glowing ash, avoiding the gazes of those opposite him. Eventually he cleared his throat.

'I reckon that's enough about me. What about you, lass? What's the story with you and boy?'

Sasha frowned back at him. 'You mean Cole? There is no story.'

'I saw the way he looks at you.'

'He can look at me any way he likes. We've known each other for years. Garrett is my mentor too. Cole is... well, you've seen how he is. He's the only person I know who can scrape through the most dangerous situations by the sheer power of his own bullshit.'

'Aye, there's some gap between the man he is and the man

he sees in the mirror. Still, I get the feeling his heart's in the right place.'

Sasha sighed. 'Somewhere deep down inside him, it is. But he's been raised to believe he's some great hero. Garrett spoiled him.' She shook her head. 'Cole lives in a bubble. One day it's going to burst and his whole world will come crashing down.' There was a hint of concern in the girl's voice. Concern and perhaps something more.

The old barbarian was wise enough to say nothing.

Footsteps squelched on soggy turf and Jerek reappeared, soaked through to the bone. His face was thunder.

'Fucking things don't work,' he said, pointing down at the faintly glowing leather boots on his feet.

Sasha rolled her eyes. 'That's because they're *bondmagic*. The enchantment only functions for the person linked to them. Salazar isn't stupid enough to allow powerful artefacts such as those to be turned against him.'

Jerek looked down at the boots in disgust and spat. 'Could have told me that before I prised them from the stinking feet of that bastard. Waste of fucking time, this whole journey. And roll those pretty eyes at me again and you'll regret it.'

Kayne flexed his neck, loosening muscles that had grown stiff during his convalescence. 'We've got a two-day march until we reach Dorminia. I reckon it'll go smoother if we all make the effort to be civil.' No one answered. Sasha and Jerek stared daggers at one another. Isaac busied himself tidying the camp. Kayne sighed. 'Fine. Silence suits me just as well.'

'I spotted a small town a few miles west of here,' Jerek said abruptly. 'We can buy supplies. Maybe rest until this shitty weather passes.' He rubbed at his scarred face as if he could do with a break, but Brodar Kayne knew the truth of the matter. In spite of everything, the realization pricked at him.

Wounded pride? Stupid old fool. You never learn. He climbed to his feet, niggling pains assailing him from every direction, so many he didn't even bother to try and count them all. He forced his stubbly face into a rictus of a smile.

'A few miles, eh? We can make that before nightfall. Let's get some shelter over our heads. You lot could use a break from the rain.'

A Precious Gift

BARANDAS RUBBED AT his tired eyes, yawned and glanced back
down at the ledger he had been studying. The numbers had
started to blur together. He sighed and closed the book, leaning
back in his chair.

Moist lips brushed the back of his neck and he turned to see
Lena watching him with a concerned expression.

'You've been up all night. Again.'

He glanced out of the window. Night had given way to a
grim dawn, iron-grey clouds plastering the sky from horizon to
horizon. Droplets of rain crawled down the glass panels and
pattered onto the stones below. The last couple of days had been
nothing but incessant drizzle. After the public announcement
that Dorminia was now at war with Thelassa, the depressing
weather was oddly appropriate. The news had been received by
the populace with all the enthusiasm one might expect. That
was to say, none at all.

He got to his feet, stretching out the tightness in his back.
Lena was still looking at him with worry on her face. He leaned
forwards and kissed her quickly.

'I'll manage,' he said. 'The Marshal still isn't fit to return to
his post. While he is indisposed, I have a war to plan and the
commissioning of new Augmentors to oversee.'

Lena shook her head in annoyance. 'What exactly is wrong
with Halendorf? You'd think he would be itching for revenge
against Thelassa. After all, their assassins did try to poison him.'

Barandas yawned again. 'He was deeply unsettled by his near-death experience. His acid is so bad he can barely rise from his bed, or so he claims.'

'And Ardling? Is our Chancellor also indisposed by the recent attempt on your lives?'

'I imagine the cost of a war with our neighbours has had greater implications for his well-being than all the excitement in the Grand Council Chamber.'

Lena's expression became grave. She was in no mood for jokes, it seemed. *Not that it was much of a joke. With the expense of the war with Shadowport and now this latest conflict, I'm surprised our Chancellor hasn't committed suicide.*

'I have a busy day ahead training the new servants, and visiting textile merchants and seamsters,' said his wife. 'I will not have our new staff pay for their own uniforms, despite what Kyla and the others might say. What time will you be home tonight?'

Barandas shifted uncomfortably. 'I will be at the Obelisk this evening. Lord Salazar has requested my presence. Don't look at me like that, Lena! Many of the city's magistrates are dead. It is only right that the rest of us do our duty. Especially in times of war.'

She sighed and eventually nodded. That was precisely why he loved her so much. *Compassion, concern and then acceptance. You are my rock, Lena, tethering me to my humanity when this world would make of me a monster.*

'What of Legwynd? Have you found his killers?'

Barandas shook his head. 'Not yet. They could have fled anywhere, perhaps even north to the Badlands. The mine, Lena... every man working the Rift was buried alive.'

'Whoever did this must be brought to justice.'

'They will be, when the Watch can spare the men to conduct a widespread search. In the meantime, we await our first shipment from the Swell. All this effort spent training new recruits will be in vain if we don't have the raw magic to create more Augmentors.'

Lena looked up at him. The green crystal on the platinum chain around her neck matched her eyes. Even after five years of marriage, her beauty still took his breath away. 'It suits you,' he said, cupping the quartz in his palm.

'You never did tell me where you found it.'

Her tone made him grin. She always told him he had a boy's smile. 'Where I *found* it? What makes you think I didn't go to the finest jeweller in the city and have it commissioned for you?'

She raised an eyebrow in response. 'As if you could tear yourself away from your responsibilities long enough to waste time buying pretty baubles for your spoiled wife. Really, Ran, where *did* you find it?'

His smile faded away. He remembered the gruesome result of Thurbal's butchery flopping around in pools of blood, and the lurid glow of flames licking around the pile of corpses to reduce them to blackened skeletons.

'Better you don't ask,' he said. 'I appropriated it while doing my duty to Lord Salazar and the city. If you don't wish to have it, I know someone else who might...'

It was her turn to raise an eyebrow. 'What, the goodwife or whatever it is she calls herself?'

'The *goodlady*,' he corrected her. 'Truth be told I'm rather certain Cyreena will never make anyone a good wife. Though I suppose a man can but try...'

She tutted and he grinned again, pulling her towards him for a kiss. 'I have to leave now,' he said. 'I don't know how long I will be at the Obelisk this evening. Don't wait up.'

'You know me,' she said, giving him a frown.

'Yes, I do. And I wouldn't have you any other way.' He gave her one last kiss, and then went to wash his face and find something to eat before heading out into the relentless drizzle. He had a busy day ahead.

'Keep your weapon up,' Barandas instructed, launching a backhand swing at his opponent's neck. He brought his longsword to a halt at the last possible instant, leaving the blade poised a hair's breadth from the man's throat.

'Point taken, sir,' said Gorm in a strained voice. He remained perfectly still. 'I don't suppose you could take your sword away now?'

Barandas lowered his weapon and stared across at the other man. Tall and thin, Gorm had the look of a clerk or accountant rather than a warrior. For all that, he was competent enough with a spear and had served in the Watch for the best part of a decade. He had been high on the list of men Halendorf had recommended for consideration. So far he hadn't set the world alight, but neither was he the worst candidate Barandas had tested in recent days.

'Tell me, Gorm. Why do you wish to become an Augmentor?'

The lanky Watchman scratched at his bulbous nose with a thin hand and cleared his throat nervously. 'I want to serve his lordship and the city. Why else?'

Barandas blinked rainwater from his eyes. All around the small courtyard, men watched the spectacle with expressions of eagerness, curiosity or apprehension. A handful of Augmentors were among them. Thurbal stroked the pommel of his enchanted scimitar and smiled cruelly at the hopefuls. Garmond loomed near the courtyard gates, motionless, like a statue carved from obsidian in his light-devouring armour.

'You say you want to serve our lord and Dorminia, yet is this not already your mandate as a man of the Crimson Watch? To become an Augmentor is to go beyond mere servitude. The magic that is bestowed upon an Augmentor links them to Lord Salazar in mind, body and soul. Are you prepared for that?'

The tall man appeared to think about this for a moment before nodding. 'I guess I am,' he said. 'Do I get to choose what kind of magic I get? I always wanted a belt that made me as strong as a giant, like the one Kronin of Gharzia wore to repel the horse lords of the steppes in the time before the Godswar. My old grandpa used to tell me stories about it.'

206

Barandas sighed. *So this one's a dreamer, full of excitement at the prospect of carrying magic around*. He glanced across to Thurbal. *They aren't as reliable as the sociopaths once the novelty wears off. Still, better a dreamer than an idealist. Those rarely last long.*

'The answer to your question is no,' he said. 'You will be assigned bondmagic that best complements your natural aptitudes.'

Gorm looked momentarily disappointed.

'If I judge you worthy, I believe that a polearm of some kind would be fitting. There are several enhancements that could be made,' said Barandas. 'A lightning-emitting head, perhaps, or a shaft able to shape the winds to its wielder's will...'

The Watchman immediately perked up. *Yes. Definitely a dreamer.*

There was a sudden commotion near the gates. 'Get out of my damned way, Garmond,' growled an irate voice. The huge Augmentor was blocking his view of the newcomer, but Barandas recognized the speaker immediately.

'Let him pass,' he ordered. He took a deep breath. This was going to be unpleasant.

Garmond moved aside. Rorshan marched towards him.

'Commandant!' he barked. 'My magic' – he gestured to the whip on the left side of his belt, then the dagger on the other – 'has gone, and I feel like... like a part of me has died inside. Commission new bondmagic for me. Please.'

Barandas looked his erstwhile comrade in the eye. 'Rorshan, you served Dorminia well for many years. Your bravery ensured the safety of our vassal towns and villages countless times. I mourned when I learned that our lord's ritual consumed your magic. Of all the men I lost that night, your dispossession was the greatest tragedy.'

'But I can still serve,' said Rorshan. 'I was on my way to Farrowgate to confront an abomination when I was summoned to the Obelisk. Replace these weapons and I will return there

207

and do my best to protect the village – as I have always done!' Desperation coloured his voice.

Barandas shook his head. 'You ask the impossible,' he said softly. 'The binding spell can only be performed once. A second attempt will kill a man. It has been tried in the past, many times, and the result has always been fatal. I am sorry, Rorshan, but you need to put this part of your life behind you. I have recommended you for an officer's position in the Watch—'

'*Fuck the Watch!*' Rorshan exclaimed. His grip on his weapons had tightened so that his hands had turned white. 'You don't know what it's like. I can't sleep. Sometimes I start to shake and it won't stop. There's a part of me that's been ripped out, and if something doesn't fill the emptiness soon I swear I'm going to make the bastard responsible pay.'

'Easy, Rorshan,' Barandas said. 'You're suffering. That's normal when an Augmentor loses his bondmagic. I can help you—'

'I don't need your help,' Rorshan spat. He tugged his weapons from his belt. 'Fifteen years. I've been an Augmentor since you were barely more than a boy. Now you're going to tell me that's it? I'm finished? I don't think so.' He took a step forwards.

As Rorshan approached, Barandas felt despair threatening to engulf him. His sword weighed like a mountain in his hand.

He gritted his teeth. *A man has to do what is necessary.*

Suddenly Garmond was between them. He shoved Rorshan so hard that the man flew a dozen feet backwards. With a yell of rage, the ex-Augmentor leaped to his feet and charged at the giant. He easily dodged a massive right swing and flicked his wrist so that his whip snaked out and wrapped around Garmond's other hand. He pulled.

Had the magic still been present in Rorshan's weapon, not even Garmond's prodigious strength would have been able to withstand its tug. The colossus would have been dragged forwards to meet the point of the dagger in Rorshan's other hand – sharp enough to pierce even the huge man's enchanted armour.

Instead, Rorshan stared with a helpless fury as his efforts failed to budge Garmond an inch. The giant Augmentor grabbed the slack part of the whip and pulled, heaving Rorshan towards him. Rorshan was too slow to react to the crushing hands reaching around his throat. They closed, and then they began to squeeze.

Barandas looked away. Rain hammered down, almost but not quite drowning out the sounds of a man being choked to death. Eventually the noises ceased. Around the courtyard men were silent, staring at the ground or the sky with troubled faces.

He looked at Gorm. The lanky fellow wore a shocked expression. 'So,' Barandas said. 'Just to be certain, do you still wish to pledge your life as an Augmentor?'

Gorm opened his mouth, but no words emerged.

'And how is your recruitment of potential new Augmentors progressing?'

'Steadily, my lord. Sadly, a promising candidate declined us earlier this day.'

Lord Salazar waved a bony hand, dismissing the unfortunate news. 'There will be others, I am certain. Keep looking.'

Barandas nodded. The events of that morning had shaken him. Rorshan had no family, but the Supreme Augmentor had nonetheless arranged an honourable burial for his old comrade. That was the least he could do, in spite of the manner of Rorshan's passing.

'My lord, we have roughly a thousand Crimson Watchmen,' he said, finally daring to broach a subject that had been troubling him for days. 'I believe we can muster another five thousand men of fighting age, untrained or poorly trained for the most part. That is a sizeable force, yet if reports are correct, Thelassa has contracted no less than three companies of mercenaries from Sumnia.'

The Magelord narrowed his eyes. 'Then we must recruit additional soldiers from our vassal towns. Thelassa has no army to speak of, and its emasculated men are worth less than a Dorminian woman.'

'Be that as it may, my lord, three thousand mercenaries will cut down untrained men like wheat. The warriors of the Sun Lands are renowned for their discipline and effectiveness. They will overwhelm us, no matter how many civilians we conscript.'

Salazar drummed his fingers against the sides of his throne. Barandas watched him in silence. The Grand Council Chamber felt huge and empty with only the two of them present. Timerus was still recovering from the poisoning, which he had survived only by spitting out the wine he had been about to swallow. Marshal Halendorf remained indisposed. Even the grey presence of Chancellor Ardling would have leavened the atmosphere somewhat.

'We have no gold left with which to hire mercenaries of our own,' said the Magelord finally. 'The White Lady has gambled much on entrusting her war effort to Sumnians. I now regret not crushing Shadowport before Admiral Kramer's incompetence sank our navy.'

Barandas nodded. Sumnians were celebrated warriors on land and in the native desert of their homeland on the other side of the continent, but they lacked any experience of maritime conflict.

'I believe the Sumnian army will march soon,' he said. 'They know we cannot launch an assault. Not without a navy. The White Lady will be aware of your... forgive me, your weakened state, my lord. Now is the right time for her to make her move.'

The Tyrant of Dorminia narrowed his eyes dangerously. 'I am not as weak as they suspect. Nor will I allow myself to be taken unawares again. The White Lady's servants are skilled in the art of sophistry, but I am prepared now. If they dare intrude here I will kill them.'

'Sophistry, my lord?' asked Barandas.

'A form of magic focused on subtle deception and mental manipulation. The Fade were masters of it, back when they roamed these lands. They could live unnoticed within a city for decades. It was but one of many racial attributes that made them so incredibly dangerous.' The Magelord's voice trailed off as he spoke, as if he were troubled by something. Barandas knew better than to push further.

Lord Salazar suddenly rose from his throne. 'I must leave Dorminia for a time. I am owed an ancient favour, though calling on it will not be pleasant. There are some things that time can never heal. As I have learned all too well.'

Barandas was shocked at the sorrow in his master's voice. 'My lord... you are leaving the city? Who will govern in your name, with Grand Magistrate Timerus still unfit for office?'

'I will not be gone long, Supreme Augmentor. I am sure you can manage in my absence. The Halfmage will assist you. He possesses a keen intellect as well as a certain cunning. Keep an eye on him.'

Barandas bowed his head. 'I will, my lord.'

Salazar nodded. 'I will detain you no longer.' He paused for a moment. 'Your dedication is appreciated, Supreme Augmentor.'

Barandas almost gasped. One learned to expect many things from a Magelord, but gratitude was not among them. For the second time in his life, he had been handed a precious gift by the master of Dorminia.

City of Towers

THE LADY'S LUCK docked in Thelassa four days after setting out from the Swell. The weather had held and the ship made good time. Although Cole was confined to a small cabin under the silent watch of one of the crew, he had found the journey almost pleasant when compared with the torturous conditions aboard the *Redemption*.

The door of his cabin creaked open a fraction and the guard peered into the room. 'We have arrived. Follow me,' she said. Cole got up from the tiny bed and followed her out of the cabin and up onto the deck. The sight that greeted him caused him to stop abruptly.

Cole had never travelled much beyond Dorminia's walls, but he had often spoken with merchants and others who had visited the City of Towers. Their tales had seemed wild and impossible at the time.

They didn't seem so far-fetched now.

Where Dorminia slumped in a chaotic mass of buildings shoved together so haphazardly that they seemed likely to collapse in a shower of grey stone, Thelassa was a soaring testament to the vision of the most skilled architects of the Age of Strife. Delicate towers reached for the clouds, framing wide avenues of white marble that gleamed in the morning sun. Lining the flawless streets were trees and shrubbery cultivated into wondrous shapes: griffins and unicorns and other beasts that were said to have roamed the world before the Godswar.

Now the forests north and west of the Trine held nothing but scattered game, and even they were beginning to disappear.

'It's like a dream,' he whispered, awestruck. He despised Salazar more than ever then, for his grey city and the grim, tyrannical rule that bled the life from his subjects. Here, in this place, was proof that humanity was not beyond redemption.

'Get your hands off me, you pox-ridden whore,' snarled an angry voice, and he turned to see Three-Finger being prodded along the ramp connecting the ship to the docking platform where he waited.

'You're alive!' Cole exclaimed. He couldn't keep the grin off his face. The other man looked up and grunted in acknowledgment. Others survivors from the *Redemption* began to emerge onto the deck, but before he could identify individual faces a firm hand took hold of his arm and pulled him around.

He gasped. The grip was ridiculously strong and unnaturally cold. The hand withdrew almost immediately, but it left a burning pain where it had touched his flesh. He looked up into the face of the pale woman who had addressed him when he had first regained consciousness aboard *The Lady's Luck*. Cole had come to understand she was the ship's captain.

'You will accompany me to the White Lady,' she said. 'Please do not try to escape. You would not get far and the consequences would be unpleasant.'

Cole rubbed at his arm. The woman's touch had left him feeling slightly nauseous. 'I'm on your side,' he said reproachfully. 'I despise Salazar. Nothing would please me more than to see him brought down.'

The captain stared back at him with a blank expression. 'That is for my mistress to judge. Keep close to me. The palace is not far.'

Cole did as he was ordered, trailing the captain as they passed down a broad promenade lined with oak and elm; at an intersection they branched off to the right, cutting through the shadow of a pair of large humanoid statues with the heads of bulls.

The sense of wonder that had filled him on seeing the city for the first time had turned to awe. He inhaled deeply, marvelling at the myriad floral scents that filled his nostrils instead of the stench of human effluence that permeated the Grey City.

How have they managed it? A city the size of Dorminia, yet it smells like a garden.

They passed men and women who glanced at them curiously. Rather than the scowls that were a permanent feature of most Dorminians, the faces of these Thelassans wore content expressions. One man smiled, bowing slightly to the captain of *The Lady's Luck*. Cole noticed other women like her, pale as ghosts and with eyes that seemed to lack any hint of colour. All of them wore the long white robes of their order.

He glanced up often as they walked, admiring the towers that rose majestically into the sky. They were tall, thin structures, rendering the Obelisk an ugly and stunted thing in comparison. He concluded that they must belong to the nobility and ruling classes. However, unlike Dorminia, where the Noble Quarter was strictly sequestered from the rest of the city, here small residences and towers stood side by side. Even the humblest buildings were attractively designed, constructed from the white marble that comprised the vast majority of Thelassa's buildings.

They passed close to a modest estate with angelic effigies smiling beatifically down upon them. For a moment Cole thought he heard the sounds of crying from within. The captain quickened her step and they were soon out of range.

Eventually they approached the centre of the city. The passing crowds thinned and in their place stood Sumnian warriors wearing leather vests and carrying swords, spears and other weapons of war. Cole couldn't help but stare at the soldiers, who were blacker of skin than even the darkest Gharzian merchants that sometimes visited Dorminia.

There were hundreds of them. They patrolled the streets

with furrowed brows, clearly impatient to see to some action – a direct contrast to the placid Thelassans, who kept their distance. The woman who had guarded his cabin back on *The Lady's Luck* noticed his confusion.

'You are surprised to see so many foreigners here. These Sumnians are my mistress's hired swords. They are unmatched in the arts of war. Dorminia has no hope of withstanding them.'

Cole was inclined to agree. Dorminia's Augmentors were an elite force, ruthless and deadly, but they were few in number. The Crimson Watch was little more than a collection of thugs and degenerates. Against an army of Sumnians, they would crumble like sand.

'The palace is close at hand,' said the captain just ahead of him. 'You will show humility in the presence of our glorious mistress. Bow down and avert your gaze until you are asked to do otherwise. And do not speak unless you are commanded.'

Cole nodded in response. Yet again fate had intervened to put him on the path to his ultimate destiny. He was certain the White Lady would be impressed by this brave young rebel marching into the palace and pledging his blade to her cause.

He reached down for Magebane, a split second before he remembered, yet again, that it was in the hands of Brodar Kayne.

With a sigh, he ran a hand through his hair and prepared for an audience with the fabled White Lady of Thelassa.

'You've prostrated yourself for quite long enough.'

He straightened, managing not to wince at the sudden lancing pain in his bruised ribs. His eyes were immediately drawn to the figure upon the ivory throne on the raised dais in the centre of the chamber. Sunlight filtered through a window set high in the arched ceiling directly overhead, bathing her in a radiant glow. His breath caught in his chest.

The White Lady wore an exquisite gown of the palest silk, so translucent he fancied he could see her curves beneath the fabric. Her platinum-blond hair was light enough to appear almost silver and framed a face so perfect the finest sculptors would have wept gazing upon it. Her skin was as flawless as the marble beneath his feet. He stood there, mouth agape, transfixed by her unearthly beauty.

Movement to both sides of the White Lady drew Cole's attention away from the intoxicating sight. To her left, up on the dais with her, a gigantic black-skinned Sumnian stood with arms folded. To the right of the Magelord, a gangly woman of middling years cleared her throat and looked pensive.

'Avert your eyes, maggot!' commanded the massive warrior in an absurdly deep voice. He was head, shoulders and most of a chest taller than Cole, the biggest man the young Shard had ever set eyes on. Pink scars crisscrossed his prodigiously muscled body, which was naked from the waist up. The giant Sumnian carried a golden spear topped by a wickedly curved blade, and he pointed it at Cole before taking a single huge stride onto the first step leading down from the dais.

Cole felt very alone all of a sudden. The giant Sumnian took another step.

'Enough, General,' ordered the White Lady. Her voice was soft and perfectly modulated and carried effortlessly across the chamber. 'Our guest is clearly unfamiliar with our customs.' She turned her face to Cole and he gasped. Her eyes were a violet hue unlike any he had ever seen before.

'In Thelassa, a man does not stare at a woman with such lust in his eyes. Not unless she welcomes the attention.' She glanced at the massive Sumnian beside her, meeting his gaze and holding it for longer than was strictly necessary to make her point. The man's answering smile was huge and proud. She turned back to Cole. 'You will learn our ways in time.'

'Heed the words of the mistress, maggot,' the Sumnian said, gesturing again with his spear. 'Or I will tear your eyes from their sockets.'

The White Lady lifted a perfect hand. 'Thank you, General.'

She turned her gaze back to Cole. 'I understand you were rescued from a Dorminian ship. What were you doing on the Swell?'

Cole took a deep breath. This was his moment. He needed to make a good impression. 'We were sent there to mine for magic,' he said. 'Most of the men on board were prisoners and had no choice in the matter.'

'You were one such prisoner?'

He nodded. 'There were two ships. The *Redemption* and *Red Bounty*. I was on the former.'

'My captain tells me the ships had become separated. It appears you were fleeing your captors before the Swell capsized you.'

Cole rolled his shoulders. 'It turns out they'd bitten off more than they could chew with a few of the prisoners.' He placed his hands together and pushed his palms outwards, giving his fingers a good crack for effect. 'One in particular. Some men just refuse to be chained.'

The White Lady raised an eyebrow. The gesture was so ridiculously perfect that he couldn't stop himself from ogling the Magelord with undisguised admiration. The Sumnian general scowled. 'I warned you, maggot.'

Cole decided he'd had enough of being called a maggot.

'My name is Davarus Cole,' he declared. 'I am the son of Illarius Cole, a hero of great renown. I was eight years old when I witnessed my father murdered by Salazar's men. I swore that, one day, I would see the bastard dead. I stand before you not as an enemy – but as a friend.'

The woman to the right of the White Lady looked up suddenly. '*Illarius Cole?*' she said. There was a strange edge to her voice, but her accent was unmistakably that of Dorminia.

The White Lady appeared not to have heard her. 'I possess three thousand Sumnian warriors under the command of brave General Zahn here. My spies in the Grey City provide all the intelligence I could possibly need. What can you offer that I don't already have?'

Cole frowned. This wasn't going quite as he had planned.

'You're probably not aware,' he ventured, 'but I belong to a rather important organization – a rebel group that opposes Salazar at every turn. *The Shards*. Your spies may have heard of us.'

The White Lady said nothing. She turned to the tall woman next to her, who whispered something and then shook her head.

'It appears not,' the Magelord said. Cole's shoulders sagged.

There was a commotion behind him and suddenly Three-Finger was brought into the throne room and shoved forwards to stand beside Cole. His scabby face was covered in bruises and a stream of bloody snot dribbled from his right nostril. Clearly he had ignored the captain's instructions not to attempt an escape.

'And who is this?' the White Lady asked.

'His name's Three-Finger,' Cole replied quickly, before the convict had a chance to reply. 'He's my henchman.'

Three-Finger shot him an annoyed glance. 'I'm not your henchman.'

Cole decided to ignore that. 'Tell her how I saved you all, Three-Finger. Tell them about my plan.'

Three-Finger shrugged. 'What do you want me to say? They don't care about us, kid. Once we're done being questioned they'll have us both killed.'

The White Lady waved a finger and suddenly Three-Finger floated up into the air, his arms and legs pinned in place. He gasped and cursed as he rotated slowly around. The sight was almost comical.

'You make a strange pair,' the Magelord observed. 'An arrogant youth and a rapist. I've always believed one can tell a person's nature by the company they keep. Now, what to do with you both...' She tapped a manicured finger against her perfect lips.

General Zahn smiled, revealing a mouth filled with golden teeth. He placed his spear on the floor. 'Hand them each a blade,' he pronounced as he straightened. 'I'll have at least one new scar to add to my collection before I put them out of their misery.' He pointed at his massive chest, where knitted flesh formed a tapestry dedicated to countless battles won.

Cole gulped. Three-Finger was a large enough fellow, but General Zahn made even the Urich brothers look like children in comparison. He doubted whether a half-dozen trained soldiers could have overcome this huge Sumnian – with or without a weapon.

'Wait.'

Everyone looked at the speaker. It was the scholarly woman with whom the White Lady had consulted a moment ago.

'Forgive me, mistress, but this boy's father was known to me. I would question him further, with your leave.'

The Magelord nodded her assent. General Zahn looked profoundly disappointed.

'Tell me, Davarus Cole. What do you remember of your father?' She was a remarkably plain woman, but there was a quiet strength to her that commanded respect.

'I know that he was a great man,' Cole replied proudly. Garrett had not spoken much of his father, probably out of shame that he had never managed to step out from his shadow. 'He died fighting three Augmentors. Before he passed away he gave me his magical dagger, Magebane. It was his final gift. One day I shall use it to avenge his death.'

All of a sudden he remembered the green quartz crystal Garrett had presented to him when he joined the Shards. He had surrendered that particular gift himself, had hurled the crystal into a fire in a fit of anger. He regretted that now. Garrett wasn't a great man like his father, but he had done the best he could.

He felt tears threatening. Embarrassment warred with sadness. Perhaps he had been unfair to the old merchant. He had the sudden urge to return to Dorminia and put things right between them.

'And your mother?' the woman continued, interrupting his moment of weakness. *Get a hold of yourself*, Cole thought. *Heroes don't cry.*

'She died giving birth to me.'

Sophia had been the only child of a successful shipwright. She and Cole's father had met when they were both young. With her unfortunate death, Sophia had left her husband a considerable estate inherited from her own wealthy father. Illarius and young Davarus Cole had lived there alone but for their maid, who had helped raise him during his father's frequent absences. He had never learned what exactly it was that his father did for a living. Not until the moment of his death.

'What became of this enchanted dagger?' the Magelord's adviser asked. There was a hint of excitement in her voice. Excitement and... *fear*?

'Magebane? I, ah, don't have it with me.'

'Where is it?'

'An old Highlander stole it from me.' The admission stung. Yet again he cursed Brodar Kayne. *Interfering old fool. I didn't even need your help.*

'Where is this Highlander?'

'The last I saw of him he was headed to the Wailing Rift, a day's ride east of Dorminia.'

The White Lady shifted irritably. 'Are you finished, Brianna?'

The adviser, Brianna, looked pensive. 'Mistress, this boy is heir to a weapon that is anathema to our kind. I should know. I barely made it out of Dorminia alive. Tell me, Davarus Cole. Did you ever have cause to test Magebane against one possessed of magic?'

Cole was unsure where all this was going, but he thought it best to keep talking – especially with General Zahn glowering down at him. 'No,' he said in answer to the woman's question. 'There are no mages alive in Dorminia except for Salazar. And I plan to kill him one day.'

Brianna nodded. She turned to the White Lady. 'I would speak with you alone, mistress. This boy could yet be of great use to us.'

Cole held his breath as the Magelord seemed to consider her adviser's request. 'Very well,' she said eventually. 'Take him to the Tower of Stars. I will send for him once his fate has been decided.'

Three-Finger cursed again. The White Lady glared at him, revulsion plain in her enchanting purple eyes.

'Drag this offal away and have him imprisoned alongside the boy. He has abused his privilege of strength, and now he must suffer for his crimes.'

'You should have let me deal with him,' the Sumnian general grumbled as the White Lady's servants approached to encircle Cole and the convict. 'See how he likes a spear shoved up his arse.' He reached down and grabbed the surprising bulge of his manhood beneath his leather skirt, and there was the glitter of something almost like amusement in his eyes. 'Or my cock.'

The thought made Cole queasy all over again.

Farrowgate

S QUELCH.

Brodar Kayne lifted his boot, placed it down in front of him. Felt it sink down into the mud. His skin was on fire and his body shook as if it was about to seize up, but they were almost there. One foot in front of the other. One foot in front of the other. One foot—

Sasha yelped as he stumbled into her, almost knocking them both into the muck. He kept his balance, but the effort caused some of his stitches to split open. Agony exploded around the wound in his stomach.

'Sorry, lass,' he gasped, trying futilely to disguise the pain. The village was further than it had initially appeared. The sun had disappeared some time ago and now they struggled on in the darkness, battered by a merciless downpour that had turned the hills into a slippery marsh. He'd fallen on his arse several times and was covered in filth, and over the last hour he had developed a fever. Only the lure of the faint glow of torchlight in the distance had kept him moving.

'Fucking rain.'

The Wolf was in obvious discomfort, the downpour causing his burns to itch uncomfortably. His mood had started off foul and had only deteriorated the closer they got to the village. Isaac trudged along at the rear of the despondent group. The torrid conditions seemed to have subdued even his perpetual cheerfulness.

'You all right?' Sasha asked Kayne. She looked annoyed. He pulled his hand away from his stomach and stared at it. It was hard to tell in the poor light, but it looked red.

'I reckon I might've opened this damned scratch back up. Nothing to be done about it now. No use grumbling.'

'You don't have to do this, you know.'

'Do what, lass?'

'Keep up this macho act. You're not made of stone. You shouldn't even be moving around, never mind marching in this kind of state.' Her tone softened a fraction. 'You need a physician.'

'We have Isaac.'

'Yes, and his supplies are exhausted. If you need to rest, just say it. We'll leave you here and go on ahead. Isaac can gather what you need and bring it back here. We shouldn't be long.'

He shook his head. 'I'm all right.'

Sasha made an exasperated noise and turned away from him. He clenched his teeth. *How much further? Can't be more than half a mile. Come on, you old bastard. Walk.*

A rumble of thunder suddenly split the sky overhead. The lightning struck a moment later, illuminating the small settlement ahead of them in blue fire. The village wasn't much to look at, but it would serve.

The girl had the right of it. If he didn't rest soon he would collapse – and there was no guarantee he would get back up again.

By the time they finally reached the village his legs had turned to water and he was shaking like a leaf in the wind. There was no one around. Fortunately the rickety old gates were unlocked. Sasha frowned.

'That's odd,' she said. 'These villagers evidently don't care much for security. There isn't even a guard posted.'

Jerek spat. 'I ain't surprised. Bit of rain and you Lowlanders curl up in your holes like worms.'

'There's light over there,' said Isaac. 'By the farmhouse.'

Kayne squinted, but it was no good. All he could see was an indistinct yellow blur. 'Guess we should go and have a look,' he managed.

There was a barn next to the farmhouse. The doors were flung wide open, revealing a pair of torches hanging from brackets on the walls just inside. The place reeked of dung, but there was no sign of any livestock within. The old barbarian wanted nothing more than to collapse on a mound of straw in one of the empty stalls just then, cow shit be damned.

'Might want to wait here, Kayne—' Jerek began, but a piteous whining noise cut him off. It came from one of the stalls at the very rear of the barn, where the light from the torches couldn't quite reach.

The Wolf pulled one of his axes from its harness. 'Wait here,' he said in a gruff whisper. He wrenched a torch from its sconce and approached the shadowy corner. He stopped as he drew near, stared for a second, and then spat. 'Now ain't that a pretty sight.'

Brodar Kayne stumbled over to see what his friend was referring to. He immediately wished he hadn't.

A cow rested on its side in the middle of the stall, pink tongue lolling out of its mouth. Its eyes were wide and staring madly at the roof. From its rear end, glistening obscenely in the torchlight, long tendrils of intestine snaked out over the blood-matted straw. Someone, or *something*, had reached into the rear of the animal and literally torn half its innards out from its rectum.

He heard Sasha gag behind him. 'These villagers got some queer ways and no mistake,' he said. He noticed someone was missing. 'Where's Isaac?

'Here,' came the manservant's voice from outside the barn. He was barely audible above the drumming of the rain. 'No one is answering. I think this place is deserted.'

'Bullshit.' Jerek raised his axe and brought it down on the cow's head, splitting its skull in half. The animal jerked once and went still.

Sasha wiped her mouth with the back of her hand. Her face was pale. 'The villagers can't *all* have left. Where would they go? And why?'

'Perhaps they're hiding from us,' Isaac suggested.

'Could be. Or could be that they're hiding from something else,' Kayne muttered. He stared at the ruined body of the cow. *Ain't no man did that. Something ain't right in this village.*

The warmth of the torches and the temporary respite from the rain had calmed his fever a little. He felt gingerly around his stomach, prodded at the wound. The sudden pain made him grunt. He looked down and winced. The left side had opened up and was leaking bloody pus.

'Urgh,' he said.

Sasha bustled over and examined him. She shook her head. 'It's become infected. You'll die if this isn't treated.'

Jerek scowled. 'Then we'll turn this village upside down. Any of the locals got a problem with that, they can go fuck themselves.'

Brodar Kayne sighed and pulled the filthy dressing back down over the festering wound. *Back out into the rain. Again.*

And to make matters worse, he needed to piss.

'Empty.'

It was dark within the modest dwelling, the fire in the small hearth having burned out long ago. Clothes were scattered across the floor. A chair was upended next to a table covered in the abandoned remains of a meal. Thick black flies hovered over the table and crawled over a large ham that had begun to putrefy.

'They didn't even stop to lock the door,' said Sasha. Her face was troubled.

'I don't reckon we'll find anything in here.' Kayne turned and walked back outside. They had searched half a dozen homes already, and every one of them had been abandoned. Jerek and Isaac emerged from a nearby building. An angry shake of the Wolf's head confirmed that their search had also failed to turn up anything useful.

'Looks like they all just upped and left.' Kayne's body was trembling again and he had begun to sweat. His insides felt as if they were on fire. For once he was grateful for the rain, which cooled his burning skin.

'Kayne,' Jerek rasped from across the way. 'You should see this.'

He hurried over to where the Wolf crouched over a row of mounds in the earth. There must have been a dozen of them, at least.

'Graves,' Jerek grunted.

He examined the mounds. They looked fresh, and shallow, as if whoever had done the shovelling lacked the time to make a decent job of it. A couple of the mounds had been disturbed: the graves had been dug up and since filled with rain. There was no sign of the occupants.

Sasha bent over one of the empty graves and stared into the filthy water sloshing around within. 'What's happening in this village?' she whispered.

There was a scrabbling sound. The mound Jerek was crouching upon suddenly shifted, sending wet earth sliding away. The Wolf leaped backwards just as a hand emerged from the soil, grasping wildly at the air. The other hand followed a second or two after, pushing up through the earth to clutch and claw like the talons of some wild animal.

'Someone's alive down there,' Isaac exclaimed. He scrambled over and began scooping away dirt. 'Don't worry – we'll get you out of there!' He reached down to try and take hold of one of the flailing hands.

Brodar Kayne felt a deep sense of foreboding. Everything about this village felt wrong. You didn't reach his ripe old age without having a good instinct for this kind of thing.

'I wouldn't do that if I were you, lad...'

With a blood-curdling moan, the head of the villager burst

226

out of the ground. Worm-eaten eyes stared from his ruined face with undisguised hatred. The villager opened his mouth unnaturally wide, revealing a cavernous hole full of maggots and broken teeth. Isaac yelped in surprise as the thing grabbed hold of his arm and pulled itself out from the grave.

'Fuck this,' Jerek snarled. He barrelled into the creature, slamming it down onto the ground. His head snapped forwards, shattering the thing's nose. It moaned pitifully as he dragged it along the ground for a few yards before bringing his boot down repeatedly on its head, breaking its skull open. One more stomp and its head collapsed with a sickening crack. It twitched a few times and went still.

Sasha screamed. Kayne glanced across to see a rotting figure lumbering towards her. He closed his eyes for a second. *I thought I'd left this shit behind me.* He tugged his sword free of its sheath.

A crossbow bolt thudded into the villager. It staggered from the impact but otherwise displayed no sign of having felt the quarrel. Sasha looked at her crossbow in disbelief.

'Strollers, we call them up in the High Fangs,' the old barbarian said. He raised his greatsword high in the air, swept it around and cut off the creature's head in a single swing. 'They appear sometimes after an abomination shows up in one of the Reachings. They're none too bright and stubborn to kill, but they're slow. Take off their heads and they die easy enough.'

Isaac had stabbed another of the shambling things multiple times, but it kept on coming at him. 'The head, lad,' Kayne shouted.

Sasha raised her crossbow again and fired.

The bolt sailed through the air and would have taken the creature dead in the back of the skull had the Wolf, who had been busy smashing another into the side of a tree, not inadvertently stepped into its path.

Brodar Kayne froze. Time seemed to stand still.

The bolt sank into Jerek's shoulder in almost the exact spot the Watchman's quarrel had struck a week before.

'Fucking *whore*,' Jerek snarled. His face was rage personified. 'You'll pay for that.' He stalked towards her.

'I didn't mean—' Sasha began, but his backhand snapped her head around and knocked her to the ground. He reached behind him, pulled an axe free with his good arm.

'Jerek.'

The Wolf spun around. 'Stay out of this, Kayne.'

'I can't do that.'

His old friend scowled. Blood ran down his arm from the bolt in his shoulder but he hardly seemed to care. 'You gonna try and stop me?'

Kayne shrugged. 'I reckon I will.'

The Wolf chuckled, a horrible grating sound devoid of humour. 'Always the hero.'

'I ain't no hero and I never claimed to be. I'm an old man trying to do the right thing in what little time I got left. I ain't letting you harm the girl.'

'You're half dead, Kayne.'

'And you've only got one good arm. Hardly a duel for the ages.'

Jerek snorted. 'Like in the sagas of the great Highlanders of old? I reckon we're both too old for that shit.'

'Aye.' The sword quivered in his hands. His arms were shaking.

Brodar Kayne had lost count of the number of men he had killed over the years. The young and the old, good men and bad men both – the latter when he could, but the Shaman was a capricious master and it wasn't for his champion to decide right from wrong. He had been the Sword of the North, a man feared and respected in equal measure.

The time was well past when he took pride in any of that, but facts were facts. He had never lost a fight, though others had possessed reputations to rival his own: Borun, his sword-brother; Mehmon, who had been as hard as the ice that covered his Reaching before he had grown old and soft. The Butcher of Beregund was said to be peerless on the field of battle, and if there was one Highlander he would have relished matching steel against it was that murderous, raping bastard.

They were hard men all, but he wouldn't have backed any of them against the one staring him in the face just then. Jerek was as relentless as the Reaver himself, and as tough and brutal a fighter as Kayne had ever known.

He drew a deep breath and gasped at the pain in his stomach. Readied himself for a fight he was certain would be his last. The sword hilt felt slick in his fevered palms.

Jerek's eyes narrowed. 'Fuck this,' he said. He lowered his axe. He turned to Sasha, who was struggling back to her feet. She had an angry red mark on the left side of her face. 'You ain't heard the last of this. For now, keep the fuck out of my way.' That said, he stormed off into the night.

Kayne heaved a weary sigh and let his sword dip towards the ground. *That didn't go too badly, all things considered.*

They walked over to Isaac. The manservant appeared to be unharmed. He had succeeded in lopping off the head of the stroller that had been attacking him and was scanning the area for more of the creatures. 'I think I've read about these things,' he said. 'Sometimes, when enough wild magic is present, souls will cross over from the realm of the dead and return to their former bodies.'

Kayne glanced down at the headless corpse near Isaac's feet. 'Huh. They don't seem very grateful for another crack at life, all things considered.'

There was another flash of lightning and the manservant jumped. He smiled sheepishly. 'The spirits are consumed with hatred and rage. Their deaths were not happy ones.'

'You seem to know a lot about it.'

'I read a lot of books. It's one of the perks of working at the depository.'

'I ain't never read a book in my life.'

'But you've fought these creatures before?'

'Aye. Them and worse. Strollers ain't the worst of what plagues the Fangs. The demons that come down from the Devil's Spine, they're as tough as most abominations and a good deal smarter. And there's been more of 'em as the years go by.'

'Demons are little more than children's tales in these parts.'

Kayne shrugged. 'The witch doctors say the barrier between the realm of men and the realm of demons is weak up in the Spine, and getting weaker. They say the murder of the gods broke the world.'

For a moment Isaac's dull face seemed to register a keen interest. 'What does the Shaman say?'

'Nothing. He don't talk about the gods. He don't talk about the past at all.'

Isaac was about to say something else when a loud gasp nearby drew their attention. Kayne turned, afraid he would find the Wolf making good on his promise to Sasha. Instead the girl was staring off at something across the village.

'What is it, lass?' he asked.

She pointed through the rain to a large building in the distance. 'There's a granary over there. I saw a light flickering inside. And… there was something else. It didn't look human.'

'One of these?' Isaac asked, pointing at the motionless stroller Jerek had battered against a tree. The Wolf was nowhere to be seen.

Sasha shook her head. 'Bigger. And it had too many arms.'

'Can't say I like the sound of that,' Kayne muttered. His voice shook. The fever was getting worse and, with the adrenalin from the recent excitement wearing off, he was feeling as bad as before. His wound needed urgent attention. There was nothing else for it. 'If there's light, could be there's villagers within. One of them might be a physician, or know where we can find supplies.'

'What about the thing I saw? What happens if it attacks us?'

Brodar Kayne gripped his sword tighter and tried to disguise the weakness in his voice. 'I ain't dead yet.'

The granary was an old cylindrical structure set back near the fence that surrounded the village. It was built on a low platform accessible by a short set of wooden steps. A couple of holes set high in the structure emitted the faint glow of torchlight, but no one answered when they knocked on the door. On further investigation they found it was barred from behind and likely barricaded within.

'Shit,' said Brodar Kayne.

A twig snapped behind them. He whirled around, his sword in his hands and up to strike before his ears had barely registered the noise.

It was the Wolf. 'Like that then, is it?' he asked. He sounded almost hurt.

'Where did you get to?' Kayne asked.

'For a walk. Needed to let off some steam.'

Kayne noticed Sasha and Isaac staring at him. 'What?' he said.

The girl had an astonished look on her face. 'I've never seen you move like that before,' she said.

'Like what?'

'Like... *that*. I thought you were hurt.'

'Ain't the first time I've been hurt, lass. I got a lifetime's experience of not dying. My body's learned to take care of itself without any help from my old brain.'

'You must teach me!' Isaac said excitedly. 'Oh, I've read a lot about swordplay, but to learn from a legend such as the Sword of the North... Now that would be a dream come true!'

'If we manage to survive the night I might just do that,' the old Highlander replied. 'Now probably ain't the time, though—'

'Saw some nasty shit,' Jerek cut in abruptly. They all looked at him. 'Villagers choked to death. Some with entrails hanging out of their arses,' he added darkly. 'Just like that cow. Killed a

231

couple more strollers, too.'

Brodar Kayne felt a shiver run up his spine. 'That thing you saw, lass. Think it might be responsible?'

Sasha thought about it for a moment and nodded. 'Yes,' she said. 'And it's out there somewhere.' Her hand went to the crossbow under her cloak.

Kayne rapped on the granary door again. 'Let us in,' he said as loudly but amicably as he could manage. 'We're friends.'

There was no response.

Jerek strolled up to the door and slammed a boot into it. It hardly budged. 'Open the fucking door!' he bellowed. When there was no answer, he reached behind him and unsheathed an axe.

Kayne was about to restrain him when suddenly he heard it: a susurration, as of a handful of snakes slithering over snow. The air smelled rotten, like a dozen corpses left to rot in the sun for a week. He knew that odour, had learned to read the signs when he served the Shaman as the protector of the High Fangs.

An abomination was approaching.

As one they turned. There it was, emerging from behind rain-swept trees like a nightmare made flesh. Its torso was humanoid in shape but supported on two thick tentacles instead of legs, and it spouted a dozen writhing tendrils in place of arms. They twisted and curled obscenely, probing as if tasting the air. A small and vaguely human head perched on top of the body, but it possessed no eyes or nose or ears – only an oversized mouth frozen in a death rictus.

One of the tendrils snaked out in their direction, paused for a second, and then retracted. Suddenly the lower tentacles pushed down hard on the muddy ground, raising the abomination high into the air so that it hovered above them. The head began to vibrate, faster and faster until it became a blur.

Jerek shifted and then his axe was hurtling towards the horror, end over end. It sank into the puffy grey flesh, splitting

232

it open. From the sundered chest of the abomination poured a torrent of pus, as though a giant blister had burst. The stench made Kayne want to vomit. The head continued to vibrate, and then the abomination was writhing towards them on its hind limbs like some gigantic spider preparing to engulf its prey.

'Get out of here!' he yelled, pushing Isaac and Sasha away. Jerek had his other axe in his hand. The Wolf looked at him, nodded once, and then sprinted forwards, ducking under one flailing tendril to roll and come up just behind the abomination.

His old bones protesting with every movement, his abused flesh slick from fever and the relentless rain, Brodar Kayne lifted his greatsword and strolled to meet the horror. *Just need to hold it off long enough for the girl and Isaac to escape*, he thought grimly.

A tendril shot down, reaching for his head, but he leaned back at the last moment and it passed in front of him. Another darted towards his chest. He pivoted, felt it brush harmlessly against his leather. Foul mucus dripped from its length, which tapered to a hardened barb at the end.

Jerek was to the right of him, a dozen feet away. The Wolf was chopping away at two of the probing tendrils. He severed one. The other wrapped itself around his ankles and jerked upwards. Uttering a stream of curses, the Wolf was tugged from his feet and pulled along the mud as he tried desperately to line up another slash at the grappling appendage.

Isaac suddenly sprinted into view, a torch in one hand and his longsword in the other. 'How do you like this?' he shouted at the apparition, and hurled the torch at its lower tentacles.

Kayne watched the torch land and brush against the wormy flesh of the abomination's leg-tentacles. He half expected it to catch fire and flare up like a pile of dry old kindling. Instead the flame flickered for a second and fizzled out. He looked across at Isaac.

'What was that lad?', he was about to ask, but a tendril swooped around and lashed the manservant across the chest, sending him flying. He struck the ground hard and didn't get back up. Jerek was still struggling unsuccessfully nearby.

'Shit,' said the old barbarian again. He raised his sword and held it horizontally before him. 'Come on then. Just you and me now.'

The eyeless head turned away from Jerek to face him. He gritted his teeth. That damned vibrating was giving him a headache.

Tendrils shot down, one from the left and then two from the right, grasping and probing. Kayne stepped back, ducked under one, leaped another, brought his sword around and was rewarded by the sight of a twitching appendage flying away into the night. His momentary satisfaction evaporated as another limb flailed down and raked his hide armour with its barbed claw. It sliced through the leather with ease, scoring a deep gouge in his chest. He felt blood well up from the wound. Something snapped inside him.

'That the best you got?' he snarled. He whirled around, ducked under one tendril and severed it. He switched his sword to his left hand, reached out and wrenched Jerek's axe from the monster's torso with his right. It came loose in a spray of vile fluid that coated him from head to foot, but he was beyond caring.

'I've been half drowned,' he said, bringing the weapons together with a clash. 'Gutted like a fish.' *Clash*. 'Got a fever that's left me feeling worse than death.' *Clash*. 'And to add to my woes, this fucking rain is making me piss like a horse.' *Clash*. He pointed both weapons at the abomination. 'So – I ain't in the mood to stand here and be buggered up the arse by the likes of you.' *Clash*.

He burst into motion, each weapon dancing independent of the other, swatting away and slicing at the snaking limbs that converged on him. He rolled away from one, dived under another, somehow keeping ahead of the torrent of spongy flesh. He was buffeted in the shoulder and back, one tendril locking around his leg before he hacked it away an instant later. His heart hammered in his chest and his breaths came in laboured gasps, but he didn't dare stop moving for a second.

Before he knew it the attacks slowed and then stopped completely. He blinked rainwater and foul discharge from his eyes, in time to see Jerek free himself from the last remaining appendage. He looked mighty pissed off and was covered in filth, but he was otherwise unharmed.

The torso of the abomination loomed before him, now bereft of limbs save for the two tentacles supporting it from the ground. The head suddenly ceased quivering.

'Had enough?' he panted. He doubled over, his heart feeling like it would tear free of his chest. *Just need to catch my breath.*

'Kayne,' Jerek rasped. It sounded like a warning. With a mighty effort, he raised his head back up.

'Shit.'

The severed tendrils were growing back with alarming speed, sprouting from the shoulders of the humanoid torso like unholy vines. Jerek shook his head and spat. He looked worried. 'How the fuck do we kill this thing?'

Brodar Kayne didn't have an answer. He was spent, his body pushed to breaking point and beyond.

'Out of the way!'

The shout came from behind them. *The girl.* He tried to turn, to yell at her to flee, but the effort was too great. He saw Jerek grimace, dive to the side. A crossbow twanged, and suddenly the magical horror had a bolt lodged in the back of its mouth.

'Run!' Sasha screamed. Jerek took hold of him, pulled him away—

Not for the first time that week, the world exploded.

'Urgh.'

'Easy, now. Your body has endured a great deal of abuse. Even a young man would be lucky to survive the wounds you have suffered.'

He didn't recognize the voice. It sounded like it belonged to an old fellow. An *older* fellow, at any rate.

He tried to open his eyes. Couldn't. 'Where am I?' he asked, battling a rising sense of panic.

'The village of Farrowgate. You're inside my home. Your friends are with me. The combustion temporarily blinded you – or it may have been the ichor in your eyes. In any case, I am confident your vision will return.'

'I'm here, Kayne.' It was Jerek's voice – gruff, unfriendly and, at that moment, the most comforting sound in the world.

'What happened?' he managed.

'I had some of Vicard's powder,' said a woman. It was Sasha, he realized. 'I took it from his backpack just after the Rift. Isaac hollowed out a bolt head for me a while back and I filled it with the stuff. I didn't really think it would work.'

'It was purely theoretical,' droned Isaac. 'You might just have revolutionized warfare. Imagine – a mere girl blowing apart a magical abomination!'

'A mere girl?' Sasha's voice had turned frosty.

'Uh, no offence,' Isaac said quickly. 'I was trying to pay you a compliment.'

'Don't.'

Silence.

'First useful thing the bitch has done, shutting you up,' said Jerek. More silence. 'The second,' he amended grudgingly. 'Though I reckon we'd have taken the fucker ourselves if it came to it. Right, Kayne?'

Kayne sighed. Somehow they'd all survived. With any luck, the remainder of the journey back to Dorminia would be uneventful and they would collect their gold and be on their way. Assuming his sight returned and he didn't die of his wounds between now and then.

Well, a man could hope.

The Chosen One

'**W**HY DO BAD things happen to good people?'

Three-Finger didn't answer. He hadn't moved for hours, or uttered so much as a word in response to any of Cole's numerous questions. The convict was curled up on the shiny black marble that formed the circular roof of the Tower of Stars, his back to the young Shard and his battered cloak pulled tight around him, though it wasn't a particularly cold night.

'We've been stuck up here for three days now. How much longer before the White Lady decides what to do with us?'

There was no reply.

'It's enough to drive you mad. No wonder they call it the Tower of Stars.' He stared glumly at the marble beneath his feet. The polished surface was a perfect reflection of the clear night sky above. 'I think I'm losing my mind.'

He walked over to the edge of the tower and risked a glance down at the city. From this height the various buildings looked like models from the hand-crafted diorama Garrett had given him on his twelfth naming day. He had thought it a silly toy, until he learned its true purpose had been to help him understand the layout of a certain section of the Noble Quarter he would later rob – in particular the quickest escape route in the event of an emergency.

He suppressed a shudder. The Tower of Stars was the tallest structure in Thelassa, or so he had been told. It was completely open to the elements, with no barrier around its circumference.

According to the captain of *The Lady's Luck,* who had brought them both to the tower, the Magelord of the city encouraged the accused to take matters into their own hands. Suicide was viewed as a welcome admission of guilt that saved everyone a lot of time and bother.

Except, Cole supposed, for the unfortunate souls tasked with keeping the streets of Thelassa clean. He imagined a jumper would make quite a mess when they finally splattered onto the streets hundreds of feet below. He had no intention of ending his own life, but the boredom was starting to get to him.

'I just don't understand it,' he said, deciding that if Three-Finger wasn't going to participate in this discussion then he might as well talk for both of them. 'All I've ever wanted is to make the world a better place. I risked my life trying to save an old man from the Black Lottery, did you know that? A waste of time that was.'

Three-Finger said nothing.

'Even among the Shards I never seem to receive the recognition I deserve.' He sighed and stretched out his muscles. It was another mild evening, at least.

'The problem is envy,' he said quietly. 'Sometimes I wish I wasn't the son of a legendary hero. If I was just a common sort – like you, Three-Finger – no one would begrudge me respect. I've worked so damned *hard* to become the man I am. That's what people don't appreciate.'

Three-Finger grunted and shifted slightly. He took that as an encouraging sign.

'I've faced prejudice throughout my life. I suppose others might have become bitter long ago. Me, I've always seen it as a challenge. Just one more obstacle to overcome. Like when I became the youngest Shard in our history.' That wasn't strictly true – Sasha had been seventeen when she was inducted into the group, a good few months younger than him – but she was a girl and therefore didn't really count.

238

Three-Finger fidgeted again and made a growling noise that sounded suspiciously like a fart.

'Did I ever tell you about Sasha? She has eyes you could lose yourself in. I knew from the moment we met that she was the one.'

He stared out across the city. Torchlight flickered far below like fireflies, illuminating very little from this height. Other towers loomed in the darkness here and there, like ghostly fingers in the starlight. For a moment Cole thought he could hear distant screams. He cocked his head and listened intently, but this time he heard only silence.

He sighed. Being stuck on top of this tower was making him paranoid. 'When I finally make it back to Dorminia, I'm going to tell Sasha how I really feel about her,' he ventured. 'She isn't like other girls. I think something bad happened to her when she was young. She's hard work, but I'm slowly winning her around.' He grinned suddenly. 'It would take a girl like Sasha to keep a man like me in check.'

Three-Finger finally rolled over to face him. His head was hidden underneath his cloak, but he sounded exasperated. 'I can't take much more of you talking bollocks, kid. Give it a rest.'

Cole frowned. 'I'm just trying to stave off the boredom,' he replied. 'Maybe you should have a walk around and stretch your legs. You've been huddled up like that for hours.'

'What's the point? It's not like there's anything to see.'

Something had been bothering Cole. He decided now was the time to bring it up. 'You know what the White Lady said – about you being a rapist. It's not true is it? The Watch just made up those charges against you, didn't they?'

Three-Finger looked up at him. The corner of the convict's mouth twitched slightly. 'Of course it ain't true. Do I seem like that kind of man to you?'

Cole frowned thoughtfully. 'No,' he said. 'You don't.'

'Well then. There you are.' Three-Finger stuck one of the fingers of his maimed hand inside his ear, wriggled it about, and then withdrew it to examine the contents. 'Get some sleep, kid.'

That night the weather took a turn for the worse. The gusting wind set Cole's teeth to chattering, and he warmed himself with thoughts of Sasha and their eventual reunion. He would have some tales to share with her and Garrett and the rest when he returned to Dorminia. Whenever that might be.

The following night his captors came for him.

The metal grate in the roof shifted slightly. Cole watched it glumly, expecting two meagre platefuls of bland food and a jug of water to be shoved up through the bars. Instead, he was shocked to see the steel hatch spring open and two of the White Lady's pale servants climb out onto the roof. They were followed by a third figure, this one wearing a cowl that completely hid its face.

The taller of the two women clutched a dark metal collar. It was connected to a chain of interwoven links. 'You will come with us,' she said simply. She gave the collar a shake.

Cole's excitement drained away like piss down a latrine as he stared at the contraption. 'I want to know where you're taking me.'

The shorter woman stared at him. As he had come to expect from the White Lady's servants, her eyes were ghostly orbs that revealed no shred of emotion. 'You will not ask questions,' she said.

'Do not be afraid,' said the hooded figure. The voice was that of a man, but it had a whispering, velvety quality only the truly sinister could successfully cultivate. 'The White Lady has plans for you. You will not be harmed.'

He heard Three-Finger shift around to face their visitors. 'What about me?'

'You will remain here.'

'Fuck that. I'm not staying here a second longer, you pale-faced piece of shit—'

The convict's words became a grunt. With incredible speed, the shorter of the women dashed across to him and wrapped her hands around his throat. Three-Finger must have outweighed her by eighty pounds, but he might as well have tried to shake off a bear. Within seconds he ceased struggling and went limp. The woman lowered his unconscious body to the floor. Angry red marks encircled his neck where her hands had gripped him.

'Now,' said the woman with the collar. 'Will you come willingly or must you also be subdued?'

'I'm coming,' Cole said hurriedly. 'Let me help you with that.' He presented his neck and the woman lowered the collar over his head. For a second he contemplated ducking away as it descended and trying to make good an escape – but one look at the comatose Three-Finger convinced him that, for now, he was better off doing as he was told.

'Lead on,' he said. The collar snapped shut.

He wandered through a monochrome cityscape. Dark shadows flickered ahead of him, blinking into and then out of existence. Tendrils of fog twisted and curled around the ground, obscuring the bottoms of his legs. A thick wall of mist hung in the air all around him so that he could barely see twenty feet in front of his face. From beyond that impenetrable blanket came a cacophony of weeping, a thousand souls voicing their sorrow.

Something brushed against his boots. He looked down, peering through the unnatural fog.

It was a hand, impossibly small. It twitched a few times, and then tiny fingers reached out towards him. He stared in increasing horror as a doll-like arm emerged from the white haze, and then another, dragging the creature along the ground. Finally the head emerged, hairless, a pale, fetal mass of flesh that stared up at him with white eyes and a mouth opened wide in anguish...

The collar came off and suddenly the real world flooded back. Cole staggered and almost fell. He stared in confusion at the woman before him, who was clutching the collar.

'What just happened? How long has it been since we left the tower?' He glanced around. They appeared to be standing in what looked like underground catacombs.

'Less than an hour,' replied the taller of the pale women who had led him to this place. She finished wrapping the chain around the collar and hid the contraption beneath her robes. 'As for your other question, the secrets of Thelassa are not yours to know at this time. We leave you in the hands of the Darkson. Do exactly as he tells you. Fail him, and you will answer to us.'

The servants of the White Lady turned and seemed to drift away, resembling nothing so much as a pair of spectres in their spotless white robes.

'The sense of unease never goes away,' whispered a voice behind him. Cole almost jumped out of his skin. He spun around to face the speaker. It was the hooded man.

'You're the Darkson?'

'Yes,' replied the figure in his sibilant manner of speech. 'I am... not the same as them. I am human.' He reached up with his gloved hands and pulled back his cowl.

Cole half expected to be met with some loathsome visage. As it happened, the face staring back at him was sharp-featured – some might even say handsome, though Cole was no judge in such matters. The man looked to be in his late thirties, with cropped black hair and skin as dark as ebony. Like Cole, he wore a short beard beneath his chin. It was flecked with a few hints of grey.

'You're Sumnian?'

'Shamaathan.'

Cole tried to recall what he knew of Shamaath. The small country was further south even than Sumnia, bordering the immense jungles that formed the absolute boundary of civilization where the Sun Lands ended and the unknown began. A nation infamous for its intrigues, political turmoil and extensive use of poison in times of both war and peace, Shamaath was also commonly known by another name: the Kingdom of Snakes.

'You're a long way from home,' he observed. At that moment he felt like he, too, was a long way from home – though compared to Shamaath, Dorminia was barely a stone's throw away.

'The more distance between my homeland and I, the better,' the Darkson replied. 'You ask a great many questions. My time is precious, so allow me to curtail further interrogation and fill you in on the basics. This,' he said, sweeping a gloved hand around to take in the dank, crumbling walls surrounding them, 'is your home for the next fortnight.'

Wherever they were, the place bore little resemblance to the Thelassa Cole remembered. The sandstone from which the small chamber was built looked ancient and the air smelled of damp and decay. Torches burned on sconces on the walls, but they were the only sources of light the young Shard could discern.

'Where are we?' he asked.

'Deep underground,' the Darkson replied. 'In the ruins of the metropolis that existed here before it was razed and Thelassa rebuilt on its corpse. The holy city. *Sanctuary.*'

'Sanctuary?' Cole was lost.

'During the Age of Strife, before the wizards rose up to smite their creators from the skies, Sanctuary was the stronghold of the Mother's faith in these lands. Her high priestess ruled the city with wisdom and compassion.' He paused for a moment. 'Or at least so the history books tell us. One can never be sure of anything without first ascertaining the motives of the writer.'

'Why build Thelassa on a pile of ruins? That doesn't make much sense.' Cole felt somewhat embarrassed by his lack of knowledge. Garrett had encouraged his protégé to pursue a broad range of studies to prepare him for the time he would assume command of the Shards, but Cole had quickly grown bored of poring over dull texts. He was a hero, not a scholar.

The Darkson pursed his lips. 'Who can guess at the White Lady's motives? Perhaps my employer has a sentimental side. More likely she chose to make a statement. Where better to display her power than standing upon the bones of the faith she renounced and later destroyed?'

It took Cole a moment to digest the Shamaathan's words. 'You mean the White Lady was once high priestess of this ruined city?'

The man opposite him sighed. 'We should not speak of such matters. The White Lady tolerates no discussion of the past. In that, she is not unlike other Magelords. It is not for you or me to question. We are here to *serve*.'

Quick as a flash, the Darkson pulled a curved dagger from beneath his black, thigh-length robes and launched himself at Cole. The young Shard tried to turn and roll out of the way but the Shamaathan was on him with the speed of a striking cobra. The dark-skinned man kicked out, collapsing Cole's knees from under him. Before he knew it, he was on his back with the edge of the Darkson's dagger tickling his throat.

'I was told you would be more formidable,' said the Shamaathan. He sounded vaguely disappointed. 'We have much work to do.'

Cole winced. His back hurt from where it had struck the floor, but the wound to his pride irked him even more. 'I was unprepared,' he protested. 'What do you mean, "We have much work to do"?'

The Darkson pulled his dagger away and sheathed it in one of his sleeves. The motion was so smooth and fast that Cole barely registered the movement. The southerner reached down one gloved hand and pulled the younger man to his feet.

'You are to be the White Lady's secret weapon in the coming

war with Dorminia.'

Secret weapon? Cole liked what he was hearing. 'Go on,' he said.

'The dagger you so foolishly lost. Magebane, I believe. It is the only thing that can guarantee Salazar's defeat. There is but one man who can harness its power against the Magelord.' He was silent for a moment. 'That man is you.'

Cole's heart skipped a beat. Excitement flooded his veins. 'I knew it!' he exclaimed. 'All of the pain and suffering... It was all to prepare me for this. My moment. My chance to shine!'

The Darkson frowned slightly. 'If anyone but you should attempt to wield the dagger they will find that its magic does not function. Your attunement to Magebane is an accident of birth.'

Cole couldn't keep the smile off his face. 'It was no accident, my friend,' he said. He reached across to give the Shamaathan a companionable pat on the shoulder. 'I was chosen. It was destin— *argh!*'

He gasped in agony as the other man grabbed his arm and twisted it around, pinning it behind him. 'Rule number one,' said the Darkson in an angry hiss. 'You do not touch me without my say so. Ever. Rule number two,' he added. 'Do not presume I am your friend. I am here to teach you the ways of the assassin in the little time we have available to us. You will refer to me only as "master". Am I understood?'

'Yes,' Cole managed. His arm felt as if it was about to be wrenched from its socket. 'Yes, master.'

'Good.' The Darkson released him. 'I trust your time in the Tower of Stars was not too debilitating. You will need to be at your best for the trials that lie ahead.'

Cole nodded. He still ached in places, and his nose would never be as straight as it once was, but he comforted himself with the fact that such minor imperfections could often prove endearing. *Like Sasha's thighs*, he thought with a sudden smile. *Let's be honest, they always were a little on the hefty side.*

'Something amuses you?' The Darkson's expression was grim.

'No, master,' he replied quickly. 'I'm ready when you are.'

'Five minutes,' lisped that velvety voice. Cole barely heard it over his own gasping. He dropped to his knees, sucking in air. 'An impressive time,' the Darkson continued. 'You might yet make a passable assassin.'

He wanted to retch. Instead he straightened up, placing his hands on his hips as if the gauntlet he had just navigated was a trifling matter. 'The pit nearly had me,' he admitted.

The Darkson nodded. 'You are agile enough. But can you handle yourself with a blade?' He reached under his robes and pulled out a dagger that looked very similar to Magebane. 'The White Lady's adviser, Brianna, had this made for you. She is... familiar with your erstwhile weapon. It should handle very similarly.' He tossed it over to him.

The young Shard retrieved the dagger from the floor. The assassin had spoken truly. It was exactly as he remembered Magebane feeling in his palms.

'Now then,' the Darkson said. 'Let's see what you can do. Attack me.'

Cole looked at the assassin uncertainly. 'Are you sure about this?'

'Don't concern yourself with me. Worry about you.' The Shamaathan lifted a hand and beckoned him forwards.

Cole went into a crouch, holding the dagger up before him in a fighting stance. He and the other Shards had sparred often, and he had usually bested them in their mock duels. The Urich brothers were the exception – the twins often overcame him with sheer strength, though they usually walked away from their sparring with almost as many bruises as he did.

'Get ready,' he said, and he feinted one way only to spring in the opposite direction. Somehow the Darkson had anticipated his ploy and moved out of the way. Cole spun at the last moment, dodging a kick aimed at his head. 'Missed,' he said with a satisfied smile.

The Darkson's other leg swept around and knocked his legs from under him.

'You are fast, but you lack focus,' the assassin proclaimed as Cole crashed to the ground. 'Keep your mouth shut and worry about taunting your opponent *after* the fight is won.'

Cole wasn't finished yet. He planted his palms on the floor, rocked himself back and then kicked up in the air, springing forwards so that he landed on his feet. 'I'm just getting started,' he said.

The Darkson looked unimpressed.

This time he took more care, probing for openings and staying just out of reach of the other man's legs. He darted forwards suddenly, aiming a stab at the assassin's chest. The Darkson swivelled with incredible speed and grabbed his lunging arm, twisting it so that the young Shard was forced to drop the dagger.

Just as he had anticipated.

'Got you!' he cried, pressing the Darkson's own curved dagger against the man's stomach with his other hand. The assassin blinked in surprise, and then his eyes widened in alarm. Cole had a small nick on his hand from where he had touched the blade while pilfering the dagger from the Darkson's robes.

'You idiot!' the Shamaathan exclaimed. 'Do have any idea what that blade is coated in?'

Cole hadn't, but the intense self-satisfaction he was feeling at his clever ploy quickly evaporated as he stared at the cut on his finger. He let the assassin's dagger clatter to the floor.

'My chamber,' said the Darkson quickly. 'I have an antidote there. We don't have much time.'

He sped off, sprinting through the doorway of the crumbling chamber and out into the corridor. Cole gulped, and then ran after him.

'That was close. Manticore venom can kill a man within minutes. An excruciating death, I understand.'

Cole was lying on his back on a bedroll in the Darkson's personal quarters. The section of the ruined city in which they were based appeared to have once housed Thelassa's ruling priestesses. Enough light filtered down from the city above that he could make out the murals of the Mother in her many forms painted on the dilapidated walls of the ruins.

The black-skinned assassin had chosen a remarkably well-preserved chapel as his lair. The furnishings were sparse, with only a couple of bedrolls, a large chest, and some cooking apparatus occupying the chancel.

'Manticores?' Cole groaned. While the antidote had saved his life, the side effects were unpleasant and would last for several hours. The Darkson had not been pleased.

'Exotic beasts possessing the head of a man, the body of a lion and the tail of a scorpion,' the assassin replied. 'Extinct for centuries north of the great jungles. Their venom is worth a king's ransom in Shamaath.' He sniffed and made a sour face.

Cole gave him an apologetic look. 'What are you doing so far from the Kingdom of Snakes?' he asked, if only to divert attention away from the smell. His stomach rumbled again.

The assassin sighed. 'I am no longer welcome there. In fact, I would be killed on sight. I suspect there are assassins hunting me throughout the Sun Lands still, even after so many years.'

'What happened?'

The Shamaathan grimaced, though whether because of the question or the next wave of unpleasantness that assaulted his nostrils Cole couldn't be sure. 'A familial dispute,' he said. 'A most unfortunate one, for my family is powerful and entirely ruthless.' He reached around his neck and pulled away the black scarf that encircled it. Even in the poor light, Cole could see the ugly scar around his throat. 'By their standards, a public hanging was charitable. I was disinclined to accept their mercy.'

Cole shook his head. 'Your family sound vile.'

The Darkson replaced the scarf and frowned at the fire between them. 'It is the nature of Shamaathan society. The Trine does not seem much better.'

'Salazar is a tyrant,' Cole agreed. 'He murdered an entire city. A crime he will one day answer for.'

'And does the White Lady seem so much fairer?' the assassin asked curiously.

Cole shrugged in response. 'The people of Thelassa seem happy enough. There are no mindhawks in the skies or Crimson Watch thugs terrorizing the streets. I wasn't happy about being locked up in the Tower of Stars,' he added. 'But I guess the White Lady wanted to be sure I posed no threat. I can't say I blame her. Apparently I can be bad for a Magelord's health.' He grinned at his own joke.

The Darkson seemed to ignore it completely. The assassin went quiet for a time. 'Things are rarely so simple,' he said eventually. 'You will learn that, as you become older.'

The man's words confused Cole. 'But you work for the White Lady,' he said.

'Yes,' the Darkson agreed. 'She pays me handsomely. The coffers of Thelassa are deep indeed, and I require a great deal of gold.'

'Why?'

'Mind your own business.'

It was Cole's turn to sit in silence. 'How many men have you killed?' he asked, when the lack of conversation became uncomfortable.

The Darkson looked at him. 'About the same as the number of women you have bedded.'

Cole whistled to himself. 'That many. I had no idea.'

'I meant, for the second time, that you should mind your own business.' The assassin sounded exasperated. 'Enough talk. We have much to do. Can you cope?'

Cole struggled to his feet. His stomach still felt like he had an iron ball lodged inside it. Still, silent stoicism was the hero's lot. 'I'll be all right,' he said. 'I'm a hard man.'

The Darkson appeared to grit his teeth. 'You're not a hard man,' he replied in an annoyed tone. 'You're barely even a man. But I mean to change that.'

The Cleansing Fire

'**S**HRANREE REQUESTS YOUR presence, sister.'

Yllandris closed her eyes for a moment. It was time. She had not been looking forward to this. 'I will be there shortly,' she said, waving a dismissive hand in the mismatched face of Thurva. The short, girlish sorceress was the most junior member of the circle besides herself.

'Shranree says you must come immediately,' Thurva protested. She might have been irritated; it was hard to tell, what with the way her left eye seemed to be staring a hole in the side of her nose. Her appearance was almost comical, but Yllandris knew better than to doubt Thurva's intellect. She had proved to be a shrewd and manipulative creature, ever eager to ingratiate herself with Shranree and the other senior sisters.

Yllandris sighed. 'Very well. Wait a moment.'

The journey back to Heartstone had been considerably quicker than the trek in the opposite direction. They had lost close to a hundred men, many at the hands of the opposing circle, but overall the storming of Frosthold had been an overwhelming success. The proud town that had once straddled the edge of the Blackwater had been reduced to a blackened ruin scattered with the charred and butchered remains of its people.

Three nights had passed since the war party had arrived back in Heartstone. Each night, her dreams had been plagued by terrible images from the massacre: the face of the young

251

sorceress from the Lake circle melting away to reveal her skull; Old Agatha's brittle bones snapping under the clubs of furious rebels fleeing from the devastating magic Shranree had unleashed; three small pairs of eyes staring at her in abject terror, utterly helpless, while their mother perished nearby...

Yllandris felt her heart quicken and took a deep breath to calm herself. No one had seen her flee the ruthless slaughter that had followed their victory. At least, none of her sisters had learned of it. If they had, she would have been disciplined already. She remembered her momentary glimpse of the giant winged creature in the skies far above Frosthold, recalled the way its mere presence seemed to freeze the blood in her veins. Mentioning it to her sisters would only invite awkward questions. Better to say nothing.

The destruction of Frosthold had been a blood-soaked testament to the savagery of the Shaman's will. An entire town of starving Highlanders had been put to the sword as punishment for rejecting the Treaty.

And for the chieftain who had made the decision to defy the King and their immortal overlord, the worst was still to come.

Yllandris followed a short distance behind Thurva as they made their way towards the Great Lodge, more out of a lack of desire to engage the woman in conversation than any respect for her slight seniority. Highlanders thronged around them, all moving in the same direction. Mothers clutched at children wrapped so heavily in furs that they waddled along in the snow like baby seals. Their faces were eager, matching the excitement of the warriors striding proudly alongside them. Some of the men bore scars from the recent battle. With their enemies vanquished, the surviving sorceresses were free to dispense their healing magic. The few unfortunates with injuries too grievous to heal were brought back to Heartstone for a proper burial.

The crowds grew thicker as they neared the great structure that dominated the centre of town. Yllandris caught up with Thurva and pushed her way through the press, ignoring the dirty looks and muttered oaths thrown her way. The anger soon faded once they realized she was a sorceress.

The rabble eventually parted and she stepped out to join her circle. They stood apart, just inside the wide ring of humanity that had formed before the Great Lodge. The sun was high in the sky, a brilliant white orb that reflected off the thawing snow to blind the pathetic figure at the centre of the ring. Mehmon was as thin as a skeleton, his emaciated body supported only by the rope that bound him to a thick wooden stake driven deep into the ground.

Shranree raised one fussy eyebrow when she saw that Yllandris had joined them. 'I do believe you were summoned almost two hours ago. It is troubling that I needed to send Thurva to retrieve you. It behoves a sister to show some respect for her superiors.' Her voice was sickly sweet and her chubby face wore a friendly smile, but there was no disguising the anger in her eyes. Yllandris drew back a fraction.

This is a woman who would hum cheerfully to herself while she burned you alive, she thought. She remembered the utter ruthlessness Shranree had displayed back at Frosthold. The senior sister had handled the task of massacring women and children as calmly as if she had been preparing dinner.

'You have much to learn from your betters,' Shranree continued. 'It breaks my heart that Old Agatha was so cruelly taken from us before fully imparting her wisdom to you. I hope you will one day prove worthy of her tutelage.'

Thurva smiled in a manner that was possibly intended to be smug but merely looked ridiculous. Even so, Yllandris wanted to slap her irritating face. She was seething inside. *You're all a bunch of tools. Puppets of the Shaman, doing his bidding like a herd of sheep. Old Agatha got what she deserved.*

She forced herself to look abashed and lowered her head slightly so that Shranree wouldn't see the lie in her eyes. 'My humble apologies, sister. I am still young and have much to learn.'

That seemed to satisfy the rotund sorceress. She brushed at some imaginary dirt on her robes. 'Indeed you do,' she huffed. 'The road is going to be a long one, but we will get there eventually, I am sure.'

Yllandris gritted her teeth and nodded. She stared across to where King Magnar sat upon his mighty throne. His steely eyes met her for a moment and the ghost of a smile passed across his lips. Then it was gone as he turned his attention back to the chieftains either side of him.

Orgrim Foehammer and Krazka One-Eye would return with their men to their respective Reachings once Mehmon had been brought to justice, but for now they awaited the arrival of the Shaman. Orgrim appeared troubled, while the Butcher of Beregund's lone eye positively glittered with anticipation.

Yllandris had been present the last time the Shaman ordered a public trial. She had been with the circle only a short time, and she still remembered the screams of the accused. The woman's wails had been unearthly, like those of the banshees that were said to haunt the highest peaks. She recalled the poor old bastard in the wicker cage and the indescribable torment on his face as he watched his wife burn.

There was a sudden commotion behind her. Shranree jabbed a thick finger in the direction of the Great Lodge. 'There he is,' she whispered reverentially. 'The Shaman comes.'

Yllandris looked up see a large black raven perched on the edge of the roof high above. It regarded them all with its beady eyes for a second and then leaped off, plummeting down towards the ground. *Crash and die*, she wished fervently, but the bird checked its fall at the last possible moment and hopped down to land unharmed on the snow. It shimmered and then began to stretch, first one way and then the other, unfolding like a sheet of parchment in an expansion of mass that made her brain hurt to watch. When the coruscation finally faded, the Shaman stood before them.

The assembled Highlanders went silent. As always, the

Magelord was naked except for a tattered pair of breeches. His olive skin glistened with sweat despite the frigid conditions; he seemed not to feel the cold. That blunt, angry face stared across the open circle with blue eyes as harsh as a glacier. Yllandris felt herself wilting when his gaze passed over her, as if his stare was enough to bare her soul for the world to see.

The Shaman turned to the sagging figure that was Mehmon. Yllandris realized she had forgotten to breathe. Had she really considered plotting to kill this immortal? This *Godkiller*? The thought now seemed as absurd as reaching out and plucking the moon from the sky.

'Mehmon,' growled the Shaman. 'I find you guilty of disobeying the will of your king and rejecting the terms of the Treaty under which all Highlanders abide. The penalty for rebellion is death by fire. Speak your last words.'

The old Highlander raised his head and coughed once. '*Rebellion?*' he managed. 'That's a joke. I'm guilty of nothing but looking after my people.'

The Shaman crossed his massive arms over his chest. His muscles were like knotted steel. 'You refused tribute. The fish that swim the Blackwater? The deer that roam the forests? This is *my* domain,' he growled, revealing his teeth. 'You rejected the Treaty and you stole from *me*. I care not for your excuses. The weak deserve only death. This is how it has always been.'

'Crazy,' Mehmon muttered. 'You're crazy. I should have thrown my sword in with Kayne when I had the chance.'

There was a collective gasp from her sisters and those townsfolk close enough to hear Mehmon's words. The Shaman said nothing, but Yllandris could see the vein throbbing in his neck as his jaw clenched. All in Heartstone knew the subject of the Sword of the North was taboo. The miraculous escape of his infamous champion still gnawed at the Shaman, for it was his failure that the man had got away. Weakness was something the Magelord would not tolerate – most especially, it seemed, in himself.

'How many of the Brethren did you send after Kayne?' Mehmon continued. He forced an ugly chuckle out from between parched lips. 'I heard he led them a merry chase. It's a shame that bloodless puppet on the throne never inherited any of his father's balls.' He spat in the direction of the King, though it was a weak effort and most of the frothy saliva dribbled down his chin.

There was another gasp from the crowd, who as one turned their gaze to Magnar. *Magnar Kayne*, the youngest man ever to rule the High Fangs in the name of the Shaman. He had sided with the Magelord against Brodar Kayne, the Sword of the North.

His own father.

Magnar's loyalty to the Shaman had won the respect of the ten chieftains of the Reachings. Respect as well as fear – for if he could condemn his own mother and father to death, what would Magnar Kayne do to a chieftain who betrayed him?

The anguish Yllandris had seen in both father and son's eyes the day the woman Mhaira burned would haunt her forever. She remembered the terrible shame on Brodar Kayne's face as he pleaded with the King to refuse his immortal master and end the horrible spectacle of his mother being burned on the pyre.

Magnar had not done so. He had watched in silence as she was consumed by flame.

At the time, Yllandris had admired him for his pragmatism. He had done what was necessary. He had passed the Shaman's test. After what she had witnessed at Frosthold, however, she was no longer certain Magnar had done the right thing.

There was a scraping sound. It was the Shaman's teeth grinding together. The Magelord gestured at one of the Six standing beside the King. The warrior had a torch in one hand. 'Burn him,' he ordered. The bodyguard moved forwards to ignite the kindling beneath Mehmon.

'Another one put to the fire, eh? Heard a funny tale about that, from a Lowland trader no less.' Mehmon's words came quickly as the flames began to take hold. 'See, as the story goes there was once a powerful wizard who fell for the daughter of another. He loved her more than anything in the world. The Age of Strife had never seen two stars shine so brightly together—' He gasped suddenly as the flame licked at his boots.

Yllandris watched her sisters turn to one another in confusion. *What is he doing*, she saw Thurva mouth to Shranree. When she looked back at the Shaman, however, she knew. His face had grown ominously dark, like a towering thunderhead in the moments before an epic storm was unleashed.

'So the tale goes, the Divine Inquisition eventually got hold of the girl. They did things to her no man should bear witness to. *Urgh.*' He gasped again. His feet had caught fire. The pungent smell of burning leather drifted through the chill air.

Agony filled Mehmon's voice as his words poured out in a torrent. 'The wizard couldn't do a damned thing. The Inquisition blocked his magic somehow. The experience fucked him up good. He exiled himself to the mountains, far away from his peers, burned everything that reminded him of the man he had been and how he had failed— Fuck, *fuck*—'

Mehmon's curses turned into incoherent screams. The smell of burning flesh reached her nostrils and Yllandris felt as if she was going to gag.

There was a blur of motion followed by the sound of tearing and suddenly the Shaman was directly before the pyre, clutching Mehmon's detached head in one hand, the top half of his spinal cord trailing out like a glistening white snake. Blood gushed from the neck of the headless body and sizzled down into the flames.

Yllandris turned away and this time she was sick, heaving her breakfast onto the thawing snow. She heard others doing the same. Even Shranree had gone pale. The Shaman raised Mehmon's head up near his face and stared into its lifeless eyes.

She suddenly felt very scared.

'Are you done, Mithradates?'

There was a collective gasp from the sisters beside her, as well as those at the front of the crowd just behind. An old man had appeared near the King's throne, seemingly from nowhere. He wore crimson robes that were overly large for his slight frame and his thin beard and moustache made him look like an elderly fop. He supported himself on a slender cane, and was the very picture of weariness.

One of the Six immediately sprang towards the intruder, his longsword raised high to smite this strange Lowlander.

The elderly man raised one eyebrow and suddenly the warrior's sword was plucked from his hands. It floated up into the air and rotated slowly around so that its tip was pointing down at the man. The bodyguard grimaced but did not move, keeping his body between the sword and Magnar.

There was movement to the side of Yllandris. 'Sisters, attend me!' cried Shranree, and she spread her hands towards the interloper. Golden light leaped out from her outstretched palms, raced towards her target – but then, instead of striking him, the arcing light bent *around* him to dissipate harmlessly. The old man crooked a finger and suddenly Shranree was clutching her throat. Her ruddy face turned purple as she struggled desperately to breathe. The other sorceresses prepared to launch their own magic as some Highlanders went for their weapons and others turned to flee.

The Shaman finally spoke. 'Enough, Salazar. Release her.'

Salazar? Yllandris recognized that name: the Magelord of Dorminia, one of the original champions of the Godswar uprising and perhaps the most powerful man in the north.

The crimson-robed figure did as he was asked. Shranree dropped to her knees, sucking in deep breaths, tears rolling down her face. 'Sheathe your weapons,' ordered the Shaman. 'All of you.'

Those Highlanders who had pulled steel put their weapons away, though the King's guards kept their hands close to their hilts. The hulking form of the Shaman walked slowly across to the crimson-garbed man. Yllandris watched, filled with awe. Despite his frail appearance, if this wizard really was Salazar, he possessed enough power to collapse the very mountains around them.

'Why have you come here?' the Shaman asked. His voice was unusually quiet, almost apprehensive.

The old man stared down at his counterpart's hand in distaste. The Shaman saw the look, grunted and tossed Mehmon's head backwards into the fire which now blazed behind them. The chieftain's body was already engulfed in flame. Mehmon had saved himself several minutes of intense agony with his desperate story. Whatever one might say about the former chieftain of the North Reaching, he was wily until the end.

Salazar leaned on his cane and tried to blink the tiredness from his eyes. 'You once made me a promise,' he said simply. 'A promise to repay a vow you broke. The time has come to honour it.'

The Shaman narrowed his eyes. 'What do you need of me?'

'You know of events in the Trine?'

'I care not for the outside world.'

'I destroyed Shadowport. I believe Marius perished within.'

'Marius,' the Shaman muttered. 'He was ever the slyest among us. I would not consider him dead until I saw proof.'

Salazar nodded. 'Be that as it may, Thelassa now moves against Dorminia. The White Lady has three companies of mercenaries from Sumnia in her employ. They plan to invade. Without help, we cannot hope to win – and my magic is near spent. I lacked the reserves even to Portal here. My journey has taken the best part of a week, using what little power I have available to me.'

The Shaman growled low in his throat.

Salazar stared boldly back. 'We once fought side by side, Mithradates. United in our tragedy. United in our desire for *vengeance*. Do you remember that much, at least?'

'I remember. There are some things I cannot forget. I try –
but I *cannot forget*.'

'It is our curse, Mithradates. Our curse and our blessing. I
would speak somewhere more private.'

The Shaman shot the King a glare and Magnar rose from his
throne. 'Go back to your homes,' he ordered loudly. 'Anyone
still here in the time it takes a man to piss will spend a night in
the stocks.'

At once relieved and disappointed to be dismissed, the
assembled Highlanders began to depart. Yllandris was
preparing to follow her sisters when a strong hand seized her
firmly by the shoulder. She spun around to stare into the steely
gaze of King Magnar himself.

'Walk with me,' he said softly. He seemed uncertain – and,
Yllandris thought, at that moment, very young.

'Of course,' she said. Her smile couldn't quite reach her eyes,
however.

How can a son watch his mother burn?

Grim Tidings

'HURRY THIS UP. I have things to do.'
Eremul shot the hard-eyed woman a look of undisguised anger. She smirked slightly in response.

You believe you can read my thoughts. I see that glowing bauble beneath your ear. Well, you conceited harpy, I have ways to guard against unwelcome intrusions.

The effort of maintaining a mental shield to defeat the Augmentor's probing had given him a splitting headache. In fairness, that was almost a welcome distraction from the throbbing lump protruding from his arse, which had swollen to the size of an orange. All in all, he had seen better days.

Recent events in the city had done nothing to improve the Halfmage's mood. The Tyrant of Dorminia had been absent for a week, leaving that damnable Supreme Augmentor to assume temporary command of the city while Grand Magistrate Timerus regained his strength. The golden-haired commander of Salazar's elite enforcers had wasted little time in putting Eremul to work, employing him in the dual role of both adviser and errand boy. His latest task was to gather every book he could find containing information about the distant nation of Sumnia. At first he had been secretly pleased with the assignment, thinking he might get a few hours' respite back at the depository. He had not counted on being shadowed at every turn by Goodlady Cyreena, whose company was about as welcome as a poker up the arse.

Still, much as he despised the malevolent bitch glaring at him from across the room, the true depths of his loathing were reserved solely for himself.

He had held Salazar's very life in his hands. He could have liberated Dorminia and its people from the grip of its tyrannical, murderous lord and ushered in a new age of justice and prosperity for all. Oh, the city would have been seized by Thelassa in short order, he had no doubt, but life under the White Lady's banner would surely be better than the random executions and systematic terrorization that were part of everyday life in this festering heap of shit.

He could have been a *hero*, or at the very least an unsung martyr. Instead he had chosen to save his own skin, as befitted the coward he undoubtedly was. He only hoped the Magelord of Thelassa never learned of his actions. In one fell swoop, he had ruined the White Lady's plan for liberating the Grey City without the need for a bloody war.

Preparations for Dorminia's defence were well under way. The Crimson Watch had already begun sweeping the poorer districts and conscripting young men into the makeshift army that would defend Dorminia from Thelassa's hired mercenaries. Eremul doubted the forced enrolment of the city's dregs would prove to be of much benefit. When given a choice between a known tyrant and a potential saviour, only a fool would fight tooth and nail for the former.

The Halfmage had seen enough of the White Lady's agents up in the abandoned lighthouse to predict a swift end to the conflict – especially with half the city's Augmentors forcibly retired and probably suicidal. Dorminia was slipping from Salazar's grasp, and there was little the ruthless old bastard could do about it. Even a Magelord has limits, and Salazar had exhausted himself destroying Shadowport. And no one knew quite what the White Lady herself was capable of.

'What do we have so far?' he asked irritably. There was a small stack of books on a table next to Goodlady Cyreena. She glanced at the spines.

'*Before the Fall: A History of the Events Leading up to the Godswar. A Grand Tour of the Sun Lands. The Soaring Spires: An Examination of Thelassan Society. The Warrior Princes of Sumnia*. What's this one?' She picked up a small tome covered in purple leather. '*Staring into the Abyss: The Planar Convergence*. What does this have to do with the war?'

'It doesn't,' he snapped in response. 'It's something I'm studying in my spare time: That book shouldn't be in the pile.'

The Augmentor flicked through the pages, her lips pursed in concentration. He had thought her pretty, he recalled – until it became clear she was a barely functioning sociopath. That had killed any latent desire he might have felt.

Not that my passions amount to anything worth a damn. He hadn't been intimate with anyone except his right hand for longer than he cared to remember.

'You believe this? All this nonsense about demons and bogeymen?' The woman's voice was scornful.

Eremul sighed in irritation. 'My wizardly forebears stormed the heavens themselves, did they not? It follows that there is a dark counterpart to the celestial plane.'

'Your time would be better spent researching how to protect our northern borders from the abominations that plague us. Those are real threats – not childish nonsense.'

He couldn't resist giving the goodlady a scornful look. 'I am led to understand it is *your* duty to combat these menaces when they threaten Dorminia. Perhaps it is difficult to find the time. After all, you are so very busy terrorizing the populace.'

Cyreena stared back at him. There was something vaguely familiar about that face, but at that moment all he could focus on was the seething hatred burning behind her eyes. 'I do as I am commanded,' she said. 'Nothing more. As should you.'

'Oh, don't you worry about my dedication,' he spat back. 'After all, did I not save Salazar's very life? I ought to be posing now for a sculptor. I deserve a statue somewhere in the city, surely. Why, it would barely count as half a job. Ardling could surely negotiate a discount.'

The Augmentor's voice softened. 'You sound bitter. I would not blame you for hating our master.'

Her words surprised him. He narrowed his eyes. 'This is what you do, isn't it?' he said accusingly. 'You tempt the gullible into treacherous thoughts so you can arrest them for treason later on. You fucking *succubus*.'

She stared at him and said nothing.

'You're worse than the rest of them,' he continued. He knew he should probably keep his mouth shut, but recent events and his subsequent treatment as some kind of skivvy for that perfect golden-haired bastard lording it up at the Obelisk had enraged him. 'How many careless fools have you led to the noose with your tastefully exposed tits and serpent's tongue? How many families have you destroyed? Do you take some kind of sick pleasure from this?'

Goodlady Cyreena sneered in response, a look of such utter contempt that Eremul was impressed in spite of himself. 'That's rich coming from you, Halfmage. You've been informing for his lordship for years. The only difference between us is that I do this willingly – not because I'm too much of a coward to choose otherwise. You're like an abused dog that still tongues his master's arse hoping for a pat on the head.'

The woman's words cut him like a blade. She had struck him right where he was weakest. He felt the blood pounding in his head, closed his eyes and gripped the sides of his chair so hard his fingers hurt. *You bitch. You ruthless, perceptive bitch.*

His magic burgeoned inside him. He was a hair's breadth from evoking and unleashing it at the Augmentor when he felt a prick on his hand. He looked down.

There was a tiny speck of blood on his palm. The woman had crossed over to him and stabbed him with her hairpin, which had been hidden underneath her hair. He had forgotten it was there. He felt himself go numb. When he tried to wriggle his fingers they refused to respond.

Goodlady Cyreena watched him like a hawk, her hairpin poised to stab him again. When she was certain he was fully paralysed, she relaxed and placed the pin back in her hair.

He tried to summon his magic again. It was useless. The enchantment that numbed his body also dampened his ability to channel his own magical reserves. He was as powerless as a newborn babe.

Wonderful. The day just gets better and better. He couldn't even move his mouth to hurl an obscenity at the damned woman.

'I want to show you something,' the Augmentor said. She grabbed his chair and spun him around to face the door, then pushed him outside. A child was kicking a stone down the street. The boy looked up curiously as they emerged into the afternoon sun.

The clouds that had hung over Dorminia like a shroud for the last few days had finally dispersed. Now a new problem faced the city. Bodies were beginning to wash up, hundreds of them, bloated corpses floating in on tides that had travelled all the way from the flooded remnants of Shadowport. The City of Shades was slowly regurgitating its dead.

Eremul watched the clean-up operation in the harbour as the goodlady wheeled him slowly down towards the docks. He had no idea what the woman planned to do with him, but he suspected it would not be pleasant.

Maybe she's going to throw me into the harbour. Will my chair carry me straight to the bottom like a stone, or will I float free to enjoy a more leisurely drowning? I can hardly decide which I prefer. Perhaps a net will sweep me up and deposit my corpse on one of those trawlers.

He felt strangely calm. If he was going to die, drowning probably wasn't such a bad way to go.

As it turned out, it appeared his tormentor had other

intentions. They stopped short of the harbour and took a left turn into a narrow street piled high with stinking rubbish on either side and peopled with rough-faced men and women. Whether it was Goodlady Cyreena's demeanour or just the sheer absurdity of an attractive woman wheeling a legless cripple around in one of the scummiest parts of town, no one bothered to molest them as they made their way down the alley. Eventually they stopped in front of a run-down house, little more than a shack, with a broken door and a roof that sagged in the middle and was coated in bird shit.

The Augmentor stood there for a time, staring at the decrepit little building. 'This is where I was born,' she said. Her voice was carefully neutral but the words shocked him nonetheless. He found that he could move his eyebrows now. One of them arched up in surprise.

'You won't remember the riots that took place during the Culling,' she continued. 'I imagine you were indisposed at the time.'

What gave you that idea, he wanted to say, but his lips still refused to form the words. He made do with a frown.

'The city was in chaos. The mages fought back, as you might expect, which gathered support for an uprising. This particular area was a hotbed of unrest.' She looked up and down the dirty streets. 'I was one of the loudest calling for change. I was in my early twenties then, in love with one of the ringleaders of the rebellion.'

She stared at the busted door hanging off its hinges. This time there was a hint of emotion in her voice. 'My parents were loyalists. They wanted no trouble. When the revolt was in full swing and there was fighting out on the streets, out *here*' – she gestured, sweeping her hand around to take in the filthy row of houses – 'my lover convinced me to let his gang into my home. He knew I was sympathetic to the rebellion and assumed my family were the same. They demanded my father and brother join them in fighting the soldiers.'

Eremul sat and listened in silence. It wasn't as if he had much choice in the matter, but hearing this cold-blooded Augmentor reveal her past was oddly compelling. Besides, she seemed to be finding the experience cathartic. He hoped that boded well for his continued existence when she got around to deciding what to do with him.

'My family... exchanged harsh words with the rebels. My brother took a knife in the throat. That set my father off. He, too, was murdered while my lover held me back. I screamed and kicked but he wouldn't let me go.'

Goodlady Cyreena went silent for a time. There was a strange glint in her eyes now. 'My lover dragged me from the house as his friends raped my sister. She was little more than a child.'

Eremul fancied he saw a tear, though it could have been a trick of the light. *I suppose I should be grateful I'm paralysed*, he thought. *I might be expected to rise from my chair and give her a supportive hug. That would be awkward for both of us.*

The Augmentor blinked and suddenly her momentary vulnerability was gone. 'My lover was cut down by soldiers barely a second after we stepped out of the house. I was arrested and released a few weeks later. When I returned, I found my mother had committed suicide. My sister was nowhere to be seen. I never learned what became of her.'

She turned to him and crossed her arms in front of her ample chest. 'Civilization functions only because strong men do not permit weaker men to indulge their baser instincts. Freedom and liberty are the means by which anarchy reigns – and anarchy is the natural state for men to freely express the evil that lurks within them. Within all of them. Within *you*,' she added, staring down at him with an expression that froze his blood.

This woman is insane.

'I was young and naive. I am no longer that person. I no longer answer to the same name. There is but one man I believe in, and he is no man at all. He is a *god*.'

She bent down so her face was close to his. 'Feel no sorrow for those you betray,' she said softly. 'Embrace what you do. You serve Salazar, whose wisdom is beyond reproach by the likes of us. Do not lament the loss of your legs. Instead, celebrate the fact they have liberated you from the evil you would have otherwise committed. You are half a man – yet by virtue of that simple fact, you possess only half the evil of a man.'

She turned away from Eremul and so, fortunately for him, didn't see the look of pure poison he shot her. *Batshit insane. She's batshit insane.*

The Augmentor looked up at the sinking sun. Evening was near. 'I will bring the books we gathered to the Obelisk,' she said. 'You can make your way home in your own time. The paralysis shouldn't last much longer.'

Goodlady Cyreena walked away without a backward glance.

It was growing dark by the time he recovered enough feeling in his arms to begin wheeling himself up the side street and back towards the depository. This was the worst day he could remember since the Obelisk dungeons had changed his life, and that was no small feat – there was the time he had fallen out of his chair while taking a shit and wallowed in his own excrement for six hours waiting for Isaac to return, to name but one possible contender.

He wondered what had become of Isaac and the rest of the small band that had set off for the Wailing Rift two weeks past. The ship sent up Deadman's Channel to investigate the collapsed mine had failed to discover any sign of the saboteurs. That gave him hope they were still alive. Despite his maddening enthusiasm and annoying knack for effortlessly picking up new skills, Isaac had proved a loyal assistant.

Lost in sudden melancholy, he didn't realize how close he had come to the harbour until he heard the sound of lapping water below. His curiosity got the better of him and he wheeled his chair out until he overlooked the vast expanse of water. The cleaning operation was winding down for the night. Crew were disembarking all around him. He gazed out, amusing himself with the thought of Isaac and the others slipping furtively through the detritus of floating corpses on their tiny sailing boat, wondering what disaster had befallen the city in their absence.

An odd noise suddenly caught his attention. It almost sounded like a baby crying, and it came from somewhere below him. He peered down into the murky water.

There. A tiny bundle fidgeted pathetically on a small piece of flotsam bobbing towards him. He glanced around to make sure no one was watching and then, with a brief unveiling of magic, he levitated the twitching figure up to drift slowly into his arms.

It was a dog – a scrawny little thing with patchy grey fur and drooping ears. It watched him nervously with watery brown eyes.

Eremul felt something strange stir within him. This poor creature had somehow lived through the absolute destruction of its city. Even more miraculously, it had survived a voyage across the Broken Sea clinging to a fragile piece of furniture.

The dog leaned forwards and licked his nose. He flinched away, then reached forwards and patted its head. *We're the same, you and I*, he thought. *A pair of mongrels, cast adrift, clinging to whatever we can to make it through the day.*

He remembered what Goodlady Cyreena had said to him. *You're like an abused dog that still tongues his master's arse hoping for a pat on the head.*

The Augmentor had been wrong about that. He had saved Salazar's life only because his own had depended on it. He would have his vengeance when the time was right, when the old bastard least expected it. He wasn't like her – a broken, vicious, evil thing. All right, perhaps he was broken and occasionally vicious, but *evil*? He patted the dog on the head again.

Would an evil man rescue a stranded animal from certain death? I'm taking you back to the depository with me. Hopefully that crazy bitch has left by now. There's some offal in the larder if I can get it out. I might even have a tasty leg of pork down there. If you're a really good boy you can—

'Argh.'

He jerked back as a warm stream of piss spurted from between the dog's legs and splashed onto his face, dribbling down his chin and then his robes. Instinctively he thrust the animal away. It slipped from his grasp and he heard the splash as it hit the water below. He wiped his face with the back of his hand and squinted down, searching for any sign of the animal.

It was gone.

He sat there for a time, staring at nothing in particular. Then, very slowly, he turned his chair around and began the lonely journey back to the depository.

The Final Test

'LEFT. RIGHT. THRUST. *Good.*'
He turned aside the assassin's curved dagger, this one thankfully devoid of venom, and stepped back.

His training had been intense, harder than anything he had ever known. Day and night were meaningless in this dark place – it felt as though no sooner had he collapsed on his bedroll than he was being prodded awake again for more countless hours of sparring. He had learned the best spots to stab a man so that he died quickly and quietly. He and the Darkson had stalked each other through the ruined streets of the holy city, both seeking to avoid detection and take the other by surprise. While Cole had yet to get the better of the Shamaathan, the Darkson had commented frequently on his progress.

'You were a tool,' the dark-skinned man was telling him now. 'Rough-edged, unfocused, and yet not without a certain promise. Now you are becoming a weapon.'

'A weapon,' Cole repeated. 'An angel of death.'

The Darkson frowned. 'That remains to be seen. Your final test awaits you before we are done here. It will test everything you have learned.'

The assassin led him across a wide avenue of collapsed buildings, holding a torch in one gloved hand to light the way. Eventually they came to a jumble of leaning walls that formed a narrow passage. Darkness lay within.

'The section of ruins ahead is a veritable maze of alleys,' the

Darkson explained. 'Somewhere within is your target. You are to hunt him down. When you find him, you are to kill him.'

'Kill him?' Cole repeated, somewhat uncomfortably. 'What has he done to deserve death?'

The Darkson paused. 'Does it matter? He is an enemy of Thelassa.'

Cole thought about this for a moment. He had sunk the boat that had been pursuing the *Redemption,* but that had been full of Watchmen intent on harming him and his fellow escapees. Besides, that had been an almost impersonal act. He had never actually killed a man face to face. Not with steel in hand.

'What kind of enemy?' he persisted.

The Shamaathan narrowed his eyes. 'The worst kind. The kind who would see Thelassa put to the sword.' He paused for a moment. 'You told me you were an angel of death.'

'I'm a hero,' Cole replied.

The Darkson sighed. 'The difference between a hero and a killer lies only in the ability of the former to justify every dark deed they perform to anyone who cares to listen. Even themselves. *Especially* themselves.'

'My father wasn't like that,' Cole said. 'He always did the right thing. He stood up for the weak and oppressed.'

'As will you,' the assassin replied. 'Once you've planted Magebane in Salazar's back and freed Dorminia from his tyranny, then you will have earned the right to call yourself a hero.'

Cole took a deep breath. *I'll show him I have what it takes.* He drew his dagger and entered the maze.

It was dark, so dark he could see no more than a few feet in front of his face. There was the sound of running water nearby. He continued on down the corridor, took a left turn and then a right. He moved as the Darkson had taught him, on the balls of his feet to avoid making any noise. He heard rats scurrying past him, but he paid them no mind. Somewhere in this sprawling labyrinth was a man who deserved to die.

He had to believe that.

There was a slight flicker of light ahead. He crouched low in the shadows, hugging the wall behind him. He waited. Another slight flicker of light, and then it was gone. He rose and padded softly towards the spot where he had glimpsed the illumination.

He listened. All was silent now, save for the sound of running water, rats squeaking... and yes, there it was, the slight *clank* of an armoured man moving carelessly some distance ahead of him.

He clutched his dagger tighter, following the sound as quietly as he could. The light returned and then grew stronger. Finally, at an intersection where two alleyways met, he located his target.

The man was a good few inches taller than him. He wore bronze chainmail armour and a full helm that covered his head, and carried a longsword in his right hand and a lantern in his left. He was heedless of the racket he made as he turned one way and then the other, holding his blade out before him and raising the lantern to inspect the shadows that surrounded him on all sides.

Cole waited until his target was facing away from him and then crept forwards. He was only a dozen feet away when the armoured warrior suddenly turned and raised the lantern in the air. The young Shard rolled away from the light, concealing himself behind a broken wall that barely rose to his waist. He could hear the warrior moving closer. He held his breath and cursed inwardly. If it came down to a direct confrontation, he would be in a whole lot of trouble.

The light drew nearer and then halted abruptly. The footsteps ceased. He could hear ragged breathing from behind the helm. He tensed, preparing to dive out of the way the instant the warrior charged around the wall.

The light flickered and then suddenly began to recede, the footsteps carrying his target away from him. He released his breath. That had been close.

When he was certain he had not been spotted, he slunk out of his cover. The armoured figure was facing in the opposite direction once again. Cole padded forwards, inching closer and closer. He positioned himself behind his target, so close now he could smell the man's sweat. There was no margin for error. If he missed his chance the warrior would likely shake him off and run him through. Images from his disastrous confrontation with the Watchmen reminded him of the terrible consequences of failure.

I'm Davarus Cole, he reminded himself. *This is what I do.*

He steadied himself. In one smooth motion, he wrapped an arm around the man's head and tilted it upwards. With his other arm he slid the dagger underneath the helm and tugged it across the man's neck. He felt it cut through flesh. His target let out a wet gasp and struggled weakly. Cole held him close, felt the warmth and the wetness soak his arm.

In moments it was over. The man jerked once and then stopped moving. Cole lowered the body gently to the ground. He felt strange. There was nothing noble in this act. No sense of pride or achievement. This wasn't what a hero was supposed to do. He reached down and grasped the helm. With a tug, he pulled it free of the corpse.

He froze in shock. The fallen lantern illuminated the weather-beaten face of Admiral Kramer. The man's tongue appeared to have been cut out, and his blue eyes were wide in death. They seemed to stare at him accusingly.

He remembered their time together back on the Swell. Kramer had been a harsh captain but also a fair one, a man who commanded respect. He was no criminal, just another of Salazar's puppets who had become caught up in events over which he had no control.

And I killed him.

'You did well,' came that whispering voice from behind him. Cole didn't bother turning around.

'A decent enough death,' the Darkson said. There was no

gloating or amusement there, just a statement of fact. He was grateful for that, at least. 'Ask yourself what the Tyrant of Dorminia would have done, had the tables been turned and this man had been his hostage. Worse than this, no?'

'I killed him.'

'Yes,' agreed the Shamaathan. 'And so, too, you will kill those who stand between you and Salazar. Men no better or worse than this one. Men who are simply doing their duty.' The assassin sounded tired, almost melancholic.

The lantern burning on the ground suddenly winked out, plunging them into utter darkness. Before Cole had a chance to react it flared back to life. Standing before him was one of the White Lady's pale servants. He stared at her in shock. *Who are these women?*

'It is done?' she enquired emotionlessly.

The Darkson nodded. 'He's ready.' He paused for a moment. 'Or as ready as he can be. This kind of training usually requires months.'

The pale woman turned to him. 'Davarus Cole, it is time for you to fulfil your destiny. A ship has been prepared to sail you around the coast to Deadman's Channel. The Darkson, Lady Brianna, and several of my sisters are to accompany you. You will seek out Brodar Kayne and reclaim Magebane.'

'How?' asked Cole. 'He could be anywhere by now.'

'Some manner of disaster befell the mine at the Wailing Rift,' the woman replied. 'If the Highlander perished there, Brianna will help you locate and recover the weapon. If this Brodar Kayne still lives, we will hunt him down.'

'It is imperative that you recover your birthright,' the assassin explained. 'Thelassa cannot liberate the Grey City while the Tyrant of Dorminia draws breath. The longer we delay the greater the threat posed by Salazar becomes. Only the unique power of Magebane can get you close enough to kill him.'

'What should I do once I have it in my possession?' The thought of going up against Salazar was thrilling, but Cole couldn't shake the feeling there was something he wasn't being told.

'Brianna will send a message back to Thelassa. Our army will then attack from the west and draw Dorminia's defenders. You will infiltrate the Obelisk during the chaos and do what you have been trained to do.'

Cole thought about this for a moment. 'What will happen to Dorminia and her people after Salazar's gone?'

'You will be free,' the pale woman replied. 'Of course, Thelassa will demand certain concessions in return, such as sole ownership of the Celestial Isles. That is fair, is it not?'

Cole nodded. 'I guess so,' he said. 'I would like to take Three-Finger with me.'

'You mean the rapist?'

'He's not a rapist. Three-Finger's a bit coarse sometimes, but he has a heart of gold. Besides,' he added, 'he's my henchman.'

The pale woman's expression was, as always, unreadable. 'I will communicate your wish to the White Lady. In the meantime, I must insist that you wear this while you are escorted from here.' She reached down under her white robes and produced a collar.

Cole grimaced. Being a hero was a much more complicated business than he had thought.

He stared again at the corpse of Kramer. *A decent man, forced to do evil things by the bastard up at the Obelisk. I will avenge you, Kramer. You, my father, and everyone else who has suffered because of the Tyrant of Dorminia.*

He looked at the bloody dagger in his hand.

I really am very sorry about that.

Duty Calls

MALBREC WAS LOCATED fifteen miles north of Dorminia. It straddled a trade route that wound up through the Demonfire Hills to continue on through to Ashfall at the very northern edge of Salazar's territory, where the Trine ended and the bandit-infested Badlands began.

A mining town, Malbrec supplied much of the granite used in the construction of Dorminia's many buildings. It also provided a lucrative source of income for the Grey City; Dorminia's incumbent Chancellor had set a high tax on the town's exports in return for its advantageous location and the protection the local Crimson Watch garrison offered from the roving abominations and bandits that haunted the region.

Barandas had been in Malbrec for only a few hours and already he wished he was back in Dorminia. His presence in the town had nothing to do with trade and everything to do with the rather grimmer business of conscription. Thelassa's mercenary army would soon cross the narrow stretch of sea dividing the two cities, and Dorminia would need every man it could muster to defend it. As a vassal of the Grey City, Malbrec had a moral and legal obligation to provide soldiers in times of conflict. It was up to Barandas to take the raw material of the town's young men and beat them into something worthwhile.

That was all very well, except that the young men of Malbrec showed scant enthusiasm for fulfilling their obligations.

Barandas frowned at the tear-streaked face of the woman before him. Her two sons loitered slightly behind her, examining the ground with mixed expressions of fear and shame. The elder sibling looked to be near twenty, the younger perhaps seventeen. Old enough to fight, Barandas judged, and didn't he himself have the scars to prove it?

'Their father perished down in the mines. Left me a widow, not a copper to my name,' the woman was saying. 'My boys, they're good lads. They work the quarry to support their mother and their sister, who's barely more than a babe. Who's going to put food on the table while they're off fighting?'

Thurbal tapped a foot impatiently. The stocky grey-haired Augmentor wasn't much for subtlety. If it were up to him, he would have thrown every likely recruit in chains and packed them off to the training camp in wagons. Barandas was fast reaching the point where he wondered if that might not be the best approach. 'You will be provided for while your boys are away,' he said. 'These are dangerous times. Magical abominations roam the wilderness. We will make men out of your sons; teach them how to use a sword so that when the threat to Dorminia is over, they may return and help protect the town from the horrors that plague this land.'

The woman looked at her boys. 'What if they don't return?'

Barandas shook his head. 'Then you will be compensated appropriately. We are at war. Every man must play his part.'

The youngest crossed his arms and shot Barandas a defiant look. 'This isn't Malbrec's fight. Why don't you all go back to Dorminia and leave us be? I'm sick of your bloody Magelord telling us what to do.'

His mother gasped. Her other son turned to remonstrate with his brother, but the damage was already done. Thurbal had drawn his scimitar. He dashed across to the youth and grabbed him by the throat with his free hand. 'Listen to me, you little prick,' he snarled. 'You'll fight, all right. You'll fight as though your life depends on it – because if you don't, I'll cut your balls off and send them back to your dear old mum here to remind her of what a gutless little whelp she raised.'

'You're choking him,' the boy's brother protested. The lad had turned red. His mother moaned pitifully.

Before Barandas could order his deputy to release the boy, the older brother grabbed Thurbal's arms from behind. He tried to pull the Augmentor away from his sibling – but quick as a flash Thurbal threw his elbow back to drive deep into the young man's stomach, causing him to release his grip and double over in agony.

'Enough,' Barandas ordered, but the grey warrior ignored his command, stepping forwards to bring the pommel of his scimitar crunching down into the lad's skull once, twice, and then a third time, each blow connecting with a sickening crunch. The quarryman flopped down onto the ground.

'*Enough,*' Barandas barked again, and this time his own sword was in his hand. 'Lower your weapon. Disobey me again, Thurbal, and I'll kill you.'

His deputy sneered back at him and waved his scimitar in the air. The pommel was covered in blood. 'That's right, defend these cowards,' he spat. 'All your softly-softly bullshit will count for fuck all when the Sumnians arrive. You know what they do to their enemies? Let me tell you—'

He didn't get the chance. With a flick of his wrist, Barandas disarmed his subordinate and sent his scimitar spinning out of his hands to land a dozen feet away. Thurbal's mouth dropped open in shock.

'I told you to lower your weapon,' said Barandas. Despite his anger he couldn't help but feel a sense of relief. Thurbal had needed a dressing down, but his disarming of the man could very well have backfired and left him holding one half of a severed sword. That wouldn't have done much to establish his authority over his rebellious colleague.

'You can retrieve your scimitar when I say so.' Barandas looked down at the fallen quarryman. Blood leaked from the top of his head and pooled on the ground next to him.

It was then that his mother started to scream.

'Someone fetch a physician,' he said loudly to the slack-faced onlookers. He turned to the woman and her younger son, who looked as if he was about to piss himself. 'I am sorry for what occurred here. Come and find me when you know if he is... likely to pull through. I would see you recompensed in some way.'

He left the sobbing woman and the small crowd that had gathered behind. Reprehensible though Thurbal's actions were, the incident had been coming ever since Barandas and his two deputies arrived in Malbrec. The town had seemingly forgotten that it was a vassal of Dorminia; forgotten that it was Salazar who kept them safe and allowed them to sleep soundly in their beds. Now that war with Thelassa loomed, the town needed reminding where its loyalties lay.

Salazar had recently returned to the city after a two-week absence. The Magelord had not yet deigned to speak of where he had been. Halendorf's condition had worsened, and the pressures of organizing Dorminia's army had taken their toll on Barandas. Grand Magistrate Timerus was sufficiently recovered from his own ordeal and was already in the process of recommending new magistrates to replace those murdered in the assassination attempt. The upper echelons of Dorminia's government would soon be crawling with men loyal to the hawk-nosed Grand Magistrate – or at least, even more loyal than the previous ones had been. Timerus was a schemer without peer, a man whose cunning had secured him a position second only to Salazar himself.

Barandas sighed. Timerus could play his games. He had more important matters to focus on. The drafting of soldiers from Dorminia's poorer districts was under way and had gone surprisingly well, but three of Dorminia's larger vassal towns had provided such a meagre yield of men that the Supreme Augmentor had decided to oversee the recruitment at Malbrec personally.

He sweated in his golden armour as he strode towards the east of town, where the gigantic quarry that was the basis of Malbrec's industry yawned like a festering wound in the land. Red-cloaked soldiers saluted as he passed them, shielding their eyes from the afternoon sun.

Eventually he found the man he was looking for. Garmond was difficult to miss, even while he was sitting down. He was clad in his enchanted plate armour from head to toe, making no concessions to the early summer afternoon heat. The only part of his raiment he had removed were the gauntlets, which lay on the table next to him.

The huge Augmentor had a sheet of parchment before him and was in the process of scribbling something down. The quill looked faintly ridiculous in his ham-sized fist. At first Barandas had been vaguely surprised that the man even knew how to write. Garmond's brutish countenance and infamous temper made it easy to overlook the fact he was a son of one of Dorminia's most renowned families.

Garmond stopped writing as Barandas approached. 'Commandant,' he said. The monstrous helm he wore caused his voice to echo ominously so that not only did he look demonic, he also sounded the part.

Barandas nodded in greeting. 'How many?' he asked. He wasn't particularly keen to hear the answer.

'Eighty-five. They came forward quickly enough once I started knocking heads together.'

Barandas raised an eyebrow. That was more than he had expected from the small part of town Garmond had been assigned. Malbrec was home to just short of four thousand, the largest of the settlements that fell within Dorminia's territory, but so far only a few hundred men had been drafted.

'Is anyone still giving us trouble?'

Garmond turned his helmed head and nodded at the hill a few hundred yards to the south. A cluster of walled estates perched on top of the hill, fronted by pretty orchards and gardens.

Barandas sighed. *Always the privileged. Too rich, too important to send their sons to war.*

'I'll speak with them,' he said. Dorminia's nobles were still resisting his efforts at securing their participation in the city's defence. He had no option but to raise that particular annoyance with Timerus, who would probably wave him away with some weak excuse. Still, there was no reason the wealthy merchants and landowners of Malbrec should dodge the draft.

He strode up the gently sloping path that meandered up the hill. The walk was a pleasant one. From this vantage point Barandas could see Crimson Watchmen going from door to door and enlisting suitable candidates. Those drafted would have a day to gather a few essential belongings and bid their farewells before they departed to the training camp just outside Dorminia's eastern wall.

Wiping sweat from his brow, he approached the first of the estates, a small manor house set behind a row of cherry trees preparing to bloom. He stopped suddenly.

He remembered trees very similar to these, on a day that had, at first, been equally glorious.

The afternoon was thick with the smells of summer. The odours that always accompanied hot days in Dorminia were there, so ubiquitous that one hardly noticed them. But nothing could overpower the rich scents of blossom, the crisp aroma of fresh grass and the sweet tang of the rose-coloured cider that was so popular during the Festival of the Red Sun – the one day of the year when Lord Salazar presented himself before his people.

Barandas recalled the pride he had felt marching alongside his comrades at the front of the procession. He had been a man of the Crimson Watch then, barely a year into his service with the army. The parade had taken them down from the Obelisk to the lush, leafy boughs of Verdisa Park, which occupied a wide space near the south-east corner of the Noble Quarter. They had proceeded to the centre of the park. There Salazar would stand silent vigil before the great oak.

The Eternal Tree, it had been called. No one knew what significance it held to their Magelord, but the tree itself was a thing of beauty, its golden leaves untouched by the turning of the seasons. The Eternal Tree had occupied the centre of the park for as long as any in the city could recall.

It was a sight to behold. A reminder of the wonders the world once held before the fall of the gods.

He remembered how he would sit beneath its gilded canopy and pray for his mother after she got sick. The malignance in her chest had killed her eventually, but he had found peace in the comforting embrace of the great tree's shadow.

Barandas closed his eyes. He remembered sensing something was amiss, glancing up to see the branches overhead rustle in a way that had struck him as strange. On an instinct that to this day he had never fully understood, he had rushed past the Magelord's Augmentors and knocked the invisible assassin to the ground before he had buried his dagger in Salazar's back. Their cover blown, the other assassins had dropped down from where they had been hiding in the boughs of the great tree. For those few seconds when everything was pure chaos Barandas had fought off the unseen assailants, taking wound after wound before the knife had plunged into his heart.

I was on my knees, coughing up blood. Salazar uttered a word and suddenly the assassins were there for all to see, their cloak of invisibility stripped from them. The Augmentors waded in, and everything from that point on was a blur.

The Festival of the Red Sun attempt on Salazar's life had ultimately proved the catalyst for the Culling. A cabal of Dorminia's most powerful wizards were found guilty of hiring assassins from foreign lands and plotting to murder the Magelord. Something seemed to break in Salazar that day, for later that year he ordered the Eternal Tree burned to the ground and every mage in the Grey City and its dependent territories killed without mercy.

As for Barandas, he had awakened with a new heart of

enchanted iron – and the most rapid promotion from Watchman to Augmentor in the city's history. He sometimes wondered if Salazar had intended the irony. *A heart of iron, to bear the burden of duty and not burst with the weight of what must be done.*

He reached the front of the manor house. A dog barked at him and then ran off around the back of the estate. He placed a hand on the pommel of his sword and cleared his throat. 'By order of Lord Salazar, Magelord of Dorminia and rightful sovereign of Malbrec, open this door.'

He waited for a minute or two. Eventually the door opened to reveal a sour-faced old man in a deerskin jacket clutching a pipe in one hand. 'I already told that armoured juggernaut of yours,' he said irritably. 'There's no one here but me. I'm far too old to be fighting in your damned war.'

There was a cough from somewhere inside, which was quickly cut off as whoever made the noise desperately tried to stifle it. 'I think I'll see for myself,' said Barandas. He pushed past into the entrance hall and through into a plush sitting room.

'This... this is *scandalous*,' the man protested, giving his pipe a furious tug. 'Do you know who I am? '

'That's of no consequence,' Barandas replied. He looked around at the leather armchairs and the fine rosewood cabinets. 'You've done well for yourself.'

The old man frowned. 'The mining business has been good to me. I ship a lot of stone to the city. I always pay my taxes. Every copper,' he added.

'Who's that?' Barandas pointed at a canvas hanging over the fireplace. It depicted a slightly younger version of the scowling merchant. Next to him was a woman of similar age with an equine face. Between them, a teenage boy wore the expression of the terminally bored.

'That's my wife, Mildra. She's been dead these past six winters.'

'I meant the boy.'

There was sudden fear on the face of the old merchant. 'Harald? He's not here. I sent him to Westrock—'

There was another cough. It came from upstairs.

'If I find you are lying to me,' Barandas said carefully, 'I will have you thrown in chains, your estate seized, and your son placed in the very front ranks when hostilities with Thelassa commence.'

The merchant's face sank and he inclined his head slightly. 'Harald is unwell. He contracted an illness while we were in Dorminia on business. I haven't found a physician who has been able to help. He's coughing up his lungs.'

Barandas frowned. This wasn't the first he had heard of this sickness. If things got much worse Dorminia would soon have an epidemic on its hands. Still, citing exemption from the draft because of some mystery illness was a claim he heard all too often recently.

'Send your son down to my man Garmond. He will have a physician examine him. If it is indeed as you say, Harald will be excused.'

The old merchant started to protest. Barandas was in no mood to hear it. He spun on his heels and marched out of the manor, pulling the door shut behind him.

'How many?'

Lieutenant Toram squinted down at the parchment in his hands. 'Four hundred and sixteen.'

Barandas sighed in frustration. The sun was sinking into the horizon and he still had an hour's ride back to Dorminia. His sweep of the hilltop residences had proved fruitless. As it turned out, many of the town's lords and wealthier merchants had anticipated there would be a draft shortly after the declaration of war and sent their sons away. It was a common story throughout Dorminia's territory.

The whorehouses and taverns of the Unclaimed Lands will doubtless enjoy a roaring trade for a while, he thought sourly.

This entire exercise had been a disappointment. Between Westrock, Ashfall and now Malbrec, they had raised barely half the numbers he had anticipated.

He turned to Symon, his squire. 'Ready my horse,' he said. 'I will return to the city shortly.'

'Yes, sir,' the lad replied, and scurried off to carry out his orders.

Toram scratched at his bristly grey moustache. 'We did the best we could, my lord. If you like, we could do one more round. I'm certain there are malingerers and cowards dodging our recruiters.'

'It's late,' he said. 'Wait until the morning. If you see anyone trying to sneak out of town—'

'Sir?'

He turned to see who had interrupted him. It was the lad whose mother had argued against his drafting earlier that day. 'Do you bring news of your brother?'

The boy looked glum. 'The physician says he will survive... but he will need months of recovery before he is fit to return to work. Or go to war.'

Barandas nodded. 'Tell your mother she will be paid the sum of three gold spires as compensation for the unfortunate incident. That should help keep food on the table while he convalesces.'

'What about me, my lord?'

'You? You're perfectly fit and healthy, are you not? Lieutenant Toram will take a few details and then he will see you at noon tomorrow outside the gates. Do not be late.'

'I'm not fighting your stupid war!' the boy cried. He backed away a few steps and then turned and ran.

'You want me to send someone after him?' Toram asked.

Barandas noticed Thurbal watching him. He had a smug look on his face. 'No,' he replied. His grip tightened on his sword. 'I'll fetch him. He needs to learn some respect.' He paused for a moment. 'You can begin another round of inquiries immediately. Use whatever methods you deem necessary.'

'Yes, my lord.' The lieutenant saluted and left to organize his men.

Barandas set off in the direction the boy had fled, intending to give him a good dressing down, when he almost collided with a horse travelling in the opposite direction. The merchant astride the beast immediately hopped down and offered up his profuse apologies.

'I am terribly sorry, my lord,' he gushed, wiping nervously at his forehead. 'I was in a rush. I have been riding for the best part of a day and night.'

'Indeed.' Barandas felt his head beginning to ache. This interruption had probably cost him the opportunity to chase down the boy. Perhaps that was for the best, all things considered. 'Would you care to elaborate on why you are in such a hurry?'

The merchant nodded, eager to make amends for his error. 'It's Farrowgate, my lord. The village has been saved! Some brave Highlanders and their companions slew the dreadful abomination that had been preying on its residents. Of course,' he added, with a conspiratorial grin, 'where there is disaster there is opportunity. The village is in desperate need of supplies. The early bird gets the worm, hmm?'

Farrowgate. Barandas had forgotten about the tiny settlement on the outskirts of the territory. He had intended to send a small detachment of Watchmen to investigate the reports of monstrous activity, but he had been so busy with war preparations the last couple of weeks that it had slipped his mind completely. 'You mentioned Highlanders?'

'Indeed. Two of them. Grim fellows. They looked in pretty rough shape, what with their injuries and all, but I tell you: I wouldn't like to be the man who got on the wrong side of them.'

Barandas stared. *Highlanders... the Wailing Rift!*

The loss of the Rift meant the creation of new Augmentors was now entirely dependent upon the successful return of the ships sent to the Swell. If he could do a single thing right this

287

day, it would be to enact justice on the bastards who collapsed the mine.

'Thurbal,' he said, moving to stand before his scowling deputy. He could hear that strange ticking sound again, the same noise he had heard during the temple massacre. 'The scoundrels who sabotaged the Rift have been spotted in Farrowgate. Retrieve your scimitar and gather Garmond and a score of Watchmen.'

The grey-haired Augmentor rose to his feet immediately. His scowl was gone, replaced by the happy grin of a child who has just been handed an unexpected gift. 'Garmond's already here.'

Barandas turned away from the deputy to see the giant Augmentor approaching. He was dragging something along the ground.

It was a body of a young man. The corpse was coated in dirt and the head was a bloody mess, but the boy's identity was unmistakable.

'Caught him trying to flee town,' Garmond said. 'He won't be going anywhere now.'

Barandas stared at the broken skull of the quarryman and then up at Garmond. *He's a monster. But what can I do? Discipline him? The boy was a deserter.* He turned to Lieutenant Toram.

'The gold you were to present to this lad's mother? Double it. Tell her... tell her there's been a terrible accident. He slipped and fell into the quarry.'

'Aye, my lord.'

Barandas closed his eyes. It had been a long and difficult day. He longed to return to his comfortable estate in the Noble Quarter and take Lena in his arms. Before he could do that, however, he needed to check in on Marshal Halendorf and review how recruitment elsewhere was faring.

When duty beckoned, a man had no choice but to answer its call. Duty was what defined him; it gave him purpose in a world of chaos and uncertainty.

A man who neglected his duty was no man at all.

Bonds of Blood

BRODAR KAYNE SHIFTED on the old mattress and looked out of the window beside him. The sun was out, casting its warmth down on the small farming settlement. Villagers went about their daily routines in a perfunctory manner, still coming to terms with the disaster that had befallen the community. Only the timely arrival of their small group had saved Farrowgate from utter destruction.

He stared up at the sun until tears stung his eyes. The physician, Gaius, had warned him to keep away from bright light as a precaution, but he couldn't resist. He had been without his sight for the best part of three days. There was a moment of absolute terror when he thought he might never see again, and that had unmanned him in a way he hadn't thought possible. To his great relief, his vision had returned shortly after.

The infection in his wound had cleared and his flesh was well on the way to knitting itself back together. As an unexpected bonus, the prolonged rest had eased the aches and pains that had been troubling him for months. All things considered, he was feeling better than he had in years.

There was a knock at the door. He sat up on the bed and then pushed himself to his feet. 'That you, lass?' he said.

Sasha entered the room, looking annoyed. She frowned at him with those big dark eyes of hers. 'You should be in bed.'

He made a face. 'It's been three weeks. I reckon that's about long enough.' He ran a rough hand over his beard and grimaced.

How long had it been since he last shaved? *Too bloody long.* 'Don't suppose you got something with an edge on you, lass? I ain't going to risk nicking myself with Magebane over yonder.'

Sasha sighed. On those rare occasions when she wasn't scowling or looking as though she was about to hit someone, she was a fine-looking girl. With him confined to bed, the fractious relationship between her and Jerek had apparently deteriorated. He hoped Isaac was doing his best to keep them apart.

'Men,' she said. 'Little more than apes, beating your chests to show the world how big and strong you are. I'd have thought a man your age would know better.' She shook her head and pointed at him accusingly. 'You're worse, if anything.'

He tried to keep the smile from his face as she glowered at him. 'Got to keep active,' he responded. 'There's a saying in the High Fangs. "A man who hangs up his sword is a man with one foot in the grave." I've still got some life in me yet.'

Sasha placed her hands on her hips. 'You'll have a lot more if you don't insist on acting like an old fool.'

He stared at her for a time, said nothing. *You could have been back in Dorminia by now. You didn't need to remain here with us. Isaac would have gone with you, kept an eye out on the road.*

As if reading his thoughts, her scowl grew even fiercer. *And it ain't like you're some helpless damsel in distress yourself.*

He cleared his throat. 'Gaius says you came to check on me while I was recovering. You didn't need to stick around. I appreciate it, I guess is what I'm trying to say.'

Sasha looked about as uncomfortable as he felt, which was to say very. 'Well, I owed you that much. You've been true to your word. Of course,' she added, 'after what happened at the Rift, you won't want to return to the city any time soon.'

'Aye. You have that right.'

A travelling merchant had brought word of recent events to the village. Shadowport had been destroyed, the entire city buried beneath the waves. Now Dorminia was preparing to repel an invasion from Thelassa. He had hardly been able to believe it when Isaac had brought him the news.

Jerek had been furious. 'Fucking priceless,' he had rasped. 'So what, now we're gonna stroll into an ant's nest of the red-cloaked cocksuckers while they're getting ready to go to war? Might as well slit our throats now.'

The fact was, setting foot any nearer the city than they already were would be asking for trouble. They were lucky the soldiers that had come to investigate the disturbance at the mine had not pursued them as far as Farrowgate; it was even more fortunate that with conscription happening all over this part of the Trine, the village had so far avoided a visit from the Crimson Watch.

We'd stick out like a sore thumb, he thought. Even if the disaster at the Wailing Rift couldn't be pinned on them, there was that incident with the two Watchmen and the Shard stripling. Someone was bound to have witnessed their bloody encounter.

Sasha was still watching him. 'Since we can't go west,' he said carefully, 'I reckon me and the Wolf will head east towards the Unclaimed Lands.'

'You don't have a copper to your name.'

He gestured at the faintly glowing dagger on the table next to the bed.

She narrowed her eyes. 'That isn't yours to sell.'

'I had an agreement with your gaffer. Thirty gold spires for accompanying you safely to the Rift. That, or the weapon there.'

Sasha sighed. 'Look, I'll get your gold. Give me Magebane and I promise that I'll have it delivered to you. You have my word.'

The old Highlander scratched his beard. It didn't seem right, pawning something as precious as that dagger. He reckoned he could trust the girl, but to say Jerek might take a different view would be like wondering if a Highland cat wouldn't mind a poke in the eye.

'Where is the Wolf?' he asked.

'Hunting. I've barely seen him for days, which suits me just fine.'

'He ain't the man you think he is, lass.'

Sasha's lip curled. 'You might have tried convincing me of that before he almost took my head off and then repeatedly threatened to kill me. Three times in the last week, in fact – and as I said, *I've barely seen him.*'

'In fairness,' the Highlander ventured, 'he was provoked. You did stick a quarrel in his arm. The Wolf's got a temper on him and I'll be the first to admit it.'

'A temper? He's a black-hearted bastard! I know all about men like him.' She paused for a moment. 'You're different to him. I don't know what kind of bond you two have, but the best thing you can do is to cut him loose. He'll bring you down eventually.'

Kayne rubbed at his forehead. He didn't want to have this conversation. 'Like I said, he ain't the man you think he is.'

'Fine,' Sasha huffed. 'Be stubborn, but don't say I didn't warn you. I'm going to find Isaac. It's time we made plans to leave this damned village.'

He watched her storm out. The girl seemed awfully tense, like a bowstring about ready to snap. She'd been that way ever since Vicard's death. *Must have been closer to the alchemist than I thought.*

With a satisfied groan he reached down and touched his toes. Then he rolled his shoulders and flexed his back, forcing his muscles into their old routine of familiarity. Age could rob a warrior of many things, but as long as the body and the mind *remembered*, everything else was trivial. You just had to fight through the pain.

There was another knock on the door, this one more hesitant. 'Come in,' he said. It was Gaius. The old physician was a

292

wrinkled prune of a man, as thin as a rake, with a balding crown covered in a few strands of grey hair.

'Ah, you're up,' said the physician. 'I see you're feeling much better. I have to say, you heal remarkably quickly. Is this a trait common to all you Highland folk?'

Kayne shrugged. 'I guess so.'

'A highly convenient attribute, I should imagine, with all the fighting and adventuring and such you people do.'

'Probably.'

Gaius walked over to a cabinet and rummaged around inside a drawer. 'I see you found the moon dust. You know, consuming so much of the drug in so short a time is unhealthy.'

'What?' He had no idea what the physician was talking about.

'The silvery powder that was inside this small pouch here. An anaesthetic with considerable mood-stimulant properties. I quite understand why you would want to dull the pain. Still, you are aware moon dust can be highly addictive? The side effects are rather unpleasant.'

Kayne frowned. 'What side effects are those?'

'Oh, they can vary depending upon the individual. Dilation of the pupils. Intense periods of depression following the initial emotional response. In prolonged cases of abuse, the membrane of the nose itself can become weak, leading to permanent scarring.' Gaius looked at him with a concerned expression. 'Are you experiencing any of these? Here, let me check...'

'Er, I think I'm all right,' the barbarian protested as the physician poked around at his face and stared up into his nose.

'You don't seem to have any lasting damage,' Gaius said. His voice took on a slightly disapproving tone. 'However, I am going to have to insist you do not consume any more of the substance once the merchant returns here with fresh supplies. There are many others in the village that would benefit from a small measure, and you appear to be in rude health.'

'Right you are,' Kayne replied. 'Sorry about that. In any case, I'll be leaving soon.'

'I'm sad to hear it. Farrowgate could use a warrior like you for protection. Who will defend us with Augmentor Rorshan gone and Dorminia at war? These are troubling times.'

'Aye,' the Highlander responded. 'They are that. If you'll excuse me, I need to get some air.'

He found Sasha and Isaac by the ancient well in the centre of the village. They were sitting on a bench overgrown with moss, enjoying the last of the sun. The manservant was instructing a small group of children on the best way to handle a sword, using a stick to demonstrate. The youngsters watched him with expressions of delight, excitement and determination. No doubt many of them had lost loved ones to the magical abomination that had ravaged the community.

Poor things, he thought. The world was a cruel place, and as far as he could see it wasn't getting any kinder as the years rolled by.

Sasha looked up as he approached. *Wide eyes. Dilated pupils. Aye, lass, I'm onto you. It wasn't just concern for my well-being that kept you here, was it?*

Isaac spotted him. A delighted grin split the manservant's face. 'Kayne!' he exclaimed. 'You're looking well! Here, come and help me out. Show these children how a true master handles a blade.'

The old Highlander tried to hide his embarrassment as the children turned and stared up at him with grubby faces full of wonder. A freckle-faced girl gave him a gap-toothed smile. The boy next to her wiped snot from his chin with the back of his hand and gave it a good hard examination.

'I reckon I'll need a sword first,' he said, nodding at the stick in Isaac's hands. The manservant tossed it to him. He stood there uncertainly. 'Right,' he said. His audience watched him expectantly.

The girl with the freckles piped up. 'How did you get that scar? Did a bear do it?'

'This one?' he said, pointing at the side of his face. 'It wasn't a bear that did that. It was outlaws, exiles from their Reaching. Bad people.'

'Did they rape you?' asked the girl.

'What? No. No, they didn't.'

'What happened?' asked one of the younger boys.

'I was out hunting with my son. They ambushed us from a stand of trees. Four of them.'

'You have a son? What's his name? What happened to him?' The girl leaned forwards, her face full of curiosity.

He glanced at Sasha and Isaac. They were watching him closely. 'His name... Magnar. His name was Magnar.'

'Where is he?' The girl again.

Kayne closed his eyes. 'Gone,' he said.

'What do you mean? Did he die?'

Might be less painful if he had. He sat there and watched his mother burn in the Shaman's fire. I never raised him to be a coward, but he sat there and said nothing as his mother's screams pounded in my skull.

'It's getting late,' he said, deciding to change the subject entirely. 'Why don't you younglings grab yourselves a stick each? We'll see if we can make warriors out of you all before the sun goes down.'

The assembled children all jumped to their feet and ran off to find make-believe swords, with the exception of the freckle-faced girl who gave him a sulky look. 'You didn't tell me what happened to your son!' She pointed an accusing finger at him.

He sighed. 'I—'

'*Kayne.* Grab your sword. *We're fucked.*' Jerek burst into the clearing, sending children scattering away in panic. His burned face was dripping with perspiration. Heedless of his surroundings, he wiped sweat from his brow and spat out a goblet of phlegm.

Kayne grimaced. His interrogator stared down at the spittle covering the bottom of her dress and, with a horrified wail, turned and ran off. Kayne gave the Wolf a disapproving frown that wasn't the least bit genuine. 'What's going on?' he asked.

Jerek's chest heaved as he sucked in air. He had obviously been running hard. 'A score of Crimson Watchmen, maybe more. Approaching on horseback from the north-west. They got Augmentors with them, one of them a giant of some kind.'

'How far?'

Jerek spat again. 'A league, could be. Maybe a league and a half. They ain't messing around. They're armed to the teeth. I reckon we got twenty minutes before they get here.'

Brodar Kayne turned to Sasha and Isaac. 'Listen. If they catch us things are gonna get bloody. We can't fight that many men, but we can lead them away from here. Give you two a chance to make good an escape.'

Sasha shook her head. 'What about you? You'll be hunted down and slaughtered.'

He gave her a level stare. 'I've escaped death often enough in the past, lass. If this is my time, so be it. But you and Isaac, you still got a chance of getting out of this alive.'

It was the manservant's turn to shake his head. 'I know the groom over at the stables. He has a few horses that didn't fall victim to the tentacled monster. They're not the quickest, but they might get us to the coast.'

Sasha nodded. 'The Unclaimed Lands are too far. We'll be ridden down and slaughtered. Maybe if we can cross over into Thelassan territory—'

'You planning to swim the channel?' Jerek snarled. 'Ain't a man alive who can do that. And we got thirty miles to the coast. I say we hole up here, give those fuckers the fight of their lives.'

'No!' exclaimed Sasha. 'We can't do that to these people. I know the Watch. They'll torch the entire village if it means getting to us.'

'Aye, she's right.' Kayne took a step forwards. 'Isaac, fetch the horses. I'll go get my sword. We'll give them a chase they'll remember.'

Jerek turned away and muttered something savage. Kayne ignored him. He was already running back towards the physician's home where his greatsword was stashed.

Three weeks, he thought. *Three weeks of peace. I've never felt so relaxed and carefree.* His feet hammered on the dry muddy ground, sending jarring impacts up to his knees. They were already starting to ache. There was something almost comforting in that.

It took him a moment before he realized he had a smile on his face.

'Not much further,' Isaac shouted. He was out in front again, having taken the lead for most of their mad gallop from Farrowgate. To the surprise of none of them, it turned out he was a skilled rider. Brodar Kayne knew how to handle a horse, but even he'd found the uncertain terrain a challenge. The manservant, however, had guided them with an assuredness the chasing soldiers could not hope to match.

It had been almost two hours since they fled the village. The sun was a red orb sinking beneath the hills to the west. He could feel his horse heaving beneath him, sucking in great gasps of air. It couldn't keep up the pace much longer, but it didn't need to. The coast was only a few miles ahead of them.

The question of what they would do when they actually reached the coast was another matter entirely, but he figured it was enough to focus on one thing at a time.

He glanced behind him. The soldiers had gained some ground over the last ten miles, but there was still a good distance between them. Gaius had evidently succeeded in delaying them for a while back at Farrowgate. He hoped the physician had followed his advice and not been too obstinate with their pursuers; he didn't want to be responsible for the kindly old man taking a beating or worse.

Sasha was clinging onto Isaac for dear life. The girl wasn't very familiar with the back of a horse. That had become apparent as soon as she had vaulted onto her mount and promptly slid off to land in an undignified heap on the other side. At least Jerek had had a good chuckle out of it.

The Wolf tugged at his reins, closing the gap between them. 'Kayne,' he rasped. 'We're almost at the coast. What's the plan?'

Right. A plan. Can't put it off any longer. 'We split up,' he said. 'I'll get their attention, try and lead them west. You look for a way across the channel. Failing that, loop back around to the north.'

Jerek took a second to digest his words. 'That's it?' he growled. 'Fuck me, and there I was thinking you knew something I didn't.'

The old barbarian shrugged. The horse beneath him stumbled suddenly, sending spasms of pain arching up his back. 'Best outcome we can hope for is that they split their pursuit,' he said between clenched teeth. 'Three against ten, I reckon you stand a chance. Ain't a hunter or tracker who can match you, Wolf, and you know it.'

'Could be,' Jerek agreed. 'But that don't help you much, does it?'

'Just lead the girl and Isaac to safety and forget about me.'

'Don't start with that shit.'

'You saved my life once already. I reckon your debt's just about paid.'

Jerek's face grew dark. 'It's paid when I say it's paid. I ain't leaving you to die. You want some noble death so maidens can get themselves wet thinking about your heroic sacrifice? Shove it up your arse, Kayne.' The Wolf spurred his mount and the horse pulled away, taking him out of earshot.

Shit. Jerek was about as stubborn as he was, which meant his hastily formulated plan was dead in the water. *Shortly to be followed by us, I reckon.* He could see the edge of Deadman's Channel now, the water glittering orange in the dying light.

His horse shuddered again. He patted the mare on the neck and his hand came away covered in lather. The beast reared suddenly, and before he knew it he was flying from the saddle as the animal stumbled to its knees.

He hit the ground with an impact that forced the air from his lungs. The pain was excruciating. He gasped, rolled three or four times down the slope before coming to a halt against a jutting slab of rock. He lay there in agony, listening to the pathetic sounds of his horse expiring nearby.

Somehow he rolled over and managed to lift his head. Jerek and Isaac had ridden on for a few hundred yards, oblivious to his misfortune. The Wolf must have noticed his absence then, as he swung his gelding around and thundered back towards him.

Kayne pushed himself up from the ground as Jerek drew near. He could see their pursuers closing on them with alarming pace.

'Grab my hand,' the Wolf snarled as he brought his horse around. Kayne reached out, grasped the scarred hand of the grim Highlander and pulled himself up behind him.

The Wolf kicked down hard, sending the animal beneath them galloping ahead at full tilt, every strike of every hoof against the hard ground igniting fresh spasms of pain throughout Kayne's body.

Isaac had slowed. They caught up with him just as they approached the edge of Deadman's Channel. The manservant shouted something and pointed down to the water. Kayne shielded his eyes from the sun and tried to make out what Isaac was gesturing at.

It was a small caravel. The ship was anchored barely fifty feet from the shoreline. He could make out a handful of figures watching their approach from the railing. *Shit*. Had another force been sent to intercept them?

As they grew nearer, however, he realized this vessel was not from Dorminia. The flag that flew from the mainmast displayed a circle of stars on a white background. Inside the circle a woman's outstretched palm supported a cluster of towers. Kayne didn't know much of the land south of Dorminia and its hinterland, but he was reasonably certain this was a Thelassan ship.

Several of the figures aboard the vessel had lowered themselves onto a tiny boat and were paddling towards them. He squinted. The man at the bow wore dark robes of some kind, but his hood was thrown back to reveal skin as black as the night. Behind him—

Sasha gasped. 'It can't be...'

The dinghy reached the shallows and the young man in the middle of the boat vaulted out and splashed towards them. That swagger, that ridiculous beard, the cocksure smile: they were unmistakable.

'Sash!' the boy exclaimed in delight. 'How long has it been? A month? I have some stories to tell you! Here, meet my new companions. This is the Darkson, a master assassin from Shamaath. And this' – he pointed at the largest of the three men wading through the surf – 'is Three-Finger. He's my henchman.' This last one was an ugly fellow with thinning hair and an unpleasant skin disease ravaging his face. He looked faintly annoyed as the boy finished his introductions.

'Greetings,' lisped the dark-skinned newcomer. Kayne narrowed his eyes. The way this one moved, the confidence with which he appraised their ragged little band – everything about him spoke of the kind of man who was as comfortable killing as he was breathing.

The assassin continued, 'I see you, too, are familiar with Davarus Cole. You must be Brodar Kayne.'

The old barbarian swung around on the horse and lowered himself gingerly to the ground. 'Aye, pleasure to meet you,' he said. He glanced back up the hill, where two dozen men approached them on horseback, outlined in red by the departing sun. He cleared his throat.

'Before we continue with the introductions, I guess I ought to mention a small matter that's going to require our attention pretty damned soon...'

Dark Omens

YLLANDRIS TURNED TO the man in the bed beside her. Magnar watched her from beneath half-closed eyes. His deep breathing was the only sound from within the bedchamber. Outside the storm raged on, the shrieking wind a terrifying animal that threatened to tear the roof from the Great Lodge and reveal their nakedness to the world.

'You are troubled,' she observed. The mingled smells of sweat and sex and smoke created an aroma that was not altogether unpleasant. She placed a hand on his face. His cheeks were smooth. Many Highland men wore their beards long in celebration of their manhood, but Magnar had always kept his face clean-shaven. It was a brave choice considering his youth, an open invitation to scorn from the older chieftains. It seemed the young king had confidence enough not to care.

'I am uneasy,' he admitted. His steely grey eyes held a hint of worry. 'The Shaman summoned the Brethren away from the High Fangs. What right does the Tyrant of Dorminia have to demand our Magelord do such a thing?'

Yllandris remembered the ease with which the frail old man had turned Shranree's magic against her. The senior sister of the Heartstone circle was possibly the most powerful sorceress in the High Fangs, yet Salazar had handled her as he might a child – and, moreover, he had been near exhausted while he had done so.

'I cannot say, my king. The ways of Magelords are not easily fathomed. Did the Shaman give any indication when they will return?'

Magnar shook his head. He was a handsome man, with a strong nose and jaw. His torso was lean but well muscled and his chest still glistened with sweat from their recent lovemaking. She felt her body stir as she gazed upon him.

'We may be without our sacred protectors for some time,' said the King. 'I have instructed Orgrim to post additional men on the northern and southern borders of the East Reaching.' He paused for a moment and sighed. 'The Foehammer was not happy with the order.'

'Orgrim took the greatest losses at Frosthold,' Yllandris replied. 'And the East Reaching has suffered the most in recent years. The Foehammer does not want to expose his largest settlements to the Devil's Spine by posting his men to the frontiers.'

King Magnar nodded. 'That was the gist of his argument. Yet the East Reaching is the barrier between our nation and the horrors that lurk in the Spine. I cannot allow demons to wander unchallenged into the other Reachings.'

A howling gust of wind rattled the roof once more and Magnar sighed again. 'I've done my best to win the respect of my chieftains. It is no easy thing to stave off famine and keep the tribes from each other's throats while managing the Shaman's whims. He listens to me sometimes, but still... I feel as if I am caught between a cave bear and a pack of wolves. I try to placate the former while the latter look for any opportunity to pounce.'

Yllandris was puzzled. 'You rule with the Shaman's blessing,' she said. 'Who would dare try to depose you?'

'Krazka One-Eye and Carn Bloodfist, to name but two. Many desire the throne. The Code dictates that all men and women swear allegiance to the king – yet it is also written that a weak king must be usurped for the good of the nation.'

'And the Shaman is the arbiter in such matters,' Yllandris said softly.

'If another proves himself more worthy, the Shaman will not hesitate to replace me.'

'As you replaced Jagar the Wise?'

Magnar nodded. 'I did not seek the throne. Jagar was dying. His rule had outlasted that of any previous king. The Shaman could have chosen any one of the ten chieftains.' He looked up at the ceiling. 'Yet out of respect for my father he chose me.'

'Out of respect for your *father*?' Yllandris repeated, shocked. 'But what he did to him... The Shaman wants nothing more than to see your father dead.'

'Yes,' Magnar replied. 'He does. But that anger is born out of the love he once held for him. Father was the closest thing to a friend the Shaman has known. He did not expect the answer he received from his champion when Beregund rebelled. And it *was* a rebellion. The Green Reaching intended to break the Treaty and begin a civil war. The Shaman's response was justified.'

He burned your mother alive, Yllandris thought, but wisely she held her tongue. Instead she said, 'Do you know where your father might be hiding?'

Magnar shook his head. 'The Unclaimed Lands, perhaps. The Brethren hunted him for two years without success. His companion is a tracker without peer.'

His companion. The Wolf. The man who freed the Sword of the North from his prison was almost as infamous as Kayne himself. Horribly burned and with a savage temper to match his prowess, no one would have guessed he would be the one to enact a daring rescue. Apparently he had owed Kayne a debt from many years past.

Yllandris had set eyes on the Wolf only once, a few months before the trial of Brodar Kayne. The thought of two Highlanders somehow evading the Brethren for months on end was difficult to credit – yet the memory of his scowling visage, so utterly implacable, convinced her that this was a man capable of anything.

When it came to the likes of Brodar Kayne and Jerek the Wolf, it seemed even the will of a Magelord could be defied. The thought gave her pause.

The King was still staring at the ceiling, a strange expression in his remarkable eyes. Yllandris decided to take a risk. She needed to know. 'It must be hard for you,' she said carefully. 'What happened to your father. What was done to your mother.'

Magnar looked at her. His expression was unreadable. 'Do you think me a monster?'

The question shocked her. She stared at him for a moment, lost for words. *Not a monster. My father was a monster.* 'I do not judge you,' she said carefully. 'You did what was necessary. Your father was guilty. Your mother...' She trailed off, unsure of how to proceed. This was so very delicate. She still desired his attentions, didn't she? She thought she did. There was no sense in angering him. Yet...

He watched his mother burn.

'My mother...' Magnar said, and she could hear the pain in his voice. 'Some things a king must do haunt him forever. It could not be helped.'

Yllandris stared at him. She remembered cowering in the corner of her small bunk, listening to those awful cries. It was the silences that followed that had terrified her the most; the moment those appalling noises ceased and her father had walked back out into the night. That handful of steps to the crumpled form of her mother – like walking out onto a frozen lake, not knowing if the ice would break and the darkness would swallow her up. Until one night it had.

That was helplessness. What Magnar spoke of was cowardice. She couldn't stop the words from bursting out. 'You're the King,' she sneered. 'You could have stood up to the Shaman. How could you allow your own mother to be consumed by fire?'

Magnar's face darkened. 'You know nothing,' he said angrily. He rose up from the bed and began pulling on his clothes.

Yllandris pushed herself up, reaching for her silk robes and the shawl that lay in a heap beside the bed. 'What of Krazka?' she asked, more quietly. 'He raped her, didn't he? Before she was brought back to Heartstone. How can you stand to look at him?'

This time Magnar's anger was not so restrained. He grabbed her hair from behind and pulled her around to face him. His eyes were iron fury. 'Krazka is the most powerful chieftain in the High Fangs,' he said, his voice shaking. 'You think it's easy for me to listen to his counsel? I want nothing more than to cut out his black heart. Were it not for the Shaman's bargain and the risk of civil war—'

A sudden howling interrupted him, so loud that the walls of the bedchamber seemed to shake.

'The Shaman's bargain?' Yllandris was intrigued in spite of the painful grip Magnar had on her hair. She could thrust him away with a brief unveiling of her sorcery, of course, but that would amount to treason – punishable by death. Fortunately the King seemed to realize he was hurting her. He let go and stepped away.

'There are many things you do not know. It is best if you leave my presence immediately. You presume too much.'

Yllandris was about to give an angry curtsy and storm off when they both heard the shouts and screams from outside.

'What is it?' Magnar demanded. His guards had their hands on their weapons and were staring up at the sky as if their eyes could pierce the flurry of snow billowing from the dark blanket of grey above them. Yllandris stood beside the King, shivering. It was late afternoon, but it might have been the middle of the night for all the visibility the snowstorm provided.

'We're under attack,' shouted a nearby warrior. He had a longbow pulled back and an arrow ready to loose at any moment. 'It struck from nowhere. Pulled Varamus into the sky and tore him clean in half.'

'It took my girl,' a woman cried. She was on her knees in the deep snow, her head in her hands. A score of men emerged from the blizzard, all with arrows nocked and ready. The biggest of them approached; she recognized Yorn. His hands were covered in blood.

'We've got a score dead already. The demon's snatching up folk and scattering parts of 'em all over town. We can't get a clear shot on the thing.' He shook his head and spat. 'It's huge. Wings like a bat, with talons that can rend a man in half.'

'Gather a hundred men,' Magnar ordered. 'Split them into groups, five men each. Have them patrol every part of town until the fiend is spotted. Yllandris, gather the rest of your circle. I want this demon blasted out of the sky.'

She did as she was commanded, hurrying off towards the small hill overlooking the west side of Heartstone. As it happened, Shranree and two other sorceresses were already on their way to the Great Lodge. They almost ran into her moving in the opposite direction.

'Sister, what is happening here?' asked Shranree, in between gasps for breath. She frowned suddenly. 'You appear rather inadequately garbed for this inclement weather, I must say.'

Yllandris sighed. She had hoped the woman's near-death experience at Mehmon's trial might have sapped some of her hubris, but the leader of the Heartstone circle was already returning to her overbearing self. 'We are under assault,' she replied. 'A winged demon haunts the skies above us. I believe it was the same monster that attacked the Brethren some weeks past.' *The same monster that was watching us at Frosthold.* She decided to say nothing of that.

Shranree clapped her hands together. 'Dastardly fiend! Does it seek to take advantage of the Shaman's absence? Come, sisters. We will hunt down this demon and make it sorry it ever left the Spine.'

There was a shout from somewhere to the north. The four sorceresses hurried towards the sound. Along the way they passed the remains of a Highlander, his belly opened to reveal steaming entrails. Yllandris wiped snow from her eyes, squinting to catch sight of the men ahead of her.

Suddenly a body crashed down into the snow nearby. They rushed over, but the man was dead before he hit the ground. A massive wound almost split his torso in half.

'It is above us,' Shranree whispered. A band of men appeared, Yorn leading them. Thurva was with the group. She saw her sisters and hurried over to join them.

'The thing is so fast,' she said breathlessly. 'My magic could barely touch it. The men's arrows have little impact. If only the Brethren were here. Or the Shaman.'

'They are not,' said Shranree. 'And so we must deal with it ourselves.'

The air rustled ominously. There was a dark streak in the sky far above and then the fiend was there among them, its taloned foot closing around the unfortunate warrior next to Yorn. The man screamed and spewed blood as those terrible claws sliced into his body.

Yllandris gasped, horrified at the sheer size of the demon. *It must be twenty feet tall.* Its wings were wider still. The head was part human and part reptilian. Three red eyes filled with malevolence stared out above a mouthful of pointed teeth resembling ivory daggers. A snaking tail whipped the ground with enough force to pulverize flesh and bone.

The warriors released their arrows. Most bounced off the thing's black hide. A couple lodged in its scales to no discernible effect. The warriors threw their useless bows to the ground and drew their swords, closing to surround the creature, but with a single mighty beat of its gigantic wings it rose above them and they were left to stare up at it helplessly.

Shranree threw her arms into the air. 'Sisters, link with me,' she shrieked.

Yllandris closed her eyes and did as the senior sister commanded, feeling her magic drain into the older woman. Shranree gasped as the power filled her. Flame danced around her hands and then lanced towards the winged horror. The demon hissed as the fire wreathed its midnight form. With another beat of its great wings it took to the skies, dropping the lifeless corpse of the Highlander like a broken doll.

The fiend disappeared from sight almost immediately, swallowed up by the relentless blizzard, but Shranree was not done. Shrieking in ecstasy, she sent the dancing flame up and after the apparition. A couple of seconds passed and then, like a rope, the flaming lasso tightened.

There was an enraged hiss from high above them. With a tugging motion, Shranree yanked downwards and the black colossus was brought crashing to the earth, the chain of fire wrapped tight around its legs. It smashed into a tavern in an explosion of flaming debris. A loud cheer went up and suddenly Heartstone's warriors were converging on the fallen demon, swords and axes bristling.

The fire wreathing Shranree's hands flickered and disappeared. She sagged in exhaustion. Yllandris, too, felt drained to the point of collapse. The magic they had expended in bringing down the fiend had sapped the last reserves of her power. It was all she could do to turn and stare at the wreckage through the waning snowstorm.

The burning ruins of the tavern shifted suddenly. Somehow the fiend was still alive. It rose, staggered a few steps, and then beat its ruined wings. Dust and rubble exploded from its blistered skin. In a lurching run, it turned and fled north towards the main gates. Arrows rained down around it, but even with its grievous injuries the demon easily outpaced the pursuing warriors. Yllandris watched on, horrified. *What manner of creature can survive such punishment?*

The sound of horses caught her attention and she turned to see Magnar seated on his mighty stallion, the Six mounted behind him. The King raised his sword in the air. 'I will hunt the demon down! Any man who wishes to join me is welcome. I want that bastard's head above my hearth.'

There was a loud cheer as the King and his elite guards passed through the town towards the gates. Men went to fetch their horses or banded together to set off after the royal war party. Within half an hour, almost every warrior in Heartstone had departed to join the hunt. Those that remained behind began the task of clearing the streets of the dead and putting out the fires that had erupted in the wake of the demon's plummet from the sky.

Yllandris counted over forty dead. Men, women and children – the fiend had not discriminated in its brief tour of destruction. *One demon did all this*, she thought. *The spirits help us if more of those creatures emerge from the Devil's Spine.*

Shranree strode up to her as she was dragging the corpse of a teenage boy from the rubble of the tavern. The older sorceress was tired and covered in sweat but her eyes were bright. *Revelling in your triumph, no doubt. Will you shed a tear for this family inadvertently killed by your hand, Shranree? I doubt it.*

'You did well, sister,' said the rotund woman with a smile. 'Perhaps you will indeed make a worthy sorceress one day.'

'I can only hope.'

Shranree looked around at the blackened corpses and tutted. 'If they had been out there helping during the attack, they would have avoided this unfortunate end. I believe there is a lesson to be learned here.'

Yllandris gritted her teeth. 'I suppose so.'

'This latest incident demonstrates the need for more sorceresses in the city.'

That was something Yllandris could agree with. 'Yes, sister.'

'Perhaps when the King returns you might speak with him? I suspect he would be most receptive to your counsel. After all, you share much, do you not?' The woman's expression was unreadable.

'I do not understand.'

Shranree smiled sweetly. 'Why, a young man's desires are

vast and often indiscriminate. And of course, one should always strive to please her king in every way possible.'

'As… as you say, sister.'

'Still,' Shranree continued. 'One must also respect tradition. A sorceress may not marry. It weakens the magic, you know.' She went silent for a time. When she spoke again, her eyes were hard. 'Put aside any girlish fantasies you may be harbouring about our handsome young king. You are mine until I deem you worthy, and quite frankly that may very well be never.' She sighed suddenly. 'Really, Yllandris. Do you seriously think Magnar would consider marrying *you*?'

Go jump off a cliff, you spiteful old hag. 'He enjoys spending time with me. I listen to him. I provide him the comfort he needs.'

Shranree shook her head and sighed in exasperation. 'So would a whore.' She turned and waddled off, casting a distasteful glance at the bodies of the family that had run the tavern.

Yllandris watched her leave. When Magnar came back she would apologize for her earlier remarks. He would forgive her, she knew. He cherished her honesty. He had his faults, but Magnar was young, handsome, and above all he was the King. And for her that meant one thing.

I will be Queen.

Beneath Notice

THE NEWS HAD reached the city earlier that morning. Thelassa's mercenary army was on the move. Over thirty ships had departed the City of Towers and would be docking somewhere to the west over the next day or two. The remnants of Dorminia's naval force were even now spread out in a defensive arc about the harbour in case the enemy fleet tried to attack the city from the sea.

Eremul shifted uncomfortably again on his chair, silently cursing the numerous physical ailments that had assailed him of late. Grand Magistrate Timerus arched an eyebrow at him. 'Is something troubling you?'

The hawk-nosed steward of the city's affairs missed little. Of all the men seated around the huge table in the Grand Council Chamber, Eremul judged him to be the most dangerous – with the exception, of course, of the evil old bastard brooding on his obsidian throne.

'Only the thought of our beloved city besieged by the White Lady's mercenaries,' replied the Halfmage. 'Ah, that and the small matter of the lump protruding from my arse.'

The new Master of Information frowned. It was the ratty old physician he had seen tending to Salazar in the dungeons. What was his name? Remy? The man had apparently earned his position for some service he had performed for the Council in weeks past. Of the thirteen magistrates that had been present during the attempt on Salazar's life, only four had survived.

New magistrates had been sworn in to replace those killed, but three seats still remained empty. It would seem that men possessed of the qualities to serve the city in the highest capacity were difficult to find. *Deceitfulness, cowardice, shameless arse-lickery. Why haven't I been made a magistrate?*

'Warm water with lavender extract,' said Remy. 'Apply twice daily, before and after rest—'

'The Halfmage is not here to discuss his well-being,' said the Supreme Augmentor, interrupting the physician-turned-spymaster. 'He is to help prepare the city's defences against the three thousand Sumnians who will soon be at our gates.'

Marshal Halendorf adjusted his collar and wiped at his brow, which was soaked in sweat. The fleshy commander of Dorminia's army looked pale and was obviously unwell, but the urgency of the situation had demanded his presence at this council meeting.

'The Watch number a thousand strong,' he said. 'The camp east of the city holds seven thousand militia. My officers are doing the best they can to beat them into an army worth a damn, but they are proving obstinate.'

'Obstinate?' repeated Salazar. Eremul almost shuddered at the annoyance in the Magelord's voice. Creator knew he wanted nothing more than to see Salazar dead, but the truth was that the Tyrant of Dorminia terrified him more than anything else in the world. 'They are reluctant to defend their homes? Their families?'

Marshal Halendorf went even paler. 'They... ah, that is to say...'

'Yes, Marshal?'

'My lord... It's been said by some that the White Lady doesn't intend to destroy the city. Rather, she wants to, ah, liberate it.'

'*Liberate it.*' The Magelord repeated the words slowly, as if every syllable was a thousand-ton hammer beating down on the men in the chamber.

Eremul could feel his heart thumping in his chest. He wished he were anywhere but here at this table. Even down in the dungeons, strapped to a cold slab. At least the men who had cut off his legs were, loosely speaking, human. They had probably felt *something* while mutilating him, even if it was only a sick pleasure. Salazar would snuff out his life as if he were an insect and not give it a second's thought.

'You will have any man who fails to show sufficient enthusiasm whipped,' said the Magelord. 'Any man who voices discontent about defending his own city will lose his tongue. Am I understood?'

Halendorf swallowed and nodded.

'We have lost the mine at the Wailing Rift. The ships we sent to the Swell have not returned.' Salazar's eyes narrowed in anger. His oiled moustache twitched. Everyone seated at the table drew back a fraction. 'I will tolerate no dissidence in this city. I want mindhawks on every corner. Anyone plotting against me will be put to death. Men and women, the young and the old. I care not.'

'It will be done, my lord,' said Timerus. The Grand Magistrate cleared his throat nervously. 'I must confess that we found no signs of the Thelassan ship which attacked us last week.'

Eremul tried to feign a bemused expression. He had already learned of the confrontation between a group of Augmentor-led Watchmen and a lone vessel from the City of Towers.

'Brianna,' said the Magelord, uttering the name like a curse. 'She now suckles at the White Lady's teats.'

According to the report the Halfmage had received, a group of soldiers had chased a small band of rebels from the village of Farrowgate down to Deadman's Channel. A brief and bloody massacre would have followed but for the timely arrival of a caravel flying the colours of the White Lady. Aboard the vessel was none other than Brianna, formerly one of Dorminia's most powerful wizards and a survivor of the Culling. She had chased off the pursuing soldiers with a magical assault that had devastated a small stretch of the coastline. Two Highlanders had been involved – as had, Eremul did not doubt, a certain insipid manservant.

The sudden appearance of a Thelassan ship to save the day struck him as fortuitous to say the least, but the exact details of what had transpired were no clearer to him than anyone else. He was trapped in the city and had no way of contacting those aboard the mysterious vessel.

'My lord,' said the Supreme Augmentor hesitantly. 'We did not count on Thelassa sending wizards. It was my understanding the White Lady has no tolerance for them.'

'She does not,' the Magelord replied. 'Brianna was... difficult to part with. Powerful, and yet demure. Loyal. Perhaps the White Lady has learned the value of pragmatism.'

'I fear even your Augmentors will be hard pressed if she brings her magic to bear against them, my lord. My men are peerless on the field of battle, but against the arcane they are as vulnerable as any other soldier.'

The Tyrant of Dorminia was quiet for a time. 'The White Lady herself will not come, that is certain,' he said eventually. 'However, her servants most assuredly will. The task of nullifying their threat falls to you and your men. I will deal with any magical assault, with the assistance of our friend the Halfmage.'

Eremul's blood froze as Salazar turned to him with a faintly mocking smile. Even in his current weakened state, the Magelord could shred his mental defences and strip his mind raw of secrets with the ease of a man crushing a maggot between his fingers. 'I will do anything to serve,' he wheedled as convincingly as he could manage.

'I know you will,' replied Salazar. 'Now then, Marshal Halendorf. Update me on the progress of the city's fortifications.'

Eremul sat in silence as the magistrates discussed the upcoming invasion. The men at the table barely looked at him unless he was called upon to answer a specific question, and that suited him perfectly. He tried to make himself inconspicuous.

An abused dog. Salazar's little plaything. He wondered what had happened to the White Lady's agents who were supposed to be contacting him.

Perhaps they, too, had decided he was beneath notice.

By the time a Watchman was assigned to wheel him back to the depository, Eremul's head felt as if it was about to explode from the tension. He was therefore less than pleased to find an unpleasant-looking fellow with a slightly panicked look in his eyes loitering before his door. He waved the soldier away and frowned at his unexpected visitor.

The man's mouth dropped open slightly. 'What happened to your legs?' he asked.

Eremul sighed. 'Why, I appear to have temporarily misplaced them. Who are you and what business do you have here?'

'My name's Lashan,' said the man irritably. 'I'm looking for a fella named Isaac. He owes me money.'

Lashan. Where have I heard that name before? 'Does he indeed. And who told you he could be found here?'

'Don't you worry about that. I need the money before nightfall. The full one hundred gold spires.'

'I know you,' Eremul said. 'You're the assistant harbourmaster.' He blinked as the man's words sank in. 'One hundred spires? Isaac's a manservant, not a bloody magistrate.'

As it happened, Isaac was paid a gold spire each month, which was a reasonable sum for a servant. A hundred was more than he had earned in his entire time at the depository.

'A manservant?' Lashan's brow wrinkled in confusion. 'That don't make no sense. This Isaac fella – or whatever he's calling himself now – he's got connections. There ain't a month goes by when he doesn't receive visitors from any place you could name. At least I assume they're here to see him.'

Eremul's eyes narrowed. This conversation was making him uneasy. 'Why does he owe you so much money?'

It was the assistant harbourmaster's turn to narrow his eyes. 'I don't see how that's any of your business.'

'Fine. Isaac isn't here. I know where he might be found – but alas, I wouldn't want to meddle in business that's none of my concern.'

Lashan looked angry. 'Don't mess me around, cripple. You're in no position to take the piss. If you won't tell me where he is, I'll just have to beat it out of you.' He cracked his knuckles menacingly.

Eremul gave the glowering little man an ugly smile. 'Why waste your energy on a legless fop like me? There'll soon be plenty of Sumnians for your mighty fists to beat into submission. Unless, of course, the vastly important office you hold prohibits you from risking yourself in defence of our fair city. I expect it might, particularly if a sizeable amount of coin greases the right palms.'

Lashan snorted. 'You're a smart bastard, I'll give you that. So I want to secure myself a position away from the fighting. Who wouldn't, given the choice?' He spat a glob of thick phlegm, which landed perilously close to Eremul's chair. 'I have a wife and three sons. Concerns a real man could understand.'

'As opposed to a half-man,' Eremul said quietly.

'You got it. Now tell me where he is or things will get ugly.' He took a step towards the Halfmage.

'I'm afraid it's too late for that.' He finished his evocation, felt the magic spiral out from his fingertips and wrap unseen around Lashan's limbs. The assistant harbourmaster yelped and then toppled over like an upset glass. He struggled to rise and got as far as raising his hips off the ground before collapsing back down. He tried again, to all outward appearances a man determined to get intimate with a particularly attractive pothole in the street.

'What's happening to me? I can't move my arms or legs,' he moaned. Eremul wheeled his chair forwards until he was looming over the struggling man. He peered down at him.

'Now, now, Lashan,' he said, his voice full of mock sympathy. 'I'm sure a small thing like the temporary loss of your extremities won't discourage you. I was quite looking forward to a good beating.'

'*You*... you did this to me.'

'Ah. Perceptive as well as brave. You should be more careful about whom you threaten.' His voice became grave. 'I would sit here all day and watch you squirm like a worm, but to tell the truth my arse aches and I quite fancy a lie down. Answer my questions and I'll let you crawl back to your hole.'

'Go fuck yourself.'

Eremul sighed. 'As if I had an alternative.' He lined up his chair and ran the wheels over the man's outstretched fingers, which were scrabbling at the dirt. Lashan howled in pain.

'Keep it down,' he said. 'You wouldn't want everyone to witness you being humiliated by a legless cripple, would you?' He reversed the chair back over Lashan's other hand. This time he felt the crack of tiny bones beneath the wheel. The cries of pain intensified.

'That sounded like it hurt,' he said conversationally. 'And you have at least eight more fingers to go. Then we can work on the toes. After that, well, things get interesting. I have a vivid imagination.'

'*Argh!* Stop, I'll talk!' The words came out in a rush. Tears tumbled from Lashan's eyes, joining a damp patch on the ground beneath his chin where drool had gathered.

'Good.' Eremul glanced around. People were beginning to take notice. He wanted this over with quickly before too much interest was aroused. 'What do you know about Isaac?'

'Nothing,' Lashan replied hurriedly. 'I've never even met him. All I know is he pays me to turn a blind eye to vessels entering and leaving the harbour. I don't know who they carry on board and I don't care.'

'How long has this been going on?'

'I don't... Three, maybe four years.'

Three or four years. How is this possible? He felt his jaw clench in anger. 'Who told you to look for Isaac here?'

'His middleman,' Lashan replied. 'Calls himself the Crow. Apparently they had a falling out.'

'Where might I find this Crow?'

'You won't,' Lashan replied. 'He told me where to find Isaac and then said he was leaving the city. He was packing his things when I found him.'

'He can't leave. The city is under lockdown and the army is encamped outside the walls.'

'The Crow does what he pleases. That's all I know, I swear.'

Eremul released the magic binding Lashan's limbs. 'Isaac isn't here. Whoever it is you're trying to bribe, he won't be signing your exemption papers. And one more thing,' he added as the balding fellow rubbed the life back into his arms and legs. 'Say nothing of this. Very few know I'm a mage. I'd like to keep it that way. Understand?'

Lashan nodded. He hovered uncertainly for a moment. The Halfmage sighed again. 'Taking bribes is practically a job requirement for those with any authority in this city. I have no interest in reporting you. Get out of my sight.' He watched the portly figure scamper away.

He felt as if he had been kicked in the balls. He had trusted Isaac. Could his manservant have been spying for Salazar? No, that was impossible. Isaac had known for months now that he was working against the Magelord. There was no conceivable way Salazar would have permitted the destruction of the mine at the Wailing Rift, so vital to the city's magic supplies.

His head throbbed. Why had he involved Isaac in his schemes in the first place? The man was clearly more adept than any servant had a right to be.

Why did I send Isaac to the Rift? The question bothered him like a scratch he couldn't quite itch. The more he thought about it, the more his head hurt. He was about to go back inside the depository and bundle the useless sack of flesh that was his body into bed for a much-needed rest when he saw the urchin approach.

'Are you normal?' the boy asked uncertainly.

Eremul stared at the lad, with his requisite grubby face and tattered clothes. 'On balance,' he said carefully, 'I would have to say no.'

'Oh.' The urchin looked momentarily crestfallen. 'What happened to your legs?'

'My legs? You mean to say they're not there?' He looked down in mock astonishment. 'Why, I do believe they've walked away of their own accord. Perhaps out of frustration at having to listen to the same question *every single day.*'

The boy looked confused. Eremul couldn't help but feel a shred of pity for him. 'I'm Eremul,' he said. 'Is that who you're looking for?'

The young waif scratched his head and repeated his name a few times before nodding. 'That's it! *Eremul.* I was told to give you this.' He reached down inside a filthy pocket and withdrew a rolled note. 'The lady who asked me to deliver it gave me six coppers.'

He took the note. 'Was this lady strangely pale and distinctly unmemorable?'

The boy nodded. 'She scared me. But Bran delivered the note last time and he returned with a whole silver! He bought us sugar cakes and so much cider we were both sick everywhere. It was real funny.' There was a hint of sadness in the urchin's voice. Eremul felt something cold worm its way inside his chest.

'How is Bran?'

'He's dead, mister. The coughing sickness killed him just last week.'

Eremul sat in silence for a time. Then he reached inside his robes and withdrew two silver sceptres. 'One of these coins is for you,' he said. 'The other is to bury your friend. You know the whereabouts of Bran's body?'

'Yes. I hid him under some leaves in an alley near the Warrens.'

'Wait here. I'll be back in a moment.' He wheeled himself inside the depository. A quick incantation later and the magically concealed words on the note were floating in the air before him. He read them once, gasped softly, and then read them again just to be sure.

He burned the note and fetched his quill and ink to pen his own brief note to the Collectors, instructing them to bring a young boy's body to the cemetery near Crook Street for burial.

Survivors

SASHA WANTED TO scream.

It had been a week since they'd fled Farrowgate and taken refuge aboard *The Caress*. She had spent almost every waking hour of the last seven days alternating between seasickness and an insatiable, terrifying craving for more of that blessed silvery powder to shove up her nose. She would have killed anyone on board the small caravel for even a single line of the stuff. In fact, she would have killed at least one of them just for being so unaware of how close he was to pushing her over the edge.

Right on cue, Cole swaggered up to her. He had a big grin on his face. 'We've just received a message from the White Lady,' he said. 'This is it, Sash. No more waiting. The army is on its way.'

Sasha sighed with relief. First they had needed to await a response from Thelassa after Brianna had sent a message indicating Magebane had been recovered. Then another message had been sent to a contact in Dorminia and they had needed to wait for his response. Finally, they had required confirmation that the army was on the move. At last, it seemed, things were in place – and not before time. She felt as though she was going crazy.

'Friends and allies,' said Brianna loudly, drawing the attention of everyone aboard the vessel. 'The time has come to push ahead with our plans.'

The two Highlanders rose from where they had been lounging against the central mast. Jerek shot Sasha an angry look. She scowled back. The man hated her, she knew, and the feeling was mutual. The dark-skinned Shamaathan joined them from where he had been talking with the equally strange pale-skinned woman at the helm. The two of them made an extreme contrast.

Still, neither unsettled her quite as much as the scabrous, leering face of Cole's new friend. She had caught the convict looking at her more than once. The hunger in his glittering stare had reminded her of things long buried in the past. The girl in her wanted to run away from him.

She wouldn't run. Men like Three-Finger and Jerek the Wolf thrived on signs of weakness. It had come as no surprise that the two seemed to get on well. What was more disappointing was that Brodar Kayne also shared in the apparent camaraderie the three had struck up. Despite herself, she was growing fond of the battered old warrior and his kindly blue eyes.

Brianna squinted at the assembled group. The noon sun was hot and growing hotter by the day. Spring had finally given way to summer. 'We will wait until night falls,' said the White Lady's adviser. 'Then we shall sail west along Deadman's Channel under the cover of darkness. If necessary, I will blanket the ship in magic to disguise our passing. Davarus Cole will disembark near Dorminia. The rest of us will continue on and join up with our forces at the specified point.'

Brodar Kayne scratched at his jaw. He had finally got around to shaving, and he looked a good deal better for it. 'Who's in charge of this army, if you don't mind me asking?'

Brianna frowned. She was a plain-looking woman, tall and thin and dressed in unremarkable blue robes. Still, Sasha had seen what she could do when she had chased off the Watchmen on the other side of the channel. No one had died in the spectacular magical assault – and she suspected that had been Brianna's intent. It had been a display of restraint that was a complete contrast to the brutal Tyrant of Dorminia. As the days passed, Sasha had found herself starting to admire the woman.

322

'Each of the three mercenary companies is led by its own general,' replied Brianna, in response to the old barbarian's question. 'However, General Zahn has overall command of the army. He is a peerless warrior and a fine tactician.'

The dark-skinned assassin spoke. 'General Zahn can be volatile,' he warned in his soft, sibilant voice. Apparently he had somehow escaped the noose back in his homeland. The near-death experience had clearly left an indelible mark on the man.

Some scars never heal, she thought. *We can cover them up and tell ourselves we're fine, but the wounds are there for the world to see.* She needed some more moon dust. She needed it so badly she could feel her palms sweating.

'Sumnian mercenary generals achieve their positions entirely through prowess in battle,' the assassin was saying now. 'Any man who is part of a company is free to challenge for the leadership position. All he has to do is defeat the current general in a fight to the death. General Zahn has not been challenged in a *very* long time...' He let the last sentence trail off ominously.

'He likes to fight with no armour,' Cole added. 'And he's huge. Bigger than anyone I've ever seen.'

Three-Finger scowled. 'He threatened to fuck me up the arse.'

The assassin rubbed at his neck. 'The general is a man of strange humour. But he is a formidable leader. Do as he says and do not question him.'

'It is my hope that Salazar's death forestalls the fighting before either side takes many losses,' said Brianna. 'I am Dorminian myself. I do not wish to see my people killed in a war to remove a tyrant they hold no love for.'

'Fear not, Lady Brianna,' Cole said, unnecessarily loudly given everyone else was only a few feet away. 'I made a vow long ago.' He paused for a couple of seconds to look them each in eye. 'And when Davarus Cole says he will do something, you can consider it done. Salazar will die.' With a flourish, he unsheathed Magebane from his belt and brandished it in the air.

It caught the sun and glinted prettily, much to his evident satisfaction.

Sasha groaned inwardly. Jerek wasn't quite so circumspect. 'I'm sick of seeing that fucking thing,' he growled. 'Put it away. Better yet, use it to shave your chin. You look like a cunt.'

Much as she disliked the bastard, Sasha had to agree with Jerek. 'You're going to be surrounded by a great many men at the militia camp,' she said. 'Some of them might recognize you. You should get rid of the beard. Cut your hair, too. I'll help.'

Cole looked as if he was about to protest until Brianna spoke up. 'Yes, a new appearance. A more rugged look. As befits a man of action,' she added with a small smile.

That seemed to do the trick. Cole looked thoughtful and then nodded.

'You must avoid suspicion until you are inside the city,' Brianna continued. 'Our contact will take care of the rest.'

Sasha had wanted to send word to Garrett and the other Shards, but Brianna was insistent that their messenger spend as little time in Dorminia as possible. The White Lady had shown her hand when her agents tried to assassinate Salazar the last time, and the tyrant would be on the alert for more of the strange pale women. If the messenger was somehow apprehended, their plot to kill the Magelord would fall apart.

Something occurred to her. 'Where's Isaac?' she asked. The manservant had been remarkably quiet ever since *The Caress* had liberated them from the chasing soldiers. For some reason Cole had taken an instant dislike to him.

'Over here,' came the manservant's muffled voice. He was hunkered down next to a pile of crates, scribbling furiously on a piece of parchment. 'I was just composing a little something. An ode to heroes, you might say.'

Sasha frowned. 'Is that a lute?'

Isaac glanced at the small wooden instrument beside him. 'Why, yes it is. I can hardly believe it survived our adventures.'

Brianna looked impressed. 'The lute is one of my mistress's favourites. Do you play it well?'

'Passably well,' the manservant replied modestly. 'I still have much to learn.'

Brodar Kayne shook his head and gave them all a rueful grin. 'Knowing young Isaac, I reckon that means he's skilled enough to make stone weep. Is there anything you can't do, lad?'

The manservant shrugged, a slightly wistful expression on his face. 'I strive to learn a little about everything. Still, there are a great many things of which I am ignorant.'

'Such is life,' the old barbarian replied sagely. 'You're a handy man to travel alongside, Isaac. Saved our skins more than once, I reckon.'

Jerek nodded. 'Aye,' he said. 'You did all right.' From a sociopath like him, Sasha thought, that was about the highest praise anyone could expect.

Cole seemed to be growing increasingly agitated. 'Yes, well, we had our own adventures, didn't we, Three-Finger?'

The ugly convict shrugged. 'Sure. If you count being imprisoned in one shithole after another and almost drowning as adventures.'

'What about the great escape? Don't you remember how I rescued Soeman?'

'Yeah, but he died anyway. That flying Augmentor put a bolt in his scrawny head.'

'And I made him pay for it,' Cole responded grimly.

'It was me that did for him.'

Cole's face darkened. 'And how many Watchmen did *you* kill? Let's see.' He raised a hand and began counting on his fingers. 'One. Two. Is that it? Funny, I can't seem to recall any more. There must have been at least a dozen in the boat I blasted from the water—'

'I'm sure your heroics are worthy of many a tale,' Brianna cut in politely. 'But your greatest deed of all lies before you. We sail at sunset.'

'Maybe we can spend a few hours ashore,' Isaac suggested. 'This region was once home to the Fade. I believe some ruins still exist nearby. I would like to study them.'

'I could do with a break from the ship,' Sasha added hopefully. They had docked only once in the last week. Brianna had wanted them ready to flee at a moment's notice.

The wizard frowned. 'I suppose it couldn't hurt. Captain, we'll anchor for the afternoon.' The pale lady at the wheel raised a hand in acknowledgment and then began to guide the craft towards the shore.

Brodar Kayne flexed his legs. 'I could do with a stretch,' he said. 'Put some life back into these limbs.' He turned to Isaac. 'I've a mind to hear that song you're working on, once it's finished.'

The manservant smiled and nodded. Cole scowled nearby. Sasha shared his annoyance, though for entirely different reasons. She wiped her sweaty palms on her trousers and rubbed at her nose. The blackness was there, clawing at the edge of her consciousness, but she wouldn't let it in.

She caught Three-Finger eyeing her and scowled back at him. He licked his lips and turned away, and she couldn't quite stop the shudder that passed through her.

The land was unsettled and surprisingly barren this far north of Thelassa. While still technically within the domain of the City of Towers, the poor quality of the soil and the proximity of the ancient Fade ruins nearby stopped anyone from settling the area.

The sun was a red circle in the sky, bathing them in a fiery glow that was unseasonably hot even for early summer. Sasha finished cutting off the last of Cole's hair and watched the dark brown locks tumble to the grass. He was sitting on a barrel, staring anxiously ahead as if expecting her to slit his scalp open at any moment. She had been sorely tempted, but self-control had won out. Just.

'Done,' she said, blowing the last few strands of hair from the blade in her hand. Cole jumped up from the barrel and turned to her, an anxious expression on his face. 'You look better,' she said, and surprisingly she meant it.

Cole ran a hand over his shorn scalp. He drew Magebane from his belt and held it up before him, admiring his reflection in the flawless steel. 'Good job, Sash,' he said with a grin. 'I wonder if Garrett and the others will recognize me.'

She crossed her arms and gave him a hard stare. 'You'll be lucky if he welcomes you back at all,' she said. 'You hurt him, Cole. He loves you like a son. He only did what he thinks is best for you.'

Cole's grin faded. He stared down at the ground. 'I know. I've been meaning to apologize. Maybe... maybe I was wrong.'

Sasha's mouth almost dropped open. She had known Cole since they were both children. She could count the number of times he had uttered those words on one hand and still have fingers to spare.

'Maybe you *have* learned something after all,' she said.

Cole nodded. 'I've been through a lot,' he replied. 'But I've come through it all a better man...' His voice trailed off and he frowned as Isaac suddenly ambled back into camp.

The manservant had been investigating the ruins a half-mile to the east, making sketches and writing notes. Sasha had gone with him, and had spent a few minutes staring at the ancient relics before heading back to the others. It wasn't that the remnants of the Fade civilization were boring – on the contrary, what remained of the twisting, alien architecture was wondrous to behold – but there had been an oppressive *feel* about the place. It seemed to prod and pull at the darkness inside her so that she couldn't bear to remain there for long.

'Many of the structures still stand,' said Isaac happily. 'It puts modern engineering to shame. The Fade were so advanced they made even Shadowport's best craftsmen and architects look like children playing with model bricks.'

Brianna glanced across from where she was conversing with the captain of *The Caress*. 'You possess an unusually keen interest in ancient history,' she remarked. 'It is my understanding the Fade departed this land at the dawn of the Golden Age.'

Isaac nodded. 'Two thousand years, give or take, and yet their influence is still felt. That tells us much, doesn't it?'

Sasha knew little about the Fade other than what was common knowledge. They were said to dwell thousands of miles to the west, across the Endless Ocean. Even before the Godswar the voyage had been a monumental undertaking. When the Lord of the Deep perished and the Azure Sea became the Broken Sea, the task grew harder still. Ships from each of the Trine city-states had attempted to cross the Endless Ocean to the Fadelands in decades gone by, and most had never returned. Those that did had admitted defeat – for even if a ship successfully navigated the vast expanse of water, some strange magic made it impossible to dock.

'The legends state that the Fade are immortal,' Brianna said. 'They do not age and die as we do. I suppose they are like Magelords in that regard.'

Isaac shook his head. 'Even Magelords were born human. The Fade are different. What use would they have for the gods, or gold, or man's obsession with, er, procreation? Time means nothing to them. No wonder they departed across the sea when humanity rose to power.'

'Departed, or fled?' asked Brianna, an eyebrow raised.

Isaac smiled his bland smile. But there was something else there, Sasha thought, something she had never seen before. It seemed almost... mocking. 'The Fade would not flee from humans. No more than we would flee a rat infestation. We are shackled by the constraints of our own mortality. Take those constraints away and what might a person become? Anything and everything, given enough time. Can you imagine a race of such beings?'

'Magic is a potent thing,' Brianna replied. 'Even the Fade must respect its power.'

Isaac went quiet for a time. When he spoke again that odd edge in his voice was gone. 'I guess that's true. Still, there isn't much magic around any more – and legends say the Fade possess formidable powers of their own.'

There was movement over where the two Highlanders, Three-Finger and the Shamaathan sat. As far as Sasha could tell the four men had been trying to out-grimace one another. She expected Jerek was winning, but this new dark-skinned southern challenger would give him a run for his money.

'I reckon it's time for a song,' said Brodar Kayne. 'It's been a long while since I heard something to stir my old bones.'

'I can't promise to do that,' Isaac replied. 'But I would be honoured to play. Where's my lute?'

Cole seemed to shuffle a few steps to the side. He had a guilty look on his face. Sasha felt a sneaking suspicion take hold. 'Cole, you brought the lute over from the boat. Where did you put it?'

'Over there,' Cole replied, pointing at the bundle of clothes, food and other items they had taken with them to shore.

Isaac walked across to the pile of provisions. 'It was a struggle to think of a fitting name,' he said. 'In the end, I decided upon "An Ode to the Survivors".'

'The survivors?' said Brodar Kayne, one eyebrow raised.

Isaac bent down to retrieve his lute. 'Well, it seems to me that every one of you has suffered much to be here. I mean, you've all faced terrible things and lived to tell the tale. It's quite inspiring really— What's this?' The manservant's eyes widened in horror. 'My lute... Two of the strings are broken! And it's full of water!'

Cole cleared his throat. 'It fell into the channel while I was unloading it from the boat.' Everyone turned to stare at him. He seemed to wilt beneath their scrutiny. 'What? It was an accident.'

Brodar Kayne shook his head slowly. Jerek turned away and spat. Brianna gave him a disapproving frown. The dark-skinned southerner raised his eyes towards the sky. Isaac stared at his ruined instrument. A ripple of anger threatened to shatter the permanent mask of insipidness that was his face.

'You did it on purpose!' Sasha accused Cole. 'I can't believe you. Just when I thought you might be starting to change.'

'But it was an accident! I promise you, it slipped out of my grasp—'

'Ah, stow it, kid.' It was Three-Finger. 'Accident or not, you're a fuck-up. That's the truth of the matter. We all had a good laugh at you playing the hero aboard the *Redemption*, did you know that?' He leaned forwards and his scabrous face twisted into a sneer. 'Why don't you tell the girl there how you really feel about her? You've got more chance of getting your dick wet with the White Lady. I reckon the girl's legs are closed up tight. Just like her pretty little ass.'

Brianna's expression became ugly and Brodar Kayne's eyes narrowed on the convict. Sasha felt her heart begin to hammer. Three-Finger looked at Jerek, obviously expecting some support from the brooding Highlander. The Wolf's face was impassive.

Cole stepped towards Three-Finger. There was hurt in his eyes, but his face was beginning to redden with anger. 'I won't let you speak about Sash like that.'

'Or what?' the convict scoffed. 'Come on, kid. We all know you're delusional. I'd stick you like a pig. With or without your little dagger.'

'*Enough.*' It was Brianna. She faced Three-Finger imperiously. Despite her plain appearance, there was a tangible aura of power about the wizard that wiped the sneer from the man's face. 'I will tolerate no discord among us. And I will especially not brook any insult to my mistress. Do so again and you will regret it.'

Three-Finger scowled and looked down at the dirt. Cole stared at him for a moment or two. Then he turned and walked over to the edge of the water, his back to them.

Sasha watched him go. Kayne and the Shamaathan had looked as if they would rise and restrain Cole and Three-Finger if necessary. Now they were settling back down, grim expressions on their faces.

Jerek met her eyes for a second. His gaze was unreadable, but she did not doubt he had enjoyed her humiliation. She gave him an angry glare, then turned and followed after Cole.

'I thought he was my friend.'

Sasha shook her head and bit her lower lip. The craving had returned, stronger than before, but she tried to ignore it. 'Men like Three-Finger don't have friends. He used you.'

Cole stared out across the water. He was handsome now that his stupid beard was gone and his hair had been shaved down to stubble; more rugged-looking. His recently healed nose was slightly crooked, but that only added to the effect. 'It *was* an accident, you know,' he said.

'I don't think it matters much now,' she replied. 'Though you owe Isaac an apology. And a new lute.'

The young Shard sighed and then nodded.

'What's your problem with Isaac, anyway? You disliked him from the moment you set eyes on him.'

Cole frowned. 'I don't trust him.'

'Jealousy doesn't suit you.'

'I'm not jealous!' he replied, a little too quickly. They stood there in silence for a time, watching the water lapping against the rocks. The sun was already on the way down. Within an hour they would be sailing west, skirting Dorminia and joining up with the army further along the coast. All except Cole, who would disembark and head for the militia camp, pretending to be a straggler from one of the smaller towns. Once the fighting started he would seek out his contact and be smuggled into the Obelisk.

'Are you ready to do this?' she asked quietly. 'Are you prepared to kill Salazar?'

Cole squared his shoulders. 'I was born—'

'None of your bullshit, Cole. This is serious. If you fail, Salazar could destroy us all. The whole army.'

'I've had training,' he said. 'The Darkson taught me everything he knew. Besides, Salazar's magic can't touch me. Not while I wield Magebane.'

She glanced across at him. He had a determined look on his face. She hesitated, and then placed a hand on his arm. 'Thanks for watching out for me back there.'

He looked at her hand. His grey eyes rose to meet her own. 'I won't let anyone harm you, Sash.'

She raised an eyebrow at him. 'You don't really have much choice in the matter. I'm about to go to war.'

Cole looked troubled. 'I know. Just… try and keep yourself safe. I'm not sure what I would do if anything happened to you.'

She wanted to roll her eyes at him – but, for some reason, she couldn't. 'I'll try not to die,' she said instead.

'I missed you,' Cole added, and this time his words really threw her. 'I thought I would never see you again.'

She stared at her feet, embarrassment warring with the sudden urge to laugh at the absurdity of the situation. 'You were only gone a month. Although it feels like a lot longer— *What are you doing?*'

Cole was leaning towards her, his lips brushing against her own. In sudden panic she threw her head back, bringing a hand around to slap him full in the face. The sound seemed to reverberate like a rockfall. He raised a palm to his cheek and stared at her with eyes full of hurt.

'I thought—' he began, but she cut him off with a snarl.

'You thought you would lure me over here, get me feeling sorry for you? Is that it? Did you plan all of this?'

'What? No, Sash, of course not—'

'You'll never change, will you?' She stared at him, fury seething within her. The darkness suddenly seemed to expand, filling her head, throbbing with the need to escape and consume everything in its path. 'You're an asshole, Cole,' she spat. 'Your father would be ashamed of you. And so would Garrett.'

She spun around and stormed off back to the others, leaving him standing alone, mouth agape.

As it turned out, they were the last words she would utter to him before he departed their grim company for the militia training camp near Dorminia.

One Last March

BRODAR KAYNE HAD seen some armies in his time, but the host that awaited them when *The Caress* docked a day's march west of the Grey City was a sight to behold. The coast was lined with ships almost as far as he could see. Carracks and galleys anchored side by side as a constant stream of smaller rowing boats ferried the three Sumnian mercenary companies to the shore.

The largest of the ships hoisted a flag depicting a stunning woman against a white background. Beneath the illustration, proudly displayed in flowing silver thread, were the words *The Lady's Luck*.

The old Highlander's breath caught as he stared up at the deck of the flagship. He squinted, just to be sure of what he was seeing. The man standing on the forecastle, if he really was a man, could be none other than General Zahn. From this distance, Kayne reckoned he looked about the size of some of the giants that roamed the High Fangs. No less than eight feet tall, certainly. The colossus was naked from the waist up, and he leaned upon a huge golden spear longer than the average Highlander was tall.

'That's the general,' muttered the Darkson beside him. The Shamaathan had his hood drawn up so that only his eyes were visible.

Kayne shook his head in amazement. 'For once, the lad wasn't exaggerating.' Davarus Cole had left them the night before, disembarking a few miles east of the city to begin his own personal quest. He had seemed unusually glum, which was surprising considering how much of a show he liked to make of things. The girl, too, appeared to be in poor spirits. He reckoned something had happened between them, but there was no point sticking his nose in where it wasn't wanted. At the end of the day, he had a job to do.

It wasn't as if he could have said no to Brianna. Not after she'd just saved their lives. Not with the promise of fifty gold spires between them if he and Jerek helped overthrow the Tyrant of Dorminia. Handing back Magebane only seemed right in the circumstances. And again, it wasn't as if he really had a choice. You didn't usually get the better of mages in an argument, not in his experience.

In any case, Brianna seemed like a pleasant and trustworthy sort. A fine figure of a woman, if he was being honest, and it was past time he should be feeling guilty about those kinds of thoughts. When it came right down to it, there were no certainties in life. The prospect of ousting a bastard of a Magelord was a job as worthwhile as any other he could think of.

The caravel he was on had a shallow enough draught to anchor close inshore, so Kayne eased himself into the water and waded towards land. He heard Jerek and the Darkson splash down and do the same behind him. The water reached up to his waist, but the late-afternoon sun was oppressively hot and the brief soaking was a welcome relief.

Curious faces turned to stare at them as they made their way up the crunchy shingle beach towards the vast camp being assembled ahead. The old barbarian returned the stares. These Sumnian warriors were a strange sight. They were dark of skin, a little paler than the assassin behind him. They wore leather vests and carried swords or spears together with circular wooden shields. With the notable exception of the monstrous general, they looked to be a fair bit shorter than the typical Highlander, though were still a shade taller than most of the Lowlanders he had met.

'Maggot!' shouted a cheerful voice somewhere ahead of him. 'Over here.' Kayne narrowed his eyes at the group of Sumnians grinning at them. The speaker was a striking man in his early thirties with amazingly thick, oiled hair that had been braided and fixed atop his head. He carried an oddly shaped sword in each hand, both blades curving near the end to form a hook. The leather he wore was bleached bone white.

'You talking to me?' Kayne asked. The man nodded in response, flashing a white smile.

'You, yes. You maggots.'

'Now that ain't no way to speak to a man. We're all friends here.' Brodar Kayne was trying his best to keep his cool, but the gleaming smile on the other man's face combined with the insults were beginning to grate on his nerves.

'Friends, yes. What is your name? And this other maggot's name? He looks angry.'

Jerek stepped towards the Sumnian, knuckles gripping the handles of the axes on his back. 'Maggot? I ain't taking that. Not from a fucking—'

'Calm.' The Darkson placed a hand on Jerek's shoulder. 'He means no disrespect. In the Sun Lands, "maggot" is a term of endearment for those with fair skin.'

'Yes,' agreed the Sumnian. 'You are white, like a maggot, no?' Something seemed to occur to him all of a sudden. 'I know that voice. The Darkson.'

The assassin threw back his hood. 'Well met, General.'

Brodar Kayne's head was beginning to ache. 'Wait... This man is a general?'

The Sumnian opposite him flashed another smile. 'General D'rak, at your service.'

The Darkson pointed at the Sumnians behind D'rak, and then at the men standing around watching them in small clusters all across the beach. There must have been scores of them, maybe hundreds. They looked ready to spring into action at a moment's notice.

'General D'rak commands these warriors. They would lay down their lives for him.'

'And these are but a handful of my brothers,' the general added. 'The rest are still on the ships, or helping prepare the camp. One thousand swords and spears – the finest company in all of Sumnia!' He brought his strange weapons together once, twice, three times. Those close enough to observe their general answered by clashing their own weapons against their shields or hammering them on the ground.

Kayne gave the man's twin blades a doubtful look. 'I've never seen swords like those. Can you fight with them?'

General D'rak laughed. It was an honest sound, sincere and heartfelt, and the old Highlander felt himself warming towards him. 'I fight like no one you have ever seen. Walk with me, friend. I will introduce you – and perhaps later I will show you how one dances with the khopesh.'

Kayne glanced behind him at the scowling Jerek and the Darkson, who nodded at him. 'I ain't much of a dancer,' he said uncertainly. 'But I guess you're never too old to try.'

By the time dusk had fallen the army was fully encamped. Fires sprang up all over the hill on which they were bivouacked. The mercenaries from the south apparently found the night air too chill for their liking, despite the heat of the day and the fact both Kayne and Jerek were still uncomfortably warm underneath their hide armour.

Kayne reckoned the Sumnians could be excused that little foible after everything else he had witnessed since coming ashore. The mercenaries functioned with a discipline he had never experienced up in the High Fangs. They moved with purpose, each man knowing his place despite all being equal under their respective generals.

These were men who lived for warfare. General D'rak had informed him that every mercenary in a company had to earn his place, and as a result there was no room for cowards or stragglers. It all seemed a far cry from the red-cloaked soldiers he had encountered back in Dorminia. If even half these Sumnians were anywhere near as skilled as D'rak, the Crimson Watch wouldn't stand a chance in hell.

He shifted again, wincing at the pain in his left calf. The general had shown him how to fight with the curved swords, sparring with and then disarming two of his own men. He had then handed the weapons over to Kayne, who had given the khopeshes a fair go, though the blades had felt strange in his hands. When the time came to start spinning around as the general had demonstrated, he had almost tripped over his own feet and fallen flat on his arse. Jerek might have fared better, considering how he favoured a weapon in each hand, but the Wolf had responded to D'rak's offer to participate with a grim shake of the head and that had been that.

'Are you all right?' Sasha asked, noticing how he kept rubbing at the muscles in his leg.

'Just a bit of a cramp,' he replied, though to be honest the pain had been so bad he'd tasted blood. As it turned out, jumping around like a lunatic without a proper warm-up was a young man's game. Just like everything else, he reckoned.

Brianna and the Darkson were off at Zahn's tent with the other two generals, no doubt discussing plans. They would begin their march on the morrow. He could hear Three-Finger's laughter from somewhere behind him. The convict was an easy man to get along with, quick with a joke and a ready smile. Still, Kayne didn't like the way he stared at the girl. He decided to stick close to her, just in case. She could look after herself, he knew, but a lone woman among so many warriors was always going to draw unwelcome attention.

'Why does he always sit alone?' Sasha asked, nodding at Jerek. He was sitting by himself at a nearby campfire, staring at nothing much.

'The Wolf likes to keep his own company,' Kayne replied. 'It's just the way he is.'

Sasha frowned. 'How did he get those scars?'

He paused a moment before replying. 'When he was a boy his family was attacked by outlaws. Men with no allegiance to any chieftain. They locked his family inside their home, set fire to the house. He was the only survivor. His mother, father, his brothers and sisters – they all perished in the blaze.'

'Is that why he's so angry?'

'Could be. He don't trust easily.'

'He trusts you.'

'I pulled him clear of the fire.'

Sasha looked at him. 'You rescued Jerek?'

He nodded. 'I killed the outlaws. Found a lad still breathing, terribly burned, and dragged him out of the wreck. Course, I was still young myself then.'

'Is that why he follows you everywhere? Because you saved his life?'

'The Wolf doesn't forget a debt.'

'But he saved you from the Shaman.'

He shrugged. 'Aye, he did. Now we're both outlaws. He don't owe me anything – and yet here he is.'

Sasha was silent for a time. She looked troubled. 'You worried about young Cole?' he asked carefully.

She scowled. 'Cole can look after himself. He's obsessed with the idea of being some great hero. Well, now's his chance.'

'He cares for you.'

'I know.'

'Then what's the problem?'

The girl sighed and ran a hand over her brow. Her pupils weren't so wide now, which was as good an indication as any that she was clean of whatever it was she had been taking. He hadn't spoken to her about it. Nothing good could come of it. 'I said something I shouldn't have,' she admitted.

Ah. Now we're getting to the root of it. 'Cole's tenacious,' he said. 'He'll bounce back. Nothing seems to faze that lad for very long.'

There was a hint of a smile on her face. 'You're probably right.'

He grinned back at her. 'There's a first time for everything.'

Isaac ambled over to them. He had a leg of roast chicken in one hand and a notebook in the other. 'These Sumnians have a most interesting culture,' he said, wiping grease from his mouth with the back of one hand. 'Did you know they are forbidden to marry until they have killed at least one warrior in battle? Once they have, they are able to take up to three wives. The generals can marry as many women as they like.'

'I reckon one woman's more than enough for any man,' Kayne replied. He raised an eyebrow. The manservant never failed to surprise him. 'We're marching off to battle tomorrow and you're making notes?'

Isaac shrugged. 'Knowledge lives on even after we're gone. That's all we really are. The sum of what others have learned before us. If I die, I hope part of my learning will remain for others to find and make use of.'

The old barbarian frowned. What would he leave behind when he died? A mountain of corpses and regrets, he supposed.

'Can a Magelord die?' Sasha asked Isaac.

'Not from natural causes. But we know at least thirty mages returned from the Godswar. There are far fewer than thirty Magelords in the world now. Maybe not much more than a dozen. Clearly many have perished over the years.'

'If Cole fails...' Sasha began. She didn't finish her sentence. Instead she shook her head and looked down at the ground.

Kayne shrugged. 'We got a job to do. We take the city and let Cole worry about the Magelord. If it comes to it, and Salazar proves too much... Well, we run like hell.'

'I'm not running,' she replied. 'I've waited for this opportunity for years. I'll do whatever it takes to kill that bastard.'

Kayne noticed Isaac watching him curiously. Again, he felt there was something odd about the manservant, but trying to pin down exactly what was akin to biting his own elbow.

'Why are you here anyway? Is it just the gold?' asked Isaac.

'Gold's always welcome.' *Twenty-five gold spires. Enough to buy a small farm in the Unclaimed Lands, maybe. Then what? Raise a family? I'm too old for that. I had a family and I lost it. And the Shaman won't ever stop hunting me, not unless I flee to the furthest reaches of the world. Maybe not even then.*

'Kayne?' Sasha said. She was looking at him with concern.

'I'm fine,' he replied. He had to stop doing that, sitting there and getting lost in his memories. It didn't do a man any good to wallow in the past. 'I'm going for a stroll,' he announced. 'See if I can walk off this damned cramp.'

He got to his feet and half limped from the campfire. Curious faces turned to stare at him. He caught Three-Finger gazing at Sasha, a hungry look in his eyes. He reckoned he was going to need to have words with the ex-convict at some point.

Hard words.

The following morning was every bit as glorious as the one previous. The sky was a clear blanket of blue without a cloud to be seen, and the sun promised a hard march ahead of them. He washed the sleep from his eyes at a nearby stream, had a bite of dry bread and an old apple, and then sat down to oil his greatsword. All around him mercenaries were doing the same. There was no telling what awaited them when they arrived at Dorminia.

Jerek strolled over and gave him a nod. He nodded in response. Nothing else needed to be said. They'd both done this often enough in the past. They knew how it went. You put your head down, kept your legs moving and focused on anything but the bloody carnage to come.

It took a little under an hour until the army was ready to march. The mercenary army decamped as quickly and efficiently as it had bivouacked, separating into the three individual companies that comprised the force. The two Highlanders,

Sasha and Isaac travelled in the foremost company under the banner of General Zahn. The giant strolled along at the very front of the army, his bald head visible above the mass of men behind him. Above him was a flag depicting a golden spear skewering what looked like a column of warriors. Brianna and the Darkson were somewhere up alongside him, Kayne knew.

He glanced behind him. He could just about see General D'rak at the head of his own company, his banner displaying what looked like a dancing skeleton. The third company was somewhere behind. He hadn't yet seen their general, who was apparently a fellow named Zolta. Chances were he was every bit as fierce as his peers. Behind the last company came the siege engines, followed by a score of the White Lady's pale servants. The women spoke to no one and kept their own counsel.

They marched eastwards, following the coast. As he predicted, the sun was merciless and bathed them in an oppressive heat that, to his frustration, the Sumnians apparently seemed to enjoy. He couldn't help but notice the glowing orb had a distinctly crimson hue this morning. He hoped that wasn't an ill omen.

By the time the sun was again sinking beneath the western horizon they neared their destination. His legs ached like something unholy and he smelled worse than that, but all things considered he had endured much longer and more unpleasant marches. The army halted a mile or so from Dorminia's walls, on a shallow hill overlooking the city.

'This is it,' Sasha said. 'Do you think we will attack tonight?'

Brodar Kayne glanced up at the darkening sky and then at Dorminia. Lights twinkled from within the Grey City, but he couldn't see much of anything else at this distance. 'It seems like a good night for it,' he answered. 'I guess we'll find out soon enough.' He looked around. 'Where's Isaac?'

'I don't know. He was right next to me until a few moments ago.'

The Highlander sighed. 'I expect he's scarpered off to do some last-minute sketching or plant collecting.'

Jerek scowled and spat. 'You ready for this, Kayne? They're watching our every move.' He jerked a thumb skywards to where a hawk of some kind had been circling overhead for the last few minutes. It screeched once and then flew off in the direction of the city.

'Mindhawks,' said Sasha darkly.

'Can't be helped now,' said Kayne. 'You set yourself against a Magelord, you don't go in expecting a fair fight.'

He should know. He had learned that lesson the hard way.

Good News, Bad News

'IT IS TIME.'

Barandas finished strapping on his sword and stared out of the window. The city was still silent at this early hour, but the first light of dawn had split the sky like a bloody wound and soon the streets would be heaving with activity.

Marshal Halendorf had taken a turn for the worse after the council meeting three days ago. According to Timerus, none of Halendorf's four captains were fit for the task of overseeing the army in his absence. As a result, Barandas once again found himself in temporary command of the Crimson Watch while the Marshal recovered.

It couldn't have happened at a more inopportune time. The Council had received the message late last night. The Sumnian force had docked yesterday afternoon and would be outside the walls by the time the sun fell this very evening.

'This is ridiculous,' Lena complained again. Her green eyes were full of worry. 'How can they expect you to lead the city's defence? You have your own responsibilities. Your own men to manage.'

He gave her a rueful smile. 'We are less than half the force we were. According to Timerus the militia need someone they can look to. Someone to inspire them.'

'It's a shame Halendorf wasn't inspired to find some better officers.'

Barandas was inclined to agree with his wife. He hadn't

realized just how bad the situation had become over the years. The Council had grown lax, content to place an incompetent bully like Halendorf at the head of the city's army in the belief the Crimson Watch would never be truly tested. And for many years that had been the case; the great cities of the Trine had been at peace for decades, and who would dare challenge a metropolis ruled by the greatest wizard in the north? Even a forest of steel would melt before a Magelord's fury.

Salazar's power was now but a shadow of what it had been. The ruler of Dorminia might never recover his full strength. For the first time in centuries, the Grey City was vulnerable – and as a result, Dorminia's armed forces had been caught with their pants down. Bullies and thugs were well suited to keeping a cowed populace under control, but they made poor soldiers.

Yet again Barandas wondered why his master had expended so much of his own vitality destroying Shadowport. Why had he not challenged Marius, decided the fate of the Celestial Isles Magelord to Magelord instead of massacring an entire city? The world was a hard place, but there were some things that could never be justified.

Those were troubling thoughts. He did his best to suppress them, to focus on what was important. Lena was looking at him with concern. 'You're tired,' she said. 'You haven't been sleeping lately.'

'I'll rest once the city is safe,' he replied. He noted with a smile that she was wearing the green crystal he had found in the Mother's temple. There was a glow about her, he thought. A radiance that made her even more beautiful than usual.

'Ran,' she said. There was something odd in her voice. His eyes met hers in sudden alarm.

'Yes? What is it?'

'I'm pregnant.'

He gasped as the world seemed to shift around him. Before he knew it she was in his arms. He felt her warmth pressing into him, the jasmine scent of her golden hair filling his nostrils.

'How long?' he managed to ask.

'I found out last week. I... wasn't sure whether to tell you, Ran. You've had so much to worry about lately—'

'Hush,' he said gently. He felt as though he was floating. 'You can't imagine what this means to me, Lena. I thought... It doesn't matter what I thought. I'm going to be a *father*.'

She smiled at him then, her eyes wet with tears. 'Promise me. Promise me nothing will happen to you.'

He held her close, stroked her hair. 'I promise,' he said.

The iron beating inside his chest seemed to swell. For that one, precious moment, the burdens he carried seemed to weigh as lightly as a feather.

He strolled through the waking city as the rising sun bathed the streets in scarlet. News of the approaching force had yet to circulate around the taverns and markets from which gossip spread like wildfire, but he knew that it would before long, and then Dorminia would be in chaos.

The spring in his step faltered slightly as he made his way through the Hook and tried to ignore the men in the gibbets above him. They stared down at him with pleading expressions, tongueless mouths emitting animal moans. Other than the gurgling of the Redbelly River nearby, they were the only sounds disturbing the dawn streets.

He turned off the Tyrant's Road and onto the old Trade Way. The ancient road ran from the west of the city across the Hook to Dorminia's eastern gates. From there it continued all the way to the borders of the Unclaimed Lands. To his left, the temple of the Mother reminded him of things he would rather forget. He wondered if Remy felt any guilt about betraying the rebel organization that had until recently operated from the old ruin. He very much doubted it.

Our new Master of Information now has a large estate in the

Noble Quarter and an allowance to shame all but the wealthiest merchants. That will doubtless assuage any lingering feelings of regret.

Barandas was not particularly keen on what he had seen of the former physician, and it irked him to have such treachery rewarded with a place on the Council, but Timerus held sway in such matters.

He approached the city's eastern entrance. The Watchmen on duty saluted him and hurried to unlock the huge iron gates, dragging them open to reveal the temporary wooden palisade beyond. Dorminia had been under a strict lockdown for over a month, with only government-approved tradesmen and soldiers of the Watch allowed to pass freely into and out of the city. The militiamen in the sprawling camp before him were allowed back inside Dorminia for only an hour every other day, and only in groups of a few hundred at any one time. The threat of rebellion or desertion was a constant concern.

Not that there were too many places for a coward to flee, he thought. Not unless a Dorminian was willing to risk the Unclaimed Lands where life was a daily struggle to survive. Beyond that lawless frontier lay the Confederation, a sprawling collection of nations loosely allied under the rule of a cabal of Magelords. Few ever made that particular journey, which was fraught with peril.

Shadowport had received a fair number of immigrants from Dorminia before the conflict over the Celestial Isles, but the Grey City had also taken in many coming in the opposite direction. Life was hard throughout the Trine, no matter where a man or woman called home.

And as ruthless as Salazar was, his rule ensured that Dorminia remained an anchor of civilization in a land that was slowly drifting to ruin.

'My lord.' A young officer saluted as Barandas entered the palisade and cast his gaze over the makeshift army stirring to life under a forest of bedrolls. The weather had blessed them:

the recent heat had turned the rain-sodden grassland to hard turf, and conditions in the temporary barracks were far pleasanter than they would have been even a week ago.

'I want every man gathered in the centre of the camp fifteen minutes from now,' he commanded the young Watchman. The officer looked startled for a moment, then saluted and scuttled off to carry out his orders.

'I am Barandas, Supreme Augmentor of Lord Salazar. I stand before you in Marshal Halendorf's absence.'

He gazed down at the thronging mass of men assembled around the platform. The tide of humanity stretched back halfway to the walls of the massive palisade, faces young and old staring up at him with a multitude of expressions. He had never seen so many people in one place. He raised his voice so that those further back might hear, though he doubted whether the men near the edges of the gigantic crowd would understand a word. 'News has reached us that the Sumnian army is but a day's march away.'

There was a stirring below as the news was relayed by the men at the front to those behind them. 'You will soon be called upon to defend your city,' he continued. 'To defend your homes. Your families. The Sumnians will show no mercy.'

Even this early in the morning the smell of unwashed bodies was strong. Barandas ignored the pungent odours of sweat and piss and wiped his moistening brow with the back of his hand. Then, in one smooth motion, he drew his sword and raised it up in the air. 'We fight for the Grey City. For freedom. If the Watch falters, I need every man here to do his duty.'

There were a few ragged cheers, mainly from the older men. A great many faces stared back at him with stony expressions. A few turned and spat on the ground. '*Freedom?*' exclaimed one voice from somewhere in the first half-dozen rows. 'That's a joke. The city won't be free until Salazar is dead.'

Barandas stared down at the makeshift army and tried to locate the speaker. He thought it might have been a young man with cropped hair, but he couldn't be sure. 'If the Lord of Dorminia falls, the city falls with him,' he shouted back. 'There are many who wish us harm.'

'Easy for you to say,' yelled another man. 'The Watch killed my brother. Dragged him away from his house and slit his throat in the middle of the street. What kind of ruler murders his own people?'

Barandas heard swords being drawn behind him. There were several hundred Watchmen assembled before the crowd, who were unarmed. If this continued things could turn ugly very quickly.

'Mistakes have been made,' he said. He knew that this was crossing into dangerous territory, but he needed these conscripts to believe in him. 'You are aware of what occurred during the Festival of the Red Sun. Rebels tried to kill our lord. Perhaps the Watch has been… heavy-handed in the years since.'

There were mutterings behind him now. He had evidently upset some of the officers. It couldn't be helped. He addressed the crowd one last time. 'You will help dismantle the camp. Then you will assemble at the nearest barracks and await further orders.'

He turned to the soldiers behind him, nodded and then stepped from the platform. He searched around for Captain Bracka. He spotted the man talking heatedly with a group of his junior officers. He strolled over, noting how quickly they fell silent when they saw him approaching. Bracka scowled and threw a desultory salute. 'Commandant,' he said in a low growl.

'How are we for weapons?' Barandas asked, ignoring the man's tone.

Bracka scratched at his huge red bush of a beard. He looked like a bear, and was said to have a temperament to match. 'Every smith in Dorminia has been working flat out,' he said. 'But there's been a shortage of iron. We used most of our reserves in the war with Shadowport. There are enough pikes to go around, but most of the swords and axes have seen better days. Some of them are more rust than steel.'

'What about bows?'

Bracka snorted and flashed a black smile. Literally black – his teeth were rotten to the core. 'Most of these bastards couldn't hit a cow's arse from five yards out.'

'They don't need to be accurate. They just need to be able to fire an arrow.'

'We should have bows enough,' the captain replied. 'As for armour, any man who gets so much as a padded jerkin can count himself lucky. If those Sumnians get close, we're fucked.'

'I don't intend that they get close,' said Barandas.

'Commandant,' gasped a breathless voice behind him. It was the young officer he had spoken with earlier.

'Yes?'

'I bring news from the city. Marshal Halendorf passed away during the night.'

'Passed away?' Barandas repeated slowly, as if the words had been spoken in a language he did not understand.

'Yes, Commandant. One of his servants found him dead in his bed, blood all over the sheets. It seems that he... coughed up his innards.'

'I was led to understand he had a bad case of acid.'

'What devilry is this?' Bracka demanded. 'The Marshal was fine last time I saw him. Just a bit under the weather.'

Barandas turned to the captain. 'Finish overseeing the disbanding of the camp. I must speak with our lord immediately.' He spun around and marched back towards the eastern gate, wondering what other news this day would bring.

'You will continue as before. The army is yours to lead now, Supreme Augmentor.'

Barandas blinked and cleared his throat. 'But, my lord... what about my other duties? I am sworn to protect you.'

Salazar pursed his lips. Grand Magistrate Timerus watched on, the only other man in the room. They were in the Magelord's private chamber on the Obelisk's sixth floor.

The chair to Salazar's right was empty – the chair normally occupied by Halendorf's fleshy arse when the Tyrant of Dorminia demanded an audience. Barandas recalled the Marshal's look of satisfaction when he had been summoned following Shadowport's destruction. That seemed like a lifetime ago now.

'I am quite capable of protecting myself,' the Magelord said. 'You and your Augmentors will be needed to defend the gates. Dorminia's walls might halt the Sumnian mercenaries for a time. They will pose little obstacle to the White Lady's servants.'

'As you command, my lord.' Barandas hesitated. 'I would have Thurbal posted here, just as a precaution. With your permission, of course.'

Salazar narrowed his eyes. 'You are persistent, Supreme Augmentor.'

'I care only for your safety, my lord.'

The Tyrant of Dorminia sat back in his throne and sighed. 'Very well. Now, you must take your leave. The Sumnians will arrive before the moon is in the sky. You have much to do.'

'Yes, my lord.' Barandas hesitated again. 'Do we know what befell Marshal Halendorf? He is not the first man to meet such an end these last couple of months.'

This time it was Timerus who answered. 'I had the corpse delivered to one of the finest physicians in the city. It will be examined for signs of anything unusual. It is not a matter with which to concern yourself, Supreme Augmentor.'

'As you say.' With a final bow to Salazar, Barandas departed the chamber. There was something odd about Halendorf's untimely death, but for now he had too many things demanding his attention. He wondered if he had time to pay Lena a brief visit before departing the Noble Quarter for the western gate.

With a great sense of regret, he decided he did not.

*

351

The grey granite wall of Dorminia rose to three times the height of a man, surrounding the city on all sides save for the south, where the harbour formed a natural barrier. The wall was three feet thick at its weakest point and could withstand all but the heaviest assault from ballista or trebuchet.

Barandas climbed the rough stone steps leading up to the gatehouse that overlooked the city's western entrance. Battlements ran down the length of the wall on both sides, with a narrow walkway providing just enough room for an archer to snipe at enemies from behind the relative safety of the merlons. The militia's training had mostly centred on the longbow. Barandas was confident he had enough men to drown their assailants in a storm of arrows if they were foolish enough to launch a head-on assault.

They won't be, he realized grimly. *These Sumnians are expert soldiers, veterans at laying siege to towns and cities. They will have a great many tricks up their sleeves.*

Fortunately, he too had a secret weapon.

The Halfmage was on the gatehouse's parapet, staring out through the crenellated wall at the western horizon. The sun was already beginning to sink, and though the approaching army was not yet within sight it was only a matter of time before their aggressors arrived and the siege would begin in earnest.

The man seated on the strange contraption looked up, a troubled expression on his face. 'Supreme Augmentor,' he said with a smile that appeared not the least bit genuine. 'Or rather, should that be Marshal? I believe congratulations are in order.'

'Supreme Augmentor will suffice,' Barandas replied. 'Do you have everything you require?'

'I could use a bottle or two of his lordship's best wine and a whore to keep me entertained while we wait. No? In that case I am as content as a pig in shit.'

Barandas moved to stand beside the wizard. He was a somewhat bizarre sight, in truth: a scholarly-looking man of a similar age to him, dressed in outlandish green robes that seemed to accentuate his missing legs. Barandas had felt sorry for the wizard, at least at first, but the man's sarcastic manner and constant barbs made him unpleasant to be around.

'You do realize I am to magic as a eunuch is to an orgy, or dear Chancellor Ardling is to the art of witty banter. If you're expecting me to eviscerate our enemies in clouds of spattering gore, you're going to be sorely disappointed.'

'I am aware of your limitations. You are to concentrate on destroying any siege weapon that gets close enough to launch an attack. In this weather they will spark like kindling.'

'It might have escaped your attention, but there is only one of me...' The mage paused for a moment. 'That is to say, there is only *half* of me, and yet there are two gates to defend. And what if they attack from the north?'

'They will not,' Barandas replied. He had discussed this with the four captains. The Redbelly River flowed into the city on the northern side from where it wound down from the Demonfire Hills. The only way the invading force could enter Dorminia from that direction was by scaling the walls or sailing down the waterway. The Sumnians had no boats. Several of Dorminia's surviving warships now patrolled the spot where the river entered the city, their artillery ready to blast apart anyone foolish enough to get close and attempt a breach.

'Lord Salazar will support the eastern wall,' Barandas added. 'The Obelisk provides the ideal vantage point from which to observe an approach on that side of the city. Our master may be weakened, but he remains formidable.'

'Yes. I am aware.'

The two men said nothing for a time. Barandas could hear the Crimson Watch trying to maintain order on the streets below. The bellmen were already doing the rounds, informing the citizenry that a hostile force was approaching and advising those not involved in the fighting to remain indoors.

He glanced down at the wizard. 'My wife is pregnant,' he

said. He had no idea where the words came from or why he decided to break the news to this strange fellow of all people, but they tumbled out before he could stop them.

The Halfmage looked at him with a blank expression. Then he laughed. It was a horrible sound, like a dying man gasping for breath. Finally he quietened, wiping tears from his eyes and snot from his chin. 'First Supreme Augmentor. Then Marshal. Now soon to be a *father*? Do you want me to shake your hand? Give you a manly embrace? I would offer you a gift as is the custom, but I am certain there is nothing one so blessed as you does not already possess.'

'I want nothing from you. It was foolish of me to expect any empathy from a hateful—'

The Halfmage held up a hand, shocking him into silence. The wizard squinted into the distance, raising his other hand to shield his eyes from the dying sun. 'Hold onto that anger, Supreme Augmentor. It will come in handy. The Sumnians are here.'

Summer Time

THE SOUND OF drums dragged her awake.

Yllandris had been dreaming of a morning long ago, when she had been a girl not yet blossomed to womanhood and the arrival of summer had been one of the highlights of her year. Her mother had been tending the hearth, a broad smile on her kindly face. Her father was nearby. The promise of the new season appeared to have softened even his dark mood, and he gave her an affectionate grunt as he passed her a warm bowl of last night's stew and a hard heel of bread.

She sat up, wiping sleep from her eyes. Had she imagined the sound?

No. There it was again. *Boom. Boom. Boom.*

She thrust the fur blanket away from her, jumped up from the pallet and pulled on some clothes: a pair of deerskin trousers, her purple shawl and some boots. The beating of the drum was growing louder. She quickly washed her face, not bothering to apply any paints, and then hurried outside.

Has the King finally returned? A full three days had passed and still no word from Magnar or his huge entourage had reached Heartstone. Additional riders had been sent to investigate. They had not returned either. With the Shaman still absent, an undercurrent of panic was beginning to pervade the town.

The sun was up already and the skies were clear. The snow had melted, revealing soggy green grass and mud underneath.

As she joined the townsfolk making their way towards the northern gate, she could hear the trickle of the last of the snow melting on the roofs of the huts and longhouses that lined the thoroughfare. Soon Lake Dragur would thaw, if it had not already, and the boats would be out on the water bringing in trout and perch and anything else the fishermen could catch. All in all it was set to be a beautiful day.

'Sister,' called a slightly shrill voice somewhere to her right. It was Thurva. The young sorceress scurried through the crowd to intercept her.

Yllandris suppressed a sigh. 'Greetings, sister,' she said with forced pleasantness. 'It appears our king returns to us.'

'With the head of the demon, I hope,' replied Thurva. She made a face. 'I don't enjoy burying the dead. It's a grisly business.'

Yllandris stared at Thurva's mismatched eyes, not bothering to hide her annoyance. *You barely lifted a finger to help*, she thought. *I did most of the hard work.*

One of the circle's duties in Heartstone was to perform last rites for the dead. Though the gods were gone, there were other, even more ancient forces in the world – the many spirits of land and sea and sky – that demanded supplication. In return for worship the spirits were said to bestow the gifts of foresight to the wise men and women and magic to the sorceresses. Males who possessed the spark underwent the Shaman's ritual and transcended, becoming one with the animal that best represented their nature.

The spirits were also said to shelter the souls of the dead once they departed their mortal shells, until it was time to be reborn in a new form. It always amazed Yllandris that the men and women of the Lowlands held no such beliefs. She didn't know how a people could survive without faith. Perhaps that was the secret of the Lowlanders' love of gold – it was their religion, one they could see and feel and spend and pretend mattered. Until, inevitably, the moment arrived when it no longer did.

She and Thurva finally reached the crowd gathered around the gates and pushed their way through to the front. The huge wooden structures were flung wide.

A loud cheer erupted as King Magnar melted out of the early-morning mist, high and proud on his stallion. He had his war helm on and his visor pulled down to shield his eyes from the sun. He saw the gathered townsfolk and raised a hand in salute, provoking a fresh round of cheers. Yllandris felt her heart flutter. *He is a king, truly.*

Behind Magnar rode the Six, his elite bodyguards. Their helms, too, covered their faces. As they emerged out of the mist she saw that their horses dragged an immense wooden sledge behind them. It was covered in a tarpaulin, pulled tight over a huge form. Another cheer went up as the sledge trundled into view.

Following the Six were the drummers, who marched on foot, beating out that same relentless rhythm. *Boom. Boom. Boom.*

'Move aside!' commanded a haughty voice that could only belong to Shranree. The senior sister waddled up to Yllandris, her cheeks flushed and her oversized chest heaving from exertion. The other three members of the circle scurried along behind her. Shranree stared out at the approaching horsemen and clapped her hands together happily. 'Finally! I was beginning to grow concerned. And it would seem our king has brought the body of the demon back with him.'

Yllandris frowned. There was something bothering her, a sense that everything was not quite as it seemed. She had grown up learning to read her father's face. The way he breathed. The way the muscles around his jaw twitched. The moment of discord – that one dreaded sign was all she had needed to seek refuge in her small room. To pull the blanket over her head and wait for the inevitable to pass.

Was it the way the King sat his horse that troubled her? She narrowed her eyes against the sun's glare.

The first of Heartstone's warriors trotted into view. He halted just as he emerged from the mist, while ahead the King and his small retinue of guards and drummers continued on towards the gate, towing the sledge behind them.

Shranree suddenly leaned in close. 'I expect our young king will desire some company shortly,' she whispered. 'Remember what we discussed. I would see our circle expanded. The damage wrought by that fiend would have been considerably less had I more sorceresses at my disposal.'

'Yes, sister,' replied Yllandris, still distracted. *The shoulders are a shade too narrow,* she thought. Perhaps the light was playing tricks on her eyes.

The King cantered through the open gates and tugged on the reins, bringing his mount to a halt. The Six did the same and drew up beside him. The drummers stopped just outside the town, but the relentless throb of their beats continued unabated.

Sudden dread seized Yllandris as she watched the King dismount and walk over to the sledge. The way he moved was too tense, his strides a fraction too short. Her eyes made their way up his legs to his backside, and one glance at that too-bony posterior was all she needed to confirm her suspicions.

'Wait! This man is not the King—'

The words died on her lips as whoever was behind Magnar's helm drew his sword and thrust it through the tarpaulin, dragging it down the length of the sledge with a tearing sound that seemed to hang in the air. With his other hand, he grabbed hold of first one side of the split canvas and then the other, yanking them apart.

Gasps and screams exploded from those close enough to see the sledge. Six headless corpses were piled on the platform, leaking black blood. The stench was nauseating.

'What is the meaning of this?' Shranree demanded, striding towards the false king. The impostor reached up to his helm, Magnar's helm, and yanked it from his head.

'The meaning?' sneered Krazka, chieftain of the Lake

Reaching, his dead eye weeping foul white mucus in the beaming sun. 'I'm seizing this town and installing myself as the new king. Effective immediately.'

'What have you done with King Magnar?' Shranree thundered.

The Butcher of Beregund grinned. 'You'll see soon enough. He's alive – after a fashion. Now, I'm going to beckon to my men over yonder and they're going to trot right in here. Any trouble and I'll start killing folk where they stand.'

'You will do no such thing,' Shranree said. She raised her hands, muttered a few words... and then stared at her palms.

Krazka tapped the blade of his brutal single-edged sword. 'You ever heard of abyssium? Me neither, until recently. Got me some new friends up in the Spine, you see.'

Shranree spun around and gestured desperately at Yllandris and the other sorceresses. Thurva immediately pointed a finger at Krazka. A flicker of lightning crackled at the tip of her outstretched digit only to sputter out harmlessly.

Krazka sighed dramatically. Then he strolled over, grabbed the cross-eyed sorceress by the hair and slit her throat. Blood welled up around the wicked sword but he kept cutting, not stopping until the blade had severed the neck completely and the head came away in his hand. He tossed the grisly trophy on the ground where it rolled a couple of times and came to a halt, surprised eyes staring off in opposite directions.

Yllandris stared dumbfounded. The crowd broke and townsfolk started to flee. Some of the hardier men went to their weapons. Krazka gestured to the fake Six, who drew their swords, and then he pointed to the horsemen who were even now approaching the gates.

'I got me three hundred warriors from the Lake Reaching,' the one-eyed killer shouted. 'Any of you greybeards or cripples cause any trouble, I'll cut your throats. Then I'll find your wives and children and cut theirs, too.'

'The Shaman will not stand for this!' Shranree gasped, her voice quivering.

Krazka grinned. 'The Shaman will be dealt with. There's older and nastier things than him.' He looked up at the sky. 'I reckon one of 'em is due any moment.'

While Krazka had been speaking the drumming had been getting faster. Now it rose to a crescendo. *Boom. Boom. Boom.* There was a sudden ripple of wind and, like an unholy comet, the black-scaled horror plummeted down out of the clouds to land just outside of town. It unfolded like a monstrous black flower, rising up a good head and shoulders above the walls to gaze down with a trio of sinister eyes. The grievous wounds it had taken only a few short days ago had already healed.

Yllandris heard her sisters turn and run, but she was rooted to the spot, too terrified to do anything but stand and stare.

Krazka faced the towering demon. He appeared to be listening to something. He nodded, and then gestured at the fiend. 'It calls itself the Herald,' he said.

'This... creature talks to you?' asked Shranree, aghast.

'It don't speak. It forms words directly inside your skull,' replied Krazka. 'And it serves another, whose name it's too afraid to even think. Aye, you heard that right. Anyways, the Herald leads those of its kind that've made it through. Most ain't as bright as he is but that don't matter, see, since killing is what it's all about. The only way more of 'em can escape into our world is by sending souls in the opposite direction. So that's what they do.'

'And you... you are allied with this *thing*?' There was a note of curiosity in Shranree's voice now.

'It made contact. Offered me a deal I couldn't refuse. You don't know how many men I had to murder to become chieftain of the largest Reaching in the High Fangs. I thought to myself, why stop there? The Lowlands, they're a hundred times the size of this place. There's a whole *world* to conquer, I figure.'

'What will you do with us?' Shranree asked quietly.

'I saw your work at Frosthold. Got to say, I was impressed. Make me a new circle. One big enough for all the sorceresses in the Reachings. Those that refuse to swear fealty...' Krazka raised his sword and examined the glistening edge, still dripping with Thurva's blood.

Shranree stared at that deadly blade, as did Yllandris. Then the leader of the Heartstone circle straightened her robes and bowed to the chieftain. 'I am yours.'

'Excellent.' Krazka leered at Yllandris with his lone eye. 'And you?'

And me? I... wanted to be Queen. To marry Magnar and have children and prove to Shranree that I am no child. You're a butcher. A monster. You're worse than the Shaman.

Krazka's leering eye began to narrow. His sword shifted a fraction.

She gulped. 'I... I will serve you.'

'Good,' grunted the chieftain-who-would-be-emperor. 'Start by rounding up a few foundlings. They're no use to me, but they'll serve.'

'What do you mean?' asked Yllandris, though deep down she knew.

'Been a while since the Herald last killed. It needs to feed.'

The Longest Night

EREMUL SLUMPED IN his chair, so tired he almost toppled forwards and down over the parapet to his doom. The stench of smoke filled his nostrils. Ash drifted through the air, carried on the light breeze that had sprung up some time after midnight. Clouds of dust clogged the sky, making it hard to tell how long remained until dawn.

He stifled a yawn and tried to focus on the endless stretch of coast before him. The last salvo had been over an hour ago. He crossed his fingers and muttered a brief prayer to the Creator, hoping desperately that the attacks had ceased for the night. He was drained, physically and mentally, the wretched limits of his magic pushed to breaking point.

The first wave of missiles from the ballistae had struck almost as soon as the sun went down. Massive bolts of iron sailed through the night air to crash into the wall below him with a concussive force that shook the entire gatehouse. The first projectile had made such a deafening noise when it struck that he almost pissed his robes. The wall had, however, withstood the ballistae. He remembered thinking the worst might be over. Then the trebuchets appeared.

He glanced down below him to where piles of smouldering rubble glowed malevolently in the darkness. The Sumnians had launched stone and flaming tar at the city, creating a nightmare storm that obliterated everything it hit. The wall was breached in three separate places, the gate below him had caught fire, and several prominent buildings had been reduced to ruin.

When he first learned of his assignment to the wall Eremul had fully intended to fake a noble offensive against the city's liberators. He would send his magic wide of his apparent targets, loudly curse his misfortune while intentionally bungling his efforts to drive off the mercenaries. He abandoned that plan the moment a ton of rock missed the gatehouse by a few feet and massacred the poor sods living in the house across the street. From that point on he had evoked all the magic available to him and hurled it against the deadly siege engines as if his life depended on it. The effort had left him so exhausted he had puked up his guts.

There was no hiding. The Halfmage had been the city's sole means of defence. Dorminia had no siege weapons of its own, at least none capable of reaching the enemy. The militia had taken to the battlements and sent arrows down at the mercenaries, but that had proved to be a spectacularly stupid tactic. The Sumnians were well out of bowshot range and almost impossible to see against the night sky. The conscripted men abandoned their position after the first wave of missiles from the trebuchets crushed a score of them beneath a shattered section of wall.

All in all, the first engagement had gone very much as anticipated. The invaders had weakened Dorminia's fortifications while taking only minor casualties of their own. The real battle would begin on the morrow, when the light of day made the task of killing all the easier. The mercenary army would seek to infiltrate the breaches created by their trebuchets. Eremul had no intention of being around when that happened. He had his own part to play in the conflict, and the time had come to put the wheels in motion. Metaphorical and otherwise.

Willing his tired arms into one last effort, he turned his

chair around and entered the abused gatehouse. The floor was covered in rubble but the building was otherwise mostly intact. Once again Eremul silently thanked his luck. He had been fortunate to survive the night. The White Lady couldn't have known her agent would be placed in such a precarious position. She would doubtless be aghast to learn how close her own forces had come to killing him and ruining the plot to assassinate Salazar.

An officer of the Watch was surveying the damage. The man scratched at his bristling moustache, which perched like a mouse below a bulbous nose threaded with blue veins. Eremul pursed his lips. *What's your name again? Lieutenant Toram? Ah yes, one of the officers from out in the sticks. Ripe for a wizard's manipulations, if my luck holds.*

'The enemy has withdrawn for the remainder of the night,' he said. 'I must return home and rest for a few hours or I shall be useless come tomorrow.'

'I was told you were to remain here.'

Eremul tried to suppress his irritation. 'I would love to, but as you can see I am hardly a peak physical specimen. A wizard's power only stretches so far. I need sleep.'

Toram looked doubtful. 'You can sleep here. I'll wake you if the enemy attacks again.'

'Look at me,' said the Halfmage. 'I've been sitting in this chair all night. My arse feels like it has been gnawed on by a pack of rabid dogs. I need my own bed. And a swig of something strong.'

'A swig of something strong?' the lieutenant repeated, slowly and carefully. His grey moustache twitched. Eremul was torn between the urge to gloat at his flawless intuition and the desire to vaporize the man where he stood for being such a dumbfuck. The Watch was so *predictable*.

'Yes,' he confirmed. 'I will gladly share a drop with the soldier who escorts me to my abode. It's near the harbour, a brisk walk from here.'

Lieutenant Toram rubbed at his moustache one more time and then nodded. 'I'll see to it myself. It's the least I can do, considering what a sterling job you've done defending the city.'

The grizzled old officer took hold of Eremul's chair by the handles and wheeled him to the edge of the steps leading down from the gatehouse. He lowered the chair one step at a time, each small *thump* sending fresh pain shooting through its occupant's arse. The Halfmage gritted his teeth and tried to ignore the agony. The first part of the plan was progressing smoothly. He just hoped his contact was where he was supposed to be.

They moved south at an impressive pace, Lieutenant Toram clearly eager to avoid any unwelcome questions from his superiors. Soldiers and militiamen were everywhere, putting out small fires and attempting to shore up gaps in the wall.

Eremul stared around at the carnage. Houses had been flattened, the timber and plaster collapsing under the weight of tons of falling rock. Several sturdier buildings constructed from granite had been hit and still stood, though the roofs were shattered in parts. He saw an arm emerging from a pile of slag near one house, clutching at the air in a death grip. Nothing was visible of the arm's owner save for a dark pool of blood oozing around the edge of the debris.

They passed south through the Bazaar. One trebuchet load had landed almost dead centre in the market, reducing several stalls to splinters. No one appeared to have been harmed by that particular projectile, but a little further along Eremul spotted a sight to make his heart shrivel up in his chest. A group of orphans were dragging tiny bodies from the Warrens to the south-west of the Bazaar. Some of the corpses were so crushed and twisted they were beyond recognition.

'What happened?' he asked thickly as the officer wheeled his chair past the children.

One of the orphans turned to stare at him. 'It fell from the sky,' he answered in a voice as dead as old bone. 'We're still pulling the bodies out of the rubble.'

As they drew nearer the harbour, Toram spoke. 'We send foundlings to the quarries up in Malbrec. No one misses them if they have an accident. It must be a right bloody nuisance, having all those little bastards underfoot.'

Eremul said nothing. Instead he gripped the sides of his chair so hard he thought the wood might split beneath his fingers.

A few minutes passed, and then the depository was in sight. The sky had lightened slightly, indicating that dawn was finally on the way. Eremul searched the murk around the building for any sign of his contact. There was no one.

'I thought a wizard might live in a grander place than this,' observed Toram as he wheeled him to the door of the depository. The lieutenant's moustache shifted slightly as he wrinkled his mouth. 'It smells like shit.'

'I appreciate the compliment.' Eremul reached into his robes and withdrew a small bronze key, unlocked the door and pushed it open. He was growing increasingly concerned. *Where the hell is the White Lady's agent? The letter said he would meet me here*. Perhaps his contact had been discovered. If that was the case he was sure to be tortured for further information – and that meant Eremul himself was royally screwed.

He wheeled himself into the depository. There was no light within, and it still smelled of damp from the recent flood. Toram followed him inside. 'It's as dark as a Sumnian's arsehole in here. How about we get a flame going and see to that drink—'

The officer was cut off abruptly as a shadow detached itself from the wall behind the door and grabbed him around the throat. 'Don't say a word,' the mysterious figure whispered, somewhat melodramatically.

Eremul squinted but was unable to make out the man's

features in the poor light. 'I assume you are the agent sent by our mutual friend.'

Toram squirmed. The unexpected guest held a dagger at his throat. It seemed to emit a faint glow. 'I am,' the figure replied. He sounded young, Eremul thought. 'My name is Davarus Cole.'

Davarus Cole. Cole was a bastard's name, a common enough appellation in Dorminia and the surrounding lands.

He had known another man named Cole once. A shiver passed through him.

Toram shifted again, pushing his captor's arm away from his throat a fraction. He managed a muffled cry for help, but no one would hear him. The streets were empty this close to the harbour; everyone was taking shelter in their homes.

Eremul sighed. 'Oh, for pity's sake. Just kill him.'

Davarus Cole seemed to hesitate for a second. Then he brought his dagger across Toram's neck in a jerking motion. The lieutenant gasped wetly and fell to his knees. A few seconds later he toppled over and lay still, to the obvious discomfort of his killer.

Eremul pushed his chair forwards an inch or two. Forcing out the last dregs of magic within him, he muttered a few words and evoked a glowing sphere of light around one trembling hand. Then he raised it, in order to better see the face of the city's would-be saviour.

He gasped. The resemblance was undeniable. That nose, crooked yet still so similar; the grey eyes staring back at him. 'Your father. Who was he?'

Davarus Cole looked proud. 'Illarius Cole. He was a great hero. You might say I take after him in many respects.'

'Illarius Cole. A great hero,' Eremul stated flatly. He stared at young Cole's face. The lad nodded solemnly in response.

The irony was too much. Eremul felt the muscles in his cheek twitch, and suddenly the mirth burst out of him. He sucked in air in great wheezing gasps, laughing so hard he almost shat himself.

'What's so funny?' asked Cole, sounding somewhat annoyed.

Eremul waved his hand, inadvertently sending the globe of light dancing over Lieutenant Toram. The man's face was frozen in an expression of shock. Blood glistened on the carpet below his open neck. 'I fear you have been... slightly misinformed.'

'Misinformed?' Cole repeated.

Eremul stared back at the lad and tried to gather himself. *Not misinformed, boy. Lied to. Fed a festering pile of bullshit that would choke the most dishonest magistrate. Your father, Illarius Cole, a hero? I could shatter your world, here and now, if I but told you the truth.*

The youngster's face was a picture of earnest confusion. Despite everything, Eremul found himself feeling sorry for the young fool. 'Do you possess his dagger?'

'You mean Magebane? It's right here.' Davarus Cole patted the side of his waist, where he must have sheathed the glowing weapon beneath his dark cloak.

Eremul remembered the feel of that blade against his throat. The way it had leached his magic away and left him powerless before he was carried off to the Obelisk dungeons to be maimed and turned into a tool of Salazar's. Bitterness filled him, and he almost blurted out the truth. Almost.

You too are a tool, he realized, studying that familiar face. *There is no sense breaking you until you have served your purpose. That is, if you do not find out from Salazar before then.*

'What did you mean by misinformed?' the boy asked again, this time sounding anxious.

Eremul shook his head. 'Forget it. You are quite right – your father was one of the greatest men I ever had the fortune to meet. I am sure you will prove equal to his heroic legacy.'

Cole grinned happily, the doubt on his face instantly replaced by glowing pride. Eremul sighed. A thought suddenly occurred to him. 'I don't suppose you were on the ship that rescued a band of rebels from Farrowgate?'

'Yes. How did you guess?'

'Brianna was aboard that vessel, was she not?' Cole nodded in confirmation. 'Tell me,' he continued. 'Did you happen to meet a fellow by the name of Isaac?'

'I know him.' The look on the young man's face told its own story.

'Did he say or do anything that struck you as... strange?'

'Now that you mention it, there was something odd about him. I tried to raise my concerns to the group. No one wanted to listen.'

Isaac, Isaac... What game are you playing? He glanced out of the window. The black sky had given way to a shade of grey. *How many will lose their lives this coming day? That all depends on the fate of one man. One Magelord. Salazar has to die or Dorminia will drown in blood.*

He glanced back at Cole. 'Morning is an hour away,' he said. 'The White Lady's army will soon be at the walls. We will make our way to the Obelisk in the confusion.'

'What if we're seen?'

'If anyone asks, we tell them Salazar summoned me. Important wizardly business of some kind. Arcane matters beyond the comprehension of regular folk. All that bullshit.'

'What sort of trouble can I expect once I'm in the tower?'

Eremul shrugged. 'Less than in normal circumstances. The Supreme Augmentor is busy leading the city's defence. I suspect that, very soon, his magic-wielding heavies will be needed at the gates. The White Lady's pale servants will not be easily turned aside by the Watch and the militia.'

'You've seen them? What are those women?'

'It's probably best not to speculate. In any case, we still have some time before we leave. I will remind you of the Obelisk's layout.'

'That would be helpful. I just have one question before we start.'

Eremul narrowed his eyes. He had a terrible suspicion he knew what was coming. 'Yes?'

'I was just wondering… what happened to your legs?'

Fire And Blood

DAWN ARRIVED ON the second day. The air felt thick and still, as if the world was holding its breath in anticipation.

Sasha wanted to vomit. She hadn't slept a wink, but her nerves were afire and she felt more awake now than she had since she'd pushed those last dregs of precious powder up her nose back at Farrowgate. Ahead of her she could see the massive holes the great siege weapons had inflicted on Dorminia's walls. The damage was far too severe to be repaired in the brief respite the trebuchet operators had afforded the city's defenders. The gate itself still stood, though that was no coincidence.

There had been a wizard on the wall last night. Two of the ballistae had been set aflame and one of the trebuchets had lost an arm. Brianna had concluded that the wizard could only be the Halfmage. Thereafter they had directed the bombardment away from the gatehouse. Apparently the strange crippled mage who had helped her small group depart the harbour unnoticed over a month ago was none other than Cole's mysterious contact. The revelation hardly allayed her fears.

General Zolta's men had circled around the hills north of the city under the cover of darkness. They had taken with them most of the undamaged catapults and ballistae. The trebuchets were too large and unwieldy to navigate the hilly ground. Zolta's company would launch a salvo from the eastern side, splitting the attention of Dorminia's defenders in half. General D'rak's men would wait in reserve until the city had been breached.

'You ready for this, lass?'

Brodar Kayne had insisted on staying close to her. Sasha would be lying if she pretended she didn't appreciate the gesture. She could feel dozens of eyes on her, crawling all over her skin. It wasn't just the mercenaries, whose attentions could at least be explained by the fact that her mere presence in the army was a bizarre sight. Three-Finger leered at her whenever the opportunity arose, stripping her naked with his dark, feral eyes. Jerek stared too – though his gaze held only honest hatred. There was almost a strange comfort in that.

'I'm ready,' she replied, gripping her crossbow tightly in her left hand. She'd strapped a short sword to the belt at her waist, for all the good it would do. She hardly knew one end of a blade from the other, and had no intention of getting involved in any kind of mêlée if she could help it.

Sasha had read unlikely tales about women who had never lifted a sword in their lives leading armies and chopping down soldiers like firewood. That was the stuff of fantasy, the delusions of cosseted fools who had never felt the terrible strength of a man pinning them to the ground.

She was no fool. She was a survivor.

Dark-skinned men jostled her on every side. The company would advance on the gate ten abreast. She found herself alongside Brodar Kayne, Jerek and several mercenaries she didn't know. Three-Finger was nearby. The Shamaathan assassin had departed with General Zolta's force.

'Still no sign of Isaac,' she whispered to the old Highlander beside her. 'It's like he disappeared.'

Brodar Kayne frowned. He was already perspiring profusely. It was shaping up to be the hottest day of the year so far. 'Isaac's a weird 'un. I expect he'll turn up somewhere.'

'This is doing my fucking head in,' Jerek grumbled. 'All this bullshit. You see the enemy, you charge in and you fuck him up. Not stand around with your cocks out.'

'Aye,' said Kayne. 'Seems these Sumnians do things a bit

different. Hang in there, Wolf. We'll get to the fighting before you know it.'

Jerek spat. Sasha looked away to hide her disgust. Unfortunately her eyes met Three-Finger's, who gave her an obscene wink. She stared back at him unflinchingly, fingering the trigger in her hand, but someone buffeted her in the back and before she knew it they were advancing on the city.

The army halted again just out of bowshot range. Sasha could see tiny faces peering at them from behind the battlements. Her palms were sweating, the handle of the crossbow so slick it felt as though it would slip from her hand. The sun was a red furnace right overhead.

Brianna's voice suddenly resounded from the very front of the column, so loud it hurt Sasha's ears from where she was positioned halfway down the line fifty yards back. From their reactions, it was evident the defenders on the wall could also hear the wizard's magically amplified words.

'Fellow Dorminians! I ask you to lay down your weapons. We come not to seize the city but to liberate it. To rid you of a dictator. Put down your bows and swords and you will not be harmed.' Silence followed as they waited to see what effect Brianna's plea would have. Sasha swatted a fly away from her face and stared up at the clouds. A mindhawk circled high above.

The archers on the walls were not soldiers, she knew. They were farmers and tradesmen, forced into service by Salazar and the Watch. Most of them probably loathed the city's Magelord, but it was a sorry truth that the familiar oppression of a despot was often preferable to the unknown.

Now they had a singular opportunity to change things for the better: to replace a ruthless tyrant with a benevolent patron who would offer Dorminia liberty as well as protection. Sasha didn't know much about Thelassa, but the wizard Brianna – whom she had so grown to respect over the last couple of weeks – gave her ample reason to trust the enigmatic White Lady.

She held her breath. The defenders were visibly agitated. For a moment she thought they were going to down arms and surrender – but then, all of a sudden, order was apparently restored. There was a pause, and the White Lady's adviser received her answer.

The volley of arrows landed just short of the mage. Brianna shook her head and turned to General Zahn beside her. She uttered a few words. The bald-headed behemoth, who still hadn't bothered to don any armour, crossed his arms in front of his scarred chest and faced his men. 'We charge!' he bellowed. The general needed no magic to carry his cavernous voice down the column.

The mercenaries in the row directly behind their general carried a huge battering ram. The ten men detached from the column and shifted around so that their burden was aiming directly at the western gate. They broke into a run.

Sasha felt her breath quicken. The mercenaries ahead of her began to trot, and then to sprint, and before she knew it she was being swept along behind them. Brodar Kayne kept pace beside her. 'Stick close to me,' he said.

A rain of arrows fell from the sky directly overhead and her heart climbed into her throat. *I'm going to die*, she thought dully, watching the missiles descend – but the hail of arrows seemed to hit an invisible barrier. They slowed suddenly and then fell harmlessly to the ground. Another wave of arrows plummeted towards them, and they too stopped short before clattering to the hard turf. She glanced at Brianna. The wizard was concentrating hard, sweat dripping from her hair. She was mouthing arcane words, clearly a spell of some kind to shield the army from the archers.

The battering ram had reached the city. It crashed against the gates with a bone-shaking impact, causing the wooden barrier to crack slightly. The mercenaries trotted backwards, lined up the ram again, and then dashed forwards once more, driving the log into the gates with enough force to buckle one.

Behind them, several groups of mercenaries broke off from the column, making for the breaches in the city walls. The rest waited, weapons readied, preparing to pour through the gates just as soon as they fell. Sasha slowed, and then gasped.

Something was wrong. There was an alien sensation in the air – a throbbing, terrifying tension that made her muscles seize up and bile rise in her throat. All around her mercenaries cried out in shock. Some dropped their weapons. Brodar Kayne's greatsword didn't waver, but the old Highlander's teeth were grinding together so hard she could hear them. 'Magic,' he managed to whisper. 'Salazar.'

There was an awful whining noise. It was coming from Brianna. The wizard was convulsing, staring up at something in the distance. Sasha followed her tortured gaze, saw the summit of the Obelisk looming above the walls and knew that the Tyrant of Dorminia was flexing his might. Red spittle ran down Brianna's chin and her eyes bulged as if they would burst from their sockets at any moment. *He's killing her.*

'So... strong...' Brianna uttered.

'No!' screamed Sasha. The dying wizard looked at her, blood leaking from her eyes to run like tears down her cheeks.

Then, incredibly, she began to straighten. Her bones splintered and jutted from her shattered body as she forced herself upright. 'Get inside... the city...' she said, her face a bloody mess. She jerked again as something snapped in her back. 'Salazar,' she managed, spitting out half of her tongue. 'This... is for *you*.'

And she exploded. Blood and viscera sprayed the mercenaries closest to her, but something else emerged from the mage's corpse: a bolt of glowing red fire that hummed for a second or two and then roared off at blinding speed towards the Obelisk. It struck the top of the great tower in an explosion of falling masonry and flame. When the dust cleared, a smoking hole the size of a house was visible.

Sasha wanted to run away and never look back. Instead she

took a deep breath and raised her crossbow. The pressure inside her was gone. Salazar's sinister magic had been broken by Brianna's final sacrifice. All around her men were reclaiming their weapons from the ground. The mercenaries in front of the damaged gates of the city hauled the great battering ram up between them. They took a few steps back, unleashed a great war cry and launched themselves forwards. The wood splintered and the gates were torn away from their hinges.

Crimson Watchmen immediately poured through the breach, swords raised. The mercenaries tossed the battering ram aside and drew their own weapons as their comrades rushed in to help. Brodar Kayne nodded, gave her shoulder a comforting squeeze and moved to join the fray.

Sasha took another deep breath and followed.

The crossbow clicked. The bolt missed her target, sailing harmlessly wide. Sasha swore, reached down and drew her sword as the burly Watchman leaped the bodies of two of his fellows and brandished his own blade. Before he could reach her a Sumnian plunged a spear into his side. It sank deep, piercing his chainmail, and he staggered. The mercenary was on him in an instant, his long dagger plunging into the soldier's neck. He went down, choking on blood. The black-skinned warrior pulled his spear free of the corpse and returned to the huge mêlée just ahead.

Sasha had no idea how much time had passed since the battle began. They had been forced back from the gates by the Watch, and now the soldiers formed a wall of crimson in front of the entrance to the city. Behind them, she knew, an unknown number of militiamen waited.

There were still a few archers on the battlements and occasionally an arrow would pick off a stray mercenary, but the bulk of the conscripts were apparently engaged in defending the breaches in the wall. From what she had seen, the archers were poor shots. With the fighters on both sides packed so closely together, they were as likely to hit their own men as the enemy.

She narrowed her eyes, trying to make sense of the chaos. The Sumnians were clearly the superior fighters, faster and more skilled, but their leather armour offered scant protection from the Watch's swords and the arrows from above. General Zahn bellowed instructions from a nearby hillock, his four guards forming a shield wall around him. In the distance she could see General D'rak's company eager to engage. They were awaiting the signal from Zahn, but it didn't look as if that was coming any time soon. The western gate and the three major breaches in the city wall formed choke points that greater numbers would do little to penetrate, and there was no sense in providing more targets for the archers.

Another Watch soldier noticed her and came sprinting over just as she finished reloading her crossbow. This time Sasha put the quarrel in his stomach, stopping him in his tracks. He lurched away, clawing at his midriff, his agonized cries haunting her from where she knelt in the shallow depression. A few archers had taken shots at her, but she was at the very limits of their range and the arrows had gone far wide.

She tried to calm her nerves as she watched Kayne and Jerek cut a bloody swathe through the Crimson Watch. The two men were like forces of nature, Jerek a whirlwind of axes chopping at arms and legs while his older companion moved as serenely as a cloud before striking like lightning. He seemed able to read every single blow before it landed. Even as she looked on, Kayne sidestepped a sword thrust and smashed the pommel of his greatsword into his attacker's face, dropping him like a sack of potatoes, and then spun around to dodge another Watchman's overhead swing. An arrow took the soldier in the back at almost the exact moment he stepped into the Highlander's path.

Sasha shook her head. The old barbarian had an uncanny knack of being in the right place at the right time.

A loud grunting drew her attention closer to her hiding spot.

Three-Finger was grappling with one of the city's defenders, stabbing him repeatedly through a hole in the man's armour. Blood splattered his scabrous face but he kept on stabbing long after the soldier had stopped twitching. He saw her watching him, gave her a yellow grin which turned to a bellow of pain as an arrow suddenly pierced his shoulder.

She squinted up at the battlements. The militiamen had returned to the wall in force and were now raining arrows down indiscriminately, hitting mercenaries and Watchmen alike. Dark-skinned Sumnians and scarlet-clad Dorminians fell to the ground, pierced by missiles.

There was a sudden blur to the side of her. Like damned souls escaping from the gates of hell, the White Lady's pale servants glided past with unnatural speed. The women went straight past the fighting, ignoring the arrow-strewn killing field, and began scaling the walls with their bare hands.

Sasha's mouth dropped open in shock. They crawled up the stone like spiders – a sight so unnatural it filled her with sudden horror.

The first of the women reached the top and disappeared over the side. A moment later the broken body of a militiaman tumbled over the wall, his head at a crazy angle to his neck. More conscripts fell from the wall, dropping like flies.

Sasha glanced at the hillock again and saw General Zahn gesturing wildly at General D'rak and his company. The thousand mercenaries raised their weapons and began to advance.

She reached for another bolt and her hand came away empty. She hesitated for a second, then discarded the spent quiver and drew her sword. The mercenaries and Watchmen were locked in combat outside the walls, while just inside the city pandemonium had broken out. The White Lady's servants were seemingly unstoppable, moving with blinding speed and striking with bare hands that carried the force of a hammer blow. They twisted and spun and attacked from impossible angles, bending like quicksilver to avoid the desperate lunges and swings of the Watch and militiamen. Soldiers fell with their heads crushed, their necks broken, their spines shattered.

She had to look away. Not even the Watch deserved this. Salazar was their true enemy. Brianna's last desperate act had disrupted his magic, but she knew he was still up there in the Obelisk, watching them, waiting until he was sufficiently recovered to launch another deadly spell.

Come on, Cole. You can't fail. If you do, there will be nothing left of the city but corpses.

You can't fail.

Come the Hour

'LORD SALAZAR IS unharmed, Commandant.'

Barandas breathed a sigh of relief. The magical assault on the Obelisk had been completely unexpected. He had feared the worst when he saw the explosion.

Kalen adjusted his ponytail and stroked his bow thoughtfully. The young Augmentor carried no quiver on his back. The weapon he held in his hands provided its own ammunition. 'I saw the Halfmage on the way to the Obelisk.'

The Supreme Augmentor grimaced in annoyance. The accursed wizard should have been on the western wall helping defend the city! 'Did he care to explain *why* he abandoned his station?'

Kalen shrugged. 'He said only that our lord required his presence. I feel sorry for the poor sod he had pushing him.'

Barandas sighed. He didn't trust the Halfmage as far as he could throw him, but there was nothing to be done about it now. If the sarcastic bastard didn't have a good reason for showing up at the Obelisk, Thurbal would send him packing soon enough. He had bigger concerns.

Captain Bracka's last report indicated the mercenaries were getting the better of the Watch at the western gate. Barandas had wanted to send more militia out to bolster the defenders, but the company approaching from the east would soon lay siege to that side of the city and he wanted men held in reserve. The situation as it stood could be better – but they need only hold the walls a few hours longer.

The nightmarish visage of Garmond loomed into view, a black silhouette against the afternoon sun. His plate armour clanked as he paced back and forth, squeezing his gauntleted fists together as if every moment spent away from the fighting was mental torture. 'When do I get to kill something?' he rumbled from behind his demonic helm. Three of his colleagues nodded in agreement.

Barandas had gathered almost all his elite enforcers to him, a dozen Augmentors in total. They made for a motley assembly, but there was no deadlier force in the Trine. Each man was worth ten normal soldiers. Some, such as the restless giant regarding him with his vambraced arms crossed, no less than twenty.

'Patience, Garmond,' Barandas replied. 'Were it not for recent events and the terrible losses we have suffered, I would not hesitate to send you against the enemy. But we are no longer forty. We are no longer even half that. I must use you wisely.'

Legwynd. Rorshan. Both gone. Falcus, too, more than likely. Whatever happened at the Swell?

The expedition to the Lord of the Deep's resting place was supposed to have provided raw crystallized magic with which to forge new Augmentors. Instead they had received nothing but silence. Falcus could have returned to Dorminia in less than a day, in the event of an emergency. That he had not done so could only mean the expedition had ended in disaster.

He shook his head. They had known the voyage would be perilous. He thought of Admiral Kramer's poor family, the relief they must have felt at seeing his death sentence rescinded only to lose him again to the vagaries of the Swell. *The world is fond of such terrible ironies.*

Someone was approaching from across the street. It was Captain Loric, judging by the hitch in his step. 'What news from the east gate?' he demanded.

'They will be within range of the city in a bell,' replied the captain.

'How many men do we have on the wall?'

Loric wiped sweat from his brow. He possessed a distinct band of white at the front of his otherwise dark hair. Unsurprisingly, that physical quirk combined with his penchant for harassing the men under him had resulted in his nickname of the Badger. 'Fifteen hundred militia. Two hundred Watchmen.'

Barandas thought for a moment. 'Keep the militia on the battlements. Launch a sortie to disrupt the siege weapons if necessary. We must hold them off for long enough.'

The captain opposite him blinked in confusion. 'Hold them off long enough for what, Commandant?'

'Let me worry about that, Captain. See to your orders.'

'Aye.' Loric saluted. He hesitated for a moment. 'I don't suppose you've seen Lieutenant Toram?'

Barandas shook his head. He remembered the moustached officer from his brief visit to Malbrec. Not a good day.

'No matter,' Loric replied. 'By your leave, sir.' He saluted again and limped back across the square, heading eastwards.

Barandas watched him go. Faces peeked at him from behind drapes and then melted away again. The streets were empty except for soldiers and the odd militiaman scurrying about. Houses stood silent, shops closed, taverns barred shut. All those not actively involved in the defence of the city – women, the young, the old, the infirm – were taking refuge behind closed doors.

He thought of Lena back at their estate in the Noble Quarter. She would be waiting for him, sick with worry – and perhaps other things. *I'm going to be a father.* He had not seen his wife since yesterday morning and the guilt gnawed at him. *I have a duty*, he reminded himself. *To the city. To the people. To my lord.*

He reached into the small bag at this belt and withdrew the silk handkerchief Lena had given him to celebrate their fourth year of marriage. It smelled of jasmine and her favourite perfume, and he smiled when he brought it close to his face.

'Sir,' Kalen called. It sounded like a warning. Barandas looked up and saw Captain Bracka leaning on another soldier as he struggled to make his way towards them. One side of the officer's face was covered in blood, which ran down his cheek to merge with the red of his beard, and he cradled his right arm in his left. Barandas could see bone protruding from the broken limb.

'Captain, what has happened?' he demanded.

Bracka's eyes were haunted. He looked as if he had seen a ghost. 'Monsters,' he said dully. 'Monsters clothed as women. They scaled the wall, killed three dozen men before we could react...' His voice trailed off.

'They came from nowhere,' the young Watchman supporting Bracka interjected. His voice shook. 'We received no warning.'

Barandas grimaced. The mindhawks had detected no sign of the pale women. Lord Salazar had warned him that the White Lady's servants possessed strange abilities – he had witnessed their potency at first hand – but immunity to thought-mining was something even the Magelord had not foreseen.

'There's more, sir. The third company is on the move. The walls will be breached within the hour.'

Within the hour. That was too soon. He had to protect the city – at all costs. He turned to his Augmentors. 'Men, draw your weapons. We go to Dorminia's defence.'

The brightness of the day suddenly intensified as glowing implements of death sprang from their sheaths. Garmond slammed one gauntleted fist into another with a force like that of two bulls butting heads. 'At fucking last,' he snarled.

Barandas placed Lena's handkerchief carefully back into the bag at his belt and drew his own sword. It whispered softly as it brushed against the scabbard, like a dying man's sigh. There was no ostentation about the cold steel. No magical luminescence. The only magic he possessed was within the mechanical instrument pumping blood around his body. Lord Salazar had told him that he required nothing more.

With a final glance across the square in the direction of the Noble Quarter, he beckoned to his men and set off towards the western wall.

When they arrived, it was to behold a scene of carnage. Bodies lay strewn all over the cobbles, twisted and broken like discarded dolls. Fighting raged ahead of them as the city's remaining defenders attempted to hold the sundered gates against the flood of dark-skinned warriors trying to force their way through.

Smaller pockets of fighting had broken out in spots just inside the wall. A group of Watchmen surrounded a pale-skinned woman and were hacking at her desperately. She was missing her left arm below the elbow, but the grievous wound did little to slow her. With stunning speed, the woman twisted out of the way of a sword thrust and flung herself on the back of one of her opponents. She reached around his neck as he tried to shake her off and almost yanked his head off. Barandas heard vertebrae snap as the man's eyes rolled up into their sockets.

Setting his jaw in a grim line, the Supreme Augmentor strode towards the pale woman, who leaped from the soldier's back as he fell lifeless to the ground. She sprang at him, almost got her hand to his throat before his sword cleaved her skull in two. Foul grey matter splattered over his golden armour but he ignored it, searching around for new enemies. He spotted two more of the pale women over by the left entrance to the gatehouse. They were standing at the centre of a heap of corpses, their white robes soaked through with blood.

One of the women noticed him. Her dead eyes revealed no surprise, no fear, no regard at all for the horror all around them. She pointed at him. Together the two pale women began moving closer.

His vision blurred for an instant as something fiery streaked across their path and then one of the women was hurtling backwards, a smoking hole in her chest. Barandas glanced to his right and saw Kalen drawing back his bow for another shot.

The ponytailed Augmentor gasped suddenly as the bloody point of a spear burst through his chest. His Sumnian killer was still trying to tug the weapon free as Garmond appeared, gore trailing from his gauntlets, and snatched the man up from the ground. With a sickening crack, he brought the southerner down over his knee, breaking his back.

Barandas tore his gaze away and focused on the unnatural creature approaching. The woman slowed a short distance from him and cocked her head as if surprised by something. 'You have no heart,' she observed in an emotionless monotone.

He gripped his sword more tightly, every muscle poised to spring into action. 'I am more human than you, creature. Whatever you are.'

The woman's lips curled into a smile, though nothing reached her eyes. 'Then I will gladly fall beneath your blade, if you are worthy. I pray it is so.'

The smile faded.

As Barandas stared at the creature, understanding dawned. This... thing, whatever it was, *wanted* to die. He would do his best to oblige her.

She darted towards him and he rolled at the last instant, springing to his feet and twisting around to meet her as she pivoted for another attack. This time his sword caught her below the knee, causing her to stumble past him. Quick as a flash he reversed his swing and severed her spine. She stumbled to the ground – and then, to his horror, began pulling herself towards him with her arms, dragging her useless legs along the blood-stained cobbles.

'*Do it*,' she rasped, staring up at him with those soulless orbs. He nodded once, brought his sword up and back down, splitting her head like a melon. *Whatever you were, I pity you*, he thought. He watched the discoloured fluids draining out

385

from the creature's cranium. The thing was rotting from the inside; it smelled as if it had been dead for months.

Ragged cheering drew his attention. The arrival of the Augmentors had given the defenders a boost. As he surveyed the battlefield he saw most of the pale women were now dead or dying, though he had lost Kalen and, it seemed, his friend Varca, whose magical helm rested fifteen feet away from the Augmentor's body. The severed head was still strapped inside the helm. Elsewhere the Sumnians had been driven back, and now the militia and the remnants of the Watch were pressing ahead, pushing them back further still.

Barandas raised his sword and gestured at the mêlée ahead of him, just outside the gates. 'Forward!' he shouted. His remaining Augmentors and the nearby defenders rushed to obey his command and together they surged into the enemy ranks. He turned away one spear, stabbed the owner through the guts and then yanked his sword free to behead another southerner.

A wall of shields suddenly loomed before them. The red-haired Augmentor, Jardwym, raised his mighty enchanted maul and swung it with all his strength. The shields exploded in a shower of splinters and the men holding them were thrown twenty feet backwards through the air from the force of the impact. Some struggled to their feet; others would never rise again.

Barandas's eyes narrowed. Over there, on the hillock: a monster of a man, unimaginably tall, towering above even Garmond. He was naked from the waist up, his chest crisscrossed with old scars. This could only be the infamous general he had heard so much about.

The Supreme Augmentor made for the leader of the dark-skinned mercenaries. *Cut off the head and the body will die.* Lord Salazar was fond of that phrase – though he had done the opposite when he had massacred Shadowport...

Barandas gripped his sword firmly. This was not the time for uncertainty. He pressed ahead, killing with surgical precision any Sumnian in his path. The enchanted heart in his chest ensured his body never tired. Mentally he required occasional rest as might anyone else, but physically he was a machine: an inexhaustible instrument of unmatched lethality.

A lone enemy appeared just as a clear stretch to the small hill opened before him. Unlike the rest of them this one was white of skin. He was panting heavily, a greatsword clutched in his gnarled old hands. A jagged scar ran down his battered face and his hide armour was covered in spots of blood.

Barandas frowned. *A Highlander? Here?*

He thrust all thoughts aside as he closed on the greybeard. He launched his attack, intending to make short work of the old warrior. His first swing was blocked just as he anticipated, so he dropped his shoulder and reversed his stroke, ready to dash by the instant his blade sliced through—

His slash was parried. Shocked, he barely got his sword back up in time as the old man launched a counter-attack, striking with alarming skill, first one direction and then the other, the massive greatsword flowing as easily as the Redbelly River. Incredibly, Barandas found himself being driven back. He knocked aside one thrust, just about parried another, and then almost gasped in shock as the pommel of the greatsword caught him a glancing blow on the nose.

The old Highlander stared at him with implacable blue eyes. 'Come at me,' he growled.

Barandas obliged.

The Hero's Destiny

D AVARUS COLE STEPPED carefully around the debris and glanced up at the black monolith soaring above him. Smoke still billowed from the top of the Obelisk. Chunks of granite – the fallen remnants of the tower's apex – littered the surrounding courtyard almost to the entrance, which was deserted. At any other time, at least twenty Watchmen would be stationed in the barracks either side of the courtyard. Right now every soldier in the city was desperately holding the walls against Dorminia's would-be liberators.

Lost in thought, Cole accidentally bumped the chair against a piece of rubble. It jerked and almost toppled over. 'Shit! Watch where you're going!' hissed his charge as he clung on for dear life.

'Sorry,' he mumbled. They had got this far on the pretence that Eremul had been summoned by the Tyrant of Dorminia, with Cole his begrudging helper. That deception would be useless once they were inside the tower. He was sweating under his leathers, and not just from the warmth of the afternoon sun.

Eremul hissed suddenly, 'There's someone coming.' A red-cloaked guard emerged from the shadows shrouding the entrance to the Obelisk. The mage shot him a warning look. 'Let me do the talking.'

The two of them continued on up to the gates. The uneven surface caused the wizard to bounce up and down like a man sat astride a particularly recalcitrant mule.

'Halt!' demanded the Watchman. He levelled his spear at them. 'The Obelisk is not expecting visitors.'

'Well met,' said Eremul brightly. 'I am the Halfmage. You may have heard of me. I am here in answer to his lordship's summons.'

The guard appeared unimpressed. 'Tough shit. I was told to allow no one through. Thurbal's orders.'

A strange expression slowly distorted Eremul's face. Cole almost shuddered, so gruesome and unnatural did it appear. It took him a moment to realize the mage was smiling. 'Come now, friend. We both know Lord Salazar does not explain his whims to the likes of us.'

The Watchman's monobrow arched in confusion and his eyes seemed to glaze over. Finally he nodded and lowered his spear. 'Right you are. I'll open the gates. Ah, about your friend here...'

'He's with me. While my compact frame bestows many benefits, traversing multiple flights of stairs by myself is not among them.'

'Of course.' The guard's face seemed frozen in a peculiar dreamy stare. He turned and unlocked the great iron gates, then beckoned Cole and Eremul through with his spear. 'How's it going on the wall?' he asked as they strolled by him. He gestured in the direction of the fighting.

Eremul gurned again. 'Your brave colleagues fight with the courage of men possessed. They will never surrender so long as our beloved ruler watches over us.' He made a show of patting his robes suddenly. 'You know, I do appear to have dropped a sceptre on the floor back there. I don't suppose you would be kind enough to retrieve it?'

Much to Cole's surprise, the guard nodded happily. 'Aye, not a problem.' He turned and began searching around for the non-existent silver coin.

Eremul shot him an urgent look and made a fierce stabbing gesture.

'What?' said Cole. 'I... Oh.' With a grimace, he drew Magebane and sidled over to where the Watchman was picking around in the dirt.

'There doesn't seem to be anything down— *Urgh.*'

The guard tumbled to the floor. Cole wiped the bloody edge of Magebane on the man's cloak and gave the wizard a reproachful look. 'We didn't need to kill him.'

Eremul sneered unpleasantly. 'That guard was not overcome by my irresistible charm alone. Sophistry is one of the hardest forms of magic to master. I was fortunate he was a dull-witted sort or manipulating him might well have proved beyond me.' The mage paused. He seemed to be trembling now, his face sweating with exertion. 'My spell would have worn off at any moment. He needed to die.'

Cole stared at the corpse. *A hero doesn't manipulate people. A hero doesn't stab someone from behind.* Sasha's words returned to haunt him again. *You're an asshole, Cole. Your father would be ashamed of you. And so would Garrett.*

He had spent the last four days turning those words over in his head. He still wasn't sure what he had done wrong, but he had evidently misread the situation back near the Fade ruins. Sasha had always been feisty and unpredictable. That was one of the reasons he found her so attractive. But what if she had meant what she said?

Damn Isaac. It was all his fault, with his stupid lute and irritating face. He had waltzed in and stolen Cole's rightful place in the group, somehow fooled them all into believing he was a boon companion when he was nothing but a dirty fraud. He would have told the man that himself, but as far as Cole was concerned Isaac was beneath him. No doubt the bastard had his eye on Sasha and had been working to turn her against him from the moment he wormed his way into her company.

He shook his head. There was no hope for deadbeats like Isaac. When it came right down to it, he was the one standing at the entrance to the Obelisk, preparing to rid the world of a foul tyrant. Not Isaac, oh no. He'd probably have pissed his pants if he'd found himself in this situation.

He would show them all that he was a hero just like his father. He would make Sasha proud of him. Make Garrett proud of him.

'Are you just going to stand there?' The Halfmage sounded vaguely annoyed.

'I was just working out the best way to make Salazar suffer,' replied Cole. He set his jaw in what he hoped was a suitably grim fashion. 'Let's do this.'

They entered a sparsely decorated hall. A scarlet carpet ran for perhaps sixty feet before terminating in a set of doors. Other doors led off the passageway into plush sitting rooms.

'The kitchens and servant quarters are near the back,' muttered the Halfmage as they progressed down the hallway. 'Keep your head down. They know me.'

A couple of old maids eyed them warily as they passed a small mess hall set with a long table covered in breads and cheeses. Cole felt his stomach rumble. The gruel that had been served in the militia camp was barely fit for a dog, but he had forced it down.

They reached the double doors. They were unlocked, and creaked open to reveal a set of steps leading up into the darkness. 'The Grand Council Chamber is on the second floor,' said Eremul. 'Keep going on up. Pass through the library and then up to the fourth floor. The Stasiseum should be unguarded. Salazar will likely be on the sixth floor, if it is not destroyed.'

Cole scratched his head. His cropped scalp was still itchy, though having caught sight of himself in the waters of the Redbelly River he had to admit he looked rather fetching. Dangerous, even. 'What's a Stasiseum?'

'You'll find out soon enough.' Eremul spun his chair around to stare him directly in the eye. 'This is where we part ways.'

'You're not coming with me?'

The wizard shook his head. 'The incident with the guard left me emptier than a magistrate's pockets after a night of moon dust and expensive whores. I will be impotent, figuratively speaking, for the next few hours. Focus on killing the Magelord and nothing else. Do you understand? We will never have a better opportunity to rid the city of that genocidal, deicidal son of a bitch. *Salazar must die.*'

Cole nodded. He gripped Magebane's hilt tightly. 'I won't fail. This is what I was born to do. My father's legacy to me.'

Eremul looked at him, a strange glint in his eyes. 'Go and make your father proud, Davarus Cole.'

The second floor of the Obelisk opened before him like the entrance to hell. Unlike the first level of the tower there were no windows to let in any natural light. Torches on brackets provided the only illumination. Cole crept down the narrow passageway, sticking to the inside wall, a loaded crossbow in hand. His booted feet made no sound on the soft carpet.

The passage curved slowly around the side of the tower. He followed it until he spotted a shadow looming on the opposite wall, moving towards him. He crouched low and prepared to shoot. The shadow suddenly wavered, then turned and disappeared in the other direction. Cole took a deep breath and padded forwards until the shadow reappeared and he could see the Watchman who cast it.

The sentry was facing away from him. He appeared to mutter something, and Cole's heart sank as another voice mumbled a reply. *Two of them. This could prove tricky.*

He retreated back down the passageway and waited. After a minute or two the shadow of the closest Watchman drifted back into view. He moved with it, keeping just out of sight. When the sentry finally stopped to turn back in the other direction, Cole made his move. He raised his crossbow and fired. The bolt hit his target in the neck. He was on him in an instant, Magebane silencing the guard before he could utter a sound.

He dragged the body along the passage all the way back to

the stairwell and hid it there. The carpet would hide the bloodstains, but he would need to be quick now. He sped down the passage as quietly as he could manage. A shallow alcove opened on his right, leading to a huge set of metal-bound doors. The other guard was just ahead. He was facing in the other direction.

Cole thanked his luck and raised his crossbow again. He was just lining up a shot when the Watchman turned. The young Shard threw himself into the alcove and back-pedalled until he was pushing up against one of the huge doors. He held his breath.

'Who's there?' the guard demanded. There was the sound of steel being drawn. Cole dropped the crossbow, drew Magebane and plunged it into the sentry's chest just as he rounded the side of the alcove. The enchanted dagger drove through the chainmail armour and deep into the flesh beneath. *Death*, Cole thought. *Death is here*.

Staring at the dying man's face, though, the desire to utter some witty remark wilted like parchment caught in a flame. *He's not much older than me*, Cole thought. *He doesn't have cruel eyes like Pock-face or that other one, the Watchmen who killed the old man back at the Hook*.

He remembered Kramer's shocked expression when he had slit his throat. *Murder isn't noble or just or heroic. It's... just murder.* Cole sagged back against the double doors. *This is Salazar's fault*, he told himself. *When he's dead there will be no more killing. Dorminia will surrender and we will be free to build a better city. A fairer city.*

He put his ear against the double doors. They were locked. The Grand Council Chamber must lie beyond, but he could hear no sound from within.

Stepping carefully over the body, he continued down the passageway, eventually reaching another set of stairs. He climbed them and emerged into the library on the third floor. There was no one about, but he flitted from bookcase to bookcase just to be safe.

When he reached the Obelisk's fourth floor, Davarus Cole's breath caught in his throat.

The entire level was a huge circular chamber. Thick transparent glass ran all around the circumference save for where the two sets of stairs connected to the lower and upper floors. Behind the glass, artfully positioned and displayed, was a wondrous array of stuffed creatures he had never before seen.

One display held a green-skinned humanoid with protruding tusks. The taxidermist had teased the beast into an aggressive pose: the spiked club in the creature's ham-like fist was raised as if it would smash open its glass prison. The display was so detailed Cole could see the individual hairs bristling from its piggish snout.

In another part of the chamber he saw what appeared to be an egg the size of a child suspended above a large brazier. He stared in amazement. There was *fire* around the edge of the brazier, so realistic it couldn't possibly be fake – and yet the flame was completely static, as motionless as ice. He put his hand to the glass and felt the warmth emanating from behind. Smoke was suspended near the top of the display, unmoving. It too was apparently frozen in time.

What had Eremul called this place? *The Stasiseum?*

The dome in the centre of the chamber stood apart from the rest of the displays. Cole walked up to it, peered inside – and was almost sick. A robed man was spread-eagled in the middle of the dome, suspended some six feet in the air by four iron spikes driven through his wrists and ankles to the small tree behind him. A fifth stake emerged from the floor vertically to impale him up the length of his body. Cole stared at the designs on the robe. He recognized the symbol of the Mother from the temple near the Hook as well as the ruins beneath Thelassa. There were other symbols too – the black horn of Tyrannus he knew, as well as the skull of the Reaver and the anchor of Malantis.

The priest's face was locked in a scream of eternal agony. Beads of blood hung suspended in the air, caught in the act of dripping from where the spikes pierced his body. Just in front of the priest was a pedestal, and in the centre of the pedestal was a golden urn. There was a name inscribed upon it. Cole peered more closely and saw that it read *Dorminia*.

He stared at the tree to which the priest was staked. It was a small oak, with leaves the colour of gold. There had been a tree like that in Verdisa Park in the Noble Quarter when he was a boy. It had burned down years ago. Shortly before his father's murder.

He tore his gaze away and headed for the stairs.

Cole hurried through the gallery on the fifth floor. He had become distracted, a mistake the Darkson would surely have chastised him for. What was his mentor doing now? What part would the master assassin play in the fighting? He didn't have time to worry about that, he realized. He had a destiny to fulfil.

Benches lined the centre of the gallery. Sculptures stared proudly at him, positioned at intervals down the chamber. Covering the walls were paintings and tapestries depicting places and events from the distant past. One of the largest tapestries caught his eye and against his better judgement Cole slowed to inspect it more closely.

It depicted a pretty young woman standing between two men, one of an age with her and the other old enough to be her father. Both men wore robes. Cole concluded they must be wizards.

He squinted at the tapestry. The mage on the left looked very much like a somewhat younger Salazar. The girl gazed at him with undisguised adoration while she held the hand of the other man, who regarded her with worshipful blue eyes. Behind the three figures, woven in exquisite detail, was a forest of the most vibrant greens and golds.

A slight noise ahead of him snapped his attention away from the tapestry. Cole's heart lurched in his chest. Staring across at him from the other side of the gallery was a burly warrior.

'The fuck you doing here?' the man growled. He wore grey chainmail, and, like Cole, his matching hair was cut short.

The warrior's hand hovered over the hilt of the weapon at his belt. Cole suddenly remembered he had a loaded crossbow in his hand. 'I'm here for Salazar,' he replied. 'Don't make me kill you.'

The drab fellow smiled, his eyes never leaving Cole's crossbow. 'If you're gonna shoot me, you'd best pray you don't miss.'

Cole's gloved fingers twitched. There was maybe forty feet between them. 'I want you to place your sword down on the bench to your left. Slowly. Then sit down on the floor over there.'

The man appeared to consider this. 'You got me,' he said, with a nod. With delicate care, he placed his fingers around the hilt of his weapon and carefully drew it. Cole relaxed an inch.

Another mistake.

The grey warrior dropped to the ground suddenly, rolling behind a bench. Cole pressed the trigger almost instantly, but it was a fraction too late. The bolt missed by a hair's breadth and struck the far wall of the gallery.

Shit. The man was back on his feet and pounding towards him before he even had time to reach for another quarrel. He hurled the useless crossbow at his attacker, who drew his scimitar and cleaved the makeshift projectile in half in a single motion. Cole saw the glow around the edge of the blade and his heart sunk further. *Augmentor.*

'Come here, you little prick,' snarled his pursuer as Cole turned and ducked behind a statue, fumbling at his belt for Magebane. There was a whistling sound just above his head and the top half of the statue simply fell away, a foot of solid stone cut through like butter.

He reeled away from the ruined sculpture and turned to face the Augmentor, who saw Magebane's glow and slowed his advance. 'How the fuck did you get your hands on that?' he snarled.

Cole didn't respond. He was weighing the odds. They didn't

look good. The Augmentor was clearly a veteran warrior – and the man carried a scimitar capable of cleaving stone. There was only one thing for it. He would have to fight dirty.

With his free hand, he reached inside a pocket on his cloak and withdrew a handful of the powder the Darkson had given him. It was mildly corrosive, capable of causing a great deal of irritation to naked skin. He took a few steps forwards and then tossed the powder at the Augmentor's exposed face.

'*You sneaky little cocksucker,*' the warrior screamed as he desperately tried to wipe away the burning substance with the back of one hairy hand. Cole was on him in an instant, Magebane plunging downwards. The Augmentor shifted at the last moment and it caught him in the shoulder rather than the chest. Cole tugged Magebane free, preparing to finish the job, but at that moment the Augmentor's knee shot out and caught him square in the fruits.

He reeled away in agony, turning back just in time to catch a headbutt to the mouth. He fell back against a bench and spat out a tooth, bloody drool spraying everywhere. The world spun.

The Augmentor's face leered into view above him. It was covered in red spots, pus-filled cysts already beginning to form. 'Like to fight dirty? You're not the only one. I'm gonna enjoy this.'

The scimitar inched down towards his face. Cole watched it descend with growing horror. As it got closer he could see that the blade was vibrating, the motion so fast it was almost imperceptible. He tried to kick out, but the Augmentor had his legs pinned. All he could do was bring Magebane across to try and cover his body – a futile gesture.

His tormentor laughed. 'Think that will protect you? This scimitar can cut through anything, boy. Even your enchanted pigsticker.' With a grin, the Augmentor brought his weapon down, lowered the edge against Magebane.

There was an explosion of white light and a noise like a horse screaming its death cry. Redness filled Cole's vision.

Clashing kaleidoscopes of colour danced across his eyes, but he could just make out his opponent's scimitar spinning wildly away across the marble floor. He shook his head desperately. It seemed to take an eternity to clear.

He heard a wet gasping noise from just ahead of him. The Augmentor was lying face down. His right arm and leg rested six feet away on the floor like a couple of tasty morsels thrown to a dog. The sinewy stumps just below the man's shoulder and above his knee squirted fresh blood with every beat of his heart, turning the marble wet and slippery.

The Augmentor's ruined scimitar lay nearby. The weapon's glow was gone and the curved blade was bent out of shape. In sudden panic Cole glanced at Magebane. It appeared to be unharmed, the magical radiance that surrounded it stronger than ever.

There was something else, another sound besides the dying man's gasps. He closed his eyes and concentrated.

Tick tock tick tock.

With a growing sense of dread, Cole bent down over the maimed Augmentor and untied the pouch hanging from his belt. He reached in and pulled out Garrett's pocket watch.

Time seemed to stand still.

'Where did you get this?' He grabbed the Augmentor's face and turned it towards him. 'Where? Tell me!'

'*Why?*' the dying man gasped wetly.

'It belongs to someone very dear to me.'

There was no reply except for an ugly chuckle. Cole turned the fallen Augmentor onto his back, heedless of the blood spurting up his trousers. 'Tell me where you got this!' he demanded again.

The Augmentor's sightless eyes stared at the ceiling, his mouth frozen in a permanent death grin. His chest had stopped moving.

Panic seized Cole. He had tried to leave a message several times while at the militia camp but had not received any response. He wanted to flee the Obelisk, to run through the city to Garrett's estate and the temple at the Hook and anywhere else his foster father might be found.

Instead he gripped the pocket watch tightly, trying to calm himself as he watched the hand tick slowly around the face. Whatever had happened to his mentor, Garrett would want him to see this through.

With a deep breath, he climbed the stairs to Salazar's personal chambers.

As it turned out, the top two levels of the tower had been forcibly merged into one. The ceiling above the sixth floor had caved in during the magical assault on the tower, leaving a sloping pile of rubble to form a makeshift staircase. Cole found no sign of Salazar or anyone else on the wasted remnants of the sixth floor, so he sheathed Magebane and began climbing towards the guest quarters above him. Rock and debris shifted beneath his feet. The air was cooler now, and he could feel a light breeze brushing against his cheek.

Grunting, Cole hauled himself up over the edge of the shattered ceiling and onto the seventh floor. Just ahead of him the Obelisk's roof had been split open, revealing a blue sky overhead. Smoke and dust still drifted through the air, obscuring his view. It seemed to be blowing from the east, so he plunged into it, pulling up his hood to shield his face and mouth. Either side of him collapsed rooms poured their destroyed contents across his path. He was forced to climb over the wreckage of four-poster beds, ornate dressers, grandiose armoires that had spilled their contents everywhere. His boots trampled silk gowns and gold-trimmed jackets into the filthy debris as he clambered across them. The wind grew stronger and the dust began to clear...

The Tyrant of Dorminia bled into view.

The Magelord was gazing out at the city, his back to Cole, scarlet robes and cloak fluttering out behind him.

He edged closer, as silent as a ghost. The yards closed between them. Fifteen. Ten. Five. He reached under his own cloak, placed a hand on Magebane's hilt. This was it. One thrust and it would all be over.

'I've been waiting for you.'

He froze. Salazar didn't turn around. The Magelord's voice was calm, measured. Cole's mind raced. Should he charge, stick the bastard before he had the chance to react?

'The White Lady sent you, did she not? A knife in the back. That was always her style.'

Salazar turned to face him.

Cole stared from beneath his hood. The most powerful man in the north seemed small up close. Small and very ancient. His skin was sagging and lined with wrinkles and he leaned on a cane, apparently unable to carry the weight of his withered body without support.

Tick tock tick tock.

The instrument at his belt, Garrett's timepiece, reminded him of the folly of judging this man by his wretched appearance. He was a despot. A Godkiller. *A Magelord.*

'I'm not here because of the White Lady,' Cole said grimly. 'I'm here because of the people of Dorminia. I'm here because of what you did to *me*.'

Salazar raised an eyebrow. 'And what have I done to upset you, young man?'

Cole threw back his hood. 'You had my father killed.'

The Magelord didn't react. He simply stared at him. His eyes were sunk so far back in their sockets he looked as if he hadn't slept in months. 'Illarius,' he said eventually. The ancient voice betrayed no emotion.

'Illarius Cole,' repeated the young Shard. 'A hero. A hero you murdered for daring to stand against you.'

The Tyrant of Dorminia cocked his wizened head slightly. 'Is that what they told you?' he asked softly.

Cole could feel the anger rising within him. 'That's the truth!

Don't try and manipulate me. Your magic won't work. My father's legacy protects me.'

For the first time he saw a flicker of emotion on Salazar's face. 'You have Magebane, then.'

Triumph flooded Cole. He tore the glowing dagger free of its sheath and brandished it before him. 'Yes. A hero's weapon. And it will be your death.'

That pronouncement wasn't met with the sudden fear he expected. Instead the Magelord closed his eyes for a moment. When he opened them again he looked tired. So very tired. 'You are aware Magebane's power functions only for you. Did you ever question why?'

Cole shrugged. 'What does it matter?'

'The weapon you hold is tied to your father's blood, which you alone share. It is bondmagic.'

'No – that's not true!' Cole felt anger take hold. Bondmagic was something only Augmentors used.

Salazar raised the thin cane on which he leaned and pointed it at Magebane. 'The blade is an alloy of unique potency. Abyssium is rarer than dragon's teeth.' He lowered the cane and leaned on it once more. 'The process of enchanting the weapon was complicated. It took me ten days spent in isolation. It is perhaps my finest work.'

Cole's mouth dropped open as the implications of what he was hearing sank in. 'You created Magebane?' he asked in astonishment.

Salazar nodded. 'After a cabal of wizards attempted to have me assassinated, I decided the city must be purged of those with the gift.' The tyrant sighed and shook his head. 'It was not an easy decision. There was a time when I defied the very gods to protect my brothers and sisters from persecution.'

'What does the Culling have to do with my father?' Even as he asked the question, Cole could feel cold dread worming its way into his heart.

The ruler of Dorminia raised an age-spotted hand to stroke

absently at his drooping moustache. 'Illarius was a man of many qualities. Loyal. Reliable. Ruthless. He alone I deemed fitting of the weapon you hold. He served me well as an Augmentor for many years.'

My father... an Augmentor? One of Salazar's killers? Cole wanted nothing more than to plunge his dagger into the wizard before more lies could spill from his mouth. 'You're lying!' he shouted. 'My father was a rebel leader! Everyone knows that!'

'Do they? How many men and women in the street, when stopped and asked, have heard the name Illarius Cole?'

Despite his rage, Cole paused to consider this. Only the older Shards, it seemed, had ever mentioned his father: Garrett, and Remy and Vicard, on occasion. They had never been very effusive on the subject. But why would Garrett and the rest lie to him? *Salazar's trying to trick me into letting my guard down.*

'If he truly did serve you, why have him killed?' Cole shot back, desperately hoping he had found a fatal flaw in the Magelord's argument.

'The abyssium that I used to forge Magebane did not react quite as expected to the binding spell. It left me... vulnerable.'

'What do you mean?' asked Cole, now genuinely confused.

'The bondmagic possessed by my Augmentors should remain bound to me. Yet I had no control over Magebane. I could not sense its presence, or that of its wielder. I could not siphon from it. Most troubling of all, I could not sever the weapon's link to Illarius when it had fulfilled its purpose.' He sighed, and there was a hint of regret in his voice. 'It pained me to order his death. There was simply no alternative. Not after witnessing his efficacy during the Culling. The threat was too great.'

Cole wanted to refute that cold logic, ridicule the words as a pack of lies. He couldn't, and so he played the last card he possessed. 'My mother would never marry an Augmentor!' he spat. 'She was a good woman.' Garrett had always told him so.

Salazar was silent for a time. 'The Illarius Cole I knew never married,' he said evenly, without humour or malice. 'His son was begat on a whore.'

His son was begat on a whore.

Cole took a step towards Salazar. 'My mother was named Sophia, you lying bastard! She was the daughter of a shipwright. We had a house on—'

'—on Leviathan Walk just north of the harbour. Yes, I recall. I had offered him an estate in the Noble Quarter. Illarius was never much for ostentation.' He paused for a moment. 'Sophia... An exotic name. The kind a harlot would choose.'

Cole's world was threatening to collapse around him. It all made sense now. The story about his father being a hero. His mother dying in childbirth. The false legacy he held in his hand, a few feet from Salazar's wrinkled old neck. Lies. All lies.

He stared out past the Magelord, towards the fierce fighting that still raged far below them in the distance, and came within a whisker of tossing Magebane over the edge of the tower. What was the point? He wasn't the hero they thought he was. He was a fraud. No better than Isaac. And Sasha had probably known it all along, which is why she had rejected him.

Tick tock tick tock. He reached down, pulled out Garrett's pocket watch. His foster father had lied to him as well. He had known the truth. He had known that Davarus was the bastard offspring of a murdering Augmentor and a whore.

He stared down at the city again. Far in the distance he could just about see the old merchant's estate west of the river. He had spent much of his time there, growing up. Despite his parentage, Garrett had taken him in. Offered him a home. Treated him like his very own son.

He swallowed the lump in his throat. Garrett had lied to protect him, he realized. Lied only because he didn't want to see him hurt.

Tick tock tick tock.

He shifted Magebane slightly, brought his hand a fraction closer to Salazar. 'We can't change who our parents are,' he said slowly. 'But we can decide who we want to be. A chance you've denied to countless innocent people.'

Salazar stared back, unafraid. 'I have always done what I thought necessary. The longer one lives, the more one understands that there is no inherent goodness in the world.' He closed his eyes for a moment, and Cole was shocked to see wetness glistening on the wrinkled skin beneath those sunken sockets. 'My daughter's heart was the purest I have ever known. If good ever really existed, it was within her. And the Inquisition burned her alive.'

Cole stared back, too surprised to speak.

'I punished all those responsible. I erected this city and named it in her honour. I planted her favourite tree, but even that was desecrated.'

Cole remembered the Eternal Tree which once had stood in Verdisa Park. He recalled the urn down in the Stasiseum. The name that was engraved there. *Dorminia.*

'You are not the first to stand here today and judge me,' the Magelord continued. He drew himself up to his full height then, straightened his robes and wiped the tears from his face. The momentary weakness was gone, and he was once again the formidable Tyrant of Dorminia. 'I would have tried to kill the other – but even at full strength I might not have succeeded. And I would not give that self-righteous bastard the satisfaction of witnessing my failure.'

There was a moment of deathly silence – and then Salazar raised one wasted hand. 'So. You wish to be a hero? Let us see if you have what it takes.'

Cole gasped as Magebane began to throb in his palm. Almost instantly it was boiling hot, burning through his glove to sear the flesh beneath.

He was across to the Magelord in an instant.

Gasping from the pain, still clutching Garrett's pocket watch in his other hand, he plunged the glowing dagger through those scarlet robes and deep into the withered body underneath.

Salazar's arm wavered and then flopped down to dangle by his side. Magebane's hilt cooled almost instantly as the Magelord's magic sputtered and died. The killer of gods, the most powerful man in the north, began to sag.

Cole held him up, staring into the wizard's eyes. He was shocked to find that he weighed less than a child. 'Why?' he asked quietly. 'You had the power to change the world for the better. Why didn't you?'

The Tyrant of Dorminia sighed softly. Cole had expected Salazar to die screaming and cursing his name, but the Magelord appeared peaceful. Almost content. His voice was a bubbling whisper.

'Things... rarely go as we hope they might. I once thought to save humanity from the gods...' He coughed suddenly, blood bubbling around his mouth to stain his beard and moustache the same colour as his robes. 'I did not realize humanity needed the gods more than they needed us. I was blinded by hatred.'

'And Shadowport? Was hate the reason you murdered an entire city?'

'"*Hate*"...' the dying Magelord repeated, his voice now so weak Cole could barely hear it. 'That was not hate. That was... compassion.'

Compassion? That made no sense. 'What do you mean?' he was about to ask, but Salazar's breathing had stopped. There was no sound but the whistling of the wind and the *tick tock tick tock* of the timepiece in his hand.

The Magelord shuddered once. His fading gaze settled on the pocket watch. '*Time... to die...*' he whispered.

His eyes closed one final time.

Cole slid Magebane free of Salazar's body. He was about to lower the corpse to the ground when suddenly it began to glow. He jerked backwards as it floated up and drifted out of the side of the tower, rising higher and higher, above even the Obelisk itself.

Without warning, blinding rays of golden light burst from

the dead Magelord's eyes and mouth. Cole shielded his own eyes as the incandescent rays shot upwards – a stream of divine energy fleeing its host to return to the heavens whence it was stolen.

The spectacle continued for two or three minutes before the light died. Salazar jerked once when the last golden motes had finally faded. Then the Tyrant of Dorminia began to fall, tumbling end over end.

The body struck the courtyard hundreds of feet below and burst apart.

The Wolf

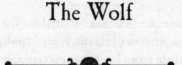

SASHA GASPED AND reached down to her side, probing at the four-inch sliver of wood stuck there. Her fingers came away bloody. A grunt ahead snapped her attention back to the fighting raging ahead of her, and before she knew it a Watchman was grappling her to the ground, his hands closing around her throat. She grabbed hold of his fingers, tried to prise them away. He was too strong. She scratched at him, attempted to bite his face, but he laughed at her clumsy efforts and squeezed harder.

She could see her short sword lying on the trampled turf. She stretched for it, every muscle in her arm straining, but it was just out of reach. She tried to scream, but the crushing hands around her throat turned her cry into a pathetic squeak.

She stared up at the leering face above her. The man's rancid breath filled her nostrils. Her vision began to blur. Her assailant's cruel eyes seemed to fill her world, sweat glistening off a nose cratered with blackheads. 'Die, bitch,' he panted.

Her right hand closed around the shield fragment protruding from her waist. With a wild effort, she wrenched it free. The pain was excruciating, but she had no time to indulge it; her strength was almost spent. Slowly, almost dreamily, as if she were detached from everything going on around her, she raised her arm from the ground and drove the makeshift dagger through her would-be killer's eye.

His scream was hideous. The pressure around her windpipe evaporated as her attacker flung his hands up to his face and reeled away from her. She choked in air, rolled over and pushed herself to her feet. Her legs almost gave away beneath her and she stumbled, but she did not fall. With deliberate care she picked her sword up off the ground.

Blood ran down her leg. She ignored it. The Watchman was still howling, his fingers plucking ineffectually at the wooden fragment extruding from his burst eyeball. She limped over to him, raised the sword, and thrust the blade straight through his face.

Sasha stood there for a time, staring at the dead man, then turned and retched. All around her the fighting continued. Thelassa's mercenary army and the city's defenders were locked in a vicious struggle. She wiped her mouth, retrieved her sword and limped over to the nearest pocket of fighting. A Sumnian almost fell into her, a pike quivering from his belly, and she pushed him away. The arrival of Salazar's Augmentors had swung the battle and now they were being pushed back away from the gates.

The blond-haired warrior in the golden armour strode the field like death itself, his sword slaying at will. He was relentless, surgical in the way he stabbed, chopped and thrust his way through the dark-skinned Sumnians. He left a trail of corpses in his wake.

Elsewhere other Augmentors had brought their magic to bear to devastating effect. Nearer to the wall, the warrior in the bronze hauberk scattered enemies like leaves with his terrible hammer. The weapon had annihilated half a dozen mercenaries in a single swing and caused the explosion of splintering wood that had knocked her to the ground and pierced her side.

The pain was growing worse. Her neck throbbed. Through the haze of agony she wondered how the assault on the east side of the city was progressing. In response to the advance of the White Lady's pale servants, the Watch had seemingly thrown the bulk of the city's militia against the western gate. If General Zolta didn't attack soon and draw some of the defenders away, two of the three companies that made up the White Lady's army could soon be routed.

An explosion suddenly rocked the ground ahead of her. The stench of burning flesh would have made her puke if there had been anything left in her stomach.

She stared through the smoke. A group of Sumnians were engaged in a desperate struggle to fight their way past a similar number of Watchmen. Behind the red-cloaked soldiers lurked an Augmentor. In one hand the man carried a wicked-looking flail, but it was his other hand, the hand he was raising above his head, that caused her heart to skip a beat. There was an ominous glow around the glove covering his fist.

As Sasha watched, the Augmentor hurled a sphere of glowing energy straight at the mercenaries. It struck the earth and exploded, sending white-hot fire blossoming outwards. Once her eyes had cleared, she saw that half the Sumnians had been reduced to smoking corpses. The others immediately fell back, screaming in agony and nursing terrible burns.

She searched around the battlefield. She had discarded her own crossbow a while back. But there, ten feet to her left, she found what she was looking for.

Half staggering, she reached the fallen Watchman and prised the weapon from his dead hands. As luck would have it, it was already loaded. She edged forwards, trying to get close enough for a clear shot. She took another couple of steps and a gap opened up. She raised the crossbow.

At the last moment, one of the Watchmen noticed her. He yelled and pointed. The Augmentor turned and raised his gloved hand.

She pulled the trigger.

This time the explosion knocked her off her feet. There was a deafening roaring in her ears. She tasted blood in her mouth and realized her nose was bleeding. Something smelled of burning. It was her hair. She reached up to touch it. A clump came away in her hand, blackened and singed. But she was still alive.

The Augmentor and those surrounding him were not so fortunate. Struck by her quarrel, the man had misdirected his fireball and launched it at the ground just in front of him. Chunks of flesh and scraps of red cloth sizzled and steamed where the Watchmen had been standing. Nothing remained of the Augmentor but a pair of smoking boots and a puddle some six feet wide.

Sasha stared numbly at the carnage. Then she released her grip on the crossbow and rolled over onto her back to stare up at the clouds overhead. She could hear the sounds of fighting nearby, but she was past caring.

Let them come. She was done.

No one would care if she lived or died. No one apart from Cole and possibly Garrett. And if they knew the truth, they wouldn't want anything to do with her either. She was a hateful, drug-addled piece of shit. She had deceived Garrett, tricking him into spending more and more of his own coin on narcotics which she had kept to fund her habit. And then she had attached herself to Vicard and used him, too.

She remembered raiding the physician's home in Farrowgate. She was a common thief as well as a manipulative, deceitful little fuck-up.

Warm blood still trickled down her leg. Just as it had all those years ago. The gang should have killed her as they had killed her father and sister. It would have been better for everyone.

There was movement ahead of her, the sound of a booted foot scuffing against the dirt. Hardly caring, she twisted her neck to see who approached. It was Jerek.

The Highlander was covered in small cuts, his hide shirt torn in multiple places. Red smears and ash covered his bald head. The axes he held at his sides dripped with the blood of countless enemies.

And his eyes were staring in her direction, burning with a hatred that promised brutal death.

The blackness inside her head receded, replaced by sudden terror. She scrabbled to her feet as the grim warrior stalked towards her. He was on her before she could think to run, his axes raised, preparing to end her miserable life. She stared dully at the strapping around his shoulder. The strapping that covered the wound she had accidentally given him. What was it Brodar Kayne had said? *The Wolf doesn't forget a debt.*

'Wait, you know I didn't mean—'

An axe came down.

And Jerek pushed her gently away from him with his forearm. He didn't take his eyes off whatever it was he was staring at. 'Get out of here,' he growled.

Sasha turned.

The hulking figure seemed to blot out the sun. It was a giant, a towering monstrosity of black metal wearing the face of a demon. 'I'm Garmond the Black,' he rumbled. 'She's mine. Once I'm done with you.'

Jerek's face twitched. 'Reckon so? I've killed bigger men than you.' He leaned over and spat. 'Ain't never seen a bigger cunt, though.'

Garmond brought his gauntleted fists together with a thud, sending splatters of gore flying in all directions. 'You're dead.'

'Get out of here,' Jerek rasped again, and this time Sasha heeded his words. She ran, half stumbling, until she had put a good distance between her and the two men. Then, unable to stop herself, she turned and watched.

The combatants circled one another warily. Jerek, himself a big man, looked shockingly small opposite the Augmentor.

The Highlander feinted and then sprinted forwards, his axes whirring. He hit the giant on the thigh, the shoulder, and then across the chest. The sounds of steel clashing against steel rang out across the battlefield – but when the Wolf ceased his flurry, Garmond's armour displayed not a single dent.

The Augmentor lunged at the smaller man, but Jerek was already out of range. The Highlander spat and then began stalking a circle around the behemoth, keeping him at a distance.

Garmond turned on the spot, maintaining the angle between them. Suddenly Jerek dropped his shoulder and dashed at the Augmentor. He was halfway to him when he hurled one of his axes at the giant's head. It whirled through the air, end over end, clashing into the demon helm with a gigantic clang and jerking Garmond's head back. At the same time Jerek launched himself at the Augmentor's armoured legs, tackling him shoulder-first with the full force of his body weight. The massive warrior stumbled and then toppled backwards, crashing to the ground.

The Wolf was back on his feet in the blink of an eye. He grabbed Garmond's head and tugged, his jaw clenching from the effort of trying to prise the great helm lose. Eventually it came free. The Highlander tossed it away and raised his remaining axe. With a grunt, he brought it whistling down.

The axe bounced off Garmond's vambraced forearm. The massive Augmentor threw his other arm back, elbowing Jerek in the stomach. He doubled up for an instant, just long enough for Garmond to get hold of him and lift him bodily off the ground. He plucked the Highlander's axe from his hand and tossed it aside, and then brought him down over his knee, once, twice, each impact striking with a sickening thud. Finally, Garmond lifted Jerek high above his head. Sasha was shocked to see the man beneath the helmet was fairly young, utterly unremarkable in appearance. With a snarl, the Augmentor hurled Jerek to the ground. He landed hard and lay still.

Sasha looked away. She hadn't liked Jerek and he hadn't liked her, but that didn't change the fact he had saved her life on more than one occasion. She thought he was done for – but then, remarkably, he began to stir.

Despite the broken ribs and worse he must have suffered, the Highlander was trying to struggle upright.

The Augmentor reached down and pulled Jerek up to his

knees; the Wolf swayed as if he might topple over at any moment. Garmond drove a steel gauntlet into his face. Sasha winced at the sickening noise of the impact. He punched Jerek again. This time Sasha heard the crack of a cheekbone shattering.

She searched desperately for a weapon of some sort. There was nothing. Not unless she wanted to charge at the giant with a sword. Hating herself, she readied herself to flee as soon as the Augmentor had finished his gruesome work.

Garmond drew his arm back again, this time as far as it would go. 'You're dead,' he grunted. Then he threw his gauntleted fist forwards with incredible force, the momentum like that of the battering ram that had sundered Dorminia's gates.

And somehow the Wolf caught the punch. Incredibly, like a dead man rising from the grave, he began to climb to his feet. Garmond growled and swung with his other fist – only to see that gauntlet, too, caught in Jerek's vice-like grip.

Like a river exploding from a fractured dam, the Wolf sprung forwards and drove his forehead into his opponent's nose, splattering it like a spoiled fruit. Garmond staggered back. Jerek headbutted him again, and again, until both men wore masks of crimson. Still Jerek would not relent. He bent down to retrieve one of his axes and swung it two-handed at Garmond's leg, a blow so powerful it sheared through the greaves, the axe lodging in his shin.

Garmond howled and collapsed onto one knee. Jerek kicked him in the face and Sasha heard the sound of the big man's jaw breaking.

Grabbing hold of the Augmentor's curly black hair, Jerek drove his own knee repeatedly into his opponent's exposed head. *Crack. Crack. Crack. Crack.* The savagery went on and on. By the time he was finished, Garmond's head was barely recognisable as anything human.

Jerek let Garmond's corpse fall to the ground and stood there panting. He met Sasha's eyes, his face a bruised, swollen mess covered in blood. Then, very slowly, he limped over to reclaim his axes.

Sasha stared at him as he turned away from her. Strange emotions whirred inside her head.

Astonished as she was, she was even more surprised when she looked to the hills to the north and saw the bestial army rushing towards Dorminia.

Ghosts

KAYNE SUCKED IN great gasps of air. Sweat stung his eyes, making it harder to track that deadly blade flickering at him from all angles. His arms were stinging with the small nicks and cuts his opponent's sword had inflicted. They were scratches, nothing that would slow the Sword of the North. No, exhaustion would take care of that.

This blond-haired bastard was one of the best he had ever faced. Maybe the best. Even so, he was managing to hang in there – except that the man didn't seem to *tire*. He grimaced as his opponent's longsword scored a shallow wound across his chest and redoubled his efforts, although his heart was hammering so hard he thought it might burst.

They'd been fighting for he didn't know how long. Bodies littered the ground all around them, not only red-cloaked Watchmen and dark-skinned Sumnians but all those poor sods who'd been handed a rusty blade and shoved out here to die: young and old, farmers and craftsmen and common labourers lying dead or groaning and weeping for their wives and mothers. He'd cut down no small number of them himself. When a man comes at you with murder in his eyes the tragedy of it all makes no difference. You kill or you get killed.

His opponent wasn't even breathing hard. The man's jaw was set in a grim line, brow furrowed in concentration. Kayne parried a thrust and then tried to take a step back; he cursed as he almost tripped over the body of a mercenary. The golden virtuoso was on him in an instant.

Concentration. That was the key. You had to note how your opponent moved, every detail, every expression. Every man had a pattern, an angle that showed in his eyes, the way his muscles twitched.

The dancing longsword missed his neck by a fraction. Kayne watched it closely, waiting for that one opening. He saw it then, the barest hint. His opponent had overreached by maybe half an inch. The old Highlander turned the greatsword around in his hands and then spun the blade in a full circle, felt it cut deep into his opponent's arm where the interlocking plates of his armour met.

This time it was the blond-haired warrior who fell back. 'Who are you?' he demanded. Blood welled up from the deep cut in his arm.

'Just a man doing a job,' Kayne replied. He seized on the opportunity – any opportunity – to catch his breath.

The answer didn't seem to please his opponent. 'You're a mercenary like the rest of them? I'm disappointed.'

The barbarian shrugged. 'When it comes right down to it, gold's as good a reason to fight as any. And more honest than most.'

There was anger in those blue eyes now. 'Is gold all that matters to you? What about loyalty? Honour? Duty?'

Brodar Kayne stared right back into that scornful gaze. 'Loyalty, honour and duty, eh? I reckon I know a bit about them. Great things, to be sure, as long as you're on the right side of 'em. They can make a man feel right good about himself, even as he's doing the most terrible things. The weak, now, they can't afford such lofty ideals. Too busy bangin' on the door while men like you sit at your high table and admire your honour and reflect on how much worthier it makes you.'

Much to his surprise, his words seemed to cut the swordsman as deeply as his blade had. There was doubt on that chiselled face, sadness in those blue eyes. 'And what about love?' he asked quietly. The fighting continued on around them, but out

416

of sheer happenstance or just unthinking deference to the skill of these two men facing off against each other, they found themselves alone on the battlefield.

Brodar Kayne blinked sweat from his eyes. 'Love? Well now, there ain't no shame in a man fighting for that.' He stared across at the troubled face. 'And I reckon if that's the case, you're a better sort than I gave you credit for.'

The golden-armoured warrior nodded slowly. 'Thank you,' he said, and he sounded as if he meant it.

Kayne glanced up at the sky. The sun was starting to go down. It would be evening soon. He sighed heavily. 'Getting late,' he said.

'Then I suppose we had better hurry up and finish this.'

It was his turn to nod. As his opponent closed, though, Kayne noticed with growing alarm that the man's wound had already stopped leaking. It had been a nasty one, ought to have worked in his favour the longer the fight wore on – but it seemed that not only did this Augmentor not tire, he didn't bleed either.

The old barbarian uttered a silent curse. He had the feeling this wasn't going to end well.

He held his own for a good few minutes longer before his body started to betray him. He wasn't a young man, that was the truth of it, and he couldn't keep this up. The greatsword started to feel like a lead weight in his hands. He twisted, dodged, parried, and with every second that passed he came a fraction closer to being just that little bit too slow.

And then it happened. He stumbled and his attacker was on him, and this time he knew he couldn't react fast enough.

This is it, he thought, watching the blade descend. *You had a good run, all things considered*. He braced himself for the inevitable.

The swordsman wavered. A confused expression spread across his face. Not about to question his good fortune, Kayne tensed, preparing to press home the advantage. Suddenly, far in the distance, the very top of the Obelisk exploded in golden light. He shielded his eyes and watched in amazement as brilliant rays the colour of dawn suddenly streamed up towards the heavens.

A choking sound snapped his attention back to his opponent. He was clutching at his chest, his eyes wide in shock. The longsword tumbled from his grasping fingers and he fell to his knees, rocking back and forth, gulping desperately as if unable to swallow enough air.

Kayne hesitated and then lowered his greatsword. All around the battlefield men had ceased fighting and were staring up beyond the city walls in astonishment. *Could it be the lad actually succeeded?* he wondered.

He caught movement at the edge of his vision and bent his neck slightly to see a mindhawk tumble out of the sky. It crashed into the ground in an explosion of feathers. Further away, another mindhawk abruptly ceased its patrol and plummeted straight down to disappear out of view behind a stand of trees.

There was a thud just ahead of him. His opponent had collapsed onto his face and was tearing up great tufts of grass in his hands, trying to drag himself along the ground. Kayne met his eyes for a second, saw the agony in those blue orbs and had to look away. Whatever had befallen the fellow, it was no way for a man so astonishingly skilled with the sword to die.

Thinking to end his suffering, Brodar Kayne walked over to the tragic figure and raised his greatsword. The man looked up at him and reached for something at his belt. Then he turned his head to stare in the direction of the city. With a final, tortured gasp, he whispered a woman's name and shuddered, his eyes closing. He exhaled once and then lay still.

There was something clutched in his hand. Kayne knelt down, examining the strange item. It was a strip of fine cloth, probably silk. It smelled faintly of jasmine and was likely worth a fair few sceptres. He hesitated for a moment, and then saw the band of gold on the man's finger. He slipped it off, gasping at the size of the emerald jutting from the ring. It had a large

'L' inscribed on the inside and was doubtless worth a small fortune.

He hesitated again. Then, very carefully, he placed the ring back on the dead man's finger and wrapped the handkerchief around it. He positioned the warrior's hands over his chest and laid his longsword down beside him. It wasn't much of a gesture, and it might not stop a mercenary from discovering the ring if and when the looting started, but it was the best he could do.

He leaned on his own greatsword, sucking in deep breaths, and surveyed the battlefield. The losses on both sides were appalling. He reckoned there were more bodies on the ground than there were still standing. All around him, combatants were starting to take notice of the fallen swordsman. He saw shocked expressions, sudden fear and uncertainty on the faces of the remaining Watchmen. The militia looked as if they were fit to piss themselves.

Kayne realized then that the man must have been some kind of commander – but it wasn't just his death that seemed to be swinging the battle. Fifty yards away, General D'rak faced off against the big fellow who had wreaked untold havoc with his glowing hammer. The Augmentor was staring at the now-dim weapon with a perplexed expression. He swung it at the Sumnian general, who caught the maul between his khopeshes. Like a whirling dervish, he spun away from the larger man only to close in again with frightening speed, his wicked curved swords slicing and chopping. The Augmentor went down in a spray of blood, the great hammer clattering uselessly from his hands. A loud cheer went up from the Sumnians nearby.

Brodar Kayne scanned the battlefield, noting how small gains were being made everywhere he looked. You developed a sense for these things, once you survived enough fights. The tide was about ready to turn, he reckoned. They'd take the city by nightfall.

He searched around for Jerek and Sasha. He couldn't

remember when he had last seen either of them, but then, a life or death struggle can do weird things to a man's sense of time.

There was a sudden commotion to the north. Once again the fighting stalled as both sides stared out at the rising hills in the distance. Kayne squinted, cursed his poor vision, and then plucked his sword up from where it stood in the dirt and moved closer for a better look.

The hills were heaving with dark shapes, and they were getting closer. The ageing Highlander stood there for a time, at first confused, then concerned, and finally unable to believe what he was seeing.

A horde of savage animals was descending upon the battlefield. It could only mean one thing.

The Brethren. Brodar Kayne's scarred hands gripped the hilt of his greatsword so tightly the blood drained from his fingers.

The Shaman's here.

He pounded across the battlefield, paying no heed to the pain in his knees. Panicked shouts were already echoing from ahead of him: Sumnian voices shouting foul curses or screaming for aid. In moments the Brethren were among them, falling upon the mercenaries in a snarling, slavering avalanche of fur that showed no mercy.

Stunned by the arrival of these unlikely allies and fearful for their own lives, the city's defenders initially fell back. When it became clear the animals were attacking the invaders, they grew bold and waded back into the battle.

As quickly as that, the city's liberators were once again on the back foot.

Kayne scanned the field wildly as he ran. His heart would have sunk if it hadn't been threatening to burst out of his chest. Everywhere he looked Sumnians were under assault by the menagerie that had suddenly appeared among them. They were hardened warriors, some of the finest soldiers in the world, but the Brethren were unknown to them. They had no idea what they faced.

To the right of him, near the city wall, three Sumnians stabbed at a bear with sword and spear while a trio of huge transcended wolves padded silently up behind them. The animals pounced, each set of massive jaws locking around a southerner's throat and dragging him to the ground before crushing his windpipe.

They think they're fighting animals, Kayne thought grimly. *But the Brethren aren't animals. They're beasts with the intelligence of a man and the Shaman's will behind 'em.* If there was one thing he'd learned in all the years spent fighting alongside the Brethren, it was that twelve inches of steel was rarely a match for razor fangs capable of crushing bone and armour – or claws sharp enough to cut through leather and flesh as easily as parchment.

A huge elk suddenly reared up before him, blood dripping from its right antler. The Transcended intended to crush him, but he rolled to the left and sliced sideways with his greatsword. He felt the blade connect, cut through muscle and bone. The elk made a high-pitched whining noise and crashed over onto its side.

Kayne was back up and running immediately. Roars, howls and shrieks filled the air. He leaped over the savaged bodies of dead mercenaries, ducked as a great eagle swooped overhead and then launched itself at him, talons clawing at his face. It screeched suddenly and tried to wheel away, a crossbow bolt protruding from its tawny feathered breast. It rose above the battlefield, careered wildly a few times, and then tumbled back down to earth, twitching spasmodically.

There was a commotion twenty yards to the right of him. He glanced over and saw the southerner who'd fired the crossbow desperately trying to reload as a monstrous grizzly closed on him, trailing gore from its gigantic jaws. With a swipe of one clubbing paw it tore open the soldier's chest, sending droplets of blood splattering across the faces of the Sumnians behind him. The bear unleashed a mighty roar and reared up on its

421

hind legs, ten feet of savage bulk and deadly claws driven by insatiable bloodlust.

Gaern. Kayne finally recognized the Transcended. There were many bears among the Brethren, but none were as huge as the great old grizzly about to fall upon the unfortunate mercenaries.

There was the flash of something golden emerging from the cowering southerners, and suddenly Gaern roared in agony, a colossal spear buried deep in his hide. The Sumnians parted and General Zahn strode forwards, both hands clutching the shaft of the spear, driving Gaern back. Half a ton of furious bear snarled and writhed, tried desperately to free itself, but Zahn had him pinned. His men quickly recovered from their shock and raised their weapons, falling upon the helpless Transcended in a flurry of chopping swords and axes.

Kayne looked away, feeling an odd sense of sadness. He'd known Gaern before the warrior transcended. He'd been a solid sort. Even after his transformation, Gaern had fought alongside him a few times – as recently as the abomination attack on Glistig in the East Reaching a scarce four years back.

He shook his head angrily. That was in the past. The Brethren had chased him and the Wolf all over the High Fangs for the best part of two years.

Kayne gritted his teeth and began running once more, his eyes narrowed on the spot where the hills began rising five hundred yards ahead of him. The hulking presence of the Magelord was unmistakable even from this distance, even with his bad eyes.

The Shaman had not bothered to keep any of the Brethren back to guard him. Neither had he shifted shape in order to watch safely from the clouds high above, or assumed his most favoured form, that of a great woolly mammoth, a near unstoppable creature. That wasn't the Magelord's style. Whatever else a man might say about him, the Shaman was no coward.

Even as he watched, the Shaman plucked a spear out of the air and snapped it between his arms with a mighty grunt. Kayne glanced at the two Sumnians facing off against him and knew instantly they were dead men. There was nothing he could do about it. Chances were he'd be joining them soon enough.

He had no idea what the Shaman was doing in the Trine, or why he had unleashed the Brethren against the city's liberators. Being honest, he didn't much care.

He had a score to settle.

Panting, filthy, covered in sweat, he arrived just as the Shaman was finishing off the two mercenaries. They'd lasted a good deal longer than he expected they would. Both men now flopped uselessly on the mud, necks broken and swords shattered. He slowed to a walk, breathing deeply, his gaze locked on the immortal he had once served. The immortal he had considered a friend.

The Shaman finally noticed him. His glacial blue eyes widened slightly in surprise. 'Kayne,' he stated in his low, rumbling voice. His muscles seemed to tense. 'You're a long way from the High Fangs.'

Brodar Kayne stared at the man who had kept him locked in a cage like an animal for a year. The man who had had his wife burned alive while he watched on helplessly.

'I ain't the only one,' he growled. He leaned on his greatsword, staring around at the chaos. The Sumnians were desperately trying to regroup, but they were fighting a losing battle. 'You here for me?' he asked.

The Shaman snorted. 'Your question is telling. I see your imprisonment did not change you.'

'I'm old and stubborn.'

The Magelord's square jaw twitched. 'I sent Borun to hunt you down.'

Kayne shrugged. 'He found me.'

The Shaman scowled in response, and then stared up at the sky. 'The ruler of this city came to me and requested my aid,' he said eventually. 'I could not refuse him. I owe him a great debt.'

Brodar Kayne fingered the hilt of his greatsword. 'Know a

bit about debts myself,' he said, his breath coming harder as he readied himself for what was coming. 'You and me, I reckon we've got one that needs settling just about now.'

He lifted his greatsword, turned it slightly so that the red sun behind him reflected off the blade and into the face of the Shaman. It was a small gesture, probably wouldn't matter a damn to the eventual outcome, but he would take any advantage he could get.

He was down and rolling away before the Magelord had left the ground. A second later the Shaman landed in the precise spot he had been standing, his fists hammering down with enough force to send mud and turf exploding out in all directions. He rose, shaking dirt from his fists. 'I gave you everything,' he growled.

'Got yourself a strange definition of everything,' Kayne replied. He took a step towards the Shaman. 'I was your tool, and that's the truth of it. A tool you grew tired of.'

'A tool that is no longer useful must be discarded. Or reforged.'

'You destroyed my life.'

The Shaman's eyes narrowed suddenly and Kayne heard someone approaching from behind.

It was the Wolf. He looked worse than hell, his face a bloody ruin and his breathing laboured. Still, he limped over to stand beside Kayne and faced the Shaman with no more fear than he had ever shown any man alive. 'Need help with this prick?' he growled, raising his axes.

Kayne could have embraced Jerek at that moment, or at least given him a manly pat on the shoulder. Instead he made do with a nod. 'I reckon so,' he said. With the Wolf beside him, he figured his chances had gone from near impossible to merely highly unlikely.

The Shaman's teeth were grinding together. 'This dog still follows you around? So be it. I will kill you both.'

Kayne gave Jerek another nod. His friend grunted, began circling to the Magelord's left as he circled around to the right.

The Shaman glared first at one man and then the other, his prodigious muscles bulging out like knotted steel.

'*Come at me*,' Kayne whispered. He fully expected to die, but he was done running. It ended now.

Suddenly the Shaman cocked his head to one side, his great shaggy mane tumbling over a shoulder as wide as a blacksmith's anvil. He appeared to be listening to something only he could hear. Both Highlanders crouched low, weapons raised, expecting some terrible magic to be unleashed. Instead the hulking Magelord unleashed a roar of utter rage that seemed to shake the very earth around them. 'I must return to the High Fangs,' he growled savagely. 'Heartstone is in grave peril.'

'You ain't going anywhere,' Kayne replied.

The Shaman clenched his fists, his bare chest heaving. 'You care not for the fate of your son?'

'Magnar let his mother burn.'

The Magelord stared at him, his mouth working silently. 'It was not Mhaira on the pyre,' he said at last.

Brodar Kayne could not have been more shocked if the Shaman had struck him full in the face. 'What did you say?'

'Magnar bargained for his mother's life. She was escorted to the furthest reaches of my domain and told never to return. Her cousin took her place on the pyre.'

'I saw her die!' His hands were shaking now.

'Magic,' the Shaman grunted in response. 'It was my intention to deliver you a harsh lesson. Nothing more.'

'You're lying.' Even as he said the words, he knew they weren't true. The Shaman did not lie.

'I was wroth. You betrayed me, Kayne. You knew the price of treason.' The Shaman's voice grew a fraction softer. There was something strange in his eyes, something he had never before seen in all the years he had served as the Sword of the North. 'Despite your betrayal, I still held some measure of respect for you. You were to be given another chance. An allowance I have never afforded any other man.'

Kayne's vision had begun to blur and he realized there were tears in his eyes. All the pain he'd kept locked away for the last two years threatened to burst out of him then and there. *Mhaira's alive. Mhaira's alive.*

The Shaman sighed heavily. The words seemed to crawl from him, as if he was unsure whether or not he wanted to speak them. 'I once watched a woman I loved die on a pyre. I would not have let you suffer the same. Even after your betrayal.'

With a sudden grunt, the master of the High Fangs threw his arms into the air and then began to shimmer. The outline of his body flickered, and then he began to shrink, growing smaller and smaller until he was a dark speck at the centre of a ball of blinding energy. Kayne watched, unmoving, barely seeing. He had witnessed the Magelord shift many times before.

The magic finally dissipated to reveal a large black raven. The Shaman took off into the air and circled the battlefield a few times. With a final caw, he soared off towards the north, leaving the two Highlanders standing alone.

Brodar Kayne sunk to his knees, the greatsword slipping from his trembling palms. Jerek watched silently. A few moments passed. The numbness began to recede.

Mhaira's alive.

Finally it sank in. He looked up to meet the Wolf's eyes. 'Mhaira's alive!' he croaked.

Jerek nodded in reply. 'Aye,' he said simply. 'Mhaira's alive.'

Before either man could say anything more, the ground beneath them began to vibrate. Kayne turned his head to see the Brethren thundering past, stampeding towards the Demonfire Hills in the direction their master had flown. Back towards the High Fangs, where ghosts he thought buried had just risen from the dead.

Sasha came stumbling over. She looked like a ghost herself, all covered in blood and ash, her pretty hair singed and blackened and her eyes telling the story of the horrors she'd witnessed. 'Zolta's men breached the east gate an hour ago,' she said, in between gasps for breath. 'They've taken the city. Someone gave the order for the militia to stand down. The Watch has surrendered.'

'Salazar?' Kayne managed to ask, though he reckoned he already knew the answer, and at that moment he wasn't much for caring either way.

'Dead,' replied Sasha. 'General Zolta confirmed it. He saw the body. What's left of it.'

There was a short silence while the news sunk in. It was Jerek who eventually spoke.

'Well, fuck me,' he said. 'The boy's a hero after all.'

The Truth

H<small>E DASHED THROUGH</small> the Obelisk, his heart racing, his mind focused on one thing only.

He had to find Garrett.

He slid down the sloping heap of debris on his arse, scraping his hands badly. He didn't care. Taking the stairs leading down to the gallery three at a time, he leaped over the Augmentor's butchered corpse and almost slipped on the slick marble. He regained his balance and ran on, praying that no guards appeared to disrupt his headlong flight from the tower.

Even the Stasiseum couldn't slow Cole's progress, though there was glass all over the floor and he saw that two of the displays had been smashed. The savage green-skinned humanoid and the huge, alien-looking egg were gone, vanished into thin air. As he sped through the chamber he heard the patter of blood dripping from the priest suspended in the central display. A hurried glance at the robed figure confirmed he was dead.

The library passed in a blur and then he was speeding down the passageway outside the Grand Council Chamber. Just as he was nearing the huge double doors he heard the sounds of voices drifting through the doorway. The left door began to rattle and then it creaked open, only to jam against the body of the Watchman sprawled there. Cole silently thanked his luck and sprinted towards the stairs down to the first floor, ignoring the corpse wedged in the corner of the stairwell.

The entrance hall was empty except for the Halfmage, who

was biting into a plum. He glanced up in surprise, wiping juice from his chin with the corner of one billowing sleeve. 'Well?' he said. 'What's happening?'

'Salazar's dead,' he said as he barged past the wizard, causing him to fumble the plum. It splattered to the floor, leaving a red mess.

'He's *what*? Where are you going? What about me?'

'There's something I need to do,' Cole shouted back. 'Let the city know. Salazar is dead.'

He glanced down at the bag hanging at his belt. *Tick tock tick tock*. Every pulse of the device sent fresh waves of dread washing through him. He gritted his teeth and ran on.

The light was fading by the time he arrived at the hidden entrance to the temple of the Mother. He pulled the snaking vines of ivy aside, noting with growing dread that they hadn't been disturbed in a while. He was about to squeeze through the narrow gap when he heard the sound of many footsteps moving in tandem. They seemed to be heading in his direction. He hesitated, and then edged back along the side of the temple's crumbling walls and peered out down the Trade Way.

A huge column of Sumnian mercenaries was marching towards the Hook. At the head of the small army was the fattest man Cole had ever seen. His ankles were as thick as most men's thighs, and his four chins bounced up and down with every waddling step he took. Behind the whale of a man, soldiers laughed and cast avaricious glances to the north, where the estates of wealthy nobles rose above the sequestering walls. Some made obscene gestures while others stared with wolfish grins.

Cole ducked back behind the temple. It looked like an entire company of Sumnian mercenaries had breached the east gate without seeing a lick of action. *Maybe the defenders learned of Salazar's death and laid down their weapons*, he thought. He should have felt some pride at that, but he couldn't. Not with the *tick tock tick* crawling in his ears like a burrowing insect. Not with the strange heavy feeling in his chest.

Taking a deep breath, Cole pushed himself through the aperture at the rear of the temple and padded down the short passageway until he reached the steps leading up, just as he had nearly six weeks ago. He had been bruised and bleeding then, late for Garrett's summons because of his own foolishness. Even so, as he slowly climbed the stairs up to the sanctuary, he would have given anything to return to that more innocent time.

When he saw that the door had been torn off its hinges, he finally knew.

The bodies had been piled in the nave and then torched.

Cole stumbled over to the blackened remains of the pyre and stood there numbly. Through blurring eyes, he took in the dark stains on the floor, the red smears covering the walls.

He reached down and grasped a tattered fragment of blue fabric. A hint of gold embroidery was visible at the edge. It was the jerkin Garrett had been wearing at the Shard meeting. The night he had stormed off, throwing the pendant his foster father had given him into the fire that had burned in this very spot.

He crouched down, desperately sifting through the ash and charred bones, growing more and more frantic as he failed to find what he was searching for.

The pendant wasn't there.

With a sudden, uncontrollable sob, he collapsed onto the filthy floor, crawling backwards until his back pressed up against a pillar.

And then he cried, and he did not stop crying until his chest was sore and his eyes were raw and there were no more tears to give.

I'm sorry, Garrett. Sorry for walking out. Sorry for being too arrogant to listen when you tried to put me on the right path.

He untied the bag at his belt and removed his mentor's pocket watch. He stared at it, remembering all the good times the two of them had shared.

Cole wiped fresh tears from his soot-covered face and rose shakily to his feet. He walked over to the altar and carefully placed the device in the centre of the pedestal. *The goddess might be gone, but perhaps the Creator will shepherd their souls.*

He said a prayer then, for Garrett and Vicard and all the others, even the Urich twins whom he had never much liked. They had been his brothers, every one of them.

At least he still had Sasha. The news would devastate her, and his heart ached more at the thought of seeing her hurt than at his own sorrow.

He swallowed hard and tried to steady himself. Garrett had spent his life seeking to liberate Dorminia from a tyrant, and now, finally, his dream had come true. Cole and Sasha would stick together and see that the Grey City became a beacon of hope in a land besieged by darkness. It's what Garrett would have wanted.

With a final farewell to his friends, colleagues and mentor, Davarus Cole departed the temple of the Mother.

He would never return.

The evening breeze was like the breath of a goddess after the carnal stench of the ruined temple. News of Salazar's death had spread, judging by the handful of revellers cheering and singing in the plaza. The gibbets had been pulled down and their captives apparently released, though Cole doubted any of them would be in much of a condition to join the meagre celebrations.

Most of Dorminia was still subdued. Despite the death of the city's tyrannical overlord, a great many men had lost their lives. There would be rivers of tears shed, months of heartbreak for those that remained.

Feeling sick with grief himself, Cole was preparing to follow the road west to try and track down Sasha when a small procession caught his attention. A thin, hawk-nosed man wearing the robes of a city magistrate walked side by side with the monstrously fat Sumnian he had spotted earlier. A dozen or so dark-skinned mercenaries trailed behind them. Between the soldiers and the mismatched pair at the front of the procession was one of the White Lady's pale servants – and hunched over next to her, looking like a mummer in gaudy magistrate's robes too large for his scrawny frame, was a man Cole knew very well.

'Remy!' he cried. The physician started as if surprised. Cole began to hurry over to him but was stopped by the bristling points of a dozen spears aiming at his face.

The procession halted suddenly. The old physician looked at him nervously from puckered eyes lined with crow's feet.

'And who is this?' queried the magistrate leading the group, in a caustic tone. Cole squinted. He looked familiar.

'Grand Magistrate Timerus, this... this is none other than Davarus Cole,' said Remy, sounding somewhat anxious.

Grand Magistrate Timerus? Cole stared around in confusion. What were Thelassa's mercenaries doing with the head of Salazar's council? And why was Remy dressed as a magistrate?

It was the corpulent Sumnian beside Timerus who spoke. 'The boy who slew the tyrant, yes? My soldiers have you to thank for the bounty that awaits us this night!' He laughed suddenly, his massive jowls wobbling. 'Every man knows that when you swear your blade to me, you wed Lady Fortune herself. The dice roll – and as always, they smile on General Zolta.'

'Indeed, General,' said Grand Magistrate Timerus. He placed a long finger on his chin and observed Cole as a lizard might regard a cockroach. 'You played your part in this to perfection, young man.'

'My part?' repeated Cole. He was lost.

Timerus raised an eyebrow. 'I took great pains to ensure the Obelisk was all but undefended. It was I who ordered the militia on the east gate to stand down when the Supreme Augmentor sadly passed away.'

'You gave the city to the mercenaries? But you're the most powerful magistrate on the Grand Council!'

Timerus tutted softly. 'You don't think a coup could have been achieved without influential support in Dorminia, surely? That cretinous half-man probably thinks himself very clever, but he too was nothing more than a pawn. And as for power... I found my ambitions uncomfortably stifled by the city's erstwhile Magelord. One does not simply wait for an immortal to die of old age. A more active approach was needed. The White Lady was most receptive to my terms.'

'She will honour the agreement,' said the pale woman in a deadpan voice. 'You will rule Dorminia as her regent. So long as *you* remember your place.'

'Of course,' replied Timerus, bowing smoothly. 'I live to serve our mistress.'

Cole's head swam. It all made sense, except...

'Garrett and the rest... They're dead. Murdered.' He frowned suddenly at Remy. 'How did you escape? You were at the temple. You fixed my nose. I remember.'

Timerus smiled, but not a single trace of warmth reached his glittering eyes. 'Ah. He doesn't know, does he?'

Remy shifted uncomfortably, glancing to the left and then the right and finally scratching at his grey stubble. 'The Shards, well... We weren't going anywhere fast. I was tired of living like a beggar. Tired of listening to Garrett's grand schemes while nothing ever changed except his pockets got deeper. I put the feelers out. Someone bit, and it wasn't quite the fish I was expecting.'

'What Remy is trying to say is that he sold out your little band of rebels,' Timerus said. 'Fortunately for all concerned, it was me he chose to rat to. Had it been anyone else the course of events might have run entirely differently.'

'I never expected—' Remy began, but Timerus raised a hand to cut him off.

'To keep up appearances and to present Remy as a credible

turncoat, it was necessary for everyone involved with the rebels to die. I had the Supreme Augmentor carry out the order. I can tell by the way your teeth are grinding together that this revelation displeases you. Well, young man, sacrifices needed to be made.'

Sacrifices needed to be made. Cole's fingers twitched closer to Magebane's hilt.

'Garrett was dying anyway,' Remy said. 'He had early symptoms of blacklung infection.'

'If you can't take a city by force, you crush its economy. The poisoning of the city's merchants began last year.' Timerus paused for a moment and inspected his nails. 'Blacklung is a most potent creation, impossible to detect and incredibly versatile. It can kill in a few minutes – as the incident in the Grand Council Chamber so ably demonstrated – or a year, depending on the level of concentration. Why, Marshal Halendorf's expiration was planned to perfection.'

'About that,' said Remy. 'I believe the poison has found its way into the Warrens. Many of the city's urchins have been dying recently.'

Timerus shrugged. 'So long as it is contained, I see no cause for concern. In fact, it is probably for the best. I understand the White Lady has little tolerance for rubbish. We will commence a more thorough cleansing operation in the near future.'

Cole had heard enough. He drew Magebane and advanced on Remy. 'You treacherous bastard!' he screamed. 'You killed them all! Men you knew for years! My family!' He raised the glowing blade – only to suddenly find himself confronted by the pale woman. She loomed menacingly close, barring his way.

Remy shook his head. 'Don't be an idiot, boy. You don't want to do this.'

Cole spat in his face.

The physician's troubled expression contorted and became angry. 'Family?' he sneered. 'Sasha was the only one who ever had a good thing to say about you. Even Garrett despaired of you.'

434

'He loved me!' Cole shouted back.

'You deluded idiot. You think Garrett became rich by being sentimental? He was a *merchant*. He took you in because of Magebane. All this talk about your father and you being some great white hope, it was all bullshit. You were an investment. Nothing more.'

'You're a lying bastard,' Cole said, his voice breaking.

Remy laughed suddenly, a thin, reedy sound that was nonetheless thick with contempt. 'The only bastard here is you. If Garrett ever did have a son, it was Sasha. And from what I heard, she's seen more cock between her legs than you ever will.'

A brief silence followed his words. After a moment General Zolta began to chuckle, a sharp whooping sound that set his men off. Suddenly it seemed everyone was laughing at him. Remy was in hysterics, snot dribbling from his chin. Even Timerus looked amused.

Cole began to shake. He stared around him wildly, at all those faces mocking him, showing him the truth of what he really was. With the guffaws of the men behind him twisting like a dagger in his back, he turned and ran.

Born To Die

SALAZAR, THE TYRANT of Dorminia, perhaps the single most powerful wizard who ever lived, was splattered all over the Obelisk's courtyard, looking like something a giant bird had shat out.

Eremul finally tore his eyes away from the pulpy mess and stared out at the darkening city beyond the courtyard. Timerus and his ratty old sidekick had passed out of the Obelisk and into the Noble Quarter an hour ago. Accompanying them, to his utter shock, had been one of the White Lady's odd creatures. The Grand Magistrate's face had been insufferably smug. It hadn't taken long for Eremul to conclude that he must have been plotting against Salazar all along. He had clearly underestimated the fellow.

He glanced again at the remains of the Magelord. It was a strange thing, seeing the man he had hated for so long come to such a spectacularly gruesome end. Now the initial rush of elation had worn off there was an uncomfortable sensation in his chest, and upon further reflection he realized what it was.

Emptiness.

Those with nothing but vengeance to live for are condemned by their own bitter victory.

He had read that in a book somewhere years ago and had thought it a heap of horseshit – the usual tripe written by authors whose aphorisms were about as relevant to the real world as his own cock was to the satisfaction of Dorminia's collective women.

As it happened, the bastard had been right on the money.

He stared out at the city again. Was that a scream he had just heard? He thought he smelled smoke on the air.

With a final glance at Salazar's corpse, he wheeled his chair out of the courtyard and began the long trek back to the harbour and the depository.

Sasha watched the lurid orange flames lighting up the night skyline behind the walls of the Noble Quarter. Mercenaries continued to pour into the district, laughing and hollering and brandishing weapons in one hand and large sacks in the other. Dark shapes flitted from house to house as the Sumnians looted and murdered their way through the homes of Dorminia's wealthiest citizens.

This isn't right, she thought, feeling despair creeping up and threatening to engulf her. *How can this be happening?* She spotted General D'rak and a group of his men near the south of the plaza and hurried over to him. She ignored the leers and whistles she received as she faced up to the mercenary in the white leather armour.

'General D'rak, what is going on? Call your men back!' she demanded.

The southerner flashed that outstandingly white smile. He reached up a callused hand and began smoothing out his oiled braids. 'They are not my men,' he said. 'They are Zolta's. As always, the Fat General emerges with the lion's share of the spoils.'

'But you were paid!' Sasha said angrily. 'This is *our* city. The nobles may be rich and selfish but they don't deserve to be murdered in their homes.'

D'rak shrugged. 'Zolta was not paid. The White Lady's purse did not stretch far enough for his services. The Fat General took the contract on the promise he would claim his share after. And that is what he is doing, yes?'

Sasha stared at the Noble Quarter again, her teeth grinding

together as she watched the pillaging continue in the distance. Someone trundled by just behind her and she turned to see the Halfmage on his strange contraption wheeling away towards the south. He seemed lost in his own thoughts, oblivious to the stares that followed his passing.

She rubbed at her throbbing head. The bleeding in her side had finally stopped, but she felt as weak as a newborn baby and she knew she looked like an absolute mess.

The mercenaries were still grinning at her. She scowled back at them and turned away. She cursed herself for not stopping the Halfmage when she had the chance and asking him where Cole might be found. Much to her annoyance, she found herself worrying about him.

The temple of the Mother, she thought. *Perhaps the Shards are gathered there now*. She pushed her way through the ever-increasing crowd gathering in the plaza. Those who had not fought in the day's battle were finally beginning to celebrate the news of the city's liberation – if liberation was indeed what it was. She was beginning to feel uneasy that the White Lady's intentions were not as altruistic as Brianna had believed.

Distracted by those troubling thoughts, she almost bumped into a woman going in the opposite direction, a hard-faced lady some years older than her with strawberry-blond hair caught up with a pretty hairpin. Their eyes met for a split second. There was something oddly familiar about the woman's face, but by the time she thought to stop and question her they had passed each other.

The temple was just ahead. She hoped her instincts were right and that Cole, Garrett and the rest were there. Cole would probably be completely insufferable now. She would have to work extra hard to keep him in check.

She wondered if she would get the chance to see Brodar Kayne again before he departed. The old Highlander had been a rock over the last few weeks, and the news that his wife still lived had gone some way to lifting her spirits after the horrors of the fighting she had seen. As for his companion, Jerek was as much an enigma now as when he had first stomped into the Shard gathering all those weeks ago. She realized then that there was no one she would rather have watching her back than that grim-faced bastard. How had *that* happened? Men never ceased to surprise her.

She reached the hidden entrance and saw that someone had recently disturbed the vines and forgotten to replace them. She allowed herself a smile. Cole might now actually be the hero he had always thought he was, but some things would never change.

There was sudden movement behind her. Too late, she reached for her short sword. A filthy hand clamped around her mouth, stifling her cry, and a hairy arm seized her around the chest. She fought madly, but whoever had hold of her was much stronger than she was.

'Don't struggle,' said a familiar voice behind her. She almost gagged at the sheer stench of the man. 'You'll only make it worse.'

Sudden, animal terror grabbed hold of her. She stared in horror at the fingers pressed over her mouth, counting them again and again as if by doing so she might arrive at a different result.

'Knew from the moment I saw you that I had to have you,' Three-Finger drawled. 'For all his bullshit, the kid spoke true. You're something, all right.'

He began dragging her backwards, away from the temple. She kicked out and threw her head back and tried to bite his hand, but the ex-convict was too big and powerful. 'Easy now,' he chuckled. 'Once we're safely out of sight I'll take my hand away. Let you scream some. You got a dirty mouth. I like that.'

She was pulled through an open doorway into an empty warehouse. The outside world faded as she was dragged back into darkness.

'I took an arrow in the shoulder thanks to you. Played dead

for near four hours. You ever hid under a pile of stinking corpses? Ain't much fun, I can tell you that.'

Three-Finger heaved her around to face the wall as he edged towards the open door. His voice dropped to a sinister whisper. She could feel his foul breath in her ear. 'You might have heard I've only got half a cock. Don't let that fool you. You won't notice the difference.'

She heard the door creak as it began to slam shut. All hope faded with the sound and she sagged, giving into despair. *Why didn't I die on the battlefield?*

There was a sudden thumping noise just behind her. Three-Finger's grip loosened and then fell away completely. She turned.

Standing in the doorway, a blood-covered stone clenched in one hand, was the woman she had passed in the Hook. The light of the moon behind her faintly illuminated that severe face. A few moments passed. Her saviour took a few steps forwards.

Sasha gasped. Long-suppressed memories flooded back. Finally, she realized the identity of her rescuer.

Her older sister casually let the stone fall next to the prone form of Three-Finger and stared back at her with an unreadable expression.

'You and I need to talk.'

Davarus Cole ran through the Noble Quarter, not caring a damn where he was going. All he knew was that he needed to get away from those jeering, laughing faces. His entire life was a lie, and it seemed he was the only person in the world who hadn't known it.

Tears stung his eyes. All those men sacrificed to liberate Dorminia from Salazar's rule, only to place the city in the hands of a snake like Timerus and his scheming mistress in Thelassa. The White Lady had used him just like everyone else.

Three-Finger had been right about him. He would have to apologize when he saw him again. And to Isaac. They were better men than him, and that was the truth. *Me, a hero?* He wanted to laugh at the absurdity of the notion now. His father had been a murderer and his mother a whore. He had no claim to heroism.

He was done pretending to be something he wasn't.

Three mercenaries suddenly burst out from the mansion ahead of him. They wore big grins on their faces. Each carried a large canvas sack bursting with valuables. One of the southerners paused to wipe his feet on the mat in the porch, and Cole saw that his boots left dark red smears behind.

'What are you doing?' he asked. The nearest Sumnian frowned.

'Taking what we're owed. Who are you, anyway?'

The mercenary with blood on his boots raised his sword and shook it at Cole. 'He's no noble. Could be he's trying to fill his own pockets.'

'Get out of here, boy. Before we kill you.'

Cole stared at the three men, and then backed away. This wasn't his business. He was done being a hero, whatever that word even meant. He ran down the street, towards the exit of the district. Other dark-skinned warriors were plundering homes to either side of him. He ignored them, carried on running.

A whooping chuckle rang out to his left, immediately grabbing his attention.

It was General Zolta, his gross profile resembling a miniature hill in the poor light. The obese mercenary captain and four of his men were standing in a small square dotted with a few cedars. They had a handful of nobles pinned against the trunks and were poking them with their spears, laughing uproariously. What was it Zolta had said? *My soldiers have you to thank for the bounty that awaits us this night!*

Cole gritted his teeth and ran on. *They're just nobles. They never gave a damn for anyone else. They're just nobles...*

He was almost at the exit now. An estate burned just to the right of him, roaring and crackling as it was consumed by flame. He was sprinting by the blaze when a sudden scream slowed him a fraction. He glanced over and saw a woman being dragged by her hair face-first over the paved veranda. The mercenary grinning over her had a table leg in one hand.

The woman screamed again; her terrified sobs pounded inside Cole's head like a hammer. *Keep running. It's none of your business. You're no hero.*

The gate was just ahead. The woman cried out one more time, a pitiful sound. His feet suddenly felt like concrete.

You're no hero.

A loud thud reached his ears. The mercenary had begun to bludgeon the stricken noblewoman with the table leg.

Davarus Cole's heart thundered, his breath coming in ragged gasps. He slowed to a walk, and then to a complete halt. Finally he turned and stared at the mercenary.

'Leave her alone.'

'What?' The Sumnian stared at him in puzzlement. 'She's my prize. I can do what I please.' He raised his club again.

'I said leave her alone.'

There was anger on the mercenary's face now. 'You want her? I don't share with maggots. But why fight over a woman? Neither of us will have her.' He gripped the makeshift club with both hands and raised it over the woman's head.

Cole's hand was a blur.

The mercenary stared down at the hilt which suddenly quivered from his throat. He gurgled once and then toppled forwards, dead before he hit the ground.

Walking over to retrieve Magebane, Cole was relieved to see the noblewoman was not badly hurt. 'Can you move?' he asked. She stirred and then nodded. 'Take my hand.' He reached down. After a moment she grasped his arm and he pulled her gently to her feet.

He stared, taken aback by the woman's beauty. Her eyes were the deepest jade, her hair like spun gold. And around her neck...

'Where did you get that?' he gasped.

'What?' The woman was distraught. She looked down at the pendant hanging just above her breasts. 'My husband gave it to me,' she said.

'Where is your husband?'

'He's... dead.' Her voice cracked on the word.

Cole closed his eyes for a moment. His grip tightened on Magebane. He raised the glowing dagger – and then placed it back in its sheath. 'Come with me. I'll get you out of here.'

A few minutes later they were safely clear of the Noble Quarter and on their way down the Tyrant's Road towards the Hook. 'Do you have somewhere to go?' he asked.

'I... I have a cousin who lives nearby.'

'Head straight there.'

She offered him her stumbling thanks and hurried away. Cole watched her go and then resumed his journey back down to the Hook. He needed to find Sasha.

'Davarus Cole.'

That voice was unmistakable. 'Master!' he exclaimed, hurrying over to the Darkson. The Shamaathan was standing on the side of the road. 'What are you doing here?'

The master assassin appeared troubled. 'Waiting for you.'

'Really? Is there something I can help you with? I – I've realized that I still have a lot to learn.'

The Darkson looked away, refusing to meet his eyes. 'I wanted to give you something.'

Cole nodded eagerly. 'Of course, master. What is it?'

'This.'

The first thing that registered was the regret in his mentor's voice.

The second was the white-hot agony in his gut.

Cole stared down at the wicked curved dagger emerging from his stomach. The Darkson jerked the blade free and he staggered, his hands desperately trying to keep the blood from gushing out. It was futile. Warm, sticky liquid ran down his fingers, splattering onto the road below. 'But… why?' he managed to gasp.

'The White Lady does not like loose ends. Or potential threats. Brianna died in battle, leaving you as the only piece left to be removed. I am sorry.'

Cole didn't reply. He reeled away, horrified at the volume of blood pouring from his body. He was growing weaker by the second. He stumbled off the road, one arm reaching out blindly, seeking something to support himself on. After what seemed like an eternity his bloody palm pressed up against a wall. It was the side of a building.

He staggered back against it and sank slowly to the ground. He was starting to feel numb. It was almost a pleasant sensation. It reminded him of when he was young, when he and Sasha would compete to see who could remain submerged in an ice bath the longest. He smiled suddenly. She usually won, but it had been good practice. Good practice for the day he would be a hero.

His eyes closed.

A familiar face was waiting for Eremul when he finally arrived back at the depository.

'*Isaac!*' he spluttered, almost slipping out of his seat in shock. His manservant was as inscrutable as ever, but there was something deeply unsettling about the way he looked in the dim light. It was as if he were seeing Isaac's face for the first time. It seemed… incomplete, as though a skilled artist had captured an uncanny likeness of his subject but missed out a few essential details.

'Hello, master.' The manservant's voice was more melodic than he remembered. 'I've been waiting for you.'

'Who are you?' Eremul demanded. He glanced left and right, but the streets were dead. Those inclined to celebrate the city's dubious liberation must have made their way to the centre or to one of the taverns a little to the north. They were completely alone.

'I don't suppose you would believe me if I told you I am your trusty manservant.'

'I had a trusty manservant? I could have sworn he was a bumbling buffoon.'

Isaac smiled faintly. 'This is why I couldn't leave without saying goodbye. Your species may have been found wanting, but there are some among you who are not without merit. A part of me will be sad when you are all gone.'

'When we are all gone?' *What is he talking about?* 'Enough games, Isaac,' he said, growing annoyed. 'I know about the harbourmaster. I know about the Crow. Who are you, really?' He paused for a moment, staring at that troubling visage. '*What* are you?'

'You may call me... an Adjudicator.'

'An Adjudicator?'

'I have spent four years among your kind. Evaluating you. I have made my decision, and so now I return to my homeland to begin the preparations. As to what I am...'

Eremul blinked, astonished by what he was seeing. It wasn't so much that Isaac was changing appearance as his brain was beginning to fill in the details it had somehow omitted before now.

Humanoid. Ivory skin. Slender, almost delicate limbs. Eyes as black as midnight... Sudden terror gripped him. He had never been subjected to a regard as utterly ruinous as that obsidian stare. Even Salazar had not unmanned him so effortlessly. The being behind that appalling scrutiny was so ancient even a Magelord's lifespan was but a flicker of a candle in comparison.

Eremul felt warm wetness trickling over the stumps of his legs. He had pissed himself.

Isaac, or the thing that had called itself Isaac, seemed not to notice. It raised one slender hand and said, almost sadly, 'Enjoy what time you have remaining, Eremul Kaldrian. Regrettably, no exceptions can be made in the coming crusade. Not even for you.'

He took a single step forwards – and disappeared. He fell away into nothingness.

Eremul sat motionless for a time. He glanced down at his soiled robes. Then he wheeled himself down to the docks, too terrified to even think about going back inside the depository alone. He sat there, staring out over the harbour, the sound of the lapping water below helping to calm his shredded nerves.

Movement caught his eye. He stared down at the dark water, mumbled an incantation to summon a globe of light and illuminate whatever it was. He saw, and his breath caught in his throat, and then he began to shake.

A moment later he held it in his hands. The creature was thinner than he remembered, barely more than a skeleton – and yet somehow, miraculously, it still breathed. *How is it possible? I fumbled you into the harbour over three weeks ago!*

The dog opened its eyes a fraction. It yelped pathetically, tried to lean forward and lick his face with its parched tongue.

Eremul held the pathetic creature close to him, as tightly as he could without harming it. *You're my little miracle*, he thought, ridiculously happy. He turned his chair around and started off back to the depository, eager to get some food and water into the animal. *The worst is over. It is time for us both to heal. Together.*

He'd even thought of a name. It had come to him just then, out of the blue, and it felt so right that he could imagine no other being quite so fitting.

Tyro.

Brodar Kayne counted out the large golden coins. Twenty-five, just as he had been promised. He pulled the drawstring tight and hefted the pouch in his hand. It felt solid and heavy, like a job well done.

'I trust you are satisfied,' said the White Lady's servant. It was a statement, not a question. He nodded.

'Shame about Brianna,' he ventured. 'She was a fine figure of a lady. Er, speaking respectfully, of course.'

The pale lady didn't deign to respond. He sighed and stared back towards the city. Sasha had left them a short while ago, saying she wanted to find Cole and check he was all right. He had mentioned he might not be here when she got back. In any case, he reckoned the two youngsters would manage fine without him around.

The fact was he'd already stayed for longer than he wanted. There was just one more thing that needed to be done.

The Wolf was sitting by himself on a small hill overlooking the city. Bodies were still being collected from the battlefield, hundreds of them, gathered in great heaps to be buried in or around Dorminia, depending on whether or not a corpse could be identified. A lot of them couldn't, and that was the trouble with magic. As far as he was concerned, if you were going to take the decision to kill another man you had better be able to look him in the eye. It kept you honest. It kept you *human*.

Magelords and their ilk, they did things differently. And it was because of the likes of Salazar and the White Lady that five thousand fresh graves would need to be dug.

Jerek gave him a nod as he approached. The Wolf was in a bad state, his face a battered mass and several ribs broken, to say nothing of the other wounds he'd suffered over the last couple of months. Kayne had never seen him so beaten up, but the last thing he was going to do was offer Jerek any kind of sympathy. He might as well pour oil on a fire.

'Here,' he said, tossing over the bag of coins. 'It's yours. My half.'

His old friend glanced at the gold but didn't say a word.

'I'm leaving,' he continued. 'Heading north. Aye, back to the High Fangs. Mhaira's still alive. I got no other choice.'

The Wolf stared straight ahead, his face as inscrutable as stone.

'We went through hell getting this far. I couldn't ask anyone to make that journey again, back the other way. I wouldn't let 'em if they offered.'

No reply.

'Call me a bloody old fool, I ain't going to argue. I know I won't be coming back. But some things a man just has to do. With fifty gold spires, I figure you can live well in one of the Free Cities.'

Jerek glanced at the bag of coins again. His silence was deafening.

'Anyway. I know you ain't much for tearful farewells and such. I don't reckon either of us is. So I guess I ought to just say thank you. For everything.'

A single muscle twitched in Jerek's cheek.

'Right then. I'll be going. Look after yourself, Wolf.'

He turned and ambled back down the hill. He supposed he could have waited until morning, but there was no time like the present.

He made it to twenty paces before the pouch struck him in the back. Golden coins exploded out everywhere, rolling all over the grass.

'Fucking unbelievable. Two years travelling together. Fighting together. Almost dying together. And you reckon you can pull this kind of shit now? That ain't fair, Kayne, and you know it.'

He turned. 'Look, this ain't your battle—'

'Like fuck it ain't. I got no more love for the Shaman than you do.' Jerek was tugging at his beard, his face an angry snarl. 'Did you hear him? Bastard called me a dog. I ain't having that. I just ain't having it. Someone needs to teach that prick a lesson.'

The rant went on for a good couple of minutes. Kayne waited until his friend had tired himself out and then nodded slowly. 'Well. It sounds like you've made up your mind.' He paused for a moment and scratched at his jaw. 'But, uh, if you're set on coming with me, I could use a hand gathering up this gold. Might come in handy in the Badlands and maybe beyond.'

Together the two began collecting the fallen coins. One had rolled some distance away. Kayne saw a young militiaman furtively reach down and pick it up while pretending to check his boots. He met the fellow's eyes and gave him a look of calculated menace. The youngster blanched and bent down to replace the coin on the ground, but stopped as Kayne held up a hand, grinned and then gestured at him to take it. Enough women and children had lost husbands and fathers in the short conflict between the two cities. He reckoned a man was due a break.

The two Highlanders stashed the last of the gold and hefted their backpacks. Then they set off towards the north, to begin the first stage of an epic journey few had ever attempted and fewer still had ever survived.

Anyone party to the odd couple's passing, such as a certain nameless soldier still musing over his good fortune, would have noted the ghost of a smile on the face of the older warrior.

In contrast, his companion wore a permanent scowl that, nonetheless, could not entirely mask the spring in his step...

ACKNOWLEDGEMENTS

This novel couldn't have been published without the help and support of the individuals listed below. I would like to extend my sincere thanks to each and every one of you.

First and foremost my agent, Robert Dinsdale, who took me on when the story was less than half written – and sold a trilogy barely six months later. He helped shape the novel into something worth publishing.

Jennifer Custer at AM Heath for negotiating various foreign language deals on my behalf.

Alan Miranda, Simon Scoltock, and Russ Davis for their feedback on the manuscript when it was it in its earliest and most fragile form. Also, Kevin Smith for pointing out a number of errors.

Mike Brooks for his support and advice from start to end. The novel wouldn't have been the same without his input.

Mathilda Imlah and the team at Head of Zeus for liking the story well enough to buy three of them, and for polishing out those rough edges.

Danielle Stockley and the team at Penguin for taking the trilogy under their wing on the opposite side of the Atlantic, and Chris Lotts for helping deliver it unto their hands.

Elizabeth Starr for her generosity in editing the entire manuscript out of the kindness of her heart – often during the early hours of the morning when the shadow of the sun was but a distant memory...

And last but certainly not least, my wife Yesica for keeping the faith.

SWORD OF THE NORTH

SOME LEGENDS NEVER DIE...

'Extraordinary,
bold and brilliant.'
TOR.COM

'Thrilling'
SFX

'Gripping'
GUARDIAN

'The best fantasy you will
read this year'
SFBOOK

LUKE
SCULL

Thirty-Six Years Ago

HE COULD HEAR THEM crashing through the trees behind him. He half-skidded down the slope, ruined boots finding little purchase on snow frozen solid. His feet were numb with cold, felt as dead as the lamb flopping wildly over his shoulder. Blood still leaked from the slit throat of the beast and soaked the filthy rags that covered his body.

There was a curse from one of the men chasing him, followed by an angry yell. He shifted the carcass on his shoulder and allowed himself a grin. He was losing them, even weighed down as he was. He reckoned a few had given up already. They were old men, most of them. Well past thirty.

He would get some distance on them and find somewhere to hide. Lay low for a bit and get a fire going. His stomach gave a mighty growl, a reminder that this winter had been desperate. Harsher than any he could remember.

He leaped a fallen tree, managing to keep his balance despite the thick patch of ice just beyond. Moments later he heard a thump and a fresh flurry of curses turned the air blue – he guessed one of his pursuers had blundered into the log and landed flat on his face.

He wondered what had become of Leaf and Red Ear – or Dead Ear, as he decided he would take to calling his hapless friend. Red Ear was supposed to be keeping watch while he and Leaf raided the farm. They were just done slaughtering the first lamb when someone raised the alarm. It turned out Red Ear was about as useless a sentry as he was a cook. How he'd survived Skarn's gang as long as he had was anyone's guess.

3

The trees finally parted. He could see the river now. Once he was across the Icemelt's surface the stubborn bastards would soon admit defeat. He ran on, rapid breaths throwing up clouds of mist – but approaching the bank he realized he had things all wrong. The Icemelt had yet to fully freeze over. Massive chunks of ice churned in the surging rapids, grinding together with enough force to crush a man to pulp. There wasn't a chance in hell of swimming across that raging deluge.

Listening for the sounds of the chase, he swerved, intending to head downstream and circle back into the forest.

Two men emerged from the trees, blocking his path.

'You've gone far enough, boy.' The nearest of the pair was panting, but there was no mistaking the grim resolve in his voice. Nor the glitter of cold steel at his waist.

He didn't waste time replying. Instead he dashed forward and drove his forehead into the speaker's face. He heard bone crack, felt cartilage crumble beneath the force of the blow. He spun immediately, shrugged the lamb off his shoulder and raised it as a makeshift shield. The other man's sword thrust wedged in the animal's flank, and his surprise lasted just long enough to get in three quick blows, dropping his assailant to the ground.

He retrieved the lamb and was tugging the sword free when someone barrelled into him from behind, knocking him down and sending both the sword and the abused carcass flying from his grasp.

He twisted around to grab the newcomer. This one was a real piece of work, as tall as he was and a good bit heavier. Though he'd always been unusually strong for his age he couldn't get the bastard pinned down for a solid hit. He took a glancing blow to the mouth, spat out blood. The other man grabbed him in a headlock and forced him down. He pushed back desperately and narrowly avoided getting his skull dashed against a rock. He swung an elbow, thought he might have cracked a rib – but if he had, his opponent didn't seem much for caring.

4

He lost all sense of time as he struggled with the big Easterman. A minute or an hour might have passed as they battered each other on the bank of the river, neither able to get the upper hand. Finally they broke apart and his opponent stepped back, breathing hard. Slowly he became aware they were being watched. He turned. Half a dozen faces stared back. One he knew well, beneath the bruises that had turned his boyish features into a discoloured mess. Leaf.

One of the men held a long dagger at Leaf's throat. Two others had arrows nocked and drawn. The meanest-looking shook his head and spat on the snow. 'Where the rest of you hiding?

'The rest of us?' He knew who the man referred to, or reckoned he did. And if that was the case, he was as good as dead.

'Your gang. Been raiding the settlements near the Boundary for the last year. Left a family murdered in their beds, mother and children and all.'

The memory made him wince. He wiped his face with the back of his hand and examined the bloody smear it left. He glanced up. The sky had grown dark as an old bruise.

'I'm waiting for an answer, boy.'

He narrowed his eyes and stared at the dead lamb lying skewered by the side of the river. 'It wasn't me what did that. Nor Leaf nor Red Ear.'

'You gonna tell me the three of you split from the group when it started killing folk?'

'It's the truth.'

The leader of the Eastermen spat again. 'We'll do this the hard way then.' He gestured at the man holding Leaf. 'Drown him in the river. Slowly, mind. Give our friend here time to ponder whether there's anything he should be telling us.'

Leaf began to struggle as he was dragged to the river. He was little more than a child in truth, and his friend's efforts to wriggle free were hard to watch, but he didn't turn away. Not

5

even as Leaf's head was forced under the churning water.

'How old are you?' the leader asked, once Leaf finally came back up again.

'Sixteen,' he replied. He could see Leaf's teeth chattering uncontrollably. The wiry youngster was struggling to catch his breath and his skin had turned an obscene shade of blue.

'Huh. Hardly more than a boy and yet you knocked two of my men senseless. Butchering that woman and her kids must've been easy work.'

He was growing angry now. 'I told you we didn't do it! All we ever did was steal some livestock. We left Skarn and the others before Eastmeet.'

Leaf went into the water again. When he reappeared his eyes had rolled back in their sockets. He wasn't struggling any more.

The leader gestured at the limp figure. 'He's done. Finish him and throw the body in the river.'

Rage surged within him. He liked Leaf, who was smart and had a cheerful nature despite the fact he'd cut his uncle's throat rather than spend another night in his bed. Leaf had watched out for him when he had joined Skarn's band; saved him from a bloody confrontation or two when his pride wouldn't let him back down.

'You drown him and I'll kill you.'

The men with bows shifted slightly, their arrows nocked and ready to loose. Their leader gave an ugly little chuckle and nodded at the man holding Leaf. 'Drown him.'

He charged.

The next thing he knew he was lying on the ground, staring up at the leaden sky. Snowflakes fluttered down to melt on his face. He reached for his knee and felt the arrow protruding there. A face loomed over him.

'That was stupid. Brave, but stupid. Men!'

He felt himself being dragged across the snow towards the sound of rushing water. They turned him roughly and held

6

him out over the river. He stared out across the Icemelt, watching as Leaf's body twisted and spun like his namesake before going under. Someone took hold of his hair and pushed his head down, down towards that freezing maelstrom of ice…

'Wait.'

His would-be executioners hesitated and his head came to a halt an inch above the water. He stared into its savage depths.

'What's your name?' asked the voice. It was deep and powerful and sounded like it was directed at him. He turned his head a fraction and saw the speaker was the big bastard he had fought earlier.

'What does it matter?' The leader was clearly annoyed. 'He's a brigand. Kill him and be done with it.'

'The boy's got fire in him. Fire and steel. We could forge him into something with purpose. The spirits know we need fighting men in the East Reaching.'

'He's a cold-blooded killer. A child-murderer. Besides, he's just taken an arrow in the knee. Few ever recover from a wound like that.'

There was a brief silence. He held his breath, the roar of the Icemelt raging below him.

A strong hand pulled him up, almost gently, and turned him around. 'I've never met a boy who put up as much fight as you did. Especially not half-starved. I'll ask again: what's your name, lad?'

He stared back at his saviour. The man's face carried a few minor injuries from their earlier struggle, but his eyes betrayed no malice or anger. Only a certain curiosity.

'My name…' he said slowly, trying not to pass out from the pain. He blinked snow from his eyes. 'My name…' he said again.

'… is Kayne.'

Wild Country

'KAYNE.'

The gruff voice snapped him awake like a bucket of ice-cold water over the head. The Wolf could rasp his name any number of ways fit to freeze the blood. One glance at Jerek's bald, fire-scarred visage was all the confirmation he needed that things were about to turn ugly.

'Bandits?' he mouthed silently. Jerek nodded and scowled at the waning night. The grim warrior's twin axes were already unharnessed, brutal implements of death that might have taken more lives than any other weapon wielded by the hand of man – save perhaps for the sword Brodar Kayne now lifted from the ground beside him.

The old Highlander pushed himself painfully to his feet, rubbing sleep from his eyes. They hadn't bothered to light a campfire. It was the height of summer and besides, they'd hoped to avoid drawing attention. Hoped to avoid a situation like this.

He squinted into the darkness. Not a damn thing, he thought sourly. His eyesight was getting worse.

Jerek's senses, on the other hand, seemed as sharp as ever. His friend did the lion's share of the sentry duty, and though neither man had spoken of it, Kayne was beginning to feel guilty. There was only so much guilt a man could take. And the older you got, the more difficult it became to bear the weight.

8

A twig snapped somewhere nearby. An arrow zinged through the air and thudded into the grass six feet from where the horses were tethered. They snorted and shifted nervously.

Kayne sighed. He hated archers. They were little better than wizards, in his estimation, though at least most had the decency not to prance around in what was, when it came right down to it, a glorified dress. A sliver of the dream he had just woken from flickered to life in the dark pits of his mind, and he glanced down at his left knee. The memory of that ancient agony made him wince.

Jerek motioned to his left and stalked off, crouching low and weaving from side to side. Kayne followed his lead, though the effort of bending caused his back to complain something fierce.

He thought he saw the shadows shift ahead. Bandits normally travelled in small groups, the better to strike hard and fast and make a quick escape. There were unlikely to be many of them. If they could take out one or two, the rest would scatter soon enough.

Suddenly, he sensed movement to his right. Careless of his creaking knees, he dived into a roll, coming out of it with his greatsword raised high, prepared to cleave whomever it was in half.

But it was only Jerek, his eyes glittering in the ghostly light. The Wolf spat on the grass and shook his head. 'They fled,' he said. 'Best we get moving. No sense waiting to be picked off in broad daylight.'

Kayne nodded. Bandits were always a risk when crossing the Badlands, as the two men knew all too well from recent experience.

They returned to camp to find their packs missing.

'Pricks stole our bags,' growled Jerek, never one to mince his words. He reached up and began tugging at his beard, the way he always did when he was on the verge of flying off into a rage.

9

Kayne closed his eyes and leaned on his greatsword. This was an inauspicious start to their journey. Three weeks had passed since the liberation of the Grey City and the wounds they'd suffered had forced them to rest for a time. Jerek's injuries in particular were nasty – at least two broken ribs and a cracked cheekbone. But the Wolf would rather pass out in the saddle than delay another week. Jerek hated crowds. He hated soft, Lowlander comforts. He hated pretty much everything, truth be told.

'At least we still have the horses,' Kayne grunted. He walked over to the mounts, shaking his head ruefully. The bandits had stolen the saddles, and he wasn't relishing the prospect of subjecting his arse to bare horseback. 'We could ride back to Ashfall and resupply,' he suggested, though he already knew what the answer would be.

Jerek shot him a dark look. 'I ain't going back there. Place is a shithole.'

Kayne couldn't argue the point. Ashfall was appropriately named. The black dust got everywhere, blown in by swirling winds from the Demonfire Hills to settle on the two-score buildings of Dorminia's northernmost vassal town. Ashfall wasn't a place either man wanted to return to in a hurry.

'I guess we ride on,' Kayne said, sheathing his sword and pulling himself on to his mount. The sky was lightening, midnight blue fading to iron grey as night gave way to morning. He studied the area as Jerek climbed onto his own horse, a black stallion that accepted his scowling burden with an ease that would have surprised the stable master who sold them the beast. Jerek had a way with animals he lacked with people.

The land ran flat for miles in every direction. Wild grasses warred with small copses of oak and elm and beech. The daylight would reveal their brilliant shades of gold and green.

Further north, Kayne knew, these vibrant colours would become muted. The grass would grow dull and sparse, and scrub would replace tree until the Badlands truly began – a vast stretch of barren country once home to the nomadic Yahan horse tribes. The last time he and Jerek had passed through, the place had been fair crawling with bandits. Given the trail of corpses the two Highlanders had left behind, Kayne figured the Bandit King would be in no mood to welcome them back with open arms.

As they rode, he watched Jerek with concern. The Wolf looked in some pain. Likely he was nursing one of his injuries. Kayne's own wounds still hurt, especially the knife slash in his stomach that had threatened to turn rotten. The flesh was clean and had knitted back together, but the scar was still raw. He paid it little mind. There were some wounds that never healed, wounds that festered deep in the soul and ultimately did more to break a man than any bodily hurt. The spirits knew he carried enough of those scars himself – but the news he'd received back at the Grey City lent him hope that the largest of them might not follow him to the grave. For the first time in many, many months, he had a reason to live.

He let go of the reins and squeezed the coin purse hanging at his belt. Forty golden spires and a handful of silver moons – a large sum of coin by anyone's standards. He and Jerek had been through hell to earn it. It wasn't every day you helped liberate a city from a tyrant. He'd made friends down in the Trine, met some good men and women – and a few some way off good, but interesting nonetheless. In different circumstances he might have been tempted to stay. Instead he and the Wolf had left Dorminia as soon as they had collected their pay. The treasure nestling inside that pouch had changed everything. It was the reason he was back riding north. Back to the High Fangs. Back to the place he had once called home.

'Kayne.'

Jerek pointed at the thicket of trees just ahead. Kayne leaned forward on his brown mare and squinted, but saw nothing save an indistinct green blur. He shook his head in frustration. He could remember a time when he had thought thirty was old. By forty, a man was past his prime. A man's fighting days should be ancient history by fifty, stories to tell the grandchildren. Yet here he was, well into his sixth decade and still doing the same old shit, except now his body was falling apart and taking a piss was a tougher battle than killing a man.

He pulled back on his reins and fell in behind Jerek. They turned away from the stand of trees and urged the horses to a run. A moment later a group of armed men on horseback burst out from behind the trees. He counted five, and Jerek grunted to draw attention to three more emerging from a thicket ahead.

'We're not getting by those without a fight,' Kayne said, eyeing the men warily. They were riding hard, wind streaming through Kayne's grey hair and dancing around Jerek's hairless scalp. Kayne risked a glance behind him. The riders giving chase were gaining fast. 'Shit,' he muttered.

They were never going to outpace the bandits. The Highlander's mounts were of reasonable stock, but the horses of these steppes were renowned the world over. The legacy of the vanished Yahan tribes had gifted the Bandit King the finest horses in the land.

As one the three riders pulled alongside them, easily keeping pace. The leader raised a hand with what looked suspiciously like a flourish. 'Surrender!' he called out in dramatic fashion. 'Flee and your lives shall be forfeit.'

Jerek narrowed his eyes and spat over the side of his horse. Surrender was the last thing on his mind, Kayne reckoned. More likely the Wolf intended to cut a bloody path right through them.

He lowered his voice so he hoped only Jerek could hear. 'Better we do this on the ground. We're outnumbered four to one, and I'm not much for fighting on horseback.'

For a moment he thought his companion would ignore

12

him, but a few seconds later Jerek tugged at his reins and brought his stallion to an abrupt halt. Kayne did the same, hoping he hadn't just made a terrible mistake.

They dismounted as the bandits moved quickly to surround them. The leader slid off his mount with an easy grace, even seeing fit to sketch a quick bow, to Jerek's evident annoyance.

'Well.' The bandit leader stroked his thin moustache, his jet-black hair bound in a ponytail. The hilt of a fancy sword stuck out from the belt at his waist, which was cinched tight around grey leather armour. Kayne swallowed a sneeze as the fragrant scent of the bandit tickled his nose. The man smelled faintly of perfume.

'Well,' the dapper outlaw repeated. He flashed a smile, revealing bright white teeth. 'I do believe we have ourselves a stick up. I would like to say you gave us quite the chase, but that would be quite the lie.'

Kayne watched Jerek out of the corner of his right eye. The Wolf's teeth were grinding together, explosive rage mere seconds away. This dandy was rubbing him the wrong way something fierce.

'I'm gonna make a suggestion,' Kayne said carefully. 'We pay you a few coin to buy safe passage. Then you bid us a pleasant journey and we part ways, all peaceful-like.'

The bandit leader raised a gloved hand to stroke thoughtfully at his chin. 'I see you are familiar with our customs. That pouch at your waist will indeed do nicely. As will your weapons – there is always need for good steel in these parts.'

'Go fuck yourself.'

Every man present immediately turned to stare at Jerek.

'I ain't handing my axes over to some faggot,' the Wolf explained, somewhat unhelpfully.

Kayne tried not to let the despair show on his face as steel whispered from sheaths all around them. To his credit, the bandit leader kept his sword at his belt. 'I do not believe,' the moustached outlaw said slowly, 'that you are in a position to refuse.' He pointed at the purse hanging from Kayne's belt. 'What's in the bag, old fellow?' he asked amiably.

Kayne's blue eyes narrowed at the insult, but he untied the pouch nonetheless and tugged it open to expose the glittering contents for all the bandits to see. 'Forty golden spires,' he said, trying his best to keep his tone friendly. He gave the purse a shake to demonstrate, but in his annoyance he misjudged and the real treasure he kept hidden within spilled out onto the grass.

Shit. He didn't know whether to laugh or cry, so he settled on a manic grin.

'Forty golden spires – and what else? A collection of precious gems, perhaps?' The bandit chuckled, a rich throaty sound. He gestured at the small bundle that lay wrapped in cloth. 'What are you trying to hide? Hand it over.'

'I can't do that,' replied Kayne. There was iron in his voice now, a hard edge he couldn't will away, though he knew where it would lead. Jerek met his eyes briefly and in that moment they both understood how things were going to play out.

The bandit leader sighed again, he looked like he was savouring the drama of it all. He shook his head in mock regret. 'Then we shall take it by force.'

'Uncle,' a small voice piped up. It was the youngest of the bandits, the lad nearest the leader. Kayne studied him with a frown. He was little more than a boy, a wiry figure with green eyes and bright red hair. Too young to be keeping such company.

'Hush, Brick.' The leader waved a dismissive hand.

'But these men...' Brick tried again. The older bandit leaned across and cuffed him around the back of the head.

'I said hush. Where are your manners? I didn't raise you to be a barbarian. Not like these brutes.'

'That's a bit harsh, boss,' said one of the bandits, a hint of reproach in his voice.

14

Their leader raised an eyebrow. 'I was talking about the Highlanders.' He placed a gloved hand on the hilt of his sword. With his other hand he drew his forefinger dramatically across his throat. 'Kill them.'

Brodar Kayne tossed the coin pouch into the air.

It sailed across the circle of bandits, their hungry eyes drawn to the gold spilling out like flies to a corpse. The distraction lasted only a moment, but in that short time several things happened.

Kayne reached behind him, tugged his sword free of its sheath, and beheaded the brigand nearest him. An axe arced through the air, spinning end over end, and thudded into the chest of the bandit opposite Jerek. The impact dropped the outlaw like a stone, blood painting the shocked faces of the men on either side. The Wolf was on them in an instant, his remaining axe cleaving through leather and bone.

Only the bandit leader reacted to this surprise turn of events, vaulting quickly onto his horse. He kicked down and sent his mount racing away without so much as a backward glance.

One bandit ran at Kayne with his scimitar raised, yelling in that pointless way men who'd never seen a real fight often did. Kayne knocked aside his awkward swing, drove a boot into the man's stomach and sent him sprawling. He was still fumbling desperately for his weapon when the old barbarian finished him off.

An arrow whistled over Kayne's shoulder. He ducked low, gritting his teeth against the spasm of pain that shot down his back. The youngster, Brick, was reaching for his quiver again, utter terror in his emerald eyes. The other bandit was already sighting down his bow. It was aimed straight at Kayne.

He caught the glint of metal in the corner of his vision and the archer's head suddenly burst like a melon, an explosion of gore and chunks of bone. The body tumbled to the ground, the handle of Jerek's axe sticking out from the broken mess that

15

had been a man's head.

And only one bandit remained.

Kayne met Brick's eyes, held them as the lad's freckled hand fumbled with the bow. There were thirty feet between them. 'You any good with that?' Kayne asked conversationally, wiping his greatsword dry on the corpse at his feet. Jerek was inching closer to the axe buried in the chest of the first man he'd killed.

'Good enough,' replied Brick, with admirable conviction. He got the arrow nocked and drew his bowstring.

'You already missed me once,' Kayne replied evenly. 'Best make your next shot a good one. Don't reckon you'll get another chance.' He nodded pointedly at Jerek, who was bending down slowly to retrieve his weapon, face grim with the promise of death.

He could see the boy's resolve beginning to waver. 'I don't want to die,' he said, sounding awfully young. He stared around wildly at the bodies of his comrades. At the ruin of a man's head, mangled brain leaking through his shattered skull.

'None of us do. But it's an ugly business, robbing folk.'

Brick's eyes jumped from Kayne to Jerek and back again, the bow in his hands twitching one way and then the other as he tried to keep both men in his sights. 'I know who you are. You're the Highlanders who killed dozens of Asander's men. The Bandit King has a bounty on your heads.'

Kayne sighed. 'Aye,' he replied. 'That's us.'

'I'll ride away and won't look back,' Brick said, desperation in his voice. 'I won't tell anyone you're here. I give you my word!'

Bit late for that now, lad. I let you go free, you'll bring every bandit in the Badlands down on us.

His heart sank at the knowledge of what had to be done. He steeled himself and walked slowly over to the boy, then thrust out a bloodied hand. 'Give me the bow and we got ourselves a deal.'

Brick sighed and let the string go slack. Brodar Kayne took the bow with a grateful nod.

With his other hand, he punched Brick hard in the face.

'We ought to kill him. Get it done quick.'

Kayne rubbed at his bristled chin. He glanced up at the stars overhead, then down at the unconscious figure strapped to the saddle on the horse beside him.

'He's just a boy.'

'You'd killed men at his age, Kayne, and you know it.'

Jerek had been less than impressed to find Brick still drawing breath. He'd calmed down now, furious rage replaced by sullen anger. In Kayne's experience, the latter tended to linger a fair old while.

'Best not to use me as a yardstick, I reckon.'

Jerek spat. They rode on in silence, heading ever northward into the wilds that lay beyond the Trine. Another day or two and they'd be well inside the Badlands.

'The Bandit King ain't forgotten about us,' Jerek finally said. 'You heard the kid. There's a bounty on our heads.'

'I know. Ain't much for it now.'

'Kid's uncle will come looking for him too. You thought about that?'

'Aye.'

'And?'

'Ain't much for it now.'

Jerek shook his head, the moonlight casting a shine on his bald scalp. 'You're turning into a right old pussy and that's a fact.'

Kayne sighed. 'Age will do that to you.'

Jerek snorted in reply.

An hour later they reined in their horses and set up camp. Brick had begun to stir, moaning softly in his saddle. They bundled him off his horse and on to the ground. The boy had a big purple bruise on his cheek, but no permanent damage.

Kayne shook his head ruefully. There had been a time when his right hook was guaranteed to break a man's jaw.

'You awake?' He gave the waterskin he was holding a shake, sprinkling a few drops over Brick's face. 'You've been out the best part of a day.'

'Urgh! Leave me alone.'

Jerek jabbed a booted foot non-too gently into Brick's ribs. 'Shift, you lazy prick.'

'Ow! Where... where am I?'

Kayne took a bite out of a chunk of bread and gave it a good hard chew. 'I'd like to say among friends,' he said, around mouthfuls. 'But the truth is that you're our captive and you'd best do what we say or we'll more'n likely kill you.'

He gave Brick a moment for this to sink in. 'Where's my uncle?' the boy asked.

'There's a question. First hint of trouble and he fled like a startled deer.'

'Uncle Glaston's the smartest man I know.'

'He was smart enough to flee, I'll give him that. What kind of man leaves his own nephew behind to die?'

'You don't understand,' said Brick. 'Asander would have killed us months ago if it wasn't for him.'

'You're not on good terms with the Bandit King?'

Brick shook his head and rubbed at his bruised cheek. 'We fled south to escape him. We only wanted your food and whatever coin we could steal. We're not murderers.'

Kayne raised a thick eyebrow but decided to let that pass. He was silent for a moment, trying to see a way forward that didn't involve murdering the lad. 'All right, Brick,' he said. 'Here's how it's going to be. You'll ride with us and act as our guide. We don't want to bump into the Bandit King's men any more than you. Do as you're told and you can have your horse back.'

'Uncle Glaston won't abandon me.'

'Then you'll just have to explain the situation when he

18

shows his face again. I'll untie your legs but your wrists are staying bound for now. Best advice I can offer for the headache is to get some food down and sleep it off.'

He cut through the rope around Brick's legs and then handed him a heel of bread and the rest of the waterskin. The boy tore hungrily into the bread, the right side of his mouth doing all the work. Kayne felt a moment of sympathy for the young bandit. He shook his head sadly, remembering a small body dragged beneath the Icemelt all those years ago.

Jerek was seeing to the horses. Kayne lowered his aching body to the ground and settled back against the trunk of an oak. Then he reached into the coin purse at his belt and rummaged around inside. It felt lighter than before – they'd lost a handful of spires and moons during the fight with the bandits. He figured it was money well spent.

With great care he removed the items wrapped inside the bag. The protective cloth had become stained with blood during the fight, but he was relieved to find none of the contents were soiled.

He counted them out, cradling them delicately in his palm. His three most precious treasures. He stared down at them.

A lock of Mhaira's hair, the chocolate brown of her youth. He remembered being embarrassed when she'd given it to him. He'd had his head wedged firmly up his arse back in those days and no mistake.

The ring she had presented to him for their joining ceremony – a plain band of silver. It was still bright despite the passing of the years.

The small knife he had fashioned for Magnar; the traditional gift a father presents to his son on his fifteenth naming day, when a boy officially becomes a man. He ran a finger softly down the dull blade, remembering.

Jerek walked over, and Kayne noticed that he limped slightly. The Wolf must have taken a wound in the fighting

19

earlier that day. He hadn't mentioned it – he never did.

Kayne felt a fresh wave of guilt, the terrible burden of things he had done, truths he had kept sealed inside for so long.

Jerek watched him, his scarred face unreadable. If the Wolf noticed the tears threatening Kayne's eyes he betrayed nothing. 'We'll find her,' he said simply. He kicked off his boots and was snoring almost as soon as he hit the ground.

Kayne rewrapped the objects in his hand and placed them carefully back inside the pouch. He glanced over at Brick, who was staring out into the night, no doubt wondering when his uncle might return and attempt a rescue.

He got himself as comfortable as he could, and then he too settled back to watch the wilderness. Time and again his failing eyes were drawn to the north.

A thousand or more miles away, the wife he had until recently thought dead waited for him. He would find Mhaira; put things right between him and his son if he could. Then he would have his vengeance.

After two long years, the Sword of the North was coming home.

20